THE UNBOUND MAN

THE UNBOUND MAN

BOOK 1 OF THE UNDYING LEGION

MATT KARLOV

IMAGO MUNDI PRESS

THE UNBOUND MAN

Maps by Maxime Plasse

Interior Art by Adam Brymora

Cover by Damonza.com

Published by Imago Mundi Press
Sydney, Australia
www.imagomundipress.com

ISBN 978-0-9925701-0-1 HB
ISBN 978-0-9925701-1-8 TPB

Typeset by Imago Mundi Press

First Printing

This book is dedicated to my father, Karl Karlov,
who first introduced me to story

Hazel and Fiver
Frodo and Sam
Siren and Splasher and Grunt

CONTENTS

ACKNOWLEDGEMENTS   *ix*

MAPS   *x*

DRAMATIS PERSONAE   *xv*

PROLOGUE   1

PART 1: THE FALLING PEBBLE   11

PART 2: THE COMFORT OF YOUR TEARS   153

PART 3: TO WAKE IN DARKNESS   367

EPILOGUE   481

ABOUT THE AUTHOR   487

Acknowledgements

My thanks to Saladin Ahmed, Adam Brymora, David Karlov, and Abigail Nathan for their feedback and editorial input at various stages in the development of this novel. Thank you also to Adam Brymora (again), Maxime Plasse, and Alisha at Damonza.com for their artistic contributions to the final book. And my grateful appreciation to my crack proofreading team: Karl, Merike, and Lisa.

Finally, a special thank you to my wife Anthea for her ongoing support throughout the writing, revision, and publication of this book.

GULF
OF SABAH

Nara

Afin

J   E   R   V

Ormande

Amherst

(PEKRATA)

Cort

Dakin

Sadurne

JERVIAN

Levente

PROTECTORATE

Marlis

CRYSLE
BAY

Farica

Cho

MIRCO
BAY

Kiarnon

Taborri

Lake
Vibo

Chayle

Talasi

Telanon

BEL HENNA

STILLWATER
BAY

Natane

Yenene

PLAINS   OF   HA

Oder

Sanam

Safak

Menefir

BAY
OF ZEVA

SE

Veda

Ira Wastes

Namir

Alba

Manelin

SEA   O

PLASSE
2014

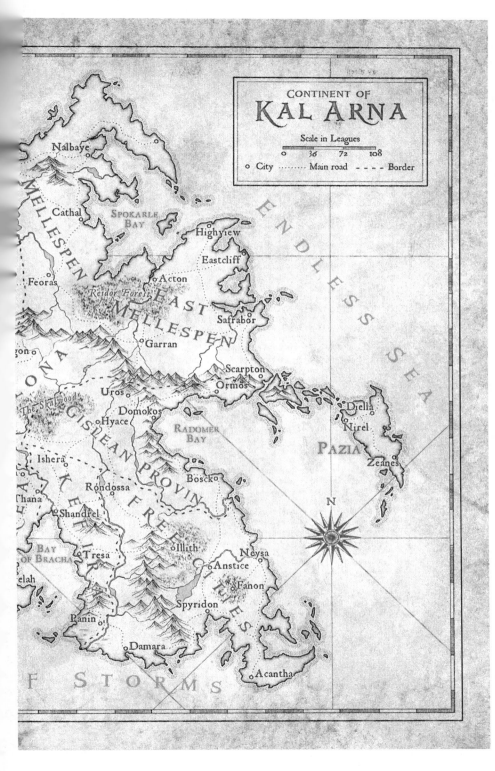

CONTINENT OF

KAL ARNA

Scale in Leagues

0   36   72   108

○ City .... Main road - - - Border

Nalbaye

Cathal

SPOKARLE BAY

Highview

Eastcliff

Feoras

Acton

Reidor Forest

EAST MELLESPEN

MELLESPEN

Safrabor

Garran

...gon

Scarpton

Uros

Ormos

The Skalwood

Domokos

Hyace

RADOMER BAY

Djella

Nirel

PAZIA

Zeanes

Ishera

GISLEAN PROVIN

FREE

Bosco

Rondossa

...hana

Shandrel

N

BAY OF BRACHA

Tresa

Illith

Neysa

Anstice

...elah

Fanon

CITIES

Ranin

Spyridon

Damara

Acantha

F   S T O R M S

ENDLESS SEA

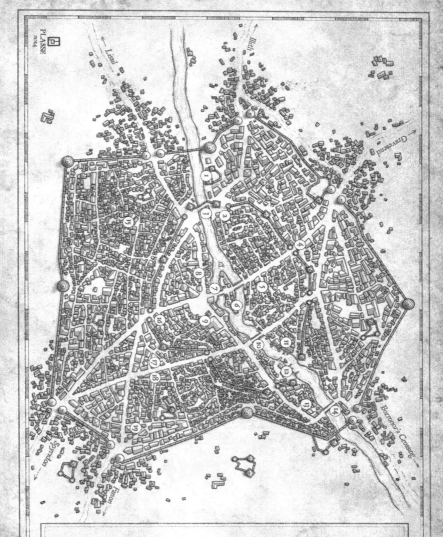

THE FREE CITY OF
ANSTICE

1. Powder Works
2. Tri-God Pantheon
3. Bastion Bridge
4. Old North Gatehouse
5. Quill Shop
6. Varek's Chocol House
7. Isle Bridge
8. Exadius Moneylenders
9. City Chambers
10. Merchants' Bridge
11. Woodtraders Guild
12. Public Docks
13. The Red Rodent
14. East Bridge
15. Quill Schoolhouse
16. Baras's Shop
17. Kefiran Temple
18. Oculus Building
19. Quilah's Emporium

PLASSE
2014

Dramatis Personae

In Spyridon

Arandras, a former Quill linguist, now poor-quarter scribe
Tereisa, his wife, deceased
Mara, a seeker of lost treasures
Druce, a thief
Jensine, a sorcerer
Onsoth, an officer of the Library
Yevin, a Library scribe
Sten, a trader of antiquities
Grae, a courier
Leff, a ditch-digger
Wil, his son

Of the Quill

Damasus, governor of the Anstice schoolhouse
Narvi, a sorcerer and researcher
Katriel, a child, Narvi's daughter
Bannard, a researcher
Senisha, a librarian
Ienn, leader of a field team
Halli, a sorcerer
Gord, a researcher
Derrek, leader of a field team
Cal, a sorcerer
Rawlen, a researcher

Of the Oculus

Clade, overseer of the Anstice unit
Garrett, his adjunct
Sinon, a sorcerer
Kalie, a sorcerer
Meline, a sorcerer
Rathzange, a sorcerer
Sera, a newly-bound sorcerer
Niele, a deserter, deceased
Estelle, a Councillor
Weneth, a Councillor
Azador, a god

Of the Woodtraders

Vorace, Guildmaster
Laris, Trademaster
Pel, her adjunct
Eilwen, a trader
Kieffe, a trader
Tammas, a hired sword, deceased
Havilah, Spymaster
Ufeus, a spy
Brielle, a spy
Caralange, Guild Sorcerer
Orom, a sorcerer
Soll, Treasurer
Phemia, Seneschal
Ged, house steward

Others

Isaias, a trader of rare items
Jasser, a trader
Peni, a trader
Qulah, a Tahisi trader

Dallin, a moneylender
Terrel, a mercenary captain
Hosk, a mercenary
Yuri, a mercenary
Noash, a boy
Jon, his brother

THE UNBOUND MAN

PROLOGUE

When a phoenix is about to die it builds a great nest upon a rock. Surrounded by twigs and leaves, it settles down among the tinder and there it gives itself over to immolation. The phoenix burns, the nest becomes ashes, and an ember is formed from which a new, younger bird will arise.

Sometimes the flame is too weak. The nest smoulders. The ember cools. The phoenix dies, yet its new self is not born. The ember hardens and dims and lies dormant, like a seed awaiting a spring that will never come.

But sometimes the flame is strong, so strong that the nest cannot contain it. It leaps and burns: a tree, a hillside, a forest. The fire spreads, and other embers that have long been cold and lifeless are kindled at last. Slowly, slowly, they awaken and remember what they are, and what they are to be.

When the fire is done, all is cloaked in ash. And who can say what embers now glow beneath the desolation, or when they might at last give birth?

So it is when empires die.

— Tiysus Oronayan, *Histories,* Third Volume

THEY WERE BEING FOLLOWED, AND Derrek was weary of it.
He lay back on the patchy grass and gazed at the glittering twilight sky. The evening was cooler than usual for summer; the breeze had turned that morning and now wafted down from the north like a whispered benediction, mild and refreshing, rustling the leaves of the trees surrounding the clearing. Somewhere in the dark, a nightbird called to its companions.

The sky had been clear the past three nights, ever since they found the small urn buried among the ruins of a modest, long-dead temple. There'd been nothing to suggest that anyone else had been there for centuries, still less that very day; but Derrek had felt eyes watching them as he pulled the urn from the earth, and again that evening as they made camp. They'd set a watch, despite the complaints — and, in the end, the somnolence — of Rawlen, but the dawn had arrived without incident.

Yet the feeling of being watched remained.

"Watch what you're doing, boy! If I want your foul tea poured all over me, I'll do it myself!"

Derrek sat up to see Callidora wiping ineffectually at her boot with a handful of grass. Cal was short and round, and had difficulty reaching her feet at the best of times. Rawlen stood frozen before her with the pot in hand, face flushed with embarrassment. Another trickle splashed over the back of Cal's hand and she yelped. "Put it down, you fool boy, before you throw the rest of it over my head!"

Jolting into motion, Rawlen lowered the pot clumsily to the ground. His mouth opened and closed until at last he turned away, stumbling around the campfire and throwing himself down with a frustrated sigh. Derrek forced himself not to glare after him. *A newborn foal would hinder us less.*

He rolled his shoulders, trying to ease the persistent ache in his back. Walking all day through a forest or sleeping on the hard earth had rarely bothered him before. Once, a long time ago, it had even been exciting. But lately he'd found himself missing the comfortable schoolhouse beds, the generous meals, the opportunities to just sit quietly for a while and read, or think, or do nothing at all. *You're getting old,* he told himself. *Old and soft.* The thought would have been distasteful even a year ago; now, it was merely resigned. *Of course it is. Submission to the inevitable — another characteristic of age.*

Even the thrill of finding their goal had been muted. He'd tucked the urn beneath his leather jerkin with barely a second look, heedless of its unblemished condition. It was made of metal — pewter, Derrek thought — its mouth sealed with a cap. But if either the urn or its contents possessed the sorcery of the long-dead Valdori, it was subtle enough to be indiscernible. *Just an antiquated trinket, no doubt. Pretty enough to look at, but nothing more.* The find would doubtless delight a Quill historian somewhere, but before long it would disappear into the archives, making its final home among the countless other inconsequential relics of the past.

Cal tossed the wad of grass into the fire and fished a strip of dried meat from her pack. Derrek thought again of the schoolhouse's hearty meals. Sighing, he settled himself beside Cal and poured himself a mug of Rawlen's tea.

"Someone's still trailing us," he said. "I'm sure of it."

"Well, good for them," Cal said, chewing noisily. "They can follow us right back to the schoolhouse for all I care." She caught his expression and snorted. "Oh, come on. If they were going to show themselves, they would have done it by now."

Derrek shrugged. "Maybe." The past few nights had been clear and moonlit. Their tracker might have merely been biding his time, waiting for more opportune conditions before... what? He sipped his tea, grimacing at the astringent taste.

"Why would someone want to follow us all this way?" Rawlen sat huddled on the other side of the campfire as though it were the middle of winter. "I mean, why bother? They must know where we're going."

Derrek's frown deepened. The boy had a point. It should have been obvious at the ruin that at least two of the party were Quill sorcerers. Now they were retracing their steps and had rejoined the trail that led back to the main road. Yet their tracker evidently still considered them worth following.

"I don't know," Derrek said. *Not very reassuring. Try again.* "But I doubt he would be foolish enough to cross the likes of us. And if he is, well, you've seen what Callidora can do. You're safe enough."

Rawlen turned his gaze back to the campfire, his chin resting on his knees.

"Tomorrow we return to the main road," Derrek continued. "We'll find an inn for the night. If our tracker wants to remain anonymous then, he's going to find it a lot harder."

Rawlen nodded slowly and Derrek looked away, trying to keep the concern from his face. Their stalker would be well aware of the road's proximity. If he had malign intent, he would never have a better chance than tonight.

They finished their meal in silence. The campfire dwindled and the stars grew brighter, a thousand gemstones embedded in the sky, each lit from within. Rawlen's eyes closed and he fell into a doze, his chin still propped up on his knees. Cal sat motionless, absorbed in her own thoughts. Derrek shifted restlessly, unable to find a position that didn't cause some part of him to ache.

"Missing the comforts of home?" Cal said at last, the hint of a smile in her voice.

Derrek chuckled softly. "Aye, something like that," he said, moving his legs to one side. After a moment he sighed and stretched them before him again. "Do you never grow weary of this endless search for ancient trinkets?"

He sensed Cal's shrug. "Some are more than just trinkets. Better we find them than someone else."

"That's not what I meant. Don't you ever want to... I don't know, just stay in one place for a while?"

"And do what?" Cal gave her familiar snort. "Research? The very word sounds tedious. Teach? Might as well raise children."

"Well, there's that." Derrek had no children that he knew of, and little patience with childish fancies. *But then, teaching the blade or training sorcerers is hardly like instructing youngsters in their letters. Such things require a certain maturity —*

Cal's hand on his arm cut short his thoughts. "Company," she said, staring at a low rise on the other side of the trail.

Derrek peered between the trees. Leaves whispered to one another, casting shadows that danced across the ground. He blinked, looked harder among the shifting patterns of darkness — and then he saw them.

Figures strode through the trees toward them, five at least, weapons in hand. They seemed to be all dressed in black, though the moonlight made it difficult to be sure. Derrek scrambled to his feet, drawing his own sword and holding it at his side, point downward.

"Stand, and state your business!" he shouted.

Rawlen started, blinking up at the others before twisting around to follow their gaze. He froze at the sight of the advancing men then scrambled to his feet and around the campfire to stand behind Derrek.

The figures continued their advance as though no-one had spoken, unhurried, their stride unbroken.

"Go and hide in the trees behind us," Derrek said to Rawlen. There were six figures, he could now see. "Don't do anything stupid. Callidora and I will take care of this."

Rawlen stammered his assent and hurried away, his rapid footfalls quickly fading.

Cal crouched by the campfire, poking at the glowing embers with a half-burnt stick. Even as Derrek glanced down, a thin flame emerged, curling reluctantly upward, and Cal stood and nodded.

"I say again, stand or be considered hostile!" Derrek called, stepping away from the campfire and raising his sword.

The figures came on, heedless of his warning, neither hastening nor slowing their pace. Blades glinted in the moonlight.

So be it.

A column of flame ripped the night apart, erupting from the ground and enveloping one of the approaching figures. Derrek raised his hand, shielding his vision from the blazing light, and glanced across to the campfire. Cal stood as though transfixed, her hand stretched toward the fiery shaft and the screaming figure within. Her other hand reached for the campfire at her back, its small flame fluttering wildly as it bent toward her.

The screams ended abruptly. Cal lowered her hand and the blazing column vanished. Where the flame had been, only a blackened circle remained, with a dark, unmoving lump at its centre. The sickly scent of charred flesh hung in the darkness.

The remaining figures glanced at each other as though suddenly uncertain. Derrek drew breath to call out again, but before he could speak, one of the black-clad men shouted a command and the figures resumed their approach on the camp. Two swift paces, a third; then they broke into a run.

Ah, shit.

They arrived in a rush, two closing with Derrek, their assault pushing him back as he worked furiously to parry their attacks. Orange light flared from Cal's position, highlighting the faces of his assailants: a scowling, pale-skinned Mellespene and a shorter man with hard eyes and a calculating frown. If either was shaken by the fate of their roasted companion it didn't show on their faces.

Gods, this just keeps getting better.

Derrek blocked one thrust and dodged another, his foot slipping on the uneven ground. His opponents pressed the attack, forcing him back and back again. The man on the left aimed a blow high and Derrek raised his sword to block, not recognising the feint until a moment too late. He disengaged, twisting desperately away. Pain bloomed across his arm and shoulder and he staggered backward, narrowly avoiding another swing.

The Mellespene stumbled, momentarily blocking his companion, but Derrek was too slow to take advantage. He flexed his wounded arm, wincing at the rush of pain. The blow had been glancing, but the leather jerkin seemed to have done little to impede it. *I need to finish this quickly.* A finger of luck was all he needed. *Dreamer, Weeper, and Gatherer, grant me victory. Deliver me from my foes, I pray.*

The man on the right launched a fresh assault, his shorter companion stepping back and moving to circle around. Derrek countered the thrusts, stepping sideways to keep both men in sight, awaiting an opening. Cal's orange light shifted and rippled, casting unsteady shadows across the clearing. *Come on. Just one little mistake. Just one...*

The taller man stumbled slightly and Derrek leapt forward, chopping at his neck and catching him off balance. The man raised his blade, somehow managing to deflect the blow, but as he hopped back his heel caught on a rock and he tumbled onto his arse. Derrek stepped in and stabbed the man through the chest. Surprise blossomed over the man's face; then he sagged, his head lolling sideways like a broken puppet.

Derrek yanked his sword loose and spun to face the second man, but even as he turned he felt fire erupt in his belly. Blinking down, he saw a blade pull free, the steel covered with his own blood and fluids. *Oh. That's not good.* He slumped to his knees, gaping at the shadowy clump of grass before him. The ground swayed and he toppled sideways, head hitting the dirt with a jarring thud.

He groaned, suddenly cold despite the mild evening, and braced for the deathblow. But as his vision cleared he saw his attacker already running across to assist his companions against Cal.

Three rings of flame enclosed Callidora and the campfire, one each at shoulders, waist, and knees. They spun and tilted, now shifting apart, now almost touching. The men prowled around her like balked dogs, snarling at the fiery barrier. A gap opened before one of them and he darted in, aiming a blow between the rings. But as his sword broached the barrier, a flaming tendril snapped out at his head and he reared away, cursing.

Derrek sucked in a mouthful of smoky air. Every breath was agony. *It's all down to you, Cal.* The woman was a better firebinder than most Derrek had known, but even she couldn't sustain a binding like this for long. *Maybe if you kill them quickly, you can think of a way to save me.* The men circled, cautious now, figures of black against the blazing rings. *Please, hurry.*

Another gap opened, inviting a blow — and this time the man stepped too close. Flame uncoiled, striking him in the head, engulfing his face. He shrieked and reeled away, stumbling sightlessly to his knees near Derrek and screaming like a gutted pig.

Yes! Wild hope surged through Derrek. But even as Cal sent another tendril just short of a swinging blade, the man who had stabbed Derrek stepped away from the others and drew something out from beneath his shirt.

A prickling sensation covered Derrek's skin, and a whimper escaped him before he knew why. *Anamnil. Gods, no.* The man crouched by the campfire at Cal's back, unfolding the object until it was about the size of a child's blanket; then, with a flourish befitting a street-corner illusionist, he tossed it *through* the lower ring. Derrek watched in horror as it floated gently onto the campfire, smothering it. Cal's vicious curse floated across the clearing. A moment later, her fiery defences winked out.

There was nothing he could do but watch. One moment Cal stood amid a blur of swords; the next, she had fallen without so much as a cry. *Gods have mercy. Cal.*

Who's going to save me now?

A sudden scramble rose from beyond the clearing, then the sound of someone crashing away through the trees. The men spun around and darted away in pursuit. *Rawlen, you idiot.* Despair welled up beside the pain in Derrek's stomach. Blundering through the forest with a pack of swordsmen at his back, the youth would be lucky to last a hundred paces.

The noise of the chase receded, leaving the clearing silent but for the low keening of the blinded attacker. Derrek wished the gods would strike him dumb. *I'm dying, and you don't hear me wailing about it.* It occurred to him to wonder whether the gods had ever actually struck anyone dumb. *The Gatherer will take me soon. Perhaps I'll ask him.* His thoughts were wandering, he realised distantly. Somehow, he could no longer summon the energy to care.

But something was gouging into his side. He dug his hand beneath his body, hissing at the pain, and pulled out a small bundle wrapped in a rag. Of course. The urn. This was what the men were seeking. Or perhaps not. Perhaps they had attacked for some other reason, and the urn, like everything else he carried, would soon be nothing more than loot. A trophy of a kill.

Rage swelled within him. To be brought down like a beast! To be killed not for who he was, nor even for what he was, but merely for what he carried. The contempt of it burned, worse even than the pain in his gut. *The gods blind you all, you murdering bastards.* And if the gods ignored this last request, as they had so many others in his life, there was still breath in him yet. He could still deny his killers this one thing.

If he had been uninjured, he might have used sorcery to drive the urn deep into the earth; but sorcery was beyond him now. Gritting his teeth, he forced himself to his knees, his injured arm clasped over his belly to hold himself together. A wave of dizziness swept over him and he swayed, sucking down air as a cry rang out from the forest. *Rawlen. Gods, I'm sorry.*

Despair flared again and he fought it, pushing it away, using it to fan his rage. He straightened, raising himself to his full kneeling height; then, with a great, gasping breath, he hurled the urn into the trees before him. The force of his throw pitched him forward, sending him face-first into the rough clearing floor. He grunted at the impact, dirt filling his senses as the last of his strength left him.

He drifted, his thoughts breaking apart and reforming like

clouds. He was badly hurt, he knew that. *My arm. No, not my arm. My gut.* Perhaps Cal could still save him if she came soon. But no, they had killed her already. And they had killed Rawlen, too; and now, at last, they had returned for him. He could hear them arguing somewhere nearby, but the words were muffled, indistinct, as though both they and he were underwater.

"This one's still alive!" The voice was right next to him. Something pushed into his side and turned him over. Strange. That was where he had been stabbed, but there didn't seem to be much pain any more.

Hands groped beneath his jerkin. A face drew near, and he felt himself being shaken. "Listen to me. Listen!"

Derrek tried to focus, but the face swam before him.

"We know you had an urn. Tell me where it is, and I'll ease your passing."

An immense satisfaction flooded through him. They were seeking the urn after all, and he had kept it from them! He wanted to smile, to laugh, but it seemed his lips had forgotten how. He gathered up saliva to spit in the face above him, but succeeded only in dribbling. Blood washed through his mouth, metallic and bitter.

The face disappeared, and Derrek heard the man move past the top of his head to where his arm lay outstretched. A moment later he felt the arm shift slightly and heard the crunch of breaking bones. *My hand? No, probably my wrist.* There was no pain at all now. Dying didn't seem so bad after all.

The face returned. "I will ask only once more. Where is the urn?"

Derrek looked sideways, toward where he thought Cal had fallen. He didn't feel so bad about the others now that he knew what dying was like. Maybe they had been allowed to wait for him, and the Gatherer would take all three of them together. He hoped so.

The argument began again, the voices distant, the words blurring and overlapping. The breeze caressed his face, whispering in his ears and sending a leaf skittering past his cheek. Sipping the mild night air, Derrek closed his eyes and waited to meet the god.

The boot stomped down and crushed his throat.

PART 1:
THE FALLING PEBBLE

CHAPTER 1

You are a child of a fallen people.
You carry a worm within you.
It coils ever tighter around your heart.
In the end it will devour you.

— Sarean birth chant

THE ARGUMENT WAS IN FULL swing when the courier from the Three Rivers Trading Company stopped by Arandras's shop to drop off the parcel of letters.

So intent was the city official on his harangue that he failed to notice the courier, putting Arandras in the awkward position of trying to acknowledge the new arrival without seeming to divert his attention from the other man. A quirked eyebrow and a flick of the fingers were not enough to convey that the courier should simply leave the bundled letters and go, and when Arandras attempted to clarify the message with a shooting glance, the official spotted it and shifted his diatribe to home in on this new display of contempt.

"This is the respect you show, yes? What is it that you find more pressing than the interests of the city? What could — *humph!*"

The official noticed Grae at last and snapped his mouth shut, blinking at the courier in bemusement. Oblivious, Grae bent his head to his bag. "Got some letters for you," he said, his voice trailing off as he rummaged through the bag. "They're just here…"

"Thanks, Grae." Arandras turned as the nameless official seemed about to object. "A moment," he snapped.

The man glared, but made no other response.

"Not those... ah." Grae pulled an unusually bulky sheaf of documents from the bag and dropped it on Arandras's writing desk with a thud. Arandras thanked him again, tossing the bundled letters into the low basket he kept for that purpose. Still absorbed in the contents of his bag, Grae paused at the door, insensible to the official's mounting irritation behind him; then, muttering under his breath, he flipped the bag shut and at last took his leave.

"Well," the official said, folding his arms with exaggerated patience. "If you're quite ready to resume our discussion?"

Weeper save me. "Of course. Forgive me, I didn't catch your name."

"Onsoth. Officer of the City of Spyridon, as I believe I mentioned. And —"

"You did," Arandras said. Onsoth scowled at the interruption, and Arandras hurried on before the man could work himself into another tirade. "Truly, I went through all this with your predecessor." *Who was able to express himself in far fewer words, and at a much lower volume.* "And he agreed that nothing I do here requires either Library membership or a licence from them."

Onsoth's scowl deepened. "I'm sure he did. But my predecessor was, perhaps, not in possession of all the facts? Such as the *fact* that your business, Arandras Kanthesi, goes beyond correspondence and the like, and in *fact* extends to schooling?"

Arandras spread his hands. "I don't know what you —"

"Of course you do. You've been teaching the local brats their letters! The ditch-digger's whelp, for one. How many others? Do you know the fine for teaching without a licence? How much is he paying? How many others are there? Well?"

"No others! He only —"

"So, private tutelage. How much is he paying you? Must be a sweet sum to make it worth your while. No wonder the kid looks like he hasn't eaten for a month. How much?"

"Nothing! He just watches me work sometimes."

"An apprentice, then! Well, if that isn't the worst of them all."

Onsoth grinned broadly. "And is this apprenticeship registered? No, of course it isn't. No scribe or notary can register an apprentice without first obtaining Library membership. And that seems to be something you just don't have."

Arandras bit back a retort. The boy in question was scarcely six years old. Calling him an apprentice was beyond absurd. *Weeper forbid that the Library should just leave me alone.*

Onsoth seemed to feel that silence was not a thing that should be allowed to linger. He leaned forward, lowering his voice to what he probably imagined to be a confidential tone. "There's no need to concern yourself with this. You know that, yes? All you need to do is become a member. Nothing you do here has to change." He glanced over the cramped shop, the unpaved street outside. "Hells, membership would likely improve your clientele no end. Up your takings. Let you find some place to work other than…" A gesture encompassing it all. "Why wouldn't you want that?"

Why not, indeed? The Library put up no barriers to membership, or none that would exclude even a moderately competent scribe. And it was certainly true that most of Spyridon would not even consider using a scribe who lacked the Library's imprimatur. Only here near the low market, where enough people were sufficiently desperate or impoverished to overlook that detail, could an unregistered scribe hope to make a living — and even here, those who used Arandras's services were looked down upon by those who could afford better. Even the illiterate poor had their pride, and Spyridon was a city of learning. The city of the Library.

No, there was no reason at all why a man in Arandras's position would not want to be a member of the Library. Assuming, of course, that being a member of anything — belonging to anything — was in any way acceptable or tolerable.

"I'm sorry," Arandras said, as pleasantly as he could manage. "I'm sure the Library is a very fine establishment, with many very fine members. But I have no interest in joining their ranks."

The words took a moment to sink in. Onsoth blinked at Arandras, bemused; then the scowl returned and a flush spread across his face. "They said you were a stubborn one," he said. "Like a mule, yes? One who doesn't know what's good for him? Well. If you will not see reason then this city has no place for you. You will abide by the rules laid down by the Library, or we will scour you from this place like the filth you are."

And there it was. The implicit made plain. The threat, unveiled for all to see.

Gatherer take you.

"You are engaged in illegal apprenticeship," Onsoth said. "Illegal apprenticeship! Your penalty will be determined by the all guilds' arbiter in ten days —"

"I contest the charge."

"Do you?" Onsoth was already red; now he began to purple. "Do you, now? Are you really —"

"Yes, I am." Arandras scowled, no longer bothering to hide his contempt. "The boy's not even as tall as this desk. The charge is ridiculous, and you know it. You want to take it to the arbiter, you go right ahead. Go and see him now, why don't you, and leave me in peace."

Onsoth glared at Arandras in fury, fists clenching and unclenching, jaw working, speech deserting him at last.

Arandras pointed to the door.

The official gave a sudden, vicious smile. "Look at you. King of your own scrapheap. Ten years from now, twenty, here you'll be, just the same, lording it over the world from your pathetic little sty."

Arandras kept his face immobile, but Onsoth seemed to sense he'd hit a nerve. He leaned over the desk, his voice soft and spiteful. "And what will you think to yourself then, hmm? When you look back at a life spent pissing in the dust, scratching out words for the other swine? What will you think when you realise you've spent your whole damn life down here in the shit?"

Arandras was on his feet before he knew it, his face a hair's breadth away from the other man's. "Get the hells out of my shop."

Onsoth straightened, satisfied, and gave a mocking bow. "As you say, your majesty." He paused at the door, offering Arandras a final smirk, then disappeared into the dusty street.

Breathing heavily, Arandras lowered himself into his chair, hands flat on the desk before him. *What do you know about it, you bastard?* There was no shame in the work he did here. Besides, this wasn't forever. Someday his side-business with Mara and the others would pay off. They'd find a relic worth enough to see them all set up for good, and that would be that.

Perhaps, if the Weeper was kind, someday soon.

~

It was not until a second courier stopped by a few hours later that Arandras remembered the bundle of letters left by Grae. The new messenger was a man from the East Mellespen Syndicate, and his delivery consisted of a single letter. Only one of Arandras's regular clients carried on a correspondence with anyone that far to the northeast, and indeed, the letter was addressed to Leff, the ditch-digger, in the spidery writing of the scribe hired by his sister. Arandras laid it aside.

Most weeks saw the arrival of three or four deliveries, each of which might consist of anything from one letter to more than a dozen. Sometimes there would be nothing from one carrier for weeks, and then a fat parcel would drop on his desk with letters that had been written a season ago. But that was the price you paid for hiring merchant companies — or, more specifically, their extensive networks of couriers and messengers — to carry your correspondence. The fees were low enough, if you picked the right network for the right destination, but the messengers were company men first and public couriers second, and the interests of their masters ultimately ran in only one direction.

Merchant companies, the Quill, even the Library: at bottom, they were all the same. Whatever purpose they claimed to espouse, in truth they all shared the same goal. They existed that they might continue to exist. They grew that they might continue to grow. All their efforts were bent toward one end: their own wellbeing.

It was, Arandras had come to see, the common sickness that afflicted all such shared endeavours, no matter where or how or why they came into being. Take the Quill, established centuries ago as refuge from the destructive, sorcery-charged bickering of the time. Beyond all reason, their efforts had borne fruit. Sorcerers and scholars had flocked to their cause. Slowly, the terror of sorcery among the ungifted had eased to distrust, then uncertainty, then enthusiasm.

And somewhere in among it all, the first shoe had dropped.

We do well, the Quill had said. *By our efforts, peace is restored. By our ingenuity, the benefits of sorcery are shared among all. The greater we are, the more we can achieve. Thus, self-interest is no vice for us, for that which serves us, serves all.*

So saying, they'd begun to equate their own interests with their purpose for being — after all, how better to serve others but to grow in power and influence? And the second shoe had begun to teeter. Until, one day, there was no longer any distinction between their ends and their own advancement. And nobody saw anything amiss, for loyalty and commitment were prized above all — not commitment to the founders' vision, nor even to any definable achievement, but loyalty to the Quill itself.

It was a kind of institutional madness, as tenacious as a Kefiran road preacher, predictable as Rondossan clockwork. None were immune: not traders, not scholars, not sorcerers, not priests. Sooner or later, every association succumbed.

But not me. Onsoth could go hang. The Library was the same as all the rest, and Arandras was damned if he was going to give a single copper duri to another establishment's dreams of self-aggrandisement.

He picked idly through the large bundle of letters. Two were for a nearby boot-maker from the man's sister in the river city of Anstice, the second dated a week after the first; one was for a local herbalist from her colleague in Poet's Corner, a town midway between Anstice and Spyridon; one for the headsman's widow from her lad, who'd been taken on as a shepherd boy on a farm just this side of the Tienette... and several dozen more, most of which had no connection to Arandras. Grae had left him someone else's letters as well as his own.

Curious, Arandras flipped through the misplaced correspondence. Most were addressed to someone called Yevin, up at the Arcade — a Library scribe, like as not. Here was a message addressed in large, awkward letters, written either by a child or by someone who rarely held a pen. Here was something formal from the Three Rivers company itself — perhaps Yevin's invoice. Here was an elegant, flowing script, the handwriting of someone who —

Arandras froze. *That writing.* As though of its own volition, his hand reached for the catch under the desk, slid open the hidden drawer. His questing fingers found the note as he had left it that morning, and the previous day, and the days and years before that; the scrap of paper folded in on itself like a dead spider. He withdrew it carefully and placed it beside the wrapped letter, smoothing out its creases with slow, practised motions.

Weeper's tears.

Side by side, there could be no mistaking it. Despite the differences in language and letterforms, the penmanship was the same: precise shapes, unusually heavy downstrokes, graceful loops. The thickness of the pen, the colour of the ink; even the finely-textured, uncommonly light-toned paper was the same.

He sucked in a lungful of air, the breath shuddering in his chest. *They told me you were dead. Found floating in the river with your throat slit.* His hand trembled on the desk, brushing the old ransom note askew, defying his efforts to still it.

He turned the letter over, but the seal showed no crest or identifying mark, just an abstract, maze-like pattern. *Still no name.* Inside would be different, though. The letter itself would surely be signed. All he had to do was open it, and —

"Arandras? Did I happen to — oh, thank the gods, there they are." Grae crossed the floor to Arandras's desk, gazing at Yevin's letters with the rapture of a man who had just found his coinpurse. Instinctively, Arandras shifted his hand to conceal the unfolded note. "Thank the gods," Grae repeated as he gathered up the bundle. His gaze fell on the sealed letter before Arandras, and he reached out an expectant hand.

Slowly, feeling as though he were watching from over his own shoulder, Arandras held the letter out. "I thought I recognised the seal on this one," he said. "Can you tell me who sent it?"

Grae took it and glanced it over. "No, sorry. Could have been someone in Anstice, but I can't be sure. Most of these are from Anstice." The letter disappeared into his bag. "These are all for Yevin. Yevin Bauk, one of the scribes up at the Arcade? You could ask him."

"Perhaps I will," Arandras said. *Alive and in Anstice, but still no name. Never a name.*

The courier nodded and left, but Arandras sat there a long while, staring at the old note and the space on his desk where the letter had been. The note was short, its brief message burned into his memory. Even now, five years on, it haunted his dreams; and when he encountered it there, the final line was always enough to tear him awake.

Speak of this to nobody, or your wife will be dead by morning.

And every time he woke, Tereisa was still dead, and he was alone.

~

Murder always left Eilwen Nasareen feeling ill.

She shifted in the saddle of her Guild-owned horse, rubbing ineffectually at the ache in her bad leg. Today was her fourth day on the road after a successful trade visit to Spyridon, and the third since the kill. Her victim's face had been bandaged. She'd never seen his eyes. Yet her stomach had been churning ever since, and even now, as she approached the end of her journey, her gorge rose at the memory of what she had done.

And of the four of them, she had killed only one.

Grimacing, Eilwen urged her horse on, her eyes narrowed to a squint against the bright sun. Fields of beans and barley crowded the road, the golden stalks of the latter waving gently in the faint breeze and filling the air with their grassy scent. Behind them stretched pastures dotted with recently sheared sheep, some grazing in small groups, others standing apart as though ashamed to be seen without their fleeces. Despite the day's warmth, a sympathetic chill stole into Eilwen and she hunched lower in the saddle.

Ahead lay Anstice, almost close enough to smell; its rooftops, spires, chimneys and redoubts all reaching skyward like trees competing for sunlight. The great forest of masonry sprawled across the landscape, spilling past the outer wall and into the surrounding farmland. She'd often felt when returning from a journey that the city had spread a little more in her absence, like a single living entity growing ever more corpulent.

One day it will grow so fat that the earth will collapse beneath it, leaving nothing but a vast chasm, she thought, and shivered at the imagined scene.

The black amber egg lay quiet at the bottom of her bag, wrapped once more in rags. She'd been a fool to take it out back at the inn; a fool to forget the hatred that stirred whenever the egg identified another of *them,* and the chafing desolation that could only be assuaged with another death. But she'd been weary, worn out by her negotiations in Spyridon and exhausted after her first day on the road. She'd not even realised what she was doing until she touched the polished egg, and then it was too late. After so long carrying the accursed object, she'd known exactly what its complex pulses meant: four servants of the Oculus, token-bearers all; three of them more distant, probably in the common room below, and the fourth in the room just across the corridor from her own.

The door had been unlocked; the room dark save for a candle by the bed in which the man lay. His head had been wrapped in wide linen bandages, but the bindings had shifted on one side to reveal angry, burned flesh across his cheek and ear. She'd been careful, creeping up beside him without a sound, not even a stumble from her bad leg. He'd had no idea she was there until she pressed the blanket over his face.

Afterwards, as always, she had resolved to cast the dark egg away. And then she had wrapped it and returned it to her pack, as she invariably did.

Never again. She looked up at the road, pressing her legs to her horse's sides and loosing an involuntary hiss as it broke into a trot. *I will never unwrap the damned thing again.*

But, of course, that was what she always told herself.

There was no single point where the fields ended and the city began. Here a slaughterhouse abutted the road, there an inn and stables; then she was riding past a cluster of partially constructed buildings, some nearing completion, others little more than timber skeletons. Builders and craftsmen laboured under the sun's steady gaze, shouting and hammering and crowding the road, many working with beams and other materials marked with the symbol of Eilwen's own guild. A high redoubt loomed away to her right, and ahead of her, the wall, cutting off her view of the city beyond. She turned her horse toward the hulking, pale grey gatehouse, its high flags of indigo and gold fluttering above the permanently open gate.

Between the flags crouched the great winged leopard of Anstice, cast in snarling, weather-stained stone.

The road split beyond the gate, bifurcating into the twin thoroughfares that passed through the city's heart and out the other side. Eilwen chose the eastern branch, resignedly settling in behind a covered wagon too wide to navigate around. *Ah, Anstice. Welcome home.* Largest of the five Free Cities worth the name, Anstice ranked among the most important trading hubs on the continent. Eilwen wouldn't have wanted to live anywhere else. *But gods, I wish this place had fewer people.*

Distracted by her thoughts, she almost missed her usual detour. She yanked the reins, steering her horse off the main road and walking it down a narrower side-street. The hunger would be near-impossible to rouse today, what with her still recovering from a kill; but avoiding the Oculus building was a good habit all the same, and in the wake of her latest lapse, she needed to make a point of reinforcing good habits.

After a few blocks, she rejoined the main thoroughfare.

Her first order of business on arrival, she decided, would be a bath. Pel would not expect her full report until tomorrow, and both her bags — one of trade samples, the other containing her personal items — would remain packed and ready for her next trip, whenever that might be. As a factor for the Woodtraders Guild, Eilwen was expected to be ready to travel whenever the instruction came down from the Trademaster. Such journeys were becoming less frequent now, as Pel did his best to allocate those assignments to others and so spare her leg the strain of travel. But Pel's influence only went so far, and so she kept her purse full and her bags packed, just as she always had.

The road split again at Merchants' Bridge, one branch a long, gently spiralling ramp lined with couturiers, moneylenders, and chocol houses, the other a wide set of steps that led directly to the bridge. Eilwen urged her horse up the steps and onto the bridge. A knot of children scattered at her approach, several waving sticks in mock combat as she rode by. Then she was down the other side, turning into Traders' Row, passing the complexes belonging to the other merchant companies and reining up outside the compound of the Woodtraders Guild.

Eilwen walked her horse through the high gate and dismounted heavily, grunting as her feet hit the ground. The main building stood before her, high and imposing, its carved stone face lit up by the afternoon sun. A wide lane on one side led to the river and the private docks at the rear. Coloured paving stones, sculpted bronze lampposts, and ornamental carvings on the older buildings all spoke of tastefully restrained wealth. But the elegance of the original design was now merely a memory. The Guild no longer confined itself to the production and sale of timber — cloth, stone, jewellery, spices, and a hundred other commodities now filled its accounts. Its range of interests had grown broad enough to rival any of its competitors, save perhaps Three Rivers, and with growth had come change. Warehouses, stables, and other, smaller buildings now crowded the compound's perimeter, their presence offering silent testimony to the triumph of practicality over display.

Abandoning her horse to a groom, Eilwen slung her bags over her shoulders and entered the main building. *First, find a maid and get that bath started. Second, tell Pel I'm back.* She made for the stairs, already imagining the caress of hot, rose-scented water drawing the ache from her leg. But as she rounded the landing, she found her path blocked by a familiar, ponderous form.

"Pel," she said. "I was just coming to see you."

Pel nodded, his face pinched in its usual disappointment. Eilwen suppressed the urge to say *I'm back* or something equally inane. Pel's typical response to such statements was that of a man listening to a once respected but now senile parent: a pained, regretful silence.

When he spoke, his words were not what Eilwen expected to hear. "Master Havilah wants to see you," he said.

"What? *Spymaster* Havilah?"

The pained silence; a momentary closing of the eyes. "The one and only," he said, making it sound like a gentle rebuke.

"Uh... right. I was just going to take a bath before I did anything else..."

Pel shook his head once. "He wanted to see you as soon as you got back," he said reasonably, as though explaining the matter to a child. "You can bathe later."

A prickle of fear stole through her. *He knows.* Somehow, after all this time, Havilah had found her out. He must have had someone there at the inn, watching her. *Who was it? What did I miss?*

Pel turned to leave. "Wait!" Eilwen yelped, and winced at the sound of her own voice. "Sorry. Um... what about my report? Do you want to hear...?"

But Pel was already shaking his head. "Later," he said.

"Right. Later."

She took a deep breath, watching Pel's back as he slouched away, leaving her alone. *Alone.* It was strange that Havilah had not already had her detained. Strange, too, that he had allowed Pel to deliver the message instead of one of his own people.

Eilwen glanced around. Nobody seemed to be paying her any attention. Below, just out of sight, the main door stood open. *I should run.* But she knew she wouldn't. She was a Woodtrader. Nothing else was as important as that.

I betrayed the Guild once before. I'll be damned if I'm going to do it a second time.

Havilah's office was on the ground floor. She turned and followed the stairs down.

∼

The door to Havilah's office was shut when Eilwen arrived. Her repeated knocking drew no response, and at last she retreated to a small, fortuitously vacant meeting chamber across the corridor. She paced, and sat, and paced again, confused and uncertain, as the sky outside the window turned pink and gold.

On reflection, it seemed unlikely that Havilah could have heard about her kill at the inn already. Nobody had seen her enter the injured man's room, she was sure; least of all the man himself. And she had left the next morning before breakfast, riding as hard as her horse and her leg could manage. For someone to have deduced her involvement and then beaten her to Anstice... no, it was impossible.

He's found out about one of the others, then. Or more than one. Enough to piece it all together.

But if so, where was he? Why keep her waiting? Eilwen racked her memory, trying to recall any contact she'd had with the man, any scrap of conversation. There wasn't much. She was a trade factor. She worked for Pel, who was adjunct to Laris, the Trademaster. She had no involvement with Havilah or his little group of spies who kept the Guild informed of its competitors' activities. No doubt parts of her reports found their way to his desk at times, but Pel coordinated all of that. It was nothing to do with her.

Her thoughts chased each other around her mind as she paced around the room, the late afternoon turning slowly to dusk outside, until at last Spymaster Havilah appeared at the door, an apologetic smile on his dark face.

"Ah, Eilwen," he said, his voice rich with the rolling accent of the Tahisi. "I'm so sorry to keep you waiting. I hope Pel let you pick up some food before sending you here?"

Eilwen hadn't felt hungry for days. "I'm fine, thank you."

"Well. Let's talk in my office."

She followed him into the next room, her confusion deepening. Havilah seemed relaxed, even friendly. *What in the hells is this about?*

Havilah shut the door and seated himself behind his desk. Eilwen perched on the edge of a simple wooden chair and glanced about the room. Books and papers filled the shelves covering one wall, but a second was given over to a large watercolour of a castle Eilwen didn't recognise. A shallow alcove concealed a door that presumably led to Havilah's private quarters. A disused raven's perch stood in the corner farthest from the entrance, half hidden in shadow.

"Now, Eilwen," Havilah said, folding his hands on the desk. "How are you enjoying your work?"

"What?" The word was out before she had a chance to think. "Sorry, I mean… my work? Fine, it's fine. I'm just back from Spyridon. Two of the big ink-makers have taken new potash contracts, plus a few smaller manufacturers. We picked up some business from Three Rivers — apparently they had trouble meeting their delivery dates last month. Word is that some fool managed to knock over a lamp and burned down a warehouse." *Gods, I'm babbling.* "Uh… was there anything specific you wanted to know?"

"Hum. No, I'll wait for your report." Havilah considered her, his expression amicable but intent. Deep creases framed his eyes and mouth, but there was no grey in his hair. Even so, she guessed him to be at least fifty, and probably closer to sixty. *Old enough to be my father. Gods, there's an unpleasant thought.*

She was suddenly aware that she was staring. Swallowing, she looked away, then down at her lap.

"You have a good eye for detail," Havilah said. "Most of the others don't report much beyond the numbers on their contracts, but you notice things." He leaned forward. "Noticing things is very important to my department."

Eilwen nodded, unsure what to say.

"Patterns of behaviour, for example," Havilah said, and stopped.

Fear filled her, stronger than ever, surging through her until she thought it would overflow. *He does know. Gods...* It was all she could do to sit there and wait for him to continue.

"Yes, I'm aware of your little hobby," Havilah said; but the words were gentle and there was no anger in his eyes. "It's going to have to stop."

"Uh, right." Her voice was a croak. She coughed and tried again. "Right. Stop. I can do that."

"Can you? It's four years since we lost the *Orenda* —"

Eilwen flinched. *Here it comes.* Four years ago she had betrayed a ship and watched it drown. There had been nothing to point back to her, no hint that the attack was anything other than a chance raid by Pazian pirates. Yet somehow Havilah had discovered the truth: that she was a traitor to the Guild, responsible for the deaths of a dozen colleagues; a liar and a snake who deserved nothing but condemnation.

She raised her head and looked Havilah in the eye. Strangely, her fear was gone. Even shame seemed absent. All she could feel was relief.

"Four years, Eilwen," Havilah said softly. "You've been sleep-walking ever since. Trying to salve your wounds with more blood. You need to accept what happened. A lot of people died. You didn't. That's how it goes."

Eilwen stared, disbelieving. *You think this is guilt over surviving, nothing more.* A second realisation followed hard on the first. *So you don't know why I kill who I kill. You must think I just select people out of the crowd, like a common murderer.* A mad urge seized her to protest; to explain that what she did was not murder, it was redress, it was *atonement*. That she had betrayed the *Orenda* but she would never, ever betray again, and that she was sorry, so very sorry. Tears pricked her eyes and she looked away, angrily blinking them back.

"There, now," Havilah murmured. "That's a start. That's good."

The kindness in the man's face was almost enough to break her. She brushed her eyes with her sleeve, willing the tears away. The weight of her secret was crushing, suffocating, an anvil on her chest. It was too much to bear. She had to be rid of it, she needed to speak, but she couldn't breathe.

"I, uh. Um. I... how did you find out?"

Havilah gave a slight smile. "That's not important. What matters is that nobody else knows. And it can stay that way, so long as it never happens again." He relaxed, leaning back in his chair. "Which brings me to the other reason I wanted to see you."

And with that, the moment was past. She sensed that as far as Havilah was concerned, the matter was now closed. He wouldn't mention it again, not if she stopped. And if she didn't, well, the warning was clear enough. *That* conversation would not be just between the two of them.

The burden settled back down inside her, a part of her once more, filling every piece of her with its weight, like lead in her bones.

She pushed an expression of interest onto her face. "Other reason?"

"Call it an opportunity," Havilah said. "As our trading interests grow, and as our competitors grow, so our need for information grows. I have nearly a dozen people now in Anstice alone, and more than three times as many in other places. I need someone to coordinate their efforts. Someone with an eye for the significant detail." He folded his hands. "Someone like you, perhaps."

"You want me to... be your adjunct?"

"Perhaps, in time. You can start with Anstice, and we'll see how you do."

The irony screamed. He trusted her! She put a hand to her head and tried to think. "Why me? Why not just promote one of your own people?"

"There, you see? An eye for the significant detail." Havilah paused.

"Unpleasantness aside, your recent activities provide one reason. You show a willingness to, shall we say, complete what you set out to do. Properly directed, that can be a tremendous asset." He raised a hand, forestalling her interruption. "Don't misunderstand me. I am not looking for an assassin. Nor is the Guild in the habit of solving its problems with a knife or a vial of poison. But I need someone who is prepared to be uncompromising in the Guild's service."

The words seemed to dance around some unspoken point. Eilwen looked away, unsure what to make of them, unsure what Havilah was expecting of her. *Not that it matters. Havilah wouldn't make an offer like this unless he believed I would accept it.* If she declined, he might think to question his other assumptions about her, and that was too big a risk to countenance.

"I accept," she said. "When do I start?"

Afterwards, as she left, Eilwen considered the reason Havilah had given her. *Am I uncompromising?* She didn't think so. Pel would never describe her that way. *I negotiate and compromise every day. Compromise is a factor's life.*

No, her kills were a singular thing. It was not ruthlessness that drove her. It was justice.

Spymaster Havilah, you've misjudged me.

It was definitely time for a bath.

CHAPTER 2

Gods do not seek equals.

— Kassa of Menefir, *Solitude*

RHOTHE'S BAR STOOD A DOZEN streets and half a world away from Arandras's shop. It occupied the narrow middle ground of Spyridon, straddling the two halves of the city: far enough from the Library to entice students seeking temporary escape from the stuffiness of academic surroundings, yet also far enough from the low market to attract those whose means had diminished but whose tastes had failed to adapt. Its interior reflected its dual nature, with a typically rowdy taproom at the front, where young scholars could indulge themselves without fearing a master's sudden intrusion, and a quieter area further back for those more interested in conversation than insobriety. Two upper levels held rooms that might equally be occupied by those climbing the social ladder or those on the way down.

The sky was darkening when Arandras arrived, his thoughts still preoccupied with the glimpsed letter. Bypassing the raucous taproom, he slipped through an unmarked door to the back room and its familiar scents of candle smoke, stewed meat, and dried apothecary's rose. Three iron chandeliers hung from the recently whitewashed ceiling, each bristling with candles. Bar staff flitted between tables, serving meals and clearing away empty plates and mugs. A groan from the centre of the room drew Arandras's attention: a party of three had one of the bar's *dilarj* sets out, though from what Arandras could see of the board, the game had only a few turns left in it. Other games at various stages of completion dotted the room, but Mara was not present at any of them.

Maybe she's not back yet.

But she was: there, in a booth by the far wall, her long black ponytail brushing her back as she glanced sideways at a second groan from the soon-to-be-defeated player, her cutlasses propped up on the seat beside her. Shaking her head, she turned back to her plate, mopping up the leftover sauce with a heel of flatbread. Arandras reached the table just as she put the last piece in her mouth, seating himself with a faint smile as she waved a greeting.

"Couldn't wait, huh?" he said as she chewed.

"For a hot meal? Gods, no." Mara swallowed, only getting part of her mouthful down. "I got back barely an hour ago. I haven't even been home." She gulped down the rest and grinned, eyes dancing with excitement. "Wait until I tell you what happened."

"What's that?"

"Well, let's see." She raised a hand and began ticking items off on her fingers. "Ambush. Sorcery. Death. Several of the latter, I think, though I wasn't exactly in a position to confirm either way. You might have warned me there were others on the trail besides us."

Arandras had no idea what she was talking about. "Uh-huh."

"Well, that's hardly..." Mara trailed off, eyes narrowed. "Has something happened, or are you just in a bad mood?"

"What? I'm not in a bad mood." His statement drew a cocked eyebrow, and he shrugged again. "It's not important."

"Crap." Mara folded her arms. "Tell me."

"It's nothing," he said. "I just... I had a visitor from the Library."

"Oh," she said, and he could hear the unspoken words in her tone. *That again.* "You know what you need to do, Arandras? Swallow your damn pride and pay the damn dues. It's just money, and not even that much. It doesn't mean anything."

Of course it does. He looked away. In any case, the morning's visit from Onsoth had rendered the question moot. Yielding to coercion only ever invited more. *Give way, and I mark myself as susceptible to such tactics. I become known as one who will bend. Until, one day, I come home to find a note on the table and my wife gone...*

"Forget it," he said, forcing a smile. "What's this about sorcery and death?"

Mara grinned. "I thought you'd never ask. Get yourself a plate and I'll tell you all about it."

Arandras snagged a passing barmaid, ordering a plate of stewed mutton and couscous for himself and ciders for them both. "All right," he said, sitting back in the booth's padded seat as the barmaid collected Mara's empty plate. "Talk."

"You were right about the temple," she began. "Finding that hill in the middle of the forest was a bitch. There was practically nothing left of the place. I'd have gone right past it if someone else hadn't been there already."

"Ah, damn."

"With someone else again looking on."

"What?"

"That's what I thought." She leaned forward, clearly enjoying the tale. "The first group were Quill. Your typical retrieval party, out of Anstice, I guess. They were just digging the thing out when I got there. I was going to leave them to it and head back when I saw someone else, perched up in a tree, watching them. He was good, too — still as a carving. Took me a while to be sure it wasn't just a trick of the light. Then I saw another one near the base of the tree, and a third further back."

Arandras frowned. "Who were they?"

"I don't know, but they got me wondering what they were up to. I figured I might have been seen too, so I started back the way I had come, hoping the Quill would stay put. Then I circled back, keeping my distance this time.

"They just stayed put that night. The next day the Quill moved off, and they followed. And I followed them. All day. Same thing the next day. I think the Quill guessed they were being followed and doubled back once or twice, making this other group backtrack." Her smile faded somewhat. "Honestly, I was lucky they didn't see me. It's just as well Druce and Jensine weren't there. They'd never have managed it."

The food and drinks arrived. Mara took a long pull from her

cider before continuing. "Anyway, on the third night they finally
got tired of following. I was woken by a scream like you wouldn't
believe, and saw this orange light flare out just past a low rise, like
someone had set a tree on fire. By the time I got there, two of the
Quill were down, and the survivors of this other group were chasing
after the last one. So none of them were there to see it. But I was."

Arandras leaned closer, drawn in despite himself. "See what?"

"One of the Quill wasn't quite dead," Mara said. "He got himself
up on his knees and threw something at me. Well, threw it away,
really. He couldn't have known I was there. But either way, it practically landed at my feet. Seems he didn't want his killers getting their
hands on what he'd dug up."

"So... you're telling me that you —"

"Grabbed it and got the hells out of there. And here I am. And
here it is."

She drew out a leather-wrapped object the size of an overlarge
scent bottle, placing it on the table with a satisfied grin. Arandras
picked it up. The bundle was light, surprisingly so; he shot a quizzical look at Mara, but she folded her arms and nodded at the wrappings. Frowning, he pushed them away and set the object on the
table.

It was a small urn, not even a hand's length in height, shaped
like two thirds of an hourglass, with a wide bulge at the bottom, a
narrow neck, and a slightly flared mouth. The surface was metal,
untouched by tarnish or corrosion, some of it elaborately carved
with images and script, other areas impossibly smooth. Its mouth
was sealed with a cap, the piece set too deep to offer any real purchase. He tried an experimental twist, but it refused to budge.

"Can you read it?" Mara asked.

Arandras squinted at the writing. It looked like a form of Old
Valdori, albeit an unusual one — he could guess at a few words, but
that was all. "Not here. Perhaps with the help of some books."

"What do you think it's worth?"

"Hard to say." The piece was obviously of Valdori make: nothing
else looked that good after centuries in the ground. "It depends
what's inside." He shook it gently, but there was no sound. "Could
be empty. Do you know how it opens?"

"No. I thought the writing might tell you."

"Perhaps it will. I'll see what I can translate tomorrow." He wrapped it again and tucked it into a pocket. "And I'll ask around, see how much people are willing to offer for it."

"Yeah, well, try to avoid the kind of people who'd rather kill you for it than pay you."

"I'll keep that in mind," he said. She tilted her head, studying his expression as though searching for something, making him feel like he needed to say more. "What did they look like, anyway?"

Her mouth twisted in a half-smile and she shook her head. "I don't know. Mercenaries of some sort, perhaps. They didn't wear big insignias on their backs, if that's what you mean, or have loud conversations about their employer."

Nodding, Arandras took a mouthful of stew and couscous; but before he could swallow, a new voice interposed.

"Couldn't wait, huh?"

Mara laughed, and Arandras looked up to see Druce hovering beside the table, Jensine a few steps behind. "Move over," Druce said, flapping his thin hands and collapsing into the booth with a sigh. "First things first," he said. "Who's sold anything?"

Good to see you, too. Arandras set down his fork. "One necklace of red porphyry disks for three sculundi, and two candlesticks of enamel and gold for one and a half luri apiece," he said. "The last of the tower haul. Comes to four sculundi and six scudi each." He produced three bundles of coin, each containing four silver lengths and six silver bits, and pushed them to the corners of the table.

"Ha," Jensine said, sliding in beside Mara and collecting her coin. "Hear that, everyone? One and a half apiece."

"Yes, yes, well spotted. I'm sure I said that at the time." Druce pulled open his bundle and immediately sought to hail a barmaid. "Gods, I'm parched."

The tip had come from the low market herbalist, who claimed to have seen the ruins of a Valdori navigation tower after venturing off the road near Lagen Cove in search of a particular weed. Arandras had been immediately sceptical — the coastal ruins in this part of Kal Arna had largely been ransacked centuries ago, their stones torn down and reused — but he mentioned it to Mara anyway, as he did all such rumours. She and the others had ridden out, and had indeed discovered the base of a ruined tower — not Valdori, but abandoned all the same, and old enough to suggest that whoever had once lived there was long gone. They'd found the trapdoor buried beneath the remains of the upper level, and the strongbox in the cellar beneath. Jensine had spied the shoulder-high candlesticks behind a creeping vine that had grown to cover two of the cellar walls, and somehow Mara had converted some cut vine into a saddle-sling and carried the candlesticks home.

Pickings since then had been slim. Arandras had discovered several leads that turned out to be false, and one that was outright criminal: a small Coridon-era watch-house that now served a senior Gislean cleric as a hideaway for his clandestine lover, a sometime galley cook from the Crimson Sails. On learning of the watch-house's owner, Arandras had warned Mara and the others off, but they'd ignored his protests and looted the place anyway, waiting until the house was unoccupied and filling a wagon with its contents. Furious, Arandras had renounced his share of the proceeds, leaving the others to dispose of the contraband as best they could. Salvage was one thing, but theft was quite another, and Arandras had no intention of sullying his hands with stolen goods. Such stains, once acquired, never truly wore off.

"Anyone else?" Druce said, slouching lower in his seat. "Mara? Tell me you've got a buyer for that damn puzzle box."

"It'll sell when it sells." Mara shot Arandras a sour look. "Of course, it'd sell a lot sooner if our man of letters here was prepared to help shop it around."

"You steal it, you sell it." The words came out sharper than Arandras intended, and he took a frowning mouthful of cider.

Jensine broke the silence. "Are you all right?"

"What? Yes, I'm fine. It's nothing."

"Arandras had the Library come knocking," Mara said, not entirely unsympathetically. "Again."

"So join them," Druce said. "Problem solved."

"I already told him that. It didn't take."

"Figures. Did he give you that look, like you just offered him a baby to eat?"

"Shut up now, Druce," Jensine said pleasantly.

"Seconded," Arandras said.

"The motion is carried," Mara said, earning a pout from Druce. "Or does no-one want to hear about our latest acquisition?"

Jensine looked up. "You found something?"

Mara grinned and began her story again, and Arandras took the opportunity to finish his dinner.

When she was done, Arandras produced the urn and handed it around. Druce took it reluctantly, his brow furrowed. "This place used to be a temple, right? Which god are we pissing off this time?"

"One that couldn't keep the walls from crumbling or the roof from falling in," Mara said. "Don't worry about it."

"Maybe it liked trees better than stone," Jensine muttered.

"It's probably just another minor deity. Weeper knows the Valdori had enough of them," Arandras said. "The urn might tell us."

Jensine gave the urn a cursory glance and handed it back to Arandras, who re-wrapped it and put it away. "Where did you say the lead came from? Seems odd that three different parties would pick the same day to check out a centuries-old ruin in the middle of nowhere."

"It was a page from some dead priest's journal. Got it from Sten, I think, up on Goldsmiths Lane." Arandras frowned. "Looked like a recent copy, as I recall — the sort of thing that might have been made forty or fifty years ago, but not hundreds. Or it could have been made last month, if someone knew what they were doing."

Druce sat up. "What, you think it was forged?"

"It wasn't fake," Mara said. "The ruins were there. And the urn, too."

"Or maybe the Quill got the urn someplace else," Druce said. "Or it was planted there for the Quill to find."

"What, so those others could watch them dig it up and then kill them? What's the point?"

Arandras gestured dismissively. "It doesn't matter." In the old days, he and Narvi and the rest of their group would no doubt have found the conundrum irresistible. But he'd left all that behind with the Quill in Chogon, and he had no desire to go back. *Besides, I already have a riddle that needs solving. All I need from the urn is silver from its sale.*

He stood. "I'll start shopping it around tomorrow. Unless any-one feels like delaying their coin for the sake of a few dead Quill?"

Nobody did.

"Right. Until next time."

"Arandras," Mara said. She leaned forward. "Don't let them get to you. All right?"

"What, the mercenaries?"

Mara rolled her eyes in mock-frustration. "The Library, of course." Her half-smile faded. "Join them or not, whatever you like. Just remember what they do if you let them in."

The same thing the Quill did. The same thing they all do, sooner or later. He nodded, and felt rather than saw the affirmation of the others: Mara, as hard and as sharp as the blades she carried; Druce, who'd have looted the strongboxes of every temple in the city by now if he wasn't so damn superstitious; and Jensine, who'd be happy simply to sit back on a green hill somewhere, a gaggle of children at her feet, and weave air and sorcery into cloud-puppets. *It's the only damn thing the four of us have in common. But it's enough.*

Druce's belch broke the moment. "Off you go, then," he said, waving his near-empty mug. "Send another my way, would you?"

"Best not," Arandras said. "The Gisleans say that the All-God forbids it, you know."

"Really?" Druce peered up at him cautiously. "What does he forbid, exactly?"

"Pickles."

He could still hear Mara's laughter as he emerged from the bar into the mild night air.

～

Clade Alsere stood motionless in the middle of his study, eyes open but unfocused, his breathing slow and steady. The slow toll of bells from the nearby Kefiran temple joined with other, more distant peals to mark the hour, but Clade ignored them all. Insensible to the vista of roofs and towers washed clean by the mid-morning sun, heedless of the rolling clamour of traffic beneath his window, Clade extended his awareness outward, groping past the limits imposed by

physical senses and on to the very edge of his perception, searching
for any sign of the familiar, hated presence.

The god was nowhere to be found.

Satisfied, Clade regathered the strands of his awareness. The
room around him snapped into focus, bringing with it a sudden rush
of sensation: the noise of lumbering wagons and shouting hawkers
from the thoroughfare outside, the cool whisper of air against his
face and neck, the scent of old paper and new timber. Four uphol-
stered armchairs faced each other around a low wooden table, the
arrangement filling the entire front half of the room. Behind him
stood his desk, the polished eucalypt surface scarcely visible beneath
weighted stacks of paper. Crowded shelves lined the walls, save for
the space near the inner door where he'd affixed a series of sketches
showing some of the sights of Anstice: the powder mill, Merchants'
Bridge, and the winged leopard that crouched above the entrance to
the city chambers. The study was light, airy and spacious; a fitting
home for the Overseer of Oculus operations in Anstice.

He would miss this suite, when the time came. He had lived
here for almost two years now, longer than anywhere since Zeanes.
Despite his eagerness to be gone, he'd developed an unexpected affinity to the place, as though at some point the walls had surrendered their indifference and become fellow conspirators in his long,
lonely struggle to find a way out, away from the Oculus, away from
the god. They had become his confidantes, the only witnesses to his
failures and frustrations and slow, painstaking progress; the only
counsellors to whom he dared speak his mind, and then only in
whispers.

A light rap on the door disrupted his thoughts. Garrett, arriving
almost on time.

A bad sign.

Clade seated himself behind his desk, the window at his back.
A slender steel pen rested beside an inkwell in a graceful lacquered
stand, half hidden by the piles of paper. Beside it, a marble horse-
head bookend gazed out from atop a stack as though surveying the
room. Clade pushed the stack aside, clearing a space where he could
rest his hands.

"Come," he said.

The door opened with the hesitant swing of a reluctant messenger. Garrett sidled into the room, blinking at Clade through floppy, straw-coloured hair, the swagger that usually animated his stride conspicuously absent. His hands were empty.

"I don't have the urn," Garrett said, his tone somewhere between apology and defiance. "They lost it."

A hollow opened in the pit of Clade's stomach. He responded instantly, walling off the feeling of despair, denying it access to the rest of him. *Control. Above all, control.* "Tell me what happened."

Garrett cleared his throat and fixed his gaze on the papers on Clade's desk. "Your estimate of the location was correct," he said. "The Quill showed up just like you said they would."

I was right. Satisfaction bloomed, weaker than his frustrated disappointment, but recognisable nonetheless. He confined it as he had the hollow in his stomach.

"The Quill led Terrel and his men straight to the site," Garrett continued. "A few hours later they had something out of the ground. Terrel was some distance away, but he's pretty sure it was the urn."

Clade grimaced. *You think I want to know his name? Fool.* But it couldn't be unheard now. He sighed, smoothed his expression. "Go on."

Garrett moistened his lips. "The Quill had a firebinder with them. Terrel waited for night, but the moon was full and the Quill set a watch. They trailed them the next day, but not well enough. Somehow the Quill realised they were being followed. In the end, Terrel had to give up on surprise."

"And?"

"He won, of course. But the Quill killed two of his men, and wounded a third badly enough that he died the next night."

"And the urn?"

Garrett swallowed. "They couldn't find it. They searched the Quill, but none of them had it. It just... wasn't there."

Clade fixed his adjunct with a cold stare. The young man was generally adept at hiding anything he considered weakness, but his reluctance to meet Clade's eyes betrayed his level of discomfort. Garrett hated to admit failure, Clade knew. *Almost as much as I hate to hear it.*

"You are a member of the Oculus," Clade said. "How are you going to repair this?"

"I've already told Terrel to go back," Garrett said, the words tumbling over each other in his eagerness to please — or was it simply eagerness to move on? "His job was to retrieve the urn. He doesn't get paid until he does that."

"Good," Clade said. His stomach no longer felt hollow. It was hard, now; a tight, heavy ball. He adjusted his barriers to compensate. "Remember that it's not just Terrel's job to retrieve the urn. It's yours."

Garrett nodded, though Clade thought he caught an edge of resentment in the gesture. "As you say."

"Pursue all avenues. Don't rely on Terrel to rescue the situation. Go out there yourself if you have to. Just find it."

"So why all this pissing about with journals and Quill and mercenaries?" Garrett burst out. "Why not just send one of our own sorcerers and be done with it?"

Anger flared. He dropped fences around it, corralled it, placed it alongside the other captured emotions.

"There is more at play than you realise," Clade said. "Suffice it to say that it would displease the Council if this operation were to become more widely known." That was true enough. They'd be more than displeased to hear that it was happening at all. "Be assured that the Council notices and values both your discretion and your effectiveness." Clade watched his adjunct absorb the meaning of the words. *That's right. Keep your mouth shut and get the job done.*

"Fine," Garrett muttered, then caught himself. "As you say. Do you have any other instructions?"

"Just find the urn. That should be more than enough to occupy you." Clade flicked a finger toward the door. "Go."

Garrett went, leaving Clade alone with his thoughts. His caged emotions were already dissipating. Only the tight knot of despair in his stomach still beat against the walls of its pen. Soon it too would fade.

It had been a mistake, perhaps, to entrust the urn's retrieval to Garrett. Within Anstice, the man seemed capable of finding or arranging almost anything. Beyond the sprawling city, though, his capacities dwindled rapidly. And perhaps his judgement was not as sound as Clade had hoped. The mercenary, Terrel, had been Garrett's choice. His failure was Garrett's failure too.

As Garrett's failure is mine.

Clade refused to permit himself the luxury of self-pity. What was, was. Wallowing would achieve nothing. But regret was different. Regret could be harnessed and forged into something else: determination, and strength of purpose. Resolve. And so Clade sat behind his desk and allowed himself to feel regret.

~

By midday his caged emotions were gone, but their departure failed to restore his equanimity. In their place rose something else: a vague, unsettled apprehension, like the tense stillness before a storm. It drifted through him like smoke, defying his attempts to wall it off. For a while he ignored it, pressing on with his task of reconciling invoices and receipts; but as the afternoon progressed, the feeling grew stronger, filling him with a deep, pervasive unease. At last he gave up, abandoning the unfinished summary of accounts on his desk and making his way outside.

The Oculus forecourt was a cool, drab rectangle, paved and walled with featureless grey stone. Two ornamental cannons stood atop the wall, pointing absurdly at each other over a plain, timbered gate that stood slightly ajar. Clade slipped through it and out onto the busy thoroughfare, picking his way between men, horses and carts to the domed Kefiran temple on the other side. The thick door swung open at his touch and he stepped inside, closing it behind him to shut out the clamour of the road.

He paused a pace in from the doorway, waiting for his eyes to adjust to the dim interior. The antechamber was a simple room of bare stone, smooth and cool to the touch. A pair of censers flanked an open portal on the other side of the room. Rich smoke curled up from the wide brass bowls, suffusing the chamber with a sweet aroma that reminded Clade of sugared almonds. He took a deep breath, filling his lungs with the cloying, familiar scent, then crossed the chamber and passed into the tabernacle itself.

The god didn't like temples. Clade had made the discovery by accident some time ago, after the majordomo employed to manage the Oculus building lost his daughter to the Brachan fever. The god had been with Clade when he arrived at the Gatherer's squat temple for the funeral, but as he entered he'd felt it shiver, and a moment later it had left. It wasn't that the temple had refused it entry, exactly; or at least, it hadn't seemed that way to Clade. Rather, the god had simply found it more comfortable to be somewhere else.

A few days later, in the middle of a discussion with several of his sorcerers about the differences between binding eucalyptus and other kinds of wood, the god had come upon him again. Curious to see whether the outcome could be repeated, Clade had halted the debate and brought the god here, slipping tentatively into the round Kefiran tabernacle; and once again, its presence had departed the moment he stepped inside. Since then, he'd repeated the experiment at a Gislean shrine, a Sarean sanctuary, and the grand Tri-God pantheon on the far bank of the Tienette, and on each occasion the result was the same. Whenever Clade entered a temple, the god preferred to be elsewhere.

The portal opened onto a large, circular room. A tall, elaborately carved box stood upright in the centre of the room, surrounded by a low velvet rope. Sunlight filtered through stained-glass windows high in the domed wall. Curved timber pews filled the outer two-thirds of the space, arranged in such a way as to form four quarters. Though the aisles between quarters approached the central ark at right angles to each other, they seemed misaligned with the encompassing building, as though whoever had arranged the seating had imagined the doorways to be a few paces around from their actual positions. It had taken Clade several visits to realise the reason for the odd arrangement: the aisles were aligned with the cardinal directions, making the large, round space into a kind of oversized compass.

At this hour the tabernacle was largely deserted. A pair of elderly men sat in the northeastern quadrant, their heads bobbing in unison as they prayed. Clade selected a pew in the next quadrant along and bowed his own head.

Anxiety rose within him, thick and noxious, plucking at the strands of his awareness and inviting him to draw deep. He closed his eyes, resisting its pull but not its advance, allowing it to range through him unimpeded. Something like a butterfly flitted through his stomach. His fingers twitched, then began to tap out a pattern on his knee. Clade retreated within himself, watching as his body gave itself over to the insistent, needy emotion. Then he turned his attention inward, striking into its billowing swells in search of the canker at its heart.

I don't have the urn, Garrett said in his mind, rueful and defensive and insolent all at once. *They lost it.* The Quill had taken the bait, providing the team and the resources that Clade had been unable to raise from within the Oculus for fear of attracting the god's attention. They'd followed the information Clade had fed them, located the urn, and raised it from its millennia-long sleep. And then, somehow, they had lost it.

Did they know? Clade experienced a genuine burst of fear, its dark stream blending with the pale, elusive currents of anxiety. If the Quill knew what the urn was and where it led...

But no. It had taken Clade years of painstaking research and investigation to discover this single thread leading back to the fabled Valdori golems. Surely the Quill could not have made the same connection from the journal page Garrett had fed them to induce their participation — and if they had, there was no way they'd have sent only a standard field team to retrieve it. *An army of soldiers fashioned from stone and sorcery by the Valdori themselves? The Quill would have burned down the entire forest to find anything even remotely connected.*

Yet the urn had vanished all the same. His one lead to the golems was gone. And without the golems, his entire plan to rid himself of the god was little more than smoke.

Heaviness returned to his stomach, leaching despair like a drenched rag. He responded instantly, dropping walls into place, sealing it off from the rest of him.

Despair. Not anxiety.

Not the urn, then. He blinked up at the red wood of the carved Kefiran ark, at the stained-glass windows and domed ceiling. *Something else.*

A sung note sounded from somewhere behind him, high and clear. It was joined a moment later by others, male and female, from various points around the perimeter of the room. The pews had filled up a little since Clade's arrival, though the two elderly men still had a complete quadrant to themselves. Clade settled into the pew, watching as the brown-robed singers filed slowly down the aisles to form a circle around the roped-off ark and commence their afternoon prayers.

Here in Anstice, the major services at dawn and dusk were conducted mostly in Yaran, the common trade language of eastern Kal Arna. Further west, it was said, Kefiran services were often held in Kharjik, and in other, more obscure languages. Prayers, however, were always and only recited in the native Kefiran tongue. Clade had come to appreciate, if not exactly enjoy, the winding, arrhythmic tapestry of voices. There was a strange, alien beauty to it, something wild and melancholy and profoundly other. Many of the olive- and brown-skinned singers had the characteristic brown-auburn hair of native Kefirans, but Clade saw others who could easily have lived in Anstice their whole lives, as well as two pale, high-browed Mellespenes. And the dark, hook-nosed woman nearest the east aisle was almost certainly Bel Hennese.

Of all the All-God religions, the Kefirans seemed to have the greatest success in attracting outsiders. Despite the compelling strangeness of their prayers, Clade found it hard to understand the appeal. The Kefiran god was obsessed with laws: what to eat, what to wear, how high to build the fences around one's roof, and what animal to kill whenever one of the other laws was broken. There was a bank of altars behind the tabernacle, where proscribed sacrifices were performed daily at the request of penitents. When the wind was right, the stench of offal and burnt animal flesh carried directly into Clade's study, where it would linger for the rest of the day in silent testimony to Kefiran sinfulness.

Yet even as he despised the mess of laws at the heart of the Kefiran faith, part of him harboured a grudging respect for the seriousness with which the Kefirans took them. Though their concept of wrongdoing seemed hopelessly tangled, their treatment of it was not. Where the Gisleans watered down the weightiness of evil, proposing acts of good with which one might somehow balance out the cosmic ledger, the Kefirans held firm. Only blood could buy atonement.

Only with death could the slate be wiped clean.

The prayer drew to a close, the singers ending on a single note, startling for its clarity. Then, heads bowed, they turned and filed back up the aisles. A man sitting a few rows in front of Clade stood with a grunt and followed the last of the singers out.

They lost it, Garrett had said. *They,* not *I.* As though the wrong-doing had belonged to someone else, someone unconnected to him. And in his eyes, a flicker of defiance.

And then the uncharacteristic outburst. Not frustration, as Clade had initially thought. Something else.

Contempt.

His unease thickened, pressing against his throat. He raised hurried barriers and drove it back, pushing the shapeless emotion down toward the cage he had prepared for it. It resisted, slithering sideways as though it might slip past his will; but he had its measure now, and he took hold of it as if it were a rebellious puppy, dropping it in its box and snapping the lid shut.

Garrett. The man had let his mask slip, there in Clade's study. And beneath it Clade had glimpsed... disloyalty? No, not exactly. Garrett was not the type to offer loyalty to anyone other than himself. In truth, Clade considered it a point in the man's favour — an absence of loyalty to the Oculus left him malleable, more receptive to Clade's direction. Loyalty was a method of control, nothing more, and where one such weakness was absent, another could usually be found. Pride, for instance, or avarice; or, in Garrett's case, ambition.

It had served them both well. Clade had promoted Garrett to adjunct, feeding the man's hunger for advancement with promises of recommendations to the Council, some of which he'd even kept; and Garrett in turn had done all Clade had asked of him, always willing and usually successful.

And now it was over.

There had been contempt on his face, and more. Resentment. Garrett no longer saw Clade as the best avenue to satisfy his ambition. He had begun to see him as an obstacle.

From such a fall there was no coming back. The man's usefulness was at an end. He could no longer be controlled, and therefore he could no longer be trusted.

Coloured sunlight from one of the stained-glass windows crept across Clade's knee, causing him to look up. Even the two old men were gone now. A still, pensive silence filled the room like a held breath, marred only by the faint noises of the street outside.

I could find a new adjunct. Clade frowned, considering the possibility. Bring in someone new, and send Garrett back to Zeanes. But there were dangers with that option. So long as Garrett was close, he had an interest in making at least a show of loyalty to Clade, and in keeping the secrets with which Clade had entrusted him. Away from Anstice, however, such discretion could not be assured.

No, Garrett would have to stay. After all, the man wasn't stupid. Even if he no longer saw Clade as an aid to his ambitions, he could hardly fail to realise that Clade could still hinder them greatly if he chose. Fear would keep him in line for a while yet.

The remaining details assembled themselves in Clade's mind. Garrett would have to retain the task of recovering the urn, at least for the time being. To insist on the urn's importance and then re-assign the task to someone else would likely be a provocation too far. That aside, Garrett would work on Oculus business only, and Clade would find someone else to assist him with his private project. A party from Zeanes was expected in a few days' time, bringing with them two new sorcerers for Anstice, including an old student of his. Perhaps he could find a way of assuring himself of her trustworthiness. Perhaps, with her, it would be loyalty after all.

Clade stood, stretching the kinks from his back. The despair he'd contained was gone now, vanished as though it had never been. He nodded, satisfied.

A sharp bray from somewhere nearby caught Clade's ear. The noise came again, then abruptly cut off. A chanted prayer took its place; a lone baritone this time, delineating the contours of the earlier song like a pencil sketch traced over watercolours. A sacrifice, conducted on one of the altars behind the temple.

He paused, a smile playing about the corner of his lips. For all their solemnity, for all the gravity with which they invested their law, somehow the Kefirans were never quite able to stop sinning. Rather than amending their actions, they chose instead to address the consequences. Forgiveness. Absolution for sins committed. Removing the sin as though it had never been.

But it had. Imagining otherwise was worse than foolish, and Clade had never been a fool.

He strode from the temple, through the smoke-filled antechamber and onto the street. The Oculus building stood opposite, tall and imposing, dark despite the afternoon sun. Arms folded, Clade squinted up at his adjunct's window, just around from his own.

You failed me today, Garrett. Be assured that you will not fail me again.

I will not permit it.

CHAPTER 3

Why does a man desire a sword, or a horse, or a son? Is it not to extend the effective reach of his will? So you see, it is foolish to question the study of sorcery, as if it were unlike any other thing upon the earth. Sorcery exists, therefore it must be obtained.

— Giarvanno do Salin I, *Meditations on Power*

"**M**ASTER ARANDRAS?"

Arandras looked up from his half-written letter and frowned at the boy sitting cross-legged in the corner of his shop. "I'm nobody's master, least of all yours. Just Arandras is fine." Wil stared back, unabashed, and Arandras set down his pen. "What is it?"

"How many words are there?"

"How many...?" Arandras shook his head. "I don't know, Wil. Lots."

The ditch-digger, Leff, had come by the shop that morning in response to the marked inkwell Arandras had left by the man's door while heading out to the bar the previous night, his usual signal to indicate the arrival of a new missive. Wil had come too, settling onto the corner table with a wax tablet on his lap and a stylus in his hand, marking out large, slanting letters as Arandras read the message from Leff's sister to them both. "You don't mind, do you?" Leff had said, as he always did when leaving his son in the shop, and Arandras had waved him off with a smile and a shake of the head. The boy was quiet, unusually serious for a child of six summers, with an uncommon capacity for stillness. Sometimes, when Wil was present, Arandras found he could think of Tereisa with something not far from repose.

"What about the Gisleans? Do they have as many words as we do?"

"More than likely," Arandras said.

"And the Kefirans?"

"The Kefirans and Gisleans mostly share the same words," Arandras said. "The Sareans, too."

"Oh." Wil considered this new development with a frown. "How come?"

Arandras smiled. "They just do." *Six years old, and already interested in comparative linguistics.* "Maybe when you're older you can go to a school and learn all about it." Though if that were to happen at all, it wouldn't be in Spyridon, where the Library had a monopoly on the teaching of languages. Because even if Leff could pay the fees, who would vouch for a ditch-digger's son?

"What about the Pazians?"

But Arandras's mood had soured. "That's enough talk for now," he said, and Wil subsided. "Let's have some quiet writing time, shall we?"

The day's most pressing task involved the production of eleven identical letters from a former Menefir guardsman to some old comrades in arms, all but two to be written in Kharjik, all to be collected tonight by the guardsman, who was organising delivery himself. Arandras bent over the writing desk, laboriously sketching out the angular characters that communicated the man's distasteful message: a plea for help in recovering his unwed daughter, who had apparently run off with a troupe of singers bound for the supposed wine and roses of the Kharjik Empire.

Arandras spelt out the guardsman's name at the foot of another copy and set it atop its fellows. The Kharjik word for *unmarried girl* gave no indication of the subject's age, but in this case it wasn't hard to guess. A year or two shy of nineteen, most likely. Old enough to make her own way here in the Free Cities, but not among the Kharjik. Not unlike Mara at that age, perhaps, though he only knew a little of her childhood or her life prior to her arrival in Spyridon. *Farm-raised, wasn't she? I wonder if her father went after her?* Probably not. By all accounts, most farmers could ill afford even a few days away from their herds, let alone weeks or months.

Good luck to you, girl. I hope you find the life you want. He drew a fresh sheet of paper from the low stack beside his desk and reluctantly began the final copy, recording once more the girl's description and her father's request that anyone seeing her advise him without delay and, if possible, separate her from her companions and confine her until his arrival. A wave of revulsion filled him and he stopped mid-sentence, struck by an overpowering urge to tear up the letters, abandon the job and refund the guardsman his coin.

He pushed the letter aside, setting the ink teetering in its cup. The guardsman had agreed to pay two and a half scudi for the eleven letters: close to Library rates, and more than Arandras typically made in a week, but not so much in light of their windfall from Jensine's candlesticks. He could have the money ready to give back when the guardsman came that evening.

Better to lose a few scudi than make himself part of such a repulsive affair.

Decision made, Arandras leaned back in his chair, mentally ticking off the tasks that remained for the hour or so before he could close the shop. *Three letters of complaint from Asan the glazier to his recalcitrant debtors, and a message from that ghastly Mellespene woman to her equally ghastly son, and half a dozen more just the same, and who cares about any of them?* Arandras shook his head with a voiceless sigh. *The hells with them.* He could write them all as well tomorrow as today. When the time Arandras had promised Wil was up, he'd close the shop and go looking for this Yevin. And until then...

He raised the hinged surface of his desk, released the catch that opened the hidden drawer beneath, and drew out the urn. In the daylight it seemed smaller than it had last night, duller somehow, less significant. Writing snaked around the urn's rounded lower half, encircling it several times. A series of images engraved below the writing showed a variety of settings: cliffs, forests, towers, and more. The human figures varied in size from scene to scene, and sometimes within a single image, but Arandras could see no pattern in the appearance of smaller figures — children, presumably — in some scenes but not others.

But it was the writing that drew his attention. The script was clearly derived from Old Valdori: the letter shapes were immediately familiar, despite their slightly stylised appearance, and he recognised a few common pronouns and adverbs which were shared by nearly all the known dialects. The bulk of the inscription, however, was a mystery. He could mouth the words easily enough, but the sounds were unfamiliar to him, their meaning frustratingly out of reach.

Arandras took a large, calfskin-bound book from the shelf and began to leaf through it. There were four major branches of Old Valdori, each comprising a host of variants and dialects. The book contained only a few examples of each group, but if he could work out which of the four branches most closely corresponded to the writing on the urn, it would at least be a start.

"What's that?" The question was soft, wondering. Wil gazed at the urn with wide eyes, stylus and tablet forgotten. Arandras suppressed a smile. To a boy for whom a new shirt was a luxury, the finely-crafted urn must have seemed as exotic as a Tahisi chocol service.

"It's an urn," he said. "Like a small vase, but metal instead of fired clay. And it has a lid." He tilted it toward the boy, showing him the cap. "I'm trying to read the writing on it."

Wil hopped down from the table, resting his elbows on the desk and bringing his face alongside the urn. "Does it open?" He leaned closer, brushing the urn with his nose.

"Careful," Arandras said as Wil hastily backed up. "I don't know if it opens or not. Maybe the writing will tell me, if I can work out what it says."

"Who does it belong to? I bet they're rich, and have a big house with servants and horses and everything."

"It belongs to a group of people. They want to know what the writing says, so they've asked me to find out." No need to tell the boy of his own share in the urn's ownership. As far as his customers knew, Arandras was little better off than any of the rest of them.

"How are you going to read it?" Wil asked, examining the

unfamiliar characters. "All the letters are strange."

"I'm hoping this book will tell me," Arandras said. "So why don't you climb back up there and let me see what I can find out."

But it seemed the language on the urn was more obscure than most. The hour passed in silence, followed by a good portion of the next, until at last Arandras turned the final page of the book, little wiser than he'd been at the beginning.

Frowning, he lifted the top of his desk and returned the artefact to its hidden drawer. *Oh, well. It was worth a try.* For some buyers, an untranslatable inscription might even increase its value. He could already think of one or two who might bite.

"Time to go, Wil," he said, standing. "I've got an errand to run, and I need to close the shop for a while."

Wil closed the tablet without complaint and slid down from the table, but when he reached the doorway he turned back. "Will you tell me what that vase says when you work it out?"

We'll sell it before I can solve it, Arandras thought, but all he said was, "I'll tell you."

He stood by the door as Wil ran off, the boy's small feet kicking up puffs of dust with each step. If Tereisa and he had had a son, the lad and Wil might almost have been of an age. Arandras wondered what name he and Tereisa would have settled on. They must have discussed the possibility of children a dozen or more times, but somehow they'd never talked about names.

But the name he truly wanted to know wasn't that of his absent son. It belonged to the man who had stolen him before he'd ever been born.

And Arandras knew where to look first.

⁓

The Arcade ran around the brow of King's Hill, overshadowed only by the Library and the old palace. According to the histories Arandras had read, the two complexes had originally comprised a single estate, built by the scholar-kings some hundred and fifty years ago after the collapse of the Coridon republic and re-establishment of the Free Cities. But Spyridon no longer had kings or queens, and though a prince still lived in the palace, the title no longer carried any real power. That now belonged to the city circle, and foremost among the circle's members was the Conservator of the Library.

Dozens of small shops lined the inner side of the Arcade, each one partly set into the hill and separated by stairs that led up to the Great Square and the Library itself. Though most shops still housed Library scribes, many were now home to pressers and typesetters, some selling printed copies of sought-after books, others offering bespoke printing to those who could afford the not-insignificant cost. The Arcade's other side opened to the city below and the sur-rounding country: tiled roofs of brown and red; the half-built walls at the city's edge — a strange design, all sharp angles and out-thrust bastions, claimed by those in charge to offer greater resistance to cannon bombardment than a simple ring; and beyond that, dis-tant orchards and meadows, all framed by the dark granite of the Arcade's balustrade and arches. Street vendors wandered back and forth along the wide gallery, calling out their wares to passers-by and the Arcade at large.

The scribes and printers in the first few shops claimed never to have heard of Yevin, though each professed themselves more than willing to satisfy whatever need Arandras possessed with their own services. Eventually Arandras tried a pie-seller, who directed him to a shop near the far end of the Arcade in exchange for the purchase of a pastry filled with carrot and eel. But the shop's door turned out to be closed, and the heavy wooden shutters fastened shut. Arandras contemplated it with a frown as he finished his pastry.

"You are seeking someone, yes?"

Arandras turned. A bear of a man in a too-small printer's smock waved an ink-stained hand from the door of the neighbouring shop. Behind him, his equally burly assistant glanced briefly at Arandras before bending his head to a partially-filled frame of type.

"I'm looking for a scribe by the name of Yevin Bauk," Arandras said, walking across. "I'm told that's his shop?"

The printer chuckled and shook his head. "Ah, you are too late. He left this morning, with the sunrise. So eager he was, he could not wait even for the second bell. Left me some books, he did, that he wished returned."

Damn it. "Left? Where did he go? Is he coming back?"

"Why yes, of course he is coming back!" said the man, laughing. "He travels only to Anstice. He will return in, what, a week? Perhaps two. Not long."

"Oh. Good," Arandras said, caught halfway between relief and frustration. *Anstice, again.* Surely it was no coincidence that Yevin should take a hurried, apparently unplanned trip to Anstice the morning after receiving that letter. *But no, there were a dozen or more letters in that bundle and Grae said most of them were from Anstice.*

"This Yevin, he owes you money? Owes you work? Do not be fearful, he will return, just as I say."

"No, it's nothing like that. I wished to consult with him on a... professional matter. Do you know what business he has in Anstice?"

The man shrugged. "Business is what business is, yes? Me, I would need very good business there to miss so much business here. But maybe his business here is not so good, not so much to miss?"

"Maybe." Arandras considered for a moment. "You mentioned some books. Could I see them?"

"Ah, no, you are too late for that, too. They are already returned to the Library. And no, I am sorry, I do not remember what they were. Just books."

"I see. Well. Thank you." Arandras nodded to the man, who returned it with another chuckle.

"A pleasure, of course. I will tell Yevin that a friend asked after him. He will be delighted, I am sure."

Yeah, I'm sure. With luck, Arandras's visit would be gone from the big man's memory by the time Yevin got back. He returned to Yevin's shop, frowning at the stout shutters. A week, then. Frustrating, to be forced to wait; but also an opportunity. He turned away, leaving the shop behind and taking the stairs that led to the hill's summit.

He emerged at the edge of a sweeping plaza paved in sandstone and granite. An elaborate fountain commanded the square, its central spout of water reaching high into the air. Small patches of lawn dotted the area around the fountain, some bright beneath the sun, others shaded by gently swaying maples. The main Library building stood on the other side, high and red, its wings extending nearly the entire width of the square. Glimpses of other structures could be seen further back, all worked in the same fiery sandstone. The old palace, Arandras knew, lay somewhere at the back of the cluster of buildings, crowded in by structures that had once served the considerable demands of the royal household but which now belonged to the city of Spyridon and its ever-expanding Library.

Arandras crossed the square briskly, passing through the Library's high doors and into a narrow foyer. To the left lay the vast reading room, which formed the sum of most people's experience of the Library — only registered scribes were permitted either to browse the shelves in person or borrow a book. A waist-high gate at the foyer's end barred access to the stairs that led to the Library proper; beside it, a man in Library grey surveyed the room, his face impassive. Doors on the right opened to the smaller enquiry room, where men and women in grey sat at high desks built into a long wooden counter, some engaged in low conversation with a scribe or other inquirer, others waiting to be approached.

All right, Yevin, Arandras thought, entering the enquiry room and scanning the open desks. *Let's find out what you've been reading.*

Most of the desks were occupied by regular library staff, but at the endmost desk he saw what he was looking for: a student of perhaps seventeen summers pushing a pair of leather-framed eyeglasses higher on her nose, the embroidered tome-and-inkpot of the Library still fresh on her grey shirt. She looked up at his approach and frowned as the eyeglasses slid back down.

"How can I help you?" she said, adjusting her eyeglasses again and tilting her head back to keep them in place.

"I'd like to check another scribe's borrowing record, please," Arandras said. "A man named Yevin Bauk."

"Oh." The girl looked at him in surprise. "People really do that?"

"On occasion." Arandras offered her a slight smile. "If you please."

As Arandras understood it, the rule had been introduced by one of the later scholar-kings, as an attempt either to undermine the growing power of the scribal class or to shore up popular support by throwing open the Library to the whole city. Whatever the reason, the borrowing records of those accorded the privilege were technically public property, and could be browsed at any time by anyone admitted to the Library. In practice, the request was rarely made, and even more rarely satisfied unless the requester was himself a Library scribe.

The girl disappeared through a door at her back, returning after only a minute or two with a handful of papers. "Here we are," she said, resuming her seat and adjusting her eyeglasses once more. "Yevin's most recent loan consisted of two volumes. There, you see?"

Arandras examined the indicated section. One of the books was an untitled treatise by Tiysus Oronayan, a historian and philosopher from the time of the Second Kharjik Expansion, comparing Valdori gods and practices with those of the even earlier Yanisinian culture. The other was simply called *Forms of Sorcery*, with no author listed. He placed his finger on a small squiggle beside the title, marked in a different ink to the rest of the page. "What's that mean?"

"That's an instruction not to return the books to the shelf. Someone else must have had them on reserve."

"Huh. Can you find out who?"

The girl smiled. "See that note at the bottom? That's a 'Q'." She paused, obviously expecting a response, but Arandras just shook his head. "As in the Quill. The sorcerers, you know?"

"Yes, I know who the Quill are," Arandras said. "I'm sorry, I'm a little confused. I thought only Library scribes were permitted to borrow books."

The girl nodded, causing her eyeglasses to slip again. "That's right, of course. Narvi of the Quill joined the Library a few months ago. He comes in quite often, almost every week."

Narvi's here? Arandras stared. *What in the hells is Narvi doing in Spyridon?* "A few months ago," he repeated. "He's been here that long?"

"Ah, I thought it was you!" came a familiar voice from just behind him, and Arandras started to turn, a smile already forming on his face; but this voice was harsh, grating, and unpleasantly triumphant. Not Narvi. More like...

"Onsoth."

The official give a satisfied smirk. "Lord Swine. Well, well. How did you get so far from your sty?"

Ignoring him, Arandras turned back to the girl. "Thank you for your assistance," he said. "You've been very helpful."

"What's this?" Onsoth picked up the page. "Checking up on who's borrowing what?" He shook his head, tutting disapprovingly. "Dear me. Feeling envious of our betters, are we?" He dropped the page and strode to the middle of the room. "Excuse me, please," he called out, and a hush descended on the room. "Staff, please take note." He pointed at Arandras. "This man is not a Library scribe. He does not have the privileges of a Library scribe. Please treat him as you would any other illiterate, low market scum." He smiled. "That's all."

The weight of the room's eyes settled on Arandras. He stood, face burning beneath his beard, and started toward the door.

Onsoth stepped into his path. "Nothing to say, Lord Swine?" he said softly, his lips curled in a smug smile.

Arandras met his gaze. "Not to you." *And still less to your masters, who will pat you on the head and tell you what a good cur you are.* "Step aside."

With a mocking flourish, Onsoth complied. "Stay in your hole next time," he murmured as Arandras passed. "We don't want your stench infesting the books."

Too late for that, Arandras thought as he reached the door at last and emerged into the plaza. Against the reek of the Library, no other scent stood a chance.

~

The benefits of being Havilah's not-quite-adjunct were soon apparent. The house steward invited Eilwen to move out of her single room and into a two-room suite.

The steward offered her a choice between a first floor suite overlooking the river and one on the ground floor by the building's interior garden. Eilwen inspected both and chose the latter, drawn by the low-branching eucalypt just outside. The suite was already furnished — desk and shelves in the front room, bed in the back — but it took the better part of the day for her to move her possessions, and each trip up and down the stairs sapped the strength from her leg a little more. Her small library was first to come down, the books freed from their crate at the foot of her old bed and placed carefully on the shelves meant for her work. Next came her travel bags, followed by armfuls of clothing, then other assorted items. By sunset, even her good leg was beginning to ache; and when at last she came in with the final sack of sundries, she dumped it in a corner and collapsed onto the bed, wanting nothing more than to lie still.

I'm aware of your hobby. It's going to have to stop. Havilah's words echoed in her ears, low and rolling and sad. *I can do that,* she'd said in response; but in truth, she wasn't sure. In the days following a kill, while she was still sick with horror and disgust, it was easy to renounce her bloodlust and swear to make an end of it. But sooner or later the horror would pass and her conviction would fade with it, turning first to desire, then to mere hope. And then, predictable as Rondossan clockwork, memories of the *Orenda* would stir once more, filling her with thoughts of justice unserved and a deep, unrelenting hunger, until eventually even hope would desert her and she would yield to the beast within once more.

What reason, then, to expect success now? What had changed that wouldn't change back? No matter how strong her intentions, sooner or later they would wane, and the whole wearisome cycle would begin anew.

But if she truly meant to stop, there was something she could do. *I can cut out the eye that shows me who deserves to die. I can destroy the black amber egg.*

Her mind shrank back even as it found the thought. The polished black spheroid was all she had of Tammas and the *Orenda,* all that was left to remind her of the two crates she'd brought on board, of the dozens of people she'd delivered up to be killed.

And why do you wish to be reminded? a traitor voice whispered in her mind. She tried half-heartedly to silence it, but it spoke on. *What good has the memory done you? The egg is a chain around your ankle, dragging you down again and again. Be rid of it. Free yourself.*

Eilwen pushed the words away. She was a trader. Persuasion was a tool she employed, not one to which she submitted. And the egg, too, was a tool, nothing more. If there was corruption to be found, it lay not with the egg but deep in her own heart, where nothing could touch it. It didn't matter what she did. Sooner or later, the desire to kill would rise again, egg or no egg.

That's what you fear, isn't it? the traitor voice whispered. *More than anything else. You fear that the urge to kill will come, but you will no longer possess the means to choose.*

The thought shook her. Was it true? Was this why she held it so tightly — because even the prospect of killing again was better than the chance she might need to kill but be unable to do so? The darkness yawned, an abyss within her, and she lay trembling on the bed, her heart pounding in her ears.

When she rose, she felt as if she were sleepwalking, as though her body were acting of its own volition. She dug the smooth, black mass out of her pack and unwrapped it. It winked in her palm, bewitching for its darkness, like a jewel of the night.

She stared at it for a long moment. Then, standing swiftly, she drew her arm back and hurled it against the stone floor.

It struck with a crack, bouncing away into the shadows at the foot of the bed. Eilwen scrambled after it, retrieving it from the corner of the room and holding it to the light; but the egg was undamaged, its glossy black unmarked by the impact. A mad panic seized her and she threw the egg again, and again, and when it remained whole she took a rock from the garden outside and struck the egg with it, over and over, trying to crush it, pulverise it, grind it to powder. But nothing she did so much as scuffed the surface; and at last she cast herself onto the bed, weeping, the hateful egg wrapped in her fist.

After a time, another thought came to her. She opened the sacks that she had brought down but not yet unpacked, scattering their contents across the floor until she found what she was seeking: an old iron trowel, its blade notched but still strong.

Outside, kneeling before the eucalypt in the light of the half-moon, she began to dig, angling around the larger roots and hacking through the smaller ones until she had a hole almost as deep as her arm was long. Then she took the egg and placed it at the bottom, reaching all the way in to be sure, releasing it only when her fingers brushed earth. Head bowed, she pressed it into the dirt with her fingertips, wishing she were a Quill earthbinder so she could send it down, deep down, out of reach and beyond recall.

Eventually she withdrew her arm and began shoving the dirt

back in, stomping it down, packing it hard. Then the wild energy left her and she stumbled back inside, undressed, and fell into bed. She lay there as the night crawled by; exhausted but unable to sleep, waiting for the grey light of dawn.

~

A loud knock woke Eilwen from her slumber. She sat up, blinking in the light — golden light, not grey. Dawn had come and gone.

She rose, cursing, and reached for her clothes. Dirt stained her sleeves and the entire lower half of her trousers. She flung them on regardless, brushing them off as best she could until a second knock sounded, harsh and insistent, and she gave up.

"A moment!" she called, hastily belting her trousers. She strode into the outer room, hissing at the sensation of cold stone beneath her bare feet, and threw closed the door to her bedchamber. A third knock came. She tied back her hair, paused a moment to catch her breath, and opened the door.

An unfamiliar man stood waiting, a large box slung awkwardly under one arm and a tight expression on his face. He squinted down his long nose at her, his eyes not quite meeting hers. "You are Eilwen Nasareen?" He proffered the box before she could respond. "These are for you."

After the exertions of the previous day, Eilwen had no desire to hoist yet another box, however short the distance. "Uh, thank you," she said, stepping aside to let him pass. "On the desk will be fine."

He brushed past her, scowling, and dropped the box on the desk with a thud. "These are agent reports for the past month," he said without turning, as if addressing the box. "Older reports are also available, should you wish to see them."

Eilwen folded her arms, frowning at the man's back. His collar and trouser hems were frayed and showed signs of clumsy repair, and his hair was beginning to thin. "And you are?"

"Ufeus." He turned, staring at a point somewhere beside her ear. "I perform low-level coordination of our agents in Anstice. Master Havilah informs me that I now report to you."

"Pleased to meet you, Ufeus. I'm Eilwen." She caught herself, smiled. "As you already know, of course."

A flicker of one eyelid was her only response.

Oh, gods, another Pel. She pressed on before her smile could slip away. "What does that mean, exactly? 'Low-level coordination?'"

"I maintain regular contact with each agent," Ufeus said stiffly. "I relay instructions from Master Havilah. I provide agents whatever resources they require. I receive each agent's reports and channel the information back to Master Havilah. I keep an archive of past reports, which I use to cross-check information as required. In short, I implement the decisions of Master Havilah."

"Or, now, you implement my decisions."

Bitterness flitted across his face, there and gone again in the space of a heartbeat. "Indeed."

"Well. Thank you, Ufeus. I'm sure I'll want to talk with you again once I've taken in all of that." She gestured at the box. "Is there anything that you feel requires my immediate attention?"

Ufeus hesitated, his gaze shifting sideways to meet her own for the first time. His eyes were hard and narrow — reassessing her, perhaps, or maybe suspicious that she was somehow mocking him. "There is an... oddity," he said at last. "A complaint from Brielle." He spoke the name with an odd emphasis, one that suggested some kind of disfavour. "She seems to think that one of our other agents is encroaching on her territory, dealing with some of her contacts directly."

Sounds like a low-level coordination problem, Eilwen almost said, but stopped her tongue in time. Ufeus's expression was bland, but the tightness about his eyes betrayed his interest. *You know what it sounds like, don't you? And if I tell you I don't care, it will be my fault later on when I complain about being kept in the dark.* It was a common enough negotiating tactic, one she'd learnt to recognise years ago. For the first time in the conversation, she began to feel confident.

"All right," she said. "I want to talk to her. Brielle, was it? Arrange for her to come and see me, please. I'd like you to be there, too. Tomorrow would be ideal."

Ufeus inclined his head, his expression unreadable. "As you say."

"Thank you." She gestured toward the door. "I'm going to go find some breakfast. Care to join me?"

"I ate several bells ago," he said, and Eilwen winced. Of course he had. He and everyone else. She realised she didn't even know what hour it was. "But if you require my presence —"

"No, no," she said hurriedly. "You go on. We'll talk later."

Her stomach growled as Ufeus departed and she looked out into the garden, trying to judge the time. Perhaps she could have a clock bought for her office? It couldn't hurt to ask. Havilah had a painting, after all.

Her eye caught on the bare patch of ground beneath the eucalypt and she turned away, regretting the impulse that had moved her to bury the egg. She should have tried other options first: fire, perhaps, or steel. But it was done, and there was no way she was going to dig it up now. *Or ever.*

Perhaps burying it was not so bad, though. Sooner or later the grass would return, and beneath it the tree's roots would thicken, wrapping around the hated object until nothing short of sorcery could pry it loose again. The egg would be lost almost as finally as if it had been destroyed.

All she had to do was wait.

CHAPTER 4

Dawn is the Dreamer's time, before the sorrow of the day begins.
Noon is the Weeper's time, and none escape its bitter toil.
Dusk is the Gatherer's time, when dreams and tears meet their end.

— Liturgy of the Bells, *Tri-God Book of Prayer*,
Pantheon of Anstice

FEW THINGS, ARANDRAS THOUGHT, PROMISED so much yet changed so little as gold.

He picked his way down the narrow, winding street, enduring the hostile glares and bored glances of the hired swords who stood watch over the close-pressed shops. Goldsmiths Lane, the road was called, and though few of the establishments that now lined the street devoted themselves solely to goldsmithery, most still had some connection to the craft that had given the road its name. Type foundries, moneylenders, and jewellers now shared the quarter, along with others who found proximity to such wealth useful.

Arandras found the street depressing. The plated doors, the barred windows, the guards watching his every step — all offered mute testimony to both the allure of gold and its ultimate impotence. *It is steel that rules the world, not gold.* Gold served only to amplify whatever it found, be it fear or charity, lust or hope. Of itself, gold changed nothing.

He rounded a bend, glancing at the faces of the guardsmen as he passed. The Menefiri with the runaway daughter had failed to appear at Arandras's shop last night; it was possible that he might encounter the man here, though an open street would be an inopportune place for the conversation Arandras intended to have. The letters Arandras had written remained intact, concealed in a locked drawer beneath his desk. During the wait of the previous evening, he'd entertained notions of tearing them up in the guardsman's face, but now, under the warm midday sun, such theatrical defiance seemed childish. It would be enough to simply return his coin. Anything more would only be an indulgence.

Gold to buy words, and words to invoke steel, if the recipients responded favourably. Even this small transaction demonstrated the limits of wealth. But then, in the end, even steel had its limits. Steel might rearrange the players, but the game was always the same, whether played in an alley for bread, or here for coin, or even between cities and kings. A single, tedious, never-ending game: compel and resist, compel and resist, over and over again.

Arandras hated it.

His mood sour, Arandras drew up at his destination: an antiquities shop, its window and door reinforced like its neighbours, but lacking a guard. The heavy door stood half-open, wedged in place by a wad of leather. The shop within was empty save for Sten, the proprietor, who sat behind the counter with a magnifying lens in his eye, peering into the ear of a seated clay idol of what appeared to be an infant boy. Shelves lined the walls, crowded with a dusty, eclectic collection of objects that had little in common apart from their apparent age.

"Like it?" Sten said as Arandras reached the counter, rotating the idol and fixing his gaze on the clay figure's vacant eyes. "It's supposed to be the Gatherer, if you can believe that, although whose idea it was to depict the god of death as a child is beyond me." He snorted. "Unless it was meant as some sort of substitute. Something for the Gatherer to take instead of their actual child. Like a god's not going to know the difference."

Arandras glanced over the round clay figure. The styling of the hands and feet suggested an early Kharjik origin, as did the infant's complete lack of hair. "Maybe it's an offering," he said. "A token of respect, perhaps, or a plea for mercy."

"Hah, right. 'Oh Gatherer, I made you this fat clay kid so please don't kill any of us.' Good one." Sten rotated the idol again, then stopped and looked up at Arandras. "Actually, that's not bad. I might use that. A token of respect, yes. Purchase it to placate the god's wrath. Should be just the thing for a superstitious merchant's wife."

Arandras rolled his eyes. "Weeper spare me."

"Not his department," Sten said with a grin. "What brings you here, then? That priest's page lead you anywhere interesting?"

"As a matter of fact, yes." Arandras pulled the urn from his bag and placed it on the counter. "How much would you say it's worth?"

Frowning, Sten picked it up and turned it over in his hands. "More children," he muttered, following the progression of images around the urn. "Must be the day for it." He ran a finger over the engraved surface. "What does the writing say?"

"I don't know. It's not in any of the major dialects."

"What's inside?"

"I don't know that, either. It might not open at all."

"Hmm." Sten squinted at the urn's mouth, poking at the cap. "And I suppose you don't know how it was sealed, either."

Arandras said nothing, and Sten didn't seem to expect a response. He put the urn down and removed the lens from his eye.

"I'll give you one lurundi and two luri for it," he said, polishing the lens. "It's pretty enough, but hardly distinctive. Best I could hope for is that it catches someone's eye and sells itself."

"One and two in gold," Arandras said noncommittally, concealing his surprise. The sum was significantly higher than his own rough estimate of the item's value. Sten would be lucky to avoid a loss if he tried selling it as a purely ornamental piece, let alone make a profit. He frowned.

"One and five, then," Sten said. "Just because I'm curious."

"Indeed." Arandras picked up the urn and hefted it, unsure. One and five was far more than he'd expected, and the prospect of a quick sale held no small appeal. But if Sten was willing to pay that much, what might the Quill offer? They'd sent a party to retrieve it, after all — though as Arandras well knew, every expedition was a gamble. Perhaps this was the piece the Quill were after, perhaps it wasn't, and perhaps they hadn't even been looking for anything specific. *And perhaps Sten is gambling too, and this is the best offer I'm going to get.*

But Sten's interest had stirred Arandras's own curiosity. How long was it since he'd come across a Valdori dialect he didn't recognise? Not since he left the Quill, at least. And then there was Mara's account of the urn's discovery. Someone else was interested in the urn besides the Quill, and if they had the resources to go up against a Quill field team, they'd have plenty to offer when it came to a straight sale.

Maybe, just maybe, this was the find they were all hoping for. Gold enough to step out of the endless, tiresome game once and for all; to leave it all behind and not look back. The only change gold could truly bring: a way out.

Besides, after his visit to the Library, he was going to have to visit Narvi anyway. He might as well ask him about the urn while he was there.

"One and five," he said, putting the urn away. "I'll keep that in mind."

"It's a temporary offer," Sten said. "Might not be available when you come back."

"I'll take that chance." Arandras turned to leave, then turned back. "That journal page," he said. "How many copies of it did you sell?"

"What?" Sten's features assembled into something like wounded indignation. "You think I'd make extra copies and sell them without telling you?"

"Of course you would. Did you?"

"Hah. You're right, I would. I didn't, though." He smirked. "Don't know anyone else foolish enough to throw silver away on something like that."

"Delighted to hear it," Arandras said. If throwing away silver brought him artefacts he could sell for gold, he'd do it every time. "Where did you get it?"

The shopkeeper spread his hands. "I really couldn't say. Are you sure you don't want to sell that urn? One and five, last offer."

Arandras said nothing.

"Look, it wasn't stolen, if that's what you're worried about. You know I respect all my customers' little peccadilloes, even yours." Sten's gaze flicked to Arandras's bag. "Are you married? Think what you could get your wife with one and five in gold. Or your lady friend. Whatever."

Arandras shook his head and turned away. As he headed for the door, Sten called after him.

"How about an idol? Appease the Gatherer, avert his eye. Protect your family!"

Arandras spun. He reached the counter in an instant and grabbed Sten by the front of his shirt. "Never mention my family again," he hissed. "Ever. Understand?"

"What did I say? What did — *yes,* yes, I understand!"

The madness passed as quickly as it had come. Arandras stared at Sten, shocked at his own reaction. "Sorry," he muttered, letting go of the other man's shirt. "Sorry." Grasping his bag tight to stop his hand from shaking, he wheeled around and strode from the shop.

The guards and shopfronts of Goldsmiths Lane awaited him, the sunlight glinting on steel as oppressive as ever. Compel and resist, compel and resist. Over and over.

And how different am I to any of them?

He quickened his pace until he was almost running, not caring if the guards stared after him. Every scrape of sword in scabbard and creak of leather armour felt like an accusation, the sounds pursuing him as he half-jogged around the corner and down the slight incline. Steel, endless rows of steel; and even when an ox-drawn wagon lumbered past, the beast bellowing its displeasure at some imagined slight, somehow he could still hear their whispered indictment.

Weeper's tears, I hate this street.

~

The Quill schoolhouse in Spyridon was as small as any Arandras had seen. Squashed between an ageing tenement on one side and a weaving house on the other, the narrow building was only three floors high. A square, weather-worn banner hung from a top floor window, the ochre feather immediately recognisable even if the black field seemed more like muddy grey. Directly beneath it stood the main doors, four steps up from the street and as narrow as the rest of the building.

The notion of Narvi being in Spyridon had settled somewhat in Arandras's mind, but the thought of a Quill becoming a member of the Library still sat strangely. After Tereisa's death, Arandras had moved to Spyridon specifically because the Quill were so few here, a consequence of the city's — which was to say, the Library's — hostility toward the sorcerers. Now, it seemed, that hostility was greatly reduced. *Of course it would be Narvi.* Arandras scratched his beard as he considered the pinched doorway. *Always the peacemaker.*

Inside, a single corridor ran the length of the building, a cramped staircase at each end. A sign hanging from the ceiling directed visitors toward a partially open door, behind which Arandras found a small waiting room containing half a dozen chairs and a second, closed door on the opposite side. An undersized handbell stood on a low corner table, and when Arandras rang it, it gave a high peal that lingered in the air like the clang of a wind chime.

The inner door opened, admitting a young man with oil-slicked hair and a practised smile. "Can I help you?"

"Yes, I'm here to see Narvi Parhenu."

"You have an appointment, of course?"

"No. I'm an old…" *Friend,* Arandras had been going to say, but for some reason the word wouldn't come. "Colleague," he said at last. "Tell him Arandras Kanthesi is here."

The young man assumed an expression of regret. "I'm sorry, but Narvi is very —"

"Please. Tell him Arandras is here." The man seemed about to object again, but Arandras spoke first. "Tell him. If he wants me to make an appointment, I will."

"Very well," the man said eventually. "A moment."

Arandras leaned back against the wall. In truth, he had no idea how Narvi would react to his presence. *We were friends, once. That was a true thing.* But it was no longer something Arandras felt — it was just something he knew, like the dates of the Calamities, or the similarities between late Yanisinian and early Valdori metalwork. *A fact of history. Just another thing that once was.*

The door swung open. Arandras looked up, expecting to see the young man again — but it was Narvi who stood before him, brushing messy brown hair out of his eyes and grinning like a Halonan fortune-carving. "Arandras? Dreamer's daughters, it really is you." He laughed, grasping Arandras by the shoulders. "Gods, it's good to see you."

"And you," Arandras said, surprised by the warmth of Narvi's greeting. He cast about for something to say, his gaze falling on the Quill feather pinned to Narvi's shirt. The ornament's point was edged in gold. "Is that...?"

"Ha, yes, I made Elector. Just like you always said I would."

Did I? Arandras didn't remember. "So, what, you're running the schoolhouse now?"

"Me? Dreamer, no. Half the time I'm not even in Spyridon." Narvi shook his head. "Come, we can't talk here. Follow me."

Narvi led him through the building to a small withdrawing room. Three large chairs faced each other around a patterned carpet of taupe and forest green, with an unlit fireplace in one wall. "Can I offer you some apple wine?" Narvi asked, fetching glasses out of a cabinet. "We've got more than we can possibly drink, don't ask why, and it's really very good. Have some, please."

Arandras accepted a glass and sat, stretching his legs. "So, what did you do to get sent to Spyridon?" he said. "Must have been something dire."

"Oh, come on, it's not so bad," Narvi said. "I looked for you when I got here, you know — must be close to a year ago, now. Knocked on the door of every single shop in the Arcade, but you weren't in any of them. Figured you must have moved on."

"Not yet," Arandras said. "But you were looking in the wrong end of town. I'm down by the low market."

"Of course you are." Narvi studied him over the rim of his glass. "I should have guessed, I suppose."

Arandras sipped the wine. It was smooth, and sweeter than he expected, though the apple flavour was only apparent in the aftertaste. "So if you're not running the place, what are you doing?"

"This and that. Building bridges with the Library, for one. Soon we'll be taking students and finally be a schoolhouse in more than just name." Narvi shrugged. "I coordinate things, some here, some in Anstice. Mostly I just solve problems so other people can do the real work."

"No sorcery?"

"Not much. And honestly, I can't say I miss it. All those hours in your own head trying to figure out why the damn construct keeps collapsing." He gave a rueful smile. "Probably sounds mad to you. Sitting and thinking — who wouldn't want to do that, right?"

Arandras shrugged. Only a handful of people could reach into the world around them and touch sorcery. Aside from a brief time during childhood, he'd never wished it for himself. "And Katriel?"

"In Anstice, and taller every day." Narvi grinned. "You'd scarcely recognise her. She's as high as my elbow now."

"You've done well. I'm glad," Arandras said, and found that it was true. "Listen, Narvi. I need to ask a favour. It's... well, it's about Tereisa."

The sorcerer's grin faded. "What about her?"

Arandras took a breath. "I think the man who killed her is still alive."

"What? No, they found him." Narvi made a face. "Dead in the river, wasn't he?"

"I thought so," Arandras said. "Until a few days ago. Just listen, please." He began a brief account of the past several days, telling Narvi about the letter, the missing scribe, and the books he'd borrowed from the Library. Narvi listened without comment, raising his eyebrows when Arandras named the books. "And so I need to know what's in those books. They're the only lead I have, at least until Yevin gets back."

Narvi shook his head. "Sounds thin, Arandras," he said. "Honestly. There must be hundreds of people with similar writing to your man."

"This wasn't similar," Arandras said. "It was the same."

Narvi gave him a long look. "All right," he said at last. He set down his wine and pushed himself to his feet. "Wait here."

"Thank you."

The door swung closed, and Arandras drained his glass. It was strange to be back in a schoolhouse again, even one such as this, drinking wine with Narvi like in the old days. How many times had they sat together on a cool Chogon evening, sometimes with Tereisa, sometimes with others, discussing the day's work, or the quality of the season's cherries, or whatever else took their fancy? Even now, it seemed, some part of him still thought of it as home. Perhaps it wasn't surprising. He'd been happy, after all. *No, more than that. I was content.*

Because I still believed.

The door swung open, and Narvi entered with two slender volumes. "I haven't even had a chance to look at them yet," he said, passing them to Arandras. "Do you know what you're looking for?"

"Not really." Arandras opened the first volume and began leafing through the hand-copied pages. The book bore the title *Forms of Sorcery,* and appeared to be an exposition on the sorcery employed by the Valdori before their fall, veering from military to religious to artistic applications and back again. Much of the content appeared to be highly speculative, if not outright fabrication. "Why did you borrow them?"

"I've got a team out in the field," Narvi said. "We got word of an old Valdori religious site — some obscure sect or order local to this region, as far as we can tell. I'm trying to find out more."

Arandras froze. "A field team," he said casually, keeping his gaze on the book in front of him. "What are they hoping to find?"

"It's — well, I can't really say. I'm sorry. You know the rules." The regret in Narvi's tone was plain. "Maybe I can tell you more when they get back. Should be any day now."

Or, perhaps, not at all. Arandras's hand went to his bag, coming to rest on the small bump made by the urn. *Was it your team that Mara saw killed?* He shivered. *And if you borrowed those books to investigate the urn, did Yevin borrow them for the same reason?*

"Arandras? I said, perhaps I can say more once they're back. If you'd like to know."

"Thank you," Arandras said. "Yes. I'd appreciate that." He took a breath. "Can you tell me why you chose those two books, specifically?"

"Simple, really. I asked the librarian for books about minor

Valdori sects and sorcery, and these were the ones he suggested."
Narvi shrugged. "For all its other resources, the Library's got barely
anything worth looking at on sorcery. And the handful of decent
books they do have never make it back to the shelves before someone else borrows them again. Any schoolhouse library on Kal Arna
has a better collection — well, except us. Chogon's sent us a few
books to get us started, but we still have to go to Anstice for any
serious research."

Arandras nodded, only half listening as Narvi chattered on
about the shortcomings of the Spyridon schoolhouse. If the Library's books about sorcery were truly so few, Yevin may well have
borrowed these two for reasons entirely unrelated to the urn. Except
Arandras didn't believe it. Tereisa had been kidnapped for ransom:
a Valdori dagger Arandras had access to at the time. Her abductor
had only killed her when Arandras, trusting the Quill to rescue her,
had refused to hand it over. *And now someone's looking for this urn,
and they've already killed some Quill to get it, and with Yevin's help
they're going to... what?* His train of thought ran out, and Arandras
breathed a sigh of frustration. He was right, he was sure of it. But
he needed more.

He closed the book and stood. "I should go," he said, handing
the books back to Narvi. "I've already taken more of your time than
I intended."

"It's no hardship." Narvi smiled, his gaze turning inward. "I still
miss it, sometimes. You and me and Tereisa and the others, back
there in Chogon. Before it all became..." He trailed off. "You know.
Complicated."

Before we knew better, Arandras thought. *Some of us, anyway.*

"Tell me what you learn," Narvi said. "About the letter, I mean.
If there's anything any of us here can do to help, just say the word."

There was no chance of Arandras doing any such thing. He'd
gone to the Quill for help in Chogon, and their actions had shown
him exactly where their interests lay. *I believe you care, Narvi. But
you don't speak for the Quill.*

In every way that matters, the Quill speaks for you.

"Thank you," he said. "I'll keep that in mind."

～

The god owned him.

Clade had given himself over to it, almost twenty years ago. At the time, of course, he'd had no idea what was happening, and when he finally discovered what he'd done the day he joined the Oculus, it was far too late. The god came and went as it pleased, watching through his eyes, listening through his ears. Sometimes it stayed only minutes before flitting away again. Sometimes it stayed for hours. Most days he wanted nothing more than for it to just leave him alone.

Today he stood in the open gallery atop the Oculus building, hands resting on the rough stone balustrade as he gazed out over the city and awaited the god's arrival.

A narrow stone tower marked the position of the city chambers to the northwest. Behind it rose the spires of the Tri-God pantheon in a cascade of blue and scarlet, gold and emerald green, the myriad coloured tiles bright in the afternoon sun. The high roofs of the merchant guilds across the river stood apart to the north, almost in line with the wide thoroughfare that ran past the Oculus building's door and, if one followed it far enough, all the way to Spyridon on the southern coast. Smoke and chanted prayer rose from the grounds behind the Kefiran dome across the road, the former drifting away on a breeze almost too faint to feel, the latter rising and falling in volume as though the singer alternated between addressing the penitent who brought the sacrifice, and raising his face to the heavens.

Sighing, Clade returned his attention to the road. The riverboat carrying the new sorcerers up the Tienette from Borronor's Crossing had been sighted approaching the city a few hours ago. Two of the sorcerers would stay in Anstice; the others would proceed to Damara, or Rondossa, or even as far west as Shandrel. The occasion of their arrival offered a rare opportunity for Clade to test the limits of his perception.

During his time at Zeanes, Clade had witnessed half a dozen binding ceremonies, and as his awareness of the god's presence grew, he began to notice its fascination with new blood. Whether the god was motivated by a desire to learn more about its new members, a determination to confirm their competence and loyalty, or a simple lust for novelty, Clade did not know; but whatever the cause, the result was the same. For a while, the god would move almost exclusively between the new additions, leaving Clade free of its presence for weeks. He had taken advantage of its distraction this time to pursue several sensitive undertakings; most significantly, his attempted retrieval of the urn. Now, as the window of its absence swung closed, he stood in the gallery and watched the road, await-ing its approach.

He saw the party before he felt it: seven or eight people on foot and a horse-drawn cart loaded with baggage, still several blocks away. He slowed his breathing, stilling his thoughts and allowing himself to rest a moment in the inner silence. Then he pushed his awareness outward, reaching down to the thoroughfare below and probing gently for the alien presence.

The group drew closer. His eyes tracked their advance, the visual report ignored by all but a small corner of his mind as he groped forward. Emptiness greeted him, flat and featureless. The horse raised its head in a whinny, the sound registered by his ears and brushed aside. They were two blocks away. One block. *Is it there?* The thought drifted across his awareness, leaving ripples in his con-centration. He let it go, stilling his mind again and nudging his perception outward, and out some more, reaching as far as his inner senses could stretch.

The party halted before the gate. A bell sounded somewhere be-low, but Clade was scarcely aware of it. Someone emerged from the building and crossed the forecourt, struggling with the gate for a moment before opening it. As the first figures passed between the cannons and stepped into the courtyard, he felt something brush the edge of his outstretched awareness: a breath of wind, almost im-perceptible at first, then condensing, still light and fragile but now also tangible, a swirl of otherness touching his mind. The presence of the god.

Clade allowed his consciousness to surface, and his sense of the god evaporated like mist on the Tienette. The cart drew up in the forecourt, the gate swinging closed behind it. Five storeys separated him from the group below. Despite an unimpeded line of sight, he'd failed to notice anything until the god was almost directly beneath him, and even then his perception had been faint and tentative.

Distance, it seemed, was still a greater barrier to his senses than he'd hoped.

Someone paid the driver, and the rest of the party began moving into the building with their bags and boxes. Clade left the gallery and headed for the staircase. *Five storeys. How far is that when turned horizontal?* Far enough, probably. Down on the thronged streets he'd be lucky to see anything that far away. And if he knew in advance where to look, the question was academic anyway.

But if he didn't know...

He descended the stairs, hand hovering over the banister, his steps beating a quick rhythm against the solid timber boards. Somewhere below, the god was entering the building. Seeking distraction, Clade turned his thoughts to spell construction, began reciting the basic forms that comprised the foundation of all sorcery. *The ground, a binding's source of power. The scaffold, to provide structure for the rest of the binding.* Converters. Connectors. Combine this piece with two of those to form a compound structure resistant to motion. Chain such resistors together like so to strengthen the effect. Add a trigger — a delicate piece in its own right — and connect it to the rest to form a rudimentary locking mechanism. Nothing a reasonably strong adult couldn't force open, of course; but if one substituted the resistors for a more complex piece that knit the two surfaces together —

A shadowy tendril touched the edge of Clade's concentration. He halted, releasing his focus, and the shadow expanded in a dark, ethereal swirl, spreading over him like unfurling wings.

Clade tensed, an instinctive reaction born of months of subterfuge and concealment. The god's presence washed over him and he resisted the urge to shudder. It was close, but not immediately so. He stood on the landing between the first and second floors, out of sight of the entry hall. Voices echoed up from below: the stern tones of the majordomo; a high, female laugh, infectious and familiar; and a thin, half-heard chuckle that Clade couldn't quite place. And somewhere among them all, the god.

One and a half floors up, and maybe a dozen paces across. Not a bad result, all things considered. Better than he'd managed the last time he'd had opportunity to test it. There was no chance any more of it sneaking up on him while riding someone else. The only way the god could surprise him now was by coming upon him directly, and that particular risk was simply unavoidable.

Satisfied, Clade resumed his descent, stepping down into the invisible fog of the god's presence and the wide space of the entry hall. The domestic staff had already begun to lead the new arrivals away to their temporary lodgings. Another laugh bubbled up from the room's edge, and Clade caught a glimpse of curly hair as a young woman disappeared around a corner. *She made it, then. Good.* An unexpected warmth rose within him, and he paused on the step to allow himself a moment's gladness.

The moment passed. Clade nudged his pleasure into a cage and shut the door. The hall was almost empty now, save for a pile of uncollected luggage and a woman leaning awkwardly on a walking stick. She turned at Clade's approach, iron-grey hair brushing her shoulders, and he blinked at her in startled recognition.

"Ah, Requiter, there you are," she said. "I was beginning to doubt my welcome."

"Councillor Estelle," Clade said, pushing a smile onto his face. "Forgive me, I didn't know to expect you. How was your journey?"

Estelle waved a gnarled hand. "Like all journeys these days. Best when over." Her expression softened. "It's good to see you again, Clade."

"And you, of course," Clade said. "What brings you here? Are you staying long?"

"A while. I have business in Anstice. I'll be staying for a few weeks, give or take."

"Indeed?" Oculus business in Anstice was usually Clade's to manage. "Well. I trust it won't occupy all of your time. I'd hate to see you leave without a chance to catch up."

Estelle smiled and leaned closer, lowering her voice. "No need to worry. We'll have plenty of time to talk on the way back."

He gave her a quizzical look. "I'm sorry?"

"The Council has an opportunity for you, something I think you'll like. You're going home, Clade."

What? Clade shook his head. "I can't leave Anstice right now. I'm sorry."

The smile faltered, just enough for him to notice. "This isn't the kind of job that waits. This is the kind you take the moment it's offered." She patted his arm. "Don't worry. You'll like it. I promise."

Estelle turned away, the clack of her walking stick echoing in the hall as she followed in the wake of her fellow travellers. At the edge of the hall she paused and glanced back.

"We'll talk later, Clade. Start thinking about what needs doing to get the place in order." She gestured with the walking stick, taking in the building, the city. "You've done well here. I'm proud. We all are."

He gave a slight bow, trying to keep his expression pleasantly neutral. She inclined her head in response and resumed her course, her progress punctuated by the staccato beat of the walking stick, the sound fading as she turned a corner and disappeared from view. The faint redolence of the god settled in his mind like a bitter aftertaste, no longer near but not quite distant enough to ignore.

It owned him, yes, but it did not control him.

And neither did Estelle.

Dinner was more lavish than usual, a gesture of welcome to the newcomers, particularly the sorcerers who would be staying with them in Anstice. Clade kept the pleasantries short. Meals were not the time for speeches.

For some reason, Estelle took a seat at the far end of the table rather than with Clade in the middle. Clade let it be, content to avoid further cryptic remarks about his future, and passed the meal in conversation with some of the party who had arrived that afternoon. The god flitted back and forth between sorcerers, occasionally disappearing entirely, but never for long. Clade watched the reactions of his dining companions as the god came and went, but saw nothing to suggest any awareness of its presence. As far as he could tell, they were entirely oblivious to it.

Sweetmeats were served, and several of the travellers excused themselves with pleas of weariness and the need to resume their journey early the next day. Clade glanced down the table. Estelle sat with her chin on her hands, absorbed in conversation with Garrett and another of Clade's sorcerers, Sinon, a brute of a man with a raw, intuitive talent and a sour temperament. Garrett said something inaudible, gazing at the ceiling in affected earnestness, and the others laughed.

Movement across the table caught his eye. Clade looked back to see Sera slipping into the vacated seat opposite him, a bright grin on her face.

"Hello, Master Clade," she said, then clapped a hand to her mouth. "Oh! I should say Overseer Clade now, shouldn't I? Overseer Clade. *Overseer* Clade. Sounds strange."

"Strange indeed." Clade bit into a piece of marzipan. "The sorcerers here call me by name. 'Overseer Clade' is what the staff call me."

"Ooh. So I should just say 'Clade'?" Sera stared at him, scandalised. "I don't know if I can do that."

Clade gave a mock-frown. "Councillor Estelle told me you'd be joining us as a bound sorcerer. Perhaps she was mistaken. Let me find her and check —"

"No!" Sera yelped, then laughed. "No, *Clade,* that won't be necessary. Oh, that sounded strange."

"I'm sure you'll get used to it." He relaxed into a smile. "It's good to see you, Sera. How was the ceremony?"

Sera pulled a face. "Horrible. You didn't tell me how horrible it could be. I felt like my insides were being squashed and stretched and twisted, all at once. I don't think I'll ever forget that feeling."

Probably not. Sensations from his own binding still haunted his dreams, even after more than twenty years: the blood pounding in his ears; the moment in which everything stopped, for what seemed an eternity; then the feeling of his heart being *wrenched,* as though ripped from his body. And then a whispered touch on his mind, the faintest smudge, barely even there; the feeling he would eventually come to know as the presence of the god.

"It's done now, anyway," Sera was saying. "Please tell me we never have to do anything like that again."

"Oh, no. Once is all it takes, believe me."

"Thank the Dreamer." She looked up, the cheer returning to her eyes. "So what will I be working on? Valdori research? Something else? Do you even do any research this far from Zeanes?"

"We do, and we'll see," Clade said, his attention snagged by Estelle as she rose from her seat and started toward them. "My adjunct, Garrett, will show you around tomorrow. But if you'll excuse me, I think the Councillor would like a word with me."

"She would indeed," Estelle said, joining them. "Overseer Clade and I have some matters to discuss."

Sera stifled a giggle. "Yes, Councillor," she said, not quite managing to keep a straight face. "Master, um, Clade. Sorry. Goodnight!"

Estelle watched her scurry away, bemused. "What was that about?"

"I suspect she's still adjusting to her new rank. Nothing that won't pass."

"If you say so." She glanced around. "Where can we talk?"

Clade opted for a small lounge tucked away behind the main dining hall. Pale panelled walls softened the light and held in the aroma of lavender-scented lamp oil. Estelle sank into a chair with a sigh, propping her feet up on a footrest as Clade poured glasses of brandy.

"Bad news first," she said, accepting the glass. "I'm afraid there's only one new sorcerer for Anstice from this group. I'm sorry. I know you were promised two."

"What happened?"

"We lost three to the binding. Your second sorcerer was one of them." She looked up. "To be honest, I thought we'd lose Sera before some of the others. She's such a flighty one."

Clade seated himself and took a sip of the brandy, savouring the feel of it as it slid down his throat. "I don't think she is, actually. High-spirited, yes, and a little naive. They all are at that age. But she completed her training. You don't do that without commitment."

Estelle gave him an arch look. "You sound like an offended father. No, no, you're right. No-one can deny she has talent, and her discipline is clearly strong enough to withstand Azador. More than we could say for three of her peers."

Withstand Azador. That was what everyone was told: that the god tested you once and then left you alone. He had never heard Estelle suggest anything else, even in private, even though he knew that the Council knew otherwise, and the Council knew he knew. When the god was with a sorcerer, it saw through their eyes, heard through their ears. Clade had seen the proof of it firsthand. But still Estelle and the Council persisted with their pretence, and nobody ever seemed to ask why sorcerers who had endured the ceremony were called *bound*.

"What brings you here, then?" Clade said. Despite Azador's connection to its members, it rarely permitted one of Estelle's rank to leave the island. The Oculus had others who were more commonly sent when the god required it — those trained to hear its voice in the artefacts of dark, twisted rock through which it spoke.

"Council business," Estelle said. "We've confined ourselves to Pazia for too long, Clade. It was necessary to begin with, I suppose. We were few. We were weak. We'd forgotten so much. But a time comes when the cradle ceases to nurture and begins to stifle."

He frowned. "The Oculus have been in Anstice for decades. We've sent people on assignment as far west as Chogon."

"A handful. And even in Anstice, our presence is barely known. You'd be lucky to find a dozen people in this city who've so much as heard of us." She looked up from her glass. "The Empire fell centuries ago. Anstice was our first attempt at crawling out of the nursery. All we've done since then is crawl a little further. It's time we learnt to stand on our feet. Time we tell the world who we are."

"Meaning what, exactly?"

"I can't tell you that. Not yet." A hint of a smile turned the corners of her lips upward. "But that brings me to my other reason for coming here."

Clade waited in silence. Once, a moment like this would have filled him with trepidation. But now, as he looked within, he found only a calm, assured stillness. *Control. Above all, control.* Without it, he'd never escape the god.

"You know that Councillor Weneth has been ill for some time," Estelle said. "The sickness comes and goes, but it never truly leaves him. He finds himself increasingly unable to leave his chambers. Some days the shaking is so bad that he can't even feed himself."

Clade nodded. The trajectory of her words was clear. "He's stepping down."

"As soon as a replacement can be found. Which is to say, at once."

He kept his voice carefully neutral. "You want me to join the Council."

"The sooner, the better. We'll leave together, as soon as my business in Anstice is done." Estelle raised her glass. "To you, Clade. The god's Requiter, now Councillor-designate. I know you won't disappoint us."

CHAPTER 5

Of the origins of the Valdori, I could find only scraps. Even the
site of their great city, Asi-Valdor, remains unclear... Yet the empire must have begun somewhere; small at first, like a seed or a
phoenix ember, or the pebble that starts the avalanche. Had the
fire not come, had the pebble not fallen, how different might the
world have been?

— Niele the Deserter, in an untitled treatise
suppressed by the Oculus

IT TOOK EILWEN THE ENTIRE day to read the box of reports.
When at last she extinguished the lamps and crawled into bed,
her head was pounding and her eyes weary of the sight of Ufeus's
handwriting. The crabbed, awkward scrawl appeared at the foot of
each report and intermittently in the margins, making reference to
other people or events or reports in a way that evidently made sense
to Ufeus but left Eilwen bewildered. She'd struggled through as best
she could, reading each report and trying to use what she learnt to
decode Ufeus's cryptic notation, but in the end she'd been forced to
admit defeat.

The reports themselves revealed a far more sophisticated intelligence operation than Eilwen had imagined. The Guild's agents
had contacts in city chambers, banks and moneylenders, rival merchant companies, even one in the Tri-God pantheon. One agent
spent most of his time furnishing the Crimson Sails with selectively
inaccurate information, apparently in the hope of sabotaging their

supply plans and luring away some of their business when they were caught flat-footed. Another had infiltrated the local office of the East Mellespen Syndicate and was working to gain access to their account ledger, with the ultimate aim of answering certain questions about the Syndicate's use of Gislean caravans. A third attempted to track the activities of the Quill and other groups of sorcerers, aided by Caralange, the Guild's own sorcerer. And this was just within Anstice. Beyond the city were other Guild agents, overseen by Havilah himself yet occasionally mentioned where their activities touched on those within Anstice, keeping the Woodtraders Guild informed of the actions and plans of parties throughout the Free Cities and beyond.

We're supposed to be a mercantile company, aren't we? Since when did buying and selling require all this? But having read the reports, she could guess the answer. *Since everyone else starting doing it to us.*

The scale and complexity of the operation made her wonder again at her selection for the role. It seemed incredible that Havilah would look beyond his own trusted agents to fill a position like this. No matter how thoroughly he had examined her past, he couldn't possibly be as sure of her as he would be of one of his own. And she had no experience in analysing such information, no idea how to piece together the myriad fragments and form a coherent picture. Nothing in her life qualified her for a job like this.

Her misgivings pursued her into sleep, and she spent a restless night drifting in and out of slumber, at times unable to tell whether she was awake or if her sleep-muddled doubts had transferred themselves to her dreams. She woke early, uneasy and unrefreshed, but relieved to avoid sleeping late for a second day.

Eilwen's interview with Brielle was scheduled for mid-morning. With nothing else demanding her attention, Eilwen picked through the reports, separating those from Brielle and trying to extract some sense of the woman behind their content. Unlike some of the other agents, Brielle seemed to lack a specific focus: her sources ranged throughout the city, from the sister of kitchen hand in the archon's palace to a beggar positioned just inside the city's northeastern gate on the road to Borronor's Crossing. The reports themselves were terse to the point of abruptness, but whether this indicated clarity of thought, disregard, or even contempt, Eilwen could not tell.

A clamour of bells sounded in the distance, marking the beginning of a new hour. Eilwen stared through the window at the enclosed garden, trying to guess at the sun's position from the depth of the slanting shadows. *I could just go outside and check the sky.* But something held her back, and she knew what it was. The egg was there, just outside her door, an arm's length below the ground.

She shuddered and pulled the curtain closed. She needed a clock. *Maybe one with a chime peg to wake me up,* she thought as she moved between the lamps, lighting them with a Quill sparker. She'd ask the house steward about it next time she saw him.

Someone knocked, loud and insistent. Brielle and Ufeus, at last. Eilwen opened the door and gestured them in. Ufeus entered first, glancing briefly at the curtained window but making no comment, his face impassive. A woman followed, taller than Eilwen by about a hand, taller even than Ufeus, with the pale skin and rough features of a Mellespene. She halted a pace in from the door, arms folded, and fixed Eilwen with a hard stare. Eilwen held the look, smiling slightly to show her amusement at the implied challenge, and after a moment the other woman snorted and broke her gaze.

Eilwen seated herself behind the desk. "You are Brielle, I take it," she said, deliberately phrasing the words as a statement rather than a question. It was an old negotiating habit: an expression of knowledge and confidence to establish oneself as worthy of respect. "My name is Eilwen. As you know by now, Master Havilah has asked me to assume oversight of all Guild agents in Anstice. I'm still familiarising myself with everything that's going on, so I'll appreciate your assistance to fill the gaps in my knowledge."

Brielle nodded once. Eilwen gave her a moment, but Brielle seemed content to stand in silence. Ufeus stood beside her, equally unresponsive, his expression as impassive as ever. But she'd seen this before, too: a show of stubbornness or reluctance, pushing her to reveal more of her position than she'd planned. Not that she had a position in this. *Perhaps I'm overthinking it. Maybe they just don't like me.*

"Ufeus tells me you have a complaint about another agent," Eilwen said. "Who is it?"

Brielle spoke at last. "I don't know," she said. She glanced across at Ufeus, then back at Eilwen, a resentful scowl on her broad face.

All right. Forget approachable. "You don't know," Eilwen repeated. "So if you can't tell me who it is, what can you tell me?"

The woman flushed. "Ufeus said he already told you —"

"I'm asking you to tell me. Now, please."

This time, Brielle's answering nod was curt, little more than a jerk of the head. "Someone in the Guild has been talking to my man in the Exadius Company."

"I see. And what has this person been saying?"

"They've been asking for things. Information about significant new loans. Repayment difficulties. Unusual transactions."

Eilwen frowned. "Sounds like the sort of thing you all ask for. Your own reports are full of that."

"You're missing the point," Brielle said. "That man is *mine*. *I* ask him these things. Nobody else."

The passion in her face took Eilwen aback. Brielle seemed furious, as though the interference of a third party was a personal betrayal. *Do all agents guard their contacts so jealously?* Eilwen had no idea. She felt as though she'd strayed into a foreign quarter of a familiar city. Everything looked the same, but all the rules were subtly different.

She turned to Ufeus. "Does any other Guild agent have an Exadius Company contact?"

"No." Ufeus's reply was definite. "Not in Anstice. If there was any such communication, I would know about it."

"But there is, and you don't," Brielle snapped, the contempt in her voice suddenly plain.

"I rely on agents to keep me informed," Ufeus said, as coolly formal as he had been with Eilwen the previous day. "If they are not sufficiently forthcoming, there is little I can do."

"'Not sufficiently forthcoming'? So the fact you can't control your agents is actually their fault?"

"Are you asking for a shorter leash?"

"If you want to know something beyond what I say, ask me!"

Eilwen watched in amazement. *A moment ago I couldn't get half a word out of the pair of them. Now look at them go.* She should have realised it earlier, but she'd been too caught up in creating the right first impression. She'd assumed there were only two sides to the discussion. But in fact, there were three.

Which gave her an opportunity.

"Enough," she said, and was gratified to see them both fall silent. She turned to Brielle. "This man of yours. He told you that someone else in the Guild has contacted him, correct?"

"Yes."

"But he hasn't given you any way to identify this other person."

"That's right."

"Right," Eilwen said. "Let's go and see him."

Brielle hesitated. "What, now?"

"Are you sure that's a good idea?" Ufeus blinked, nonplussed.

"Yes, I am," Eilwen said. "Don't argue, please. In any case, I'm not asking you to join us. Brielle and I will go."

Ufeus's eyes narrowed and he gave a stiff nod. Beside him, Brielle stared, the surprise still evident on her face. *And silence is restored,* Eilwen thought, torn between amusement and exasperation. She looked at Brielle.

"Shall we?"

~

Without Ufeus around, Brielle reverted to her earlier laconic self, speaking only in answer to Eilwen's questions, volunteering nothing. But the quality of her silence seemed to have changed; it was calmer now, and not quite so defensive. Eilwen wondered if Brielle had received the intended message of her decision: an indication of support for her and a rebuff to Ufeus. Surely she had. She was an intelligence agent, after all.

They left the compound on foot, turning south at the thoroughfare and climbing the broad steps of Merchants' Bridge. The high span was a relic of earlier times, built to accommodate the small trading ships that had once sailed all the way up the Tienette from the eastern sea. Most seafaring ships these days went no further than Borronor's Crossing, leaving the upstream reaches of the Tienette to the numerous riverboats that now plied its waters. A fleet of river galleys flying the indigo and gold of Anstice patrolled the waterway all the way to the coast, protecting cargo and travellers from piracy and guarding against the threat of mischief from any who might wish the city harm.

Not that anyone would dare attack us now. The region had become known as the Free Cities at the time of Coridon's fall, a period described in most histories as bordering on anarchic. Now, little more than one hundred and fifty years after the disintegration of the short-lived southeastern kingdom, five cities stood head and shoulders above the rest. On the southern coast, Damara and Spyridon; on the eastern, Neysa; to the northwest, hemmed in between the Kefirans on one side and the Gisleans on the other, the great craftsman's city of Rondossa. And in the centre, greatest of all, Anstice, master of no fewer than eleven client cities and dozens of lesser townships. *Only Neysa still speaks against us, and even they do so only in whispers. They need the coin to keep flowing as much as everyone else.*

On the other side of the bridge they turned west, following the river into the heart of the city. The fortress-palace of the city chambers loomed ahead, its upper levels bulging beyond the limits set out by the lower to overhang the street below. A finger of stone thrust skyward from the roof: the clock tower, as tall again as the building from which it rose, the single hand on its face a few degrees shy of midday.

"You didn't mention your contact's name," Eilwen said. Not a question, but an invitation nonetheless.

"Dallin," Brielle said. "Dallin Nourt."

Well, that's an improvement. "How long has Dallin been one of ours?"

"A few years. His sister fell in with some bad people. We helped get her out of the city."

"Any unusual behaviour lately? Asking for more money or something?"

Brielle snorted. "He asks for more money every time I see him. No, nothing unusual."

They passed beneath the city chambers and cut through the adjoining square, the Tienette on their right. The Isle split the river here, its land crowded with buildings in at least four distinct architectural styles. Isle Bridge, however, was plain and unornamented; the widest of the city's four bridges, albeit barely high enough for barges to pass beneath. Fishermen perched on the pylons, some crouching on ledges just above the waterline, others sitting on the narrow shelves with their legs dangling in the water. River gulls swooped around them, snapping at their catches with the outraged shrieks of the dispossessed.

"How did you discover something was amiss?" Eilwen said.

"He told me."

Of course he did. Eilwen kept her tone amicable. "Told you what?"

"I saw him two days ago," Brielle said. "Regular meet. He gave me what he had. I questioned him on a few points and he got frustrated, said he'd already told us about that. Then he clammed up, like he'd just realised he'd said something wrong."

"Ufeus mentioned contacts, plural. Are there others?"

"Maybe. I'm not sure."

"But you told him there were?"

"I said there may be." Brielle stopped, ducking slightly as a squawking gull flew past their heads. "We're here."

"Wait. What do you mean, you said there may be?"

Brielle shrugged. "Just that. I don't know if there are others or not." Eilwen folded her arms, waiting, and Brielle gave a frustrated sigh. "You want me to fill in the gaps for you? Try this. Ufeus is a self-important prick. He has no idea how this works. I tell him everything I learn, and it's never enough. The *facts* are never enough. He always wants more. Opinions. Suspicions. So I gave him some."

"Fine," Eilwen said. "Then give me an opinion now. Do you think it *likely* that any of your other contacts have been approached by someone else in the Guild?"

Brielle fixed her with a baleful glare; then a grin spread slowly across her face. "You're a step up, aren't you? At least you know how to ask a question."

"Well?"

She shrugged again. "It's nothing I can point to. Just a feeling. Like when they're talking to me, they're not worried about someone else finding them out any more. They're worried about me."

"How many?"

"Three or four. Maybe more."

"All right," Eilwen said. "List it for me in your next report. And from now on, I want those opinions reported too. I won't hang you if you're wrong, but I might if you're right and don't say anything." She gestured to the nearby building. "Lead on."

The Exadius Company occupied a purple-grey building with a clear view of the river. A series of fluted columns supported a covered entrance, the central frieze of which showed a faded bas-relief of a group of soldiers marching through a forest, the image carved in such a way that the men seemed to dwarf the trees around them. The sides of the building were stepped like a Yanisinian ziggurat, with small rooftop balconies on each level. Dragon-headed gargoyles at the corners of each balcony glowered down at uncaring passers-by.

As they neared the entrance, Brielle caught Eilwen's arm and steered her behind a column, away from the door. "There he is now," she murmured, pointing up the street. "The one with the shoulder bag, coming this way."

Eilwen scanned the oncoming faces, her gaze lighting on a young, angular man striding cheerfully toward them, his gaze on the river. She glanced back, wondering whether they should intercept the man on the street or follow him inside; but Brielle was already slipping away and taking up a position beside the door.

The man was so absorbed in his thoughts that he walked right past Brielle before she reached out and tapped his arm. He brushed her hand away with an absent frown; then he froze, his jaunty manner vanishing like mist.

"Gods below! What are you doing here?" He shot Eilwen a panicky glance. "And who in the hells is this?"

"Dallin, this is Eilwen. Also from the Guild. She wanted to meet you."

Dallin turned on her, his voice a furious whisper. "Are you mad? What are you doing, meeting me here? Why not shout it from the roof, make sure everyone knows! Gods!"

Eilwen stared mutely back, suddenly realising her mistake. Ufeus had tried to warn her. *Are you sure that's a good idea?* And she had told him not to argue. *Damn. That was... stupid.*

He scanned the street and shook his head. "You can't be seen here. Go. I can be at the usual place in three hours."

On impulse, Eilwen stretched out her arm, barring his way to the door. "Actually, this won't take a moment," she murmured. "I just want to know the name of your *other* Guild handler."

"Oh, no. No no no. I don't know what internal thing you've got going on and I don't care. I'm not getting involved."

"Ah, but you're already involved, Dallin. The name, that's all I want."

"Damn you!" Dallin's fearful gaze swept the street again, then fixed on Eilwen. She stared back, unrelenting. He was taller than her by a head. *If he tries to break free, I won't be able to stop him.*

"The name, Dallin. Now."

"I don't know! We don't meet! Just messages... exchanged..."

"When, and where?"

Dallin whimpered. "There's a loose stone in the old wall, near the north gatehouse."

"When?"

"Next drop... four days from now. Evening..."

Eilwen let her arm fall. "Thank you," she said brightly, and Dallin rushed to the door, shoving it open and scurrying inside.

She turned, leaning against the wall and exhaling in a rush. *That wasn't put on for our benefit. The boy was genuinely scared.* Unease stirred within her, and she hugged her arms to her chest. Ufeus was right, and Brielle too. Something was going on.

"You probably just burned him, you know," Brielle said. "I doubt he'll be giving us anything after that."

"Would you trust anything he told us now?"

"Perhaps." There was a long pause, then Brielle shrugged. "He didn't ask for more money. That's unusual."

The slow grin spread across her face, and Eilwen gave an abrupt laugh. "Right. Seems suspicious to me."

But her amusement soon faded, lost beneath her growing disquiet. She made her way back to the Guild in silence, Brielle padding alongside like a cat; and though they exchanged neither word nor glance, Eilwen found herself oddly glad of the company.

~

Arandras was last to arrive at Rhothe's Bar. The work he'd ignored the previous day to go chasing information about the urn had caught up with him today, and it had taken him all day and part of the evening to complete the most urgent tasks. By the time he joined the group at their booth in the crowded back room and ordered a meal, Mara and the others had finished theirs and had a *dilarj* set out, each of them picking through their pieces and placing their selections on the board. A fourth pile lay untouched before the vacant seat, the coloured band on each piece a matching shade of faded red.

Druce glanced up at Arandras's approach and gave a theatrical sigh. "Damn," he said. "Thought Jen or I might have a chance tonight."

"If you two were going to gang up on Mara, don't change your plans on my account," Arandras said, sitting. "Sorry I'm late."

"Hey, I think he's getting soft," Druce said to Jensine. Three mugs already populated his corner of the table, two of them empty. "Wants us to do the hard work for him. How about we take him out instead?"

"Sounds good to me," Mara interjected, her grin as sharp as one of her cutlasses. "Busy day?"

Arandras nodded. "Busy day." Frowning, he began sorting through his heap, standing the pieces in rows. An outer shell on each piece concealed its identity from other players, with a small gap on one side to allow the piece's owner to see within. As he found pieces he was sure to include — spire, dragon, both sorcerers, several fortresses — he set them aside, gradually accumulating his opening set.

"Have you sold the urn yet?" Jensine asked. Her starting pieces were already in position on the board, with the remainder — her reserves — arranged on the table in concentric circles.

"Yeah, don't keep us in suspense," Druce said. "How much did you get for it?"

"What's the rush?" Arandras said, adding two archers and an assassin to his selections. "You got a bunch of coin just the other day."

"Which went straight to the moneylender, didn't it, Druce?" Jensine said, her light tone undercut by a streak of genuine irritation.

"Oh, shut up already," Druce said, turning away from her to

focus on Arandras. "How much?"

"Nothing yet."

"But you've started shopping it around, right?"

"What? Yes, I spoke to a couple of people about it yesterday."

"And?" Druce twiddled a piece between his thin fingers. "Didn't you say it would only take you a day or two?"

So I did. Damn. His meal arrived and he perched the plate on the table's edge, dipping his flatbread into the hot tagine and taking a bite. Mara and Jensine looked at him expectantly, waiting for his reply, and beside him Druce set the piece down and folded his arms.

"It's turned out a little more complicated than I thought," Arandras said, swallowing. "I need to do more research before I can sell it."

Druce's eyebrows drew together. "Meaning what?"

"Meaning," Mara said, "that Arandras needs a better idea of what it's worth before he starts negotiating prices. Maybe it's worth no more than tonight's drinks — or maybe it's worth a great deal more."

"Really?" Jensine's tone was cautious, but she looked at him hopefully.

Arandras scratched his beard. Thoughts of the urn's monetary value had all but evaporated after his conversation with Narvi the previous day. But the artefact was not his alone. Sooner or later, he'd have to sell it. "I don't know," he said, resisting the urge to shift in his seat. "I wouldn't get my hopes up just yet. Give me a few more days and I might have a better idea."

"So, best case," Druce said. "How much are we looking at?"

"I really couldn't say. I'm not being coy, I just don't know."

Druce whistled. "That much, huh?"

"What did I just say about getting your hopes up?"

Jensine leaned forward. "I could take a closer look at it. See if there's any sign of sorcery —"

"No," Arandras snapped, and Jensine blinked in surprise. "No," he said again, struggling to remove the edge from his voice. "Thank you. I've got it covered."

An uneasy quiet descended around the table. Arandras bent his head to the game pieces before him, completing his opening set and beginning to position the pieces on the board.

"What about that puzzle box, then?" Druce said, turning to Mara.

Mara shrugged. "Nothing local. Seems there might be some interest in Anstice, if I can get there in the next week or two."

Druce slumped into the seat with a frustrated sigh. "Damn it."

The game proceeded in awkward silence. Druce lost his sorcerers early, one in a reckless foray against what turned out to be Jensine's golem, the other to a clever trap set by Mara, and failed to recover from the setback. A raid by Mara's dragon exposed his spire and eliminated him from the game. Jensine played more cautiously, but was undone when she left her defences exposed to Arandras's sappers. They destroyed most of her fortresses before she could drive them off, after which it was only a matter of time before the rest of his army finished the job, her spire eventually falling to his captain.

"Might as well not bother," Jensine grumbled as Arandras cleared the board of her remaining pieces, leaving only her surviving fortress in place. "It's always these two in the end."

"Always?" Druce sounded offended. "You're forgetting my famous —"

"Yeah, I know. Always, except the time Arandras ate some bad shellfish, and even then, Mara still beat you." She drained her mug and stood. "I'm done here. Coming?"

Druce looked mournfully at his own empty cup. "Not much point staying, is there?"

"Hold up." Arandras dug into his pouch and slapped some coppers down in front of Druce, who blinked at the assortment of coins and lengths. "Don't drink it all," Arandras said. "Just sit tight until I sell the damn thing. All right?"

Druce's expression darkened. "Hey, I'm not going to take charity from you —"

"It's an advance on your portion of the proceeds. I'll be sure to deduct it from the total."

Druce considered. "Well," he said, and began gathering up the coppers. "In that case."

Once they were gone, Mara leaned back from the game, brows raised. "So. What's up?"

"What's up what?"

"Don't give me that." Mara folded her arms. "What aren't you telling us? Did you translate something after all? Hells, if you're just trying to protect Druce from his own superstitions, I'm with you all the way. But whatever it is, I want to know."

Arandras dropped his gaze, suddenly afraid that Mara might see his thoughts in his face. "It's nothing important," he said, frowning at the board as if contemplating his position. "Nothing you need to worry about."

"You said that the other day, too," Mara said. "Is it the Library again?"

He shook his head. "Nothing like that."

"Maybe I can help —"

"You can't." Arandras forced himself to meet her eyes. "Trust me. You can't."

Mara said nothing for a long moment. He endured her regard, refusing to look away. Abruptly, she gave a crisp nod. "All right, Arandras. I trust you. Let me know when you're ready to trust me."

He winced, unable to prevent it, and he thought he spotted a fleeting look of satisfaction on her face as she turned her attention back to the game board. *Damn it, Mara, it's not like that. You don't want any part of this.* But the thoughts rang hollow in his mind, and he didn't give them voice.

They completed the game in silence, Arandras unable to think of anything more to say, Mara apparently unwilling to give him another opening. Arandras was vaguely aware that his play was loose, but Mara seemed unusually slow to take advantage. Gradually, however, she began to get the upper hand, reducing his army and destroying his fortresses by slow attrition, finally capturing his spire with a lowly scout.

She wished him a curt goodnight, leaving him to pack away the game alone. He sat there for a while, staring at the board and the jumble of pieces lying across the table — the aftermath of the evening's mock battle. *It's not you I can't trust with this, Mara. It's the whole damn world.* After all, it wasn't like he'd never tried. He'd trusted the Quill, once, with Tereisa's life in the balance. And here he was.

Eventually he stirred, clearing away the discarded pieces, leaving the board clean and unmarked: fresh ground for someone else to contest tomorrow.

~

The morning dawned grey and overcast, the sky a vast, flat ceiling of pale marble. The air hung heavy with the kind of moisture only a storm could lift. Arandras threw the door and window of his shop wide open, hungry for whatever faint breath of wind might happen to stir along the street.

The events of the previous evening weighed on his thoughts as he busied himself with the numerous small tasks of opening the shop. *I trust you,* Mara had said to him, and though the words had been barbed, they hadn't rung false. But she'd spoken in ignorance, unaware of the need that now drove him. Would she have said it if she'd known? He doubted it.

But then, he didn't need her trust. He just needed a reason to keep the urn a while longer.

He unlocked the lid of his desk and retrieved the sample correspondence for display beneath the window, then glanced up to see Wil trotting in, tablet and stylus in hand, climbing onto the corner table and seating himself there without a word. The boy caught Arandras's gaze and immediately lowered his eyes, biting his lip and beginning to sketch letters with his stylus.

"Not today, Wil," Arandras said, laying the samples in their place and putting a hand on the boy's shoulder. "Run along —"

A cough at the door interrupted him. A large man with skin almost as dark as Mara's stood there, his rough-spun shirt already stained with sweat despite the early hour. "A foul morning," he said in halting, heavily-accented Yaran. "In Menefir, air is air and liquid is liquid. None of this... uh..." He waved his hand.

"Humidity," Arandras said, then repeated the word in Kharjik.

"Yes. Humidity." The guardsman scratched his armpit. "So. My messages."

Arandras moistened his lips. "About that," he said, sitting behind his desk and folding his hands, his knee brushing the outer drawer where the letters still lay. "I'm afraid I won't be able to help you after all."

Confused, the guardsman cocked his ear. "What say?"

"I said, I can't help you retrieve your daughter," Arandras said, struggling not to raise his voice. The man wasn't hard of hearing, just Kharjik. "In the Free Cities, a young woman may do as she likes. A young man, too. I can't help you round her up like cattle."

"Cattle?" The guardsman scowled. "No. Is girl! Daughter!"

"Yes, I know that," Arandras said. "Daughter, but not girl. Woman. Old enough to decide for herself."

"No! Girl!" The man slammed a thick fist on Arandras's desk, and in the corner of the shop Wil flinched. "Twelve summers. Twelve!"

Arandras blinked. *Twelve?* "Are you sure —"

"Twelve!" The guardsman gestured angrily. "I give money. You give messages!"

"Yes, of course. A moment, please." *Dear Weeper. Only twelve.* He fetched the letters from their drawer, placed them on the desk. "Almost done," he said, holding up the final, unfinished letter. "A moment."

Arandras hastily completed the final letter, sprinkling it with sand to absorb the excess ink. The guardsman accepted the stack of letters with an air of injured dignity. "I will find," he said, the papers rustling as he closed his fist around them. "I will."

"Weeper's blessing," Arandras said as the man left, and sagged into his chair.

Wil shifted on the table, eyes wide, his tablet and stylus forgotten in his lap. "Did something happen to that man's girl?"

"She got lost," Arandras said. "But he's off to find her now, so don't worry about it." *Weeper grant she's still alive.* "And you need to run along. Come back another day."

Wil pouted, but Arandras was in no mood to humour him. Grudgingly, the boy climbed down from the table, feet dragging as he trailed out the door.

Gods. Where was I? The guardsman's visit had utterly disrupted the course of his thoughts. *The urn, that was it.* The sooner he worked out what it signified, the sooner he could find a reason to keep it a while longer.

A fresh shadow fell just inside the door, and Arandras gave a silent groan. *For the Weeper's sake, what now?*

"Hello, Arandras." Narvi stood at the threshold, picking uncomfortably at his low collar, his sleeves rolled back to his elbows. His cheer of the other day was gone, replaced with an uncharacteristic guardedness. He gave Arandras a long, searching gaze. "May I come in?"

"Of course," Arandras said, indicating the vacant chair. "Please." The moment stretched, and Arandras cleared his throat. "Guess I'm not so hard to find after all."

Narvi's faint smile did nothing to lift his countenance. "Apparently not."

"I'd offer you wine if I had any."

The sorcerer nodded. When he spoke, the words came slowly. "I need to ask you something, Arandras," he said. "I hope you won't take it amiss."

Arandras frowned. "Go ahead."

"Do you know any reason why my field team is still not back?"

Arandras went still. "I'm not sure," he said carefully. "Can you tell me what they were looking for?"

Narvi blinked. "'Were,'" he repeated softly, and Arandras gave a silent curse. "They're looking for an urn," he said, and gestured with his hands. "About so big, we think." He paused, examining Arandras closely. "Only Sten tells me someone brought one in the other day just like it."

Arandras looked away. "Your team is dead," he said, his voice low. "They were attacked by some other group, I don't know who. My associate was there. She saw it happen. I'm sorry."

Narvi's face crumpled. "You're sure they're dead?"

"The last she saw, one was still alive but in bad shape. No match for the survivors of the other group."

"Gods. Poor Rawlen. He didn't want —" Narvi broke off, brushing at his eyes. "Why didn't you say something?"

"Say what? I thought they were from Anstice. I didn't even know you had anyone operating out of Spyridon until the other day."

"What difference does it make where they're from? They're Quill, same as us!"

"Same as you, you mean," Arandras said, and Narvi bridled. "As you well know! You wouldn't even tell me what they were after."

"That's just the stupid rules! It doesn't mean anything!"

But it did, of course. Arandras bit his tongue, remembering the last and only time he'd tried explaining it to Narvi, the day he left the Quill for good. "I didn't kill them, Narvi," he said at last. "I'm sorry. I didn't know they were yours."

Narvi took a deep breath. "Fine," he said, waving a hand in dismissal. "Forget it." He closed his eyes, exhaling heavily. "Tell me what happened. Please."

Arandras recounted Mara's story, leaving out her dramatic flourishes and relating only the bare facts. Shorn of its frills, the tale lasted only a few minutes. Narvi gave a half-grunt when Arandras told of the Quill throwing the urn into the night and looked up.

"That's just like Derrek," he said, smiling through watery eyes. "Never did know when to quit."

Just like Derrek. The comment touched something unexpected within Arandras, and he fell silent. *Narvi knew them,* he realised, and the thought was at once a revelation and the most obvious banality. Of course he'd known them. They were Quill. But he'd done more than simply make their acquaintance. He knew who they were. Swallowing, Arandras dropped his gaze. Suddenly, even looking at the other man's face seemed intrusive. "I'm sorry, Narvi," he said. "Truly."

"Yeah. Me too." Narvi blotted his eyes with his sleeve. "But here we are." He shook himself, his stout form wobbling like an overweight cat's. "And we can still salvage something out of all this. Tell me you'll sell us the urn."

Ah, Narvi, not that. Regretfully, Arandras shook his head.

"I can triple Sten's offer," Narvi said. "I can go even higher. At least think about it."

"I'm sorry," Arandras said. "I can't."

Narvi sighed. "Because of Tereisa."

"Yes."

"Well. I had to ask." Narvi's mouth twisted in a sour smile, but there was no reproach in it, only regret. "You understand, I'm sure."

"Of course," Arandras said, shamed by the unexpected display of compassion. *Ah, Narvi. You always were the peacemaker, weren't you?*

Narvi shifted in his seat. "This journal page you mentioned," he said. "Where'd you get it?"

"From Sten, as it happens. Why?"

"We got a similar page." Narvi drew out a piece of paper and set it on the desk. "Not from Sten — ours came from Anstice." He leaned forward. "May I see yours?"

Arandras found it in a drawer. He unfolded it and set it before Narvi, who scanned it for only a moment before nodding.

"It's a match." Narvi looked like he had just taken a bite from something bitter. "You have the exact same page that we do."

Not quite exact. There were a few words different here and there, a few letters out of place. *But still.* "Someone's playing us."

Narvi gave him a sharp glance. "You want to find the person who set this up?" he said. "So do I. So does the Quill. We can work together on this. Help each other."

Arandras pulled back, his lips pressed together.

"No, listen," Narvi said, suddenly eager. "Come with me to Anstice. We've got people there. Resources. Add your expertise in languages, and…" He gestured expansively. "The urn is yours. You know the Quill will respect that. Together, we can solve this. Don't you want to know what that thing is?"

Arandras shook his head. "The hells with solving puzzles. I want to find the man who wrote that letter."

"What if they're the same thing?"

Then I'll solve it on my own. Arandras exhaled sharply. Inviting the Quill to join his search was a fool's move. Sooner or later, their interests would clash with his, and when that happened, theirs would almost certainly prevail.

He shook his head again. "Thank you, but no."

"I see," Narvi said. "Well." He pushed himself reluctantly to his feet. "If you change your mind, you know where to find me. I'm heading back to Anstice next week anyway. The offer is good until then."

Arandras nodded and said nothing.

"All right." Narvi headed for the doorway, then paused on the threshold and turned back. "Arandras," he said. "Do something for me, would you?"

"What's that?"

"Get yourself out of here. This shop. This life." Narvi's gesture took in the shop, the street, the city. "Accept our help or not, whatever you like. Just don't sit here writing dusty letters for dusty people the rest of your life."

Arandras bristled. "There's no shame in this," he said. "Which is more than I can say for some. These people have as much right to a scribe as anyone else."

"I never said otherwise. Only that this… well, it isn't you." Narvi stepped out into the street, his hand raised in farewell. "Be well, Arandras."

Arandras watched him leave with a frown. The drawer in which the guardsman's letters had rested was still open, the pouch containing the intended refund tucked into the corner. On the side of his desk sat a bundle of messages awaiting a courier's pickup: the headsman's widow's reply to her boy, congratulating him on his new position of sole responsibility for the farmer's second flock; a request from the herbalist for several items not readily found in the vicinity of Spyridon; and more that Arandras could not at this moment recall.

Other people's words, all of it.

Maybe Narvi had a point.

What if solving the urn and finding the man are the same thing? Narvi had said it, but Arandras had been thinking the same thing ever since his visit to the schoolhouse. *It fits the pattern. First Tereisa, now Narvi's team. First the dagger, now…*

He opened the lid of his desk, retrieving the urn from its hidden drawer, and setting it on the desk.

What are you?

CHAPTER 6

Power is the necessary companion to wisdom, and wisdom the necessary companion to power. Lacking both, a man may live a long and contented life; but he who possesses one without the other is doomed to frustration and failure. Impotent wisdom destroys a man as surely as mighty folly.

— Giarvanno do Salin I, *Meditations on Power*

To CLADE's RELIEF, ESTELLE WAS largely absent in the days following her arrival. She would leave early in the morning, sometimes even before breakfast was served, heading north along the thoroughfare toward the Tienette and the heart of Anstice. In the evening she would return from the same direction, join them for dinner, then retire to her room where, as far as Clade knew, she would remain until the next day. She made no demands of him, issued no requests, and the subject of his impending elevation to the Council was allowed to rest where they had left it the first evening.

The third night after Estelle's arrival found Clade wading cautiously through the darkness of the barren forecourt. The air was mild and still, the waning moon's pale light deepening the shadows that lay across the courtyard. Clade probed the space ahead with his foot, nudging aside something that felt like broken pottery. The heavy gate was locked for the night, but a small door beside it provided entry and egress at all hours to those permitted the privilege of carrying a key. Junior sorcerers and servants wanting passage at night could either explain their need to their betters or wait until morning.

Clade halted before the door and inserted the key, turning first one way and then the other to engage the sorcery. The hinges squeaked softly as he pulled the door open, revealing a bent-over figure on the other side, key in hand. It straightened sharply, then leaned forward, its shape silhouetted against the lamps of the street. "Hello?" it said, and Clade recognised the thin tenor and slight frame of Garrett.

"It's Clade," he said, motioning Garrett forward before realising the uselessness of the gesture. "You first."

Garrett stepped quickly through, brushing the hair out of his face as his gaze found Clade in the gloom. "Clade. I was just running an errand for Councillor Estelle," he said, and Clade thought he heard an edge of... *something* in his voice. "Is all well?"

"Fine." Clade peered at the younger man, but the darkness hid the subtleties of Garrett's expression. "An errand, you say?"

"Yes," Garrett said, his tone smug.

Frowning, Clade swung the wicker door closed and leaned near. "Speaking of errands," he whispered, "what progress have you made in recovering the urn?"

Garrett hesitated. "Ah." He lowered his voice to match Clade's. "I have several leads, but nothing solid yet. Perhaps you could speak to the Councillor, ask her for more resources, or even her own assistance —"

"No."

"Look, if you really want to find this thing, we're going to need —"

"Enough," Clade hissed. "I understand the difficulties. I do not expect the impossible. But I do expect your best, and *so does the Council.* Do not disappoint us, and whatever you do, *do not* raise this matter with Councillor Estelle yourself. Am I clear?"

Garrett nodded, his face unreadable in the darkness. "Yes."

"Good." He considered saying more, then thought better of it. "Goodnight."

"Goodnight, Clade."

The door was low, and Clade had to duck as he passed beneath its frame. He pulled the door closed behind him, the lock giving a hollow *thunk* as it re-engaged. *That was… unsatisfactory.*

He set off, reviewing the conversation in his mind as he turned off the wide road into a darker, westerly side-street. Traffic at this hour consisted mostly of small knots of pedestrians, with the occasional lone walker or larger, more raucous group. Clade moved quickly through the streets, emerging a few minutes later on the western branch of the great north-south thoroughfare that passed through the city. A closed carriage rattled past to the clop of iron-shod hooves and he fell in behind it, following its course toward the intersection with the Illith road.

It seemed Garrett's presumptuousness was developing more quickly than he'd hoped. Clade had thought it still in the early stages, but Estelle's unfortunate attention appeared to have accelerated its growth; and such conceit in a man like Garrett, rooted in his innate self-regard, would be all but impossible to remove.

I need to get rid of him. The danger of keeping him close was becoming greater than the danger of letting him go. His control over the man was already beginning to slip, and only a fool grasped a snake after it had begun to wriggle free.

Ordinarily, it would be a simple matter to have Garrett transferred back to Zeanes. As overseer, Clade would simply have put him on a ship, confident that his decision was sure to be accepted, no matter how slight the pretext. But with Estelle in town, formalities dictated that he seek her approval; and with his days in Anstice numbered — in her mind at least, if not his own — there was no guarantee she'd accede to his request. And even if she did, a transfer would achieve nothing if Clade too was forced to return to Zeanes. An image formed of Garrett and himself on the ship to Pazia, united in sullen silence, and a wry snort escaped him.

The Illith road followed the line of the old wall, curving northwest toward Bastion Bridge. Little of the original ramparts were left in this part of the city, though here and there fragments of the original wall could be spied in the facades of newer, taller structures. Clade lengthened his stride, enjoying the absence of the crowds that filled the streets during daylight. *Maybe I can cook up some other assignment, something that would take him away from Anstice for a few weeks. Long enough to see Estelle off, one way or another.*

It seemed to Clade that men like Garrett were becoming increasingly common within the Oculus; men, and women too, with no higher goal than their own ambition. Clade wondered how Garrett appeared to Azador. Did the god understand the difference between one who believed in a cause and one who believed only in himself? Did its schemes extend to individual sorcerers, plans to use this one and not another to achieve a particular purpose? Or did it regard the body of sorcerers as merely a pool of resources: something to be nurtured, yes, but ultimately to be used?

Perhaps it was pleased with the changing character of the Oculus.

Perhaps the change reflected a shift in the nature of the god itself.

High clouds drifted across the sky, alternately obscuring the scooped moon and revealing its scarred face once more. Soon the bridge appeared ahead, its lopsided walls giving it the appearance of something either unfinished or in decay. The barrier on the city side was narrow, no more than waist-high, but the crenellated wall on the opposing side rose above Clade's head, the stones large and solid. Narrow bastions projected over the river at regular intervals, the spaces now home to a series of small merchant stalls, each locked up for the night behind a pair of vertical steel-plate shutters.

The grand Tri-God pantheon crouched on the other side of the river, its coloured spires grey in the thin moonlight. A filigree gate stood ajar, opening onto a wide, many-sided courtyard. Three great carved figures looked out from the centre of the yard, each twice the size of a man: the Dreamer, the Weeper, and the Gatherer; their various expressions of rapture, sorrow, and tranquillity lost in the night's gloom. Behind them rose a vast temple, the spectacular colours of its polished marble exchanged in the dark for a solemn, obscure immensity. Lamplight shone from narrow ground-level windows and spilled out from a partially ajar door at one end.

Clade eased the door open and seated himself on one of the low stools scattered throughout the long anteroom. The sanctum itself was already closed; soon the assistant priests would come through to usher the few remaining worshippers outside and shut the gates. Clade had deliberately timed his meeting tonight to allow himself a few moments in the pantheon beforehand, just in case the god chose this night to accompany him. It was, of course, out of the question to hold the meeting itself in a temple like this. Such places were useful for ridding himself of the god, but they were far too visible for even a semi-regular rendezvous. Concealment from Azador meant little if more mundane privacy could not also be guaranteed.

A fat woman with a tear-streaked face shuffled past Clade toward the door. She paused beside the iron-bound collection box, whispering a prayer and dropping in a pair of silver lengths. They landed with a loud clink, as though reminding all who listened of the surest way to the Tri-God's favour.

And what of Azador's favour? The purpose of the Oculus was nothing less than the restoration of all that had been lost when the Valdori fell. Everything the Oculus owned and did — its silent stake in the Crimson Sails, its even more silent investments in Pazian pirates, the research, the scrambling after artefacts overlooked by the Quill — all of it was directed to that end. Such was the god's greatest passion.

So Clade had been told, and so he had believed, even as he'd begun searching for a way to free himself from its influence. But the Oculus also told its sorcerers other things, things Clade knew to be false. What if the god's supposed passion was just another lie?

A pair of assistant priests emerged from a side door and approached a thick-limbed Jervian man, murmuring to him in muted tones and gesturing toward the door. *Dismissing the faithful. Just as Estelle and the Council dismiss the rest of us.*

Only she hadn't. She'd reached out to him, invited him inside. Offered him the chance — no, the right — to speak on behalf of his god. After all, wasn't that what every worshipper wanted?

But I am not a worshipper. I want nothing from Azador, save the one thing it will never give me.

The priests turned toward him, both faces showing the same expression of sombre self-satisfaction. Clade shivered. He pushed himself his feet, thrust his hands deep in the pockets of his trousers, and hurried out of the temple into the cool night air.

The tall granite redoubt stood close to the riverbank, its heavy martial design offering stark contrast to the soaring pantheon. Fourteen such strongholds had originally been built around Anstice, but only nine had survived the centuries since their construction, and most of those were now enclosed within the city's expanded walls. This tower now served as storehouse for the city's armaments, including a sizable stockpile of gunpowder. The powder works was situated nearby, a large building with two great waterwheels protruding from its side into the Tienette. The wheels were said to drive no fewer than four separate mills within, perhaps as many as six, though Clade doubted the truth of the more extravagant reports. The building lay quiescent in the fickle moonlight, silent but for the rhythmic slap and creak of the wheels.

A short jetty extended into the water between the bridge and the powder works, and as Clade approached he saw a figure seated on the rough bench that ran the length of the jetty's downriver side. Clade stepped onto the jetty, causing the warped boards to squeak beneath his feet, and the figure raised its head, pushing back its hood to reveal the familiar features of the Library scribe.

"Pleasant evening for it," Yevin said.

"Indeed." Clade sat, stretching his legs. The Tienette lay spread out around them, undulating gently, the reflected lights at its edges dancing like giant fireflies on the shifting surface. Ahead, beyond the waterwheels, the river and its banks terminated abruptly as though cut off by a great pitch-black curtain: the new wall, the arched channels at its base hidden in the darkness. A few specks of light hovered near the top of the dark mass, just below the inky peak of the gatehouse.

Yevin withdrew a sheaf of papers from his satchel and passed it across. "It's all there," he said. "Everything the Library can tell you, including some they don't like to admit they have."

"Thank you." Clade handed Yevin a fat pouch, and the scribe tucked it away in a pocket without opening it. "Did you have any trouble?"

The man might have shrugged. "None worth mentioning."

Clade nodded, looking out at the dark river. "Were there any accounts of the actual spell?"

"Perhaps. I think so. I don't know." A wry note crept into Yevin's voice. "Honestly, I'd be fortunate to understand even half of what's in those papers. Descriptions of sorcery are like a man talking in his sleep. You recognise each word, but together they sound like so much nonsense."

Clade laughed. "I know what you mean. The archon here has a similar gift."

"A common malady." Yevin chuckled. "Still, I found several accounts of spellcraft matching your description."

"Excellent. Thank you." Clade leaned back against a wooden post, his hand on the papers beside him. Not just one account, but several. A better result than he'd anticipated.

"I had to return the books you asked me to hold," Yevin said. "Had a note from the Library just before I left. Apparently someone put them on reserve."

"Oh?" Something anxious shifted within him and he walled it off. "Who?"

"The Quill."

The caged emotion beat against its prison, but the walls held. "I see." It was hardly a surprise that the Quill, having discovered the existence of the urn, would seek to learn more about it. Clade had asked Yevin to keep the books for precisely that reason: to keep the Quill at bay until such time as he, Clade, took possession of the urn.

Pity about that.

There was nothing to be done about it now. If the Quill figured out what the urn was, nothing on Kal Arna would prevent them from joining the hunt. But with luck, it might still be a while before that happened.

Clade pushed the Quill from his mind. The black waters of the Tienette shifted all around him, mesmerising for their dark beauty. Somehow the scene put him in mind not of a river but of a lake, with wavelets moving up and down as if anchored to the spot, and the nearby waterwheels ploughing the surface as through driven by a brace of oxen marching in slow circles within the building.

Yevin stirred, his feet scraping over the rough boards. "Your letter didn't mention the additional diary copy. I assume it reached its destination? I had it sent via the shop, just like you said."

Irritation at the reminder of the failed scheme flared and was confined. The scowl evaporated before it touched his face. "Yes."

"Was something wrong with it?" Concern sounded in Yevin's voice.

"Hmm? No, no, the copy was fine —"

It came without warning, as it always did, disorienting him, forcing him to steady himself on the bench: the familiar, alien *wrongness,* swirling darkly like a swarm of invisible flies. The presence of the god, here, *right now.* The air thickened in his lungs, smothering him. He closed his eyes, fighting the urge to gasp, and held up a hand to forestall any action or word from Yevin.

I have to leave. Right now, before it sees or hears anything it shouldn't.

Fighting for air, he took a deep breath, then another, the god's presence settling over him like a shroud. The papers lay on the bench beside him; eyes closed, he gathered them up, feeling to make sure he had all of them. "I must go," he said, standing, and raised a finger to his lips to indicate silence. "Thank you for your help." There was a soft rustle of clothing from where Yevin sat. Perhaps he nodded.

Clade turned, making his way awkwardly back to land. The creak of the waterwheel and the hollow clunk of his steps rang in his ears. He cringed inwardly, lightening his steps, increasing his pace. When he reached the bank he opened his eyes a fraction, peering through the lashes just enough to get his bearings and find the road back to the bridge.

He was halfway home before he dared open his eyes fully. The god stayed with him all the way, riding him as he climbed the stairs to his suite, still there as he pulled off his clothes. He crawled into bed and lay on the thin mattress, staring up at the empty, brooding darkness, and waited for sleep to take him.

                            ∽

Eilwen had little opportunity to reflect on her encounter with Dallin, occupied as she was with the demands of her new position. There was a never-ending succession of details to be absorbed, players to become acquainted with, and connections hinted at but left unstated. At first, the sheer volume of information threatened to overwhelm her. Gradually, however, the great, tangled web of self-interest began to take shape in her mind. It was as though some vast, inhuman parasite lay at the city's heart, sucking on its wealth the way a leech sucked blood. *This is Anstice,* she thought more than once as the image formed in her thoughts. *This is my city.*

The other agents seemed little happier to meet her than Ufeus. Most were politic enough to try to hide the fact, though none tried so hard that she might actually make the mistake of thinking herself welcome. Yet what frustrated her most was neither the squalor of her city nor the disfavour of her colleagues, but the seemingly endless sprawl of her new field of responsibility. As a trader, she'd been able to focus on a single negotiation for hours or even days in advance. The world of intelligence offered no such luxury. Everything was connected to everything else, and nothing could be understood on its own.

Each morning, Havilah quizzed her on the threads of scheme and counter-scheme that permeated the city, and every day she was able to explain more, earning more of the quick, flashing smiles with which he rewarded a correct answer. When she told him about her encounter with Dallin, he listened in silence, then nodded and thanked her for her report. On its implications for the Guild itself, he said nothing.

Something is going on, Eilwen thought as she made her way down the corridor to Havilah's suite. *Not out in the city, but in here.* Dallin's drop was scheduled for this evening, and so far Havilah had neither instructed her to be present nor forbidden it. Not that it mattered — either way, she was damn well going to be there.

She pushed the door open and was greeted with the sound of a low, rasping voice, abruptly cut off. Caralange, the Guild sorcerer, stood within, his mouth half-open; and beside him, Trademaster Laris, her face hidden behind the high collar of her jacket. Havilah sat on the edge of his desk, a faint smile on his lips.

"Oh," Eilwen said. "I'm sorry. I'll come back later."

"No, come in," Havilah said. "You should hear this too."

"Should she?" Caralange pressed his lips together and shook his head. "This is pointless." The sorcerer glared at Havilah, then at Eilwen; then he turned and strode from the room, his untidy grey hair brushing Eilwen's ear as he swept past.

"Eilwen." Laris extended a hand, inviting her in. "Congratulations, my dear. Master Havilah's a fortunate man."

Eilwen stifled a laugh. *Gods, you make it sound like I've wedded him.* "Thank you."

"Truly," Laris said. "If I didn't know better, I'd think the Spymaster was running short on coin. Gods know you made more for me in your time than anyone else."

Which was a lie, albeit a flattering one. Pel had never let her near the genuinely lucrative deals. "As you say, Trademaster."

The other woman gave an easy smile. "Call me Laris." She nodded to Havilah, still perched on the edge of his desk. "Havilah."

"Trademaster," Havilah returned pleasantly to her departing back. Only when her footsteps began to fade did he tilt his chin at the open door and murmur to Eilwen, "Close that, would you?"

Eilwen hastened to obey, then turned, the door hard against her back. "Sorry for barging in like that."

"Not at all." The corners of Havilah's eyes crinkled in amusement. "In truth, I was hoping you'd come by sooner."

"Caralange didn't seem very pleased to see me."

"Caralange was unhappy before you got here," Havilah said. "So was Laris."

"What happened?"

Havilah rubbed the bridge of his nose. "Rumours," he said. "It seems there's a new player in town. New money."

Eilwen shrugged. Aspiring traders came to Anstice all the time, some seeking to expand an established business or start a new one, others hoping to quickly parlay a small sum into a fortune by means of some starry-eyed scheme dreamt up around a barrel of ale. The illusions of the latter typically lasted only days. "A rich northerner, perhaps?"

"Maybe," Havilah said. "Whoever it is, they're wealthy enough to make Three Rivers sit up and take notice. They've sent word to Neysa recalling their sorcerer."

"Their *sorcerer?* Who are they dealing with, a Kharjik prince?" A thought struck her. "I haven't seen anything about this in the reports."

"No. And that's what worries me. If someone like that's in town, we shouldn't need our agents in Neysa to tell us about it. We should already know."

Like we should have known about Dallin. But then, it wasn't that they hadn't known Dallin was an informant. It was that someone else knew, too.

"We should already know," Eilwen repeated. She looked up. "What if we do?"

Havilah's brow arched. "Meaning?"

"Dallin," she said. "Someone else is running him. Supposedly someone from the Guild. Well, what if it's true? What if someone else in the Guild is trying to cut us out of the loop? Not completely, just enough for us to miss a few things without realising we've missed them."

Havilah frowned. "A difficult thing to do well. They'd need a full list of every agent's contacts, which would be hard enough in itself. Then they'd need to work out which of them might hear whatever they're trying to conceal and suborn each one." He shook his head. "Unlikely."

"Oh," Eilwen said, deflated. "You don't think there's any connection, then?"

"I didn't say that. Right now we don't know either way." Someone laughed in the corridor outside, and Havilah lowered his voice. "Neither Laris nor Caralange can tell me anything about who Three Rivers' new dance partner is, nor why they might need their sorcerer at the party. We need to find out what they're up to. Otherwise we're just blundering around in the dark."

"What can I do?"

"Nothing. You don't know the city well enough yet." He pointed at her. "You find Dallin. Go to the drop tonight and see what you can learn about this rogue handler."

Thank you. "Where should I put him? We'll need a cell or something —"

"No," Havilah said, his voice hard. "No cells. You're not to lay a hand on him. I don't want him to even know you're there. Better to lose him than tip him off. Understood?"

"But —"

"No." His glare cut into her like steel. "We're not just talking about one man. He'll have resources and friends, possibly very powerful friends. We do nothing until we know what we're dealing with."

Eilwen lowered her head. "As you say."

"Good," Havilah said. "And go alone. Let's not involve any others in this until we have to."

That, at least, would not be a problem. Alone was how she worked best.

"You can count on me," she said.

~

Eilwen spent the afternoon alternately listening to and trying to ignore the soft, rhythmic clicks of her new clock. Somehow the steward had managed to find a Rondossan table clock for a price within the Guild's limits on personal furnishings. He'd delivered it in person the previous day, whereupon she'd given him her thanks and surrendered her bond, to be held by the Guild as surety against damage. Its polished brass face and wood-panel case drew the eye as its clicks did the ear, and as the hours passed Eilwen found herself increasingly entranced by the hand's near-imperceptible progress. She had never seen so small a clock, even from afar, and the notion that such precision could be captured in a box no larger than a clothes chest enthralled her. *Rondossan craftsmanship. Not even the Quill's devices can compare to this.*

At five hours past noon she left her suite and headed out into the city. Brielle had offered to come along, but Eilwen had declined, glad of the excuse of Havilah's instruction. She was well used to shadowing a mark alone. But there was no black amber egg tonight, no loop of sharpened wire in her boot, and though she carried daggers beneath her shirt and in her other boot, she hoped to have no occasion to use them. The absence of wire and egg gave her a strange sense of unpreparedness, and she shivered, trying to drive the unwelcome feeling away. *Nothing is missing that has any place in me. Not any more.*

According to Dallin, the drop was set to take place near the old wall's northern gatehouse. The gate itself was long gone now, the house just another building, albeit one that straddled the wide western thoroughfare. The upper rooms were now home to a school, one of many scattered throughout the city. As a child, Eilwen had never visited a school; there was no way her father could have afforded to educate them all even if he had wanted to, and so two of her brothers were schooled while she and her youngest brother spent their days on the street, fighting the rival gangs and learning skills that her father never dreamt of. But every evening she'd asked Den to tell her what he'd learnt, poring over the small, printed primers he brought home, and vowing to herself that one day she would leave and never again feel the sting of her father's hand against her face.

There were no children at the window when Eilwen reached the gatehouse. On the other side of the vacant archway lay a small square lined with shops: a barber, an oil merchant, two tailors, a locksmith. The late afternoon sun lit the wall's outer face in fiery orange, highlighting every crag and protuberance in its rough blocks. Eilwen worked her way along the wall, searching for the loose stone Dallin had mentioned; but despite its age, the wall seemed unexpectedly solid. She could find only a few stones that shifted at all, and none that could be prised free or manoeuvred to reveal a hiding place.

Frowning, she retraced her steps beneath the arch. *Maybe it's on the inside.* But the inner wall proved to be even more solid than the outer, and at length she was forced to admit defeat, scowling at the impassive stonework as its shadow slowly lengthened before her.

A loose stone in the old wall, near the north gatehouse. Well, wherever it was, she wasn't going to find it now. The afternoon was fading, and it wouldn't do to be caught poking around if Dallin arrived early — or, worse yet, his handler. With a resigned sigh, Eilwen drew up an overturned half-barrel, dragging it to a position from which she could watch the thoroughfare in both directions, as well as the alleys that ran along the wall's inner side. The barrel rocked as she sat on it, its broken rim unsteady on the rough cobbles. She shifted sideways, wedging the barrel in place as best she could; then, pulling her hood over her head, she settled down to wait.

The sun slipped behind the high gatehouse, turning the road to shadow. A lamplighter passed by, Quill sparker in hand, a trail of burning street lights in his wake. Eilwen sat motionless, her face hidden beneath her hood, marking each passer-by and disregarding them as soon as she was sure it was not Dallin. His stride the other day had been long but slightly awkward, even before he had seen Eilwen and Brielle waiting for him. Tonight, under pressure, both length and awkwardness would almost certainly be exaggerated.

All she had to do was watch, and be patient.

It was pure chance that she happened to glance up when she did. A half-hidden silhouette crouched atop the wall, black against the fading cerise clouds, stooped over something hidden from view. *Shit, I didn't cover the wall itself.* She was on her feet before she could stop herself, staring upward in dismay. The figure straightened abruptly, and she recognised the angular form of Dallin as he scurried away, vanishing and reappearing between the merlons before passing out of sight altogether.

Eilwen sat back down, her mind racing. Of course, the old wall was its own path. Its northern course was almost entirely intact. Dallin might join or leave it anywhere — and so might whoever was coming to collect the drop. The gloom was deepening by the minute; soon, any movement on the wall wouldn't be visible even in silhouette. *I need to go up. Down here, I'm as good as blind.*

But if she did, then what? Up on the wall she'd have no place to wait unseen. Besides, the handler might arrive at any moment; move now, and she risked missing him entirely. She exhaled, frustrated, eyes flicking between the wall and the road. The gatehouse door lay in plain view, as did the crenel behind which Dallin had crouched, presumably to deposit his information. *I can still see every-thing from here. And if he takes the road, I can still follow him when he comes out.*

Gods, I hope he takes the road.

The clouds lost the last of their glow, the sky shifting to deep, twilight blue, then black. Lamps flickered below the wall, spilling yellow light over the battlements and casting the spaces between them deeper into shadow. Eilwen fixed her gaze on the dim crenel, hoping to preserve as much night vision as she could; but as the minutes dragged by, the lamps seemed to burn themselves into the edges of her sight, hovering against the black like tiny, unsteady suns.

She cursed, squinting against the dancing spots of light. Nothing remained between the battlements except thick, unyielding shadow.

Damn it. Why is he taking so long?

Movement by the gatehouse caught her eye: a man with ashen hair and a long cloak wrapped tightly around his shoulders. He moved swiftly, without hesitation, opening the gatehouse door with a single motion and disappearing inside. Blinking rapidly, Eilwen flicked her gaze back up to the crenel, peering into the gloom with one hand raised to block the lamps. Something shifted between the battlements, black on black, then stopped — and was that a glint of light on pale hair? She blinked again, unsure.

The darkness shifted once more, passing behind the neighbouring gap, back toward the gatehouse. Then it paused, leaning out over the street, and a narrow face emerged from the gloom, cheeks and chin lit by the flickering lamps below, its stark features framed by shoulder-length ashen hair. *Got you.*

The man turned and vanished from view. Eilwen stood, heart pounding, and pressed herself into the locked door of the baker's shop behind her. *If he doesn't come out after fifty heartbeats, I'll have to go up. Damn, I wish Brielle was here.* The gatehouse door swung open, and she tensed; but the man who emerged was short and dark-haired, and his arm was draped around a giggling Kharjik woman. They embraced, the woman locking her arms about the man's neck, pushing him back against the door post. Eilwen grit her teeth, staring daggers at the couple until at last they broke loose of each other and moved on, the man weaving backward down the road, the woman giggling at his side.

Eilwen stared at the door, willing it to open once more. She'd lost her count, distracted by the idiot lovebirds. *Ten more, then I go looking.* But her heart was racing, and after ten beats she stood there still, counting further. Fifteen. Twenty.

On the twenty-third beat the door opened and the man emerged, a curl of ashen hair peeking out from beneath his now-raised hood. Eilwen relaxed against the wall as he turned his head, sweeping the street with his stare. Then he set off back the way he had come: south, into the heart of the city.

Between the gloom and his hood, the man was hard to keep in

sight; and when he turned off the thoroughfare it took her a moment to realise he had disappeared. She dashed ahead to where she had last seen him and peered down the side-streets, hurrying from one to the next in growing anxiety. *I can't lose you now, damn it.* She paused at the mouth of a dim lane and was rewarded with a fleeting glimpse of his hood disappearing around a corner. *There. Gods, would you just slow down?*

Eilwen ran after him, skidding to a halt at the corner and wincing at the pain in her bad leg. There he was, his long, even gait unbroken. She recognised the route, now: a shortcut through to the eastern thoroughfare, one she had used herself from time to time. *Maybe if I duck around and meet him coming the other way, I can get a better look at his face.* But no, that would be foolish. The man might turn in any direction at the thoroughfare. All she had to do was stay patient and she could follow him home right now.

When the man reached the thoroughfare, he turned south once more, and an uneasy foreboding stirred within her. *Follow him home. But I already know where he's going, don't I?* And as he led her south along the thoroughfare, then turned onto Traders' Row, her foreboding grew, so that when at last he reached the Woodtraders compound and knocked at the gatekeeper's window, she felt no surprise, only a heavy, hollow sense of inevitability.

Too late, she realised that the Row was empty save for the two of them. She froze for a moment, then forced herself to resume her approach. If she backtracked now, he might see her and recognise her. Better to hope he hadn't noticed her pursuit and continue on. She pushed her hood back, easing her pace and trying to catch her breath. He turned as she neared and she gave him a brief wave, a nod of one colleague to another. Ashen hair framed his face beneath the hood. His narrow cheeks and chin were the same as those she had seen atop the wall.

She didn't know him.

"I'm Eilwen," she said as the gate swung open. "I don't think we've met."

"Kieffe," he replied, returning the nod. His voice was soft, and she had to lean forward to hear him. "I've been away from Anstice for a while."

"A trader, right?" Eilwen said. "Where did they send you? North? West?"

Kieffe shrugged. "Lots of places. Here is better."

They passed within, the gate clanging shut behind them. Inside the main building, they parted with another nod, Kieffe heading toward the stairs as Eilwen turned aside to her own suite. Heart hammering, leg aching, she stumbled inside, kicked off her shoes, and fell onto her bed, exhausted.

Who are you, Kieffe? she thought, staring up at the gloom-shrouded ceiling. *And what are you doing to my Guild?* But there was no answer, save for the soft clicking of the clock in the next room.

CHAPTER 7

Before the tree, a shoot.
Before the shoot, a seed.
Before the seed, a thought.
Holy Dreamer, grant us a glimpse of your reverie.

— Liturgy of the First Hour, *Tri-God Book of Prayer,*
Pantheon of Anstice

ARANDRAS FANNED HIMSELF WITH SOME folded papers and tried to concentrate on the open volume before him. The booth was small and poorly ventilated, making the humid air even more oppressive, but Arandras still preferred it to the cavernous public reading room outside. The Library had only a handful of individual reading stalls, and the cost of this one was already running into silver, but the privacy it afforded was worth every copper duri. Whatever the urn was, its value was no longer in question. The fewer people who knew he had it, the better.

Four days of research had brought only marginal progress on the inscription's translation, and none at all on the question of the urn's origin or purpose. His sole achievement had come on the second day: the discovery of a similar Valdori dialect associated with a region on the other side of the Pelaseans, near where the city of Zonta now stood. With the aid of the word list and a poorly-copied sample text, he'd been able to guess at several of the words encircling the urn. But those fragments he could decipher seemed to offer little more than a rote message of good fortune, much the same as might be found on any worthless trinket, leaving him no closer to understanding the urn's true purpose.

I could ask the Quill. The thought hung in the back of his mind, feeding off his frustration. But the attraction was a mirage, he knew. There was no inviting the Quill into something like this, not without ceding them control. He rubbed his beard, frowning again at his transcription of the urn's lettering.

A knock sounded at the booth door, followed by the high forehead and narrow nose of a librarian. "You asked to be notified when two books became available," he said primly, the words a statement of fact. "They have both just been returned. You may peruse them now, if you wish."

Narvi had returned Yevin's books, at last. Arandras sat up. "Yes, that would be fine."

The door opened further and the librarian entered, wrinkling his nose at the sight of Arandras's cluttered desk, and delicately placed the two volumes in a small clear patch on one side. "Have you finished with any of these?" he asked hopefully.

"Ah, no, not quite," Arandras said. "Thank you."

The librarian sniffed. "As you wish." He backed cautiously out of the booth, closing the door with a soft click.

Arandras picked up the first volume. It was the one he'd glanced through at the schoolhouse, an anonymous work titled *Forms of Sorcery.* Clearing a space on the desk, he set the book down and began to read.

A close perusal confirmed the impression he'd received earlier. The book skipped through dozens of purposes to which the Valdori had supposedly applied sorcery, from agriculture to leisure to weapons of war. But the work's breadth only highlighted its corresponding lack of depth; and despite what Narvi had said, most of the book's references to religious practices focused on a handful of major orders. Arandras skimmed through its handwritten pages, his pace increasing as he progressed, until at last he closed the book with a snap, frustrated and none the wiser.

The second book was as slender as the first, but where the other volume was fresh and well cared for, this one reeked of mould. Arandras covered his nose and mouth with his sleeve, gingerly turning the pages with thumb and forefinger, and tried not to breathe.

Tiysus Oronayan, the famed Kharjik historian, had written more than twenty separate volumes and countless shorter pieces. This was a lesser-known work, shorter than his celebrated *Histories*, but still long enough to merit its own binding. Arandras leafed slowly through the book, moving each page as gently as he could, until he came to an illustration that stopped him dead.

It was not quite the same as his urn. It had handles, for one thing: slender stalks that curved out from the base before bending back in just where the neck began to widen. It was taller, too, or not as wide, and its surface carried writing only, not images. But the likeness was unmistakable. There was the same bulbous base, the same flared mouth, the same flat cap sealing the contents within. The writing, alas, was indistinct — the drawing too small for the copy-artist to accurately reproduce such details — but it spiralled around the same portion of the rounded body and seemed similar in length to the inscription that had so far defied his attempts at translation.

At the foot of the facing page was a reference to the drawing. The Kharjik word that stood for the urn was unfamiliar, but something about it triggered a faint recognition. Arandras paused, puzzling over the term but unable to pin it down. Then he turned the page, and the riddle was solved.

A half-page illustration showed a man lying on the ground, pierced with arrows. At his side knelt another, holding the urn to the wounded man's mouth. But the man was not drinking. He was exhaling — surrendering his dying breath to the urn, and with it all that he was, to be preserved against the passage of time. And there in the text was the word Arandras had heard the echo of, an old Yanisinian term: *zaki,* the passing of the spirit. Death.

That's it. Arandras stared at the page, the image filling his vision. *It's an ossuary, but not for the man's physical remains. An ossuary for the soul.*

The text below the second illustration was brief, describing the supposed capture of the spirit as a Yanisinian custom that had no parallel among the Valdori. That at least made sense. Preserving the dead was the stuff of Jervian savages, or the fire-cultists who burned their corpses and retained the ashes. The Valdori had buried their dead, sung songs about them, even built monuments to them, but that was all. Nowhere had Arandras ever heard of the Valdori capturing souls of the dead and putting them on a shelf.

Yet the urn was clearly of Valdori make. Only they had ever fashioned such pieces that were impervious to the passage of time. *Why would they make something with no function in their own culture?* A thought struck him, and he shivered. *Unless they made it work.* Was it possible? Could they have found a way to draw out a spirit and imprison it in a small pewter vessel — perhaps the very vessel he now held in his hand?

Was there, even now, a *person* trapped inside?

Reason returned with a rush. *No. It can't be.* Such sorcery, if possible at all, would surely rank among the most complex and laborious of all the Empire's works. Any such binding would require an immense physical anchor in which to ground it, far greater than the hand-high urn. For all their power, even the Valdori were not immune to the laws of sorcery. There was no way the urn could hold such a binding.

Arandras closed his hand over the small pewter vessel. It was smooth and cool to the touch, just as it had always been. He grasped it tightly, squeezing hard against the unyielding metal. *Don't be a fool. There is no spirit within.*

But if that was so, what was it for? The thing had clearly been designed to mimic the form of a Yanisinian receptacle, which at least explained why there was no way to open it. The inscription, too, made sense now: not a good luck charm, but a benediction for the deceased. The engraved images presumably showed scenes from the life of whoever supposedly rested within. All the details made sense. *But what is it really? And why does someone want it so much they're prepared to kill for it?*

His hand was still resting on the urn when the door slammed open. Startled, Arandras scrambled to his feet, hiding the urn behind his back and bracing himself for an attack. But the newcomer merely stood there, a self-satisfied grin on his face, and a breath later Arandras recognised the smirking features of Onsoth.

"You," Arandras said in disgust. He crouched to pick up some papers that had fallen to the floor and slipped the urn into his bag.

"What do you want?"

"Well, well," Onsoth said, his grin widening even further. "What have we here? Could it be Lord Swine himself, studying in the Library he treats with such contempt? Why, yes, I believe it is!"

"What do you want?" Arandras repeated, his voice flat. "Or is it your usual practice to harass people for no reason? No, wait, forget I asked. Stupid question."

"Harass?" Onsoth folded his arms, still smiling. "What an offensive thing to say. I'm here on behalf of the city of Spyridon. You should show the proper respect."

Arandras grit his teeth. "What. Do. You. Want?"

"I'm surprised to find you here, you know. Here in the public reading area of the Library. Open to all the citizens of Spyridon." Onsoth paused, and an unpleasant suspicion began to form in Arandras's thoughts. "But do you know what I've discovered? It's not just the Library you're too proud for. It's the whole damn city! Even citizenship of Spyridon is not good enough for Arandras, Lord of the Swine!"

It was futile to argue. Never mind that in practice, the Library opened its doors to all comers save children and criminals only — nonetheless, its mandate extended only to the citizenry. Anything more was a mere courtesy, one that might be revoked whenever, or from whomever, the city wished.

Onsoth must have seen the resignation on his face. "That's right, Lord Swine. Pack up your things. The Library is *closed* to you."

Arandras collected his papers in silence. Then he gathered the Library's books, stacking them neatly on the small desk. He reached for the musty Oronayan volume last, placing it atop the pile, and Onsoth wrinkled his nose in disgust.

"Hells, what is that smell?" he said, fanning the air with his hand. "Get out already. Take your shit back home to your sty."

It took all of Arandras's self-control not to punch Onsoth in the face as he left.

~

By evening, the street outside Rhothe's Bar was slick with moisture, the result of a brief afternoon storm that had done nothing to relieve the oppressive humidity. Inside, the usual hubbub of conversation was muted as patrons slouched listlessly around tables, most barely moving except to raise mugs to their lips or to gesture the serving staff for more. The high windows along the far wall stood wide open, admitting flashes of lamplight, the clop of passing horses and, occasionally, the faintest breath of air.

Arandras found Druce and Jensine ensconced in a booth directly below one of the yawning windows. Jensine smiled in greeting, but Druce offered only a curt nod, his fingers drumming against the table and his eyes roving the room. His drink sat on the table, untouched.

"What's with him?" Arandras said, then grimaced at the edge in his voice. Onsoth was a bastard, but taking it out on Druce wouldn't help.

Jensine shrugged. "He won't say. Not until everyone's here." Druce continued his survey of the room, showing no sign of hearing their conversation. "He's been like this all day."

Arandras took a deep pull from his cider, watching as Druce shifted restlessly in his seat, eyes flicking here and there, all the while avoiding Arandras's gaze. *Must be the only one in the city who isn't noticing the heat,* he thought sourly, cupping the cool mug between his palms. *What trouble have you got yourself into now?*

"Have you learnt anything more about the urn?" Jensine said, and Druce's attention shifted to a point just above Arandras's shoulder. "You must have translated the message by now."

"Partly, I think," Arandras said. "Seems like a blessing of some kind, but I still don't know what it means. I'm working on it."

Druce snorted and shifted his gaze back to somewhere in the middle of the room.

Arandras leaned forward. "Something you'd like to say, Druce?"

"What's going on here, then?" Mara plonked a brimming mug on the table and sank into the vacant seat with a sigh. "Hells, what a pathetic excuse for a storm. I've sneezed better storms than that." Silence greeted her pronouncement, and she glanced around the table in bemusement. "Did I interrupt something?"

"Not at all," Druce said, his voice tight. "We were just waiting for you."

"Well, here I am," Mara said, gesturing expansively. "Proceed!"

Druce sat forward, looking directly at Arandras for the first time since his arrival. "Tell us, please, Arandras," he said. "How are your enquiries progressing? I speak, of course, of the small trinket Mara recovered last week."

Arandras's eyes narrowed. *Put away the theatrics, boy. If you want to ask something, ask it.* "They continue," he said.

"I see. And tell us, if you would, have you received any offers to purchase it?"

"I told you the other night, it's not that simple. I need to find out more —"

"Let me make it simple, then," Druce said. The earlier jitters were gone; he seemed assured now, even cocky. "Just tell us the best offer you've had so far."

Arandras frowned. "I spoke to Sten, on Goldsmiths Lane —"

"No, Arandras," Druce said. "I'm talking about the Quill. How much did they offer you?" Arandras moistened his lips, and the gesture seemed to set something off in the other man. "Tell us!" Druce shouted, slamming his hand on the table.

"What is this, Arandras?" Jensine asked, her tone cautious. "What's he talking about?"

"I spoke to a Quill sorcerer," Arandras said, each word clipped. "He offered to purchase the urn. A specific sum was not mentioned." He sat back, arms folded, daring Druce to say otherwise.

Druce considered him a long moment. "Maybe that's true," he said at last. "If so, I have some good news for you. For all of us." He glanced around the table. "The Quill want the urn, badly. They're willing to give us three gold hands for it."

Three hands. Fifteen lurundi, each bar a finger of gold. Gasps sounded around the table, and Druce grinned.

"Are you sure the offer's good?" Mara said. "You know what the Quill are like."

"Oh, I'm sure," Druce said, the conviction in his tone unmistakable. "I heard a couple of them talking about it. They didn't even know I was there." He took a mouthful of ale. "They weren't joking."

"This is wonderful!" Jensine looked as if someone had offered to fetch the moon and place it in her lap. "What are you all going to do? I think... I'll buy a horse. A Halonese cross, if I can find one around here —"

The words seemed to come from someone else. "I'm not selling it."

Jensine gaped, brought up short in mid-reverie. "But... why? Three gold hands!" She blinked. "Do you think you can get even more?"

"No," Arandras said. "I'm not selling it. At all."

"I knew it!" Druce burst out. "Gods, but I knew something was up. What do you mean, you're not selling it?"

Arandras closed his eyes. The air in the room seemed completely still. "I can't."

"That's not for you to decide, is it? There are four of us with a say, and —"

"Let him speak, Druce," Mara said. She turned to Arandras. "Why?"

"I can't sell it. Not right now. I need it." The words ran out, and he shook his head.

Mara's voice was like steel. "Why?"

"Ahhh. All right." Arandras covered his head with his hands and tried to gather his thoughts. "Fine. I — um. Well, I used to be married. Really." He looked from face to face, trying to impress upon them the weight of his words. "Tereisa... she was killed. Murdered. And that urn is going to lead me to the man who did it."

"The hells it will," Druce said. "Do you truly expect us to believe —"

"*Don't.*" Arandras glared across the table. "I really don't care what you believe. I *know.*"

Something in his words seemed to reach them. They stared, or looked away: Jensine speechless, Druce uncertain, Mara impossible to read.

Eventually Druce broke the silence. "I see you believe that," he said, his tone subdued. "But this changes nothing. The urn belongs to all of us. I say we sell it. Jensine?"

Jensine hesitated. "Sell," she whispered. "I'm sorry, Arandras, truly I am. But we have to sell it. You see that, don't you?"

"Mara?"

Mara stared at the table, her hand clenched around her mug. When she spoke, her voice was thick. "No sell."

"What?" Druce stared at her, shocked. "What do you mean, no?"

Mara snapped around. "Nobody asked you to explain your vote. I don't have to explain mine." She turned back to the others. "Two votes to sell, two against. We do nothing."

"No, this is bullshit!" Druce was on his feet in an instant, fury contorting his features. "This is not what happens! We find things, we sell them. That's all! We do not just *decide* to hang on to the biggest find we've ever had!"

"You called for the vote," Arandras muttered.

"Shut up!" Druce leaned over the table, his finger practically touching Arandras's face. "One fourth of that thing is mine. You want to keep it? Buy my share. Four gold bars, minus change. Same again for Jensine, while you're at it."

"Don't be absurd. I don't have that kind of money."

"Absurd, is it? You're keeping exactly *that kind of money* from us! You arrogant bastard."

"Listen, Druce, if you need silver, I can tide you over until —"

"I don't want an advance, and I don't need your charity!" Druce dug into his coinpurse and flung a handful of coppers at Arandras, striking him in the face and chest. "There's your loan back. I don't owe you anything." He paused, breathing hard, and shook his head. "I thought you were different. Did you know that? I thought, here's a man who's straight. Here's a man who respects you enough to tell it true. But you don't respect anyone, do you, Arandras? Not even your friends. Not even yourself. Well, fuck you."

He stalked away, jouncing the table as he departed. Arandras rubbed his stinging cheek and forehead, copper coins clinking as they fell to his lap.

"So, what, that's it?" Jensine said, and Arandras looked up. "Druce is right, Arandras. This isn't what we do. You can't just change the rules like that."

"We voted," Arandras said.

"And when have we ever had to vote about anything before? No, this is wrong."

"I'll make it up to you. Just give me time."

"No. This is over." Jensine pushed herself to her feet. "You owe me, Arandras, and you owe Druce, and that's going to eat at you until you make it right. But even then…" She shrugged. "How could I trust you again?"

Arandras bowed his head as Jensine followed Druce out of the bar. He felt wrung out, as if he had been running for his life. *I have no choice. Can't you see?* But such thoughts were useless now. *This is over,* Jensine had said, and she was right. It had been over the moment Mara found the urn.

"Well done," Mara said, and it took him a long moment to recognise the sarcasm. She considered him, head tilted as though trying to discern his thoughts. He looked away, reluctant to meet her eyes.

"Are you going to leave as well?" he asked, and found he did not know what answer he was hoping to hear.

Slowly, Mara shook her head. "My lover died, too," she said, so softly that he almost couldn't hear.

Still he could not meet her eyes. "Who killed him?"

She shrugged. "Me, in the end. But he was dead long before." Her hand found his arm. "I know what it is to have questions that need answers. I'll help you, if you want it."

"Thank you," Arandras said. He swallowed, searching for more words but finding none. "Thank you."

They sat there for a time, neither moving. Arandras's tears were few, and soon ran into his beard, and he did not think Mara saw them.

~

Two days of prowling the compound yielded Eilwen frustratingly little information about Kieffe. Once, she spotted him through the high bathhouse window as he crossed the compound, but by the time she emerged he was gone. Another time she passed him on the staircase and doubled back, trailing him to a featureless door on the first floor. She was not bold enough to follow him in, and when she came back that night and tried the door, she found it locked.

At breakfast on the second morning she sought out Pel, asking him about Kieffe's past assignments, and what had brought him to Anstice. But Pel merely shook his head in disappointment and suggested that if she wished to become better acquainted with Kieffe then she might, perhaps, consider a conversation with the man himself. Then, blinking ponderously as if in surprised realisation, Pel leaned in and offered to arrange an introduction, forcing Eilwen to backtrack hastily and change the subject.

But if Kieffe was difficult to locate, Master Havilah was impossible. Eilwen saw no sign of him at all, nor any indication of activity in his suite, leading her to suspect that he had left the compound entirely. Where he had gone, and when he would be back, she did not know.

Ufeus could tell her nothing about either Havilah's whereabouts or Kieffe's assignments, past or present. Nor did he know anything about the room on the first floor. "My interests begin at the compound gate," he told her stiffly. "The details of Guild administration are not my concern. Perhaps you should try Ged."

Perhaps I should. With nothing else to go on, and with Havilah absent, the locked room seemed her only lead. Ged, the house steward, could at least tell her which master the room was allotted to. If it turned out to be Laris, it would at least be confirmation of sorts that Kieffe was indeed a trader. And if not...

Maybe I've got it wrong. Maybe Kieffe is something else entirely. She recalled Caralange's glare when she walked in on him and Laris in Havilah's office. *A sorcerer, perhaps.*

The steward's chambers occupied three adjoining suites on the second floor, the intermediate walls of which had been partially removed to form one long, twisting room. Eilwen halted by the vacant assistant's desk, looking about for someone to speak to. Crates and boxes filled the winding space, some clinging to the walls in irregular stacks, others clustered together in rough islands on the floor. Most were closed, but a few bared their contents to her gaze: plates and utensils, lamp oil and wicks, pens and ink. A faint hum rose from the far end of the room, and Eilwen stood on tiptoes, craning her neck to see past the piled goods.

"Hello?" she called. "Is someone there?"

The humming stopped. "Back here. Try not to bump anything."

Eilwen stepped around the first of the piles, making her way past boxes of sealing wax and scent bottles to the rear of the room where a small office was partitioned off from the rest by a light wooden screen. Ged sat at one end of a narrow table, a collection of papers before him, eyeglasses perched on the end of his nose. Eilwen cleared her throat and the steward waved her in without looking up.

"Eilwen," he said, running his finger down a column of numbers and pausing to scratch a note beside one of them. "How fares the clock? Running smoothly, I hope?"

"Yes, thank you." Eilwen glanced around, looking for somewhere to sit, but every available surface was covered with papers. "I'd almost think it sorcery if it weren't for the clicking. Remarkable craftsmanship."

"Good, good." Ged's finger reached the bottom of one column, moved to the top of the next. "And what can I do for you today?"

"Just answer a question, I hope," Eilwen said. "There's a room on the first floor. Could you tell me who has use of it?"

"Ah. I think so. A moment, if you please..."

The moment stretched to a minute, then two. Eilwen folded her arms, her gaze falling on a wide, shallow cabinet on the wall behind the steward's head, its doors fastened with a pair of heavy locks. The key cupboard. Even as the thought formed in her mind, she pushed it away. Havilah's instructions had been plain. *Better to lose him than tip him off.* Letting herself into Kieffe's room was out of the question.

But what if it wasn't his room? Perhaps it was a meeting chamber, or a storeroom, or —

Ged pushed back his chair with a screech and turned to a set of calfskin-bound folios at the end of the table. He selected one and laid it open, revealing a plan of the building.

"First floor, yes?"

"That's right. North side, facing the garden. Third door from the eastern corner."

"Hmm." He turned the page, scanning the rows of slanting text. "Here, this is it," he said, tapping an entry with a lined forefinger. "This room is designated for the use of Spymaster Havilah."

"What?" Eilwen leaned over to read the words for herself. "Are you sure that's the right room? First floor, I said."

"You did, yes," Ged said tartly. "This is the room, and it is allocated to the Spymaster's department."

"His department," Eilwen repeated, trying to think. What in the hells was going on? *Gods, please let Havilah not be playing both sides. The key cabinet hung from the opposite wall, silent and inviting. If he's not, going in there would be madness. But if he is...*

The steward closed up the folio and returned it to its place. "Is there anything else?"

Eilwen smiled at his back. "Do you happen to have a spare key for that room? There's an... anomaly I need to resolve."

"Master Havilah will have a key. No doubt he can tell you what lies within."

"No doubt," Eilwen said as Ged turned back, peering at her over the rims of his eyeglasses. "Unfortunately, Master Havilah is away at present. Guild business, you understand." Ged offered no reaction, and Eilwen plunged ahead. "But I am his appointed deputy, which makes me the department's ranking officer in his absence, at least where matters in Anstice are concerned. And since we are, in fact, in Anstice..."

He frowned. *Come on,* Eilwen thought, willing her smile not to slip. *Just give me the key.*

"Spymaster Havilah is away, you say." The steward rubbed his chin. "Perhaps you should wait until he returns."

"This can't wait, I'm afraid," Eilwen said, careful not to plead. Any hint of desperation would only undermine her authority.

"And where is Master Havilah?"

"I can't tell you that," Eilwen said. "I'm sorry."

"Can't wait, can't tell." Ged eyed her speculatively. "You are like him, aren't you? I did not see it before, why he chose you. Now, I see."

Eilwen smiled and said nothing.

Ged inclined his head, an amused glint in his eye, and turned to the key cabinet.

~

Eilwen left the steward's chambers with the key in her hand and questions filling her mind. If the room belonged to Havilah, why had he never mentioned it? Was Kieffe one of Havilah's agents outside of Anstice? But if so, what was he doing in the city? Or maybe he had nothing to do with Havilah. Maybe someone else had simply used Havilah's name to procure the room. But who would do such a thing, and why would they bother?

Had Ufeus been holding out on her? Had Havilah?

She found herself on the first floor, having descended the stairs without thought, her steps leading her around the corner to the northern corridor. Beech panelling lined the walls on both sides, the light tones broken only by doorways, lamp sconces, and some small plaster statues of the Coridon era. Eilwen slowed as she neared the third door. No-one else was in sight. The door was unmarked, giving no hint of whether it led to a private suite or a chamber with some other function. She slowed further, straining her ears for any sound of activity within.

Someone rounded the far corner and began striding toward her. Eilwen accelerated at once, the key clenched tight in her sweaty palm, heart thudding against her ribs. A flash of something pale caught her eye — ashen hair? — and she glanced up; but no, it was just Laris in another of her high-collared jackets, this one somewhere between the colours of cream and pearl. The Trademaster offered her a warm smile as she approached.

"Eilwen. I was hoping to see you again."

"Trad — Laris," Eilwen said, hoping her face didn't look as flushed as it felt. "You're well, I hope."

"Very well, thank you," Laris said. "And how is Havilah treating you?"

Good question. "Fine," Eilwen said. She cast about for something more to say, but nothing came to mind.

Laris's brow furrowed. "Is something wrong?"

"No." Eilwen took a deep breath. "Everything's fine."

"Ah. Good." A maid emerged into the corridor a few doors down, and Laris drew Eilwen aside to let her pass. "My door is always open to you, Eilwen," the Trademaster resumed, her voice low. "I hope you know that."

Eilwen blinked. "Uh, thank you. That's very kind."

"I mean it," Laris said, her hand lingering on Eilwen's arm. "Havilah's very good at what he does, but he has a fondness for tossing people out of the nest to see who'll learn to fly on the way down." She shrugged wryly. "It's his way, I suppose. But if you need help finding your wings, come talk to me."

"Thank you," Eilwen said again. "I'll keep that in mind."

"Good." Laris straightened. "I'm sure you'll do us proud," she said with a parting smile.

Eilwen sagged against the wall, rubbing her temples as the Trademaster's footsteps receded behind her. *Gods. Of all the times to run into a master.* She turned around just in time to see Laris stride past the locked door and disappear around the corner, leaving the corridor empty once more.

Perhaps she should just leave it be. Wait for Havilah to get back. But what if that wasn't what he wanted? Maybe Laris was right. Maybe Havilah was nudging her out of the nest and sitting back to see what happened.

Or maybe he's behind the whole thing.

The thought stretched in her mind like a great cat, all languid grace and sheathed claws. Something was going on. What if that something was him? Maybe that was why she'd been chosen for this position over one of his own. Maybe Havilah was counting on her inexperience to blind her to the truth of his own involvement.

The hells with that. Eilwen pushed herself upright, wincing at the pain in her fist: the key, still clenched in her sweaty hand, its hard edges digging into her palm like an arrowhead.

The corridor was still empty, and the sound of her steps reverberated off the stone floor and panelled walls. She halted before the door and knocked twice on its polished timber grain, leaning close to listen for movement. Nothing stirred within. *Nobody there? Or do you just want me to go away?* It didn't matter. She was done playing games.

Lips pursed, Eilwen slid the key easily into the lock and gave it a smooth twist. The lock responded with a satisfying *snick,* and she pushed the door open.

Darkness greeted her, black and impenetrable. She reached for the lamp beside the door, then reconsidered and hurried to the end of the corridor, plucking the corner lamp from its bracket. Wrapping her fingers around the leather-bound handle, Eilwen lifted the lamp high and stepped through the unlocked door.

The floor and walls were bare stone, bereft of carpets or pan-elling or other ornamentation. The wall on Eilwen's left was close enough to touch, but the rest of the room extended away to the right beyond the lamp's reach. Rough boards covered the windows facing the inner garden, edges filled so as to block the slightest glimmer of light from without. A faint scent of varnished timber hung in the air, but the room seemed entirely empty of furniture, and indeed of anything else. Eilwen glanced about the room, cursing as realisation sank in. *They knew we were coming. They knew, and got everything out before we could get here.*

She swung her lamp to the right, peering into the shadows of the far wall. There *was* something, there in the corner. Something long and narrow, bundled against the wall. It looked almost like...

The lamplight fell on a hand, pale and unmoving. *Gods preserve.* Trembling, she edged closer. There was the arm, and there the head. Ashen hair spilled over the floor beneath an upthrust chin and nose. "Hello?" she said; but the word was barely a whisper, and the figure did not respond.

Dread closed around Eilwen's heart. She crept closer, allow-ing the light to fall on the figure's face. *Kieffe.* Empty eyes gazed sightlessly past her ear, one half-lidded as though frozen mid-wink. Small spots of blood marked the skin just below the man's nostrils. The play of lamplight over his mouth revealed worn, lightly stained teeth. His limbs lay flat along the floor, the toes of his boots propped against the wall in ghastly nonchalance. Aside from the blood be-neath his nose, his body showed no obvious sign of violence.

Gods, she thought, staring stupidly at the corpse before her. *They killed him.* Her arm sagged, drawn earthward by the leaden weight of the lamp. She set it down and lowered herself onto the floor be-side it, knees pulled up to her chest, arms wrapped around her calves. *They knew we were onto them, and they killed him for it.*

A breath of air brushed her face, and she froze. The lamp flick-ered, casting wild shadows about the room. Footsteps whispered behind her; then came a rustle of fabric as someone crouched along-side.

Slowly, she turned her head.

"Eilwen?" The voice was soft, and deep, and richly accented. "Are you all right?"

"Havilah." The Spymaster's face hovered before her, concern in his eyes. She stared, then flung her arms around him and buried her face in his shoulder. "Havilah. Thank the gods."

She held him a long moment, longer than she would have dared in daylight. But it was dark, and there was a dead man in the room, and she was no longer alone.

CHAPTER 8

Wisdom? Why do you ask me of wisdom? Wisdom is pragmatism, nothing more: the ruthless winnowing of the lesser in service of the greater.

— Daro of Talsoor, *Dialogues with my Teachers*

CLADE CLOSED THE DOOR TO his suite and turned the key once, twice. The curtains behind the desk were already drawn, shutting out the bright mid-morning sun and muffling the noise of the street below. It was not merely a question of privacy today: the morning's task required his undivided attention. Distraction could prove disastrous.

Since the night of his meeting with Yevin, the god had left him alone; in fact, it had apparently lost interest in Anstice altogether. Clade had observed no sign of it with any of his sorcerers, not even Sera. The timing of its visitation still bothered him, though he could think of nothing that might have tipped the god off. No-one but Garrett knew he had been out, and even if Azador had chanced to overhear him mentioning the fact, the boy knew nothing of his purpose. Garrett could not have given him away even if he wanted to.

Perhaps he was simply being paranoid. The god came and went as it willed. Some appearances were inevitably more inconvenient than others.

A perfumed oil lamp burned steadily on his desk, adding its soft yellow light to the glimmers of daylight around the curtains' edge.

Clade perched on a cushioned armchair, intent on the low table before him and the objects on its surface: two simple earthenware mugs, almost identical but for the thickness of their handles. Ink runes snaked around the surface of one, the lines dividing and joining to form a single, unified structure.

Sera had obtained the mugs and performed the binding at his request. Though she shared Clade's primary proficiency — the binding of wood — the girl had rudimentary talent across a range of other elements, including clay. She'd screwed up her nose when he'd given her the assignment, giving her such an air of a mischievous child that he'd been hard-pressed not to grin outright. "A mug? Yuck! Do you know how nasty sorcery feels when you have to ground it in clay? All slithery and bony and quiet, like a snake." But she'd done as he asked, leaving the ensorcelled mug and its unmarked twin outside his door some time during the night for him to discover as he rose for breakfast.

The runes covering the thin-handled mug were only a representation, not the binding itself. Sorcery did not depend on runes any more than music depended on a score, or a building upon an architect's diagram. Drawing the desired structure on the target object was a beginner's technique, useful for planning the order of the binding, but feasible only for spells of sufficient simplicity. Even the keenest penmanship could not hope to match the intricacy of a master sorcerer's binding.

Clade placed his hand over the mouth of the mug. A whisper of cool air wafted against his palm. This particular binding reduced the temperature inside a vessel, enough to preserve the chill of an already cool drink for perhaps a day, if kept in the shade. Though too weak to serve any serious purpose, a chiller was the kind of spell beloved by dandies for its peculiar blend of the understated and the ostentatious: it marked the bearer as wealthy enough to afford so frivolous a binding, yet modest enough to allow such proof of wealth to go unnoticed by anyone outside the owner's immediate vicinity. Closing his hand over the edge, Clade slid his fingers inside. The feeling was like dipping his hand into a still pool of pleasantly cool water. He withdrew his hand and the sensation vanished as though pulling off a glove.

Today was his first opportunity to put his guesses to the test. The accounts Yevin had given him were more comprehensive than he'd dared hope, but the descriptions of the bindings themselves still contained frustrating gaps. Clade had spent the past few evenings studying them, extrapolating as best he could, and considering how to apply his suppositions to the spell he needed to construct. The design he had come up with was suitably balanced, and seemed consistent with all he'd learnt; yet some aspects of the binding continued to elude him.

All sorcery was built on a physical anchor. Permanent bindings were grounded in the substance of the object being bound, like the clay of the mug before him. Transient effects, those involving fire, mist, and the like, required a physical source close at hand: a flame, or a wisp of vapour. But the spell he was about to attempt did not address any physical object. It was directed at sorcery itself: the binding Sera had constructed last night. What, then, could act as an anchor for such a spell? What physical ground could exist for something that had no physical nature?

A few years ago he would have called such sorcery impossible. But then, a few years ago he would have thought golems nothing more than legend.

Clade settled himself on the chair, centring himself: feet flat on the floor, back straight, forearms resting on his legs. He had removed the table's usual collection of glassware, leaving it bare of everything save the two mugs. With an efficiency born of long practice, he cleared his mind, reducing his focus to the two objects before him: the one solid, plain and unmarked, the other wrapped around with runes and infused with sorcery. He took a deep breath and held it a moment; then, exhaling, he began to construct the spell.

For Clade, building sorcery was like crafting an elaborate mechanism, the work as delicate and precise as that of any clockmaker, but on a scope of which such an artisan might only dream. Every binding was different. The form of the object addressed by a spell dictated the spell's shape, at once imposing constraints on what might be achieved and offering opportunities to build on its inherent properties. In a way, a well-crafted binding was like a bespoke suit, made to measure for one man. Though another might wear the same clothes with more or less difficulty, there would always be some small difference between the two men that called for a subtle alteration. And the closer one came to representing the object's true shape, the more effective the binding would be.

Carefully, he laid out the first lines of sorcery, beginning with the ensorcelled mug. According to the accounts supplied by Yevin, the spell was to be constructed as if the targeted binding was its ground; and so, despite the apparent impossibility of the notion, Clade started there, feeling out the shape of the existing sorcery and moulding a foundation to its contours. Then he began to compose the spell itself, building on the base, taking care at each step to preserve the balance of the growing edifice. Some of the spell's components were familiar, common pieces of sorcery used in a wide variety of bindings. Others were entirely new to him, or of his own devising, and these he fashioned slowly, rehearsing each addition before he applied it. Gradually, one piece at a time, the structure grew, extending from one mug and reaching toward the other like an invisible, handless arm.

The spur narrowed slightly as he went, tapering at last to a blunt point. Clade reached out and nudged the unmarked mug toward the thick branch, edging it across the smooth table until the gap between binding and mug was no greater than a finger's breadth. The final connection was relatively straightforward, consisting of a lighter, simpler version of the spell's foundation. He formed the last piece, tied it to the bare mug — and it was done, an invisible span of sorcery shaped in a gentle arc between two earthenware vessels.

Clade lifted his head. The binding was complete, but not yet active. The prepared sorcery still required his concentration to hold it in place and prevent it from disintegrating. A bead of sweat rolled down his forehead, hanging in his eyebrow for a moment before dropping onto his cheek. The urge to set the binding off and so relieve its burden pulled at his will, tempting him as it always did. But the idea was foolishness, and doubly so for an experimental binding. Before the spell could be triggered, he must first examine it for flaws.

Some sorcerers claimed to be able to visualise their work, seeing it as a kind of web or lattice; others described it as sound, melodies and harmonies and chords. For Clade, sorcery was tactile, something he could reach out and touch with his mind. Taking care to maintain his concentration, he pressed his awareness against the span, checking for weakness or imbalance, verifying that each element was correct and in place. Twice he found a slipped line and stopped to repair it: one caused by an error joining one element to the next, the other a simple oversight. He felt his way along the branch, testing each point, and at last sat back, satisfied. The structure was sound.

Sound in construction, at least. Clade returned his attention to the foundation of the spell. *Now we put the design to the test.*

One gap remained in the construct's base, left there deliberately to prevent the binding from activating prematurely, like a mound of earth separating a river from a newly-dug dam. Stretching out his mind's hand, Clade formed the final piece of the spell and slotted it into place.

A thick, woody, splitting sound tore the air, almost obscuring the dull clack that sounded at the same time. Something flew past Clade's face, nipping his flesh as it went by. He pressed his hand to his cheek without thinking, rubbing it to remove the sting. His fingers came back smeared with blood.

Shit. What just happened?

The rune-marked mug rolled gently back and forth on the table, a bite-sized chunk torn from its side. A few earthenware crumbs lay nearby, but not nearly enough to account for the entire gap. Confused, Clade glanced about the room. Tiny fragments of clay dotted his shirt and chair and lay scattered across the floor behind him. The side of the mug had not just crumbled: it had burst apart, hurling its pieces outward.

Frowning, he brushed himself off and picked up the broken mug. The chill was gone. The spell had done that much at least, though it would have been incredible for the binding to survive that kind of damage. He closed his hand over the other mug — then stopped short as a thin waft of cool air brushed his palm.

A thrill ran through his body, and he snatched his hand away as though scalded. *It worked. The binding moved.* He turned inward, moving instinctively to drop walls around his astonishment, but the cage snapped shut on nothing. *I'm startled, that's all. Still taking it in. Dear gods, it worked.*

A dark slash across the table caught his eye. He pushed the mug out of the way. The crack was deep, running the entire length of the table along its grain. A dent marked the place where the mug had stood, as though the timber surface had been slammed by some superhuman fist. Clade slid his finger lightly along the shallow depression. Two power discharges, then: one at the source, and one at the target. And the binding had still been a success. *What would have happened if I'd got it wrong?* But he had not quite got it right, either. Evidently the binding was still unbalanced. He needed to work out why, find a way to balance it properly, make it safe for himself to undergo —

An urgent knock at the door interrupted his thoughts, followed immediately by Garrett's thin voice.

"Clade? It's Garrett. Can I come in?"

Frustration bloomed, and was caught. "A moment." He grabbed the mugs, dropped them on the floor behind one of the armchairs. He'd hoped to complete his experiment undisturbed — Garrett rarely bothered him before noon, and everyone else knew not to disturb him when the door was closed. Why would the boy want to see him now? *Perhaps he's found the urn.* Hope leapt at the thought and he hurriedly walled it off. *Today might be a very good day.*

With a hurried sweep of his arm he brushed the clay fragments off the table; then he stood, unlocked the door and swung it open.

Garrett strolled in, a smug smile playing about his mouth as though he were trying and failing to suppress it. He sat in a cushioned chair with a satisfied sigh and spread his arms out along the back.

Clade pulled the door closed. "Good news?"

The younger man laughed. "You could say that. But I'm sure you know already."

"Know what?"

"About my promotion to Overseer, of course. When you leave for Zeanes with Councillor Estelle."

Your what?

"I want to thank you, Clade," Garrett said. "For supporting me before the Council. I won't forget it."

Clade stared in disbelief. *My replacement? You?* The absurdity of the thought smashed past his carefully cultivated discipline. He felt an incredulous laugh welling up within, floating irresistibly to his lips.

No. He clenched his jaw, pushed back against the mad impulse; and abruptly it was gone, his iron control snapping back into place. Nobody had gone anywhere yet. He took a deep breath, holding it for half a dozen heartbeats before letting it go.

"No need," he said at last. "The Council makes its own judgements."

"Nonetheless."

Continued protest was pointless. Clade nodded, accepting the thanks. "What did the Councillor tell you about the role?"

"Only a little," Garrett said, relaxing back into the chair. "Apparently there's a new initiative in the works, something to do with Neysa. With so few Oculus stationed there, we'll be coordinating things from Anstice. What is it, do you know?"

Clade knew nothing about any plans involving Neysa. "Nothing I can share right now, I'm afraid."

"She says she'll fill me in over the next few days. Says she wants to talk about my time here, how we can do things better..."

Talk about my time here. Garrett spoke on, but Clade heard no more. He grasped the arm of the chair, abruptly aware of the precipice yawning before him. If Garrett were to tell Estelle of the tasks Clade had given him, tasks Garrett believed to have come from the Council...

"I think a small celebration is in order. In honour of the occasion." Clade rose. "Let me pour some drinks."

The glassware was on his desk where he had put it earlier that morning: a decanter of whisky, three quarters full, and a set of tumblers. He reached past the tray to the large stack of papers at the desk's edge, closing his hand over the horse-head bookend that weighed down the pile. The cool marble curved against his hand as if shaped to fit, as if created for just this moment. He picked it up, measured its heft.

It would do.

"What happened to your table?" Garrett sat forward, bent over the table's surface, his back to Clade. Slowly, Clade began to retrace his steps. "It's almost split through. What did this? Strange that the dent is so shallow. It must have been —"

Clade swung. The bookend hit Garrett's skull with a crack and burst free of his grasp. Garrett collapsed onto the table like a sack of meat. Clade strode around, grasping Garrett by the shoulders as the table folded beneath him and shoving him back into the chair. Garrett moaned, eyelids fluttering, his hand twitching spasmodically beside him.

The bookend was gone, lost somewhere beneath the table. Clade cursed, casting about for an alternative. He grabbed a cushion from the other chair, pressed it over Garrett's face. Garrett moaned again, the sound muffled now, and began to beat feebly against Clade's arms with a fist, his unclenched hand jerking back and forth. Clade pushed the cushion down harder, and harder still, pinning the man's head in place with his weight.

Abruptly, Garrett went limp, like a puppet with its strings cut, one hand flopping into his lap as the other fell still.

Clade lifted the cushion. Garrett's glassy eyes stared back at him. Hurriedly, Clade returned the cushion to its chair and turned back to the body, preparing to drag it into the other room. But as he lifted the dead man's arm, the god arrived, slamming into him like a tornado and driving him to his knees, and any hope of concealment was gone.

He stood unsteadily, stumbling across the room to the door, and began shouting for a physician.

~

It was midday, and the sky was black.

Arandras began the climb as the first fat globules of rain began to fall. The scrawled note had been short and to the point. *Yevin is back.* The writing was Narvi's, all canted uprights and wide, looping tails, but the messenger was a woman Arandras had never seen before. She'd placed it on Arandras's desk with an expression of mild distaste, her Quill brooch glinting in the lamplight, and disappeared as silently as she'd arrived.

It was a generous gesture, far more than Arandras had expected.

Thank you, Narvi, he thought as he snuffed the lamps, hastily shutting up shop and setting out for the Arcade.

Lightning flashed away to the north, followed by a long roll of thunder. Arandras quickened his pace, pressing through the traffic as the slow patter of rain began to increase. The top of King's Hill and the shelter of the Arcade were still out of sight — from here, all he could see was the winding, climbing road, and the close-packed buildings on either side jostling for position. A charged scent filled his nostrils, and Arandras breathed deep as he hurried on his way. The storm was only moments away.

Rain arrived in a wave, dropping over the street like a falling curtain, its loud, angry hiss instantly drowning all other sounds. Arandras pressed on, water coursing over his head and neck and body, filling his shoes and overflowing into the small river that now poured down the slope. A dark shape loomed before him and he dodged aside, almost losing his feet as the horse splashed past, its flank brushing his arm. He peered after it, wondering who would be mad enough to ride a horse down so steep a street in the middle of a storm; but it was already out of sight, vanished into the deluge.

Drenched, Arandras rounded a corner and pushed his water-logged body onward. The rain enclosed him on all sides, shutting out the rest of the city. Only the slope of the road kept him pointed in the right direction. Flashes of lightning drew ever closer, the accompanying thunder growing sharper, and the rain, if anything, becoming even heavier. Water rushed past his shins, cold and numbing. He trudged higher, squinting through the rain for the glimmer of lamps that marked the staircase to the Arcade.

He found it almost by accident, stumbling onto the covered porch before he realised where he was. The lamps were dark, despite being set well back beneath the roof. Apparently no-one had thought to light them. He paused to catch his breath, ineffectually mopping his face with a sodden sleeve. Even here, several feet back from the street, he could still feel the spray kicked up by the teeming rain. Turning, he squelched his way to the top of the stairs and entered the Arcade.

Lightning stabbed down with a crack that sounded like the sky being torn apart. Then, as though pouring through the rent, the

hail began. Arandras found a space at the balustrade, squeezing between a middle-aged woman and a fat youth in Library grey, and
stared out at the shifting, shadowy whiteness. It clattered over roofs
and streets like an attack from some skybound army, a hundred
thousand pellets of ice dashing themselves against the city. *Spyridon,
city of learning*, Arandras thought, awed by the sight. *The gods are at
war with you now.*

At length, the hail began to thin, revealing a strange, half-
bleached scene below. Dark chimneys rose from muted rooftops like
tree trunks on a desolate field, white streets snaking between them
like frozen streams. The shapeless sound of rushing water swallowed
all other noise, and for a moment it seemed to Arandras that he was
alone, the sole witness to a frozen monument. Then the fat youth
pushed away from the rail with a sniff, jostling Arandras as he went,
and the sensation was broken. He sighed, taking a final look at the
scene below before turning away and resuming his course.

His sodden clothes clung to his body, pulling against him as he
walked; his shoes chafed the sides of his heels. *Perhaps I should go
home, come back later in something dry.* But if the rain-bound ascent
had been difficult, a descent with hail underfoot would be nothing
short of dangerous. In any case, he was here now. Wet or not, it
didn't change what needed doing.

He followed the curved road around the brow of the hill, past
the street vendors and students and assorted citizenry of Spyridon,
until he reached the shop of Yevin, the Library scribe. The door
stood ajar, yellow lamplight spilling out onto the stones of the Arcade. Arandras halted outside, peering through the gap — but the
opening was barely half a hand wide, revealing only a section of
wall and the rounded edge of a high table. All seemed quiet within.

Cautiously, Arandras pushed the door open and stepped inside.
The shop was small, almost as small as his own. A circular table
filled the front of the room, half a dozen high stools placed around
it, its surface bare save for a box of ink bottles. Yevin's desk stood
further back, an expansive timber affair scattered with papers and
other items, a bracket at each end holding a glass-shielded lamp. But
of Yevin himself there was no sign. The room was empty.

Arandras eased the door closed, clicking the latch into place and shutting out the bustle outside. The tall flames of the lamps burned bright and steady. He rounded the table, reluctant to break the silence, each soft step leaving a small puddle on the stone floor. Slowly, he approached the desk, eyes fixed on a half-written page in its centre. Perhaps it would tell him something of what Yevin was up to, or why he had found it necessary to leave the city. He was almost close enough to read it —

The door banged open and Arandras whirled around. A man stood in the doorway, a half-eaten pastry in his hand. He was older than Arandras had expected — perhaps fifty, judging by the lines in his face and the grey spreading through his hair. He looked quizzically at Arandras, the expression made faintly comical by the up-and-down motions of his jaw. The silence stretched as the man chewed until Arandras felt obligated to speak.

"Um," he said. "The door was open."

A raised eyebrow was the only response. Arandras rubbed his beard, conscious of the expanding puddle at his feet.

"You are Yevin, yes?"

The man swallowed at last. "Yes. I'd welcome you to my shop, but at this point that seems redundant." He moved briskly past Arandras and sat behind the desk. "What can I do for you?"

"You're a difficult man to get hold of," Arandras said, as Yevin put the remainder of the pastry in his mouth. "I'm told you've been away in Anstice."

Yevin nodded. "Back yesterday," he said, the words emerging more or less intact around his mouthful.

"Good journey?"

"Just business." Yevin sucked his fingers clean and looked narrowly at Arandras. "What did you say your name was?"

"I didn't. Your —"

"Perhaps you'd like to tell me now, then."

"Your business in Anstice," Arandras said, refusing to be turned. "Who was it with?"

Yevin sat back, eyeing Arandras speculatively. "Well, my anonymous friend, that's not your concern, is it?"

"I'm afraid it is."

"And why is that, exactly?"

The cold of his wet clothes was beginning to seep into his skin. Arandras suppressed a shiver. "I know about the urn," he said, and was rewarded with a twitch of Yevin's eyelid. "I know about the letters, and I know about the Library books. All I'm asking for is the name of your correspondent."

"Sounds to me like you're doing pretty well all by yourself." Yevin turned his attention to the half-written page on his desk. "See yourself out, won't you?"

Arandras snatched up the paper and scanned its lines — but it was only a child's grammar, setting out the five classes of letter and the rules governing how they could be combined. He set it back down, feeling foolish.

"Careful with that," Yevin said. "My niece is going to want to crumple it herself." He put his pen in its holder and folded his arms. "You're sure you don't want to check it for secret messages?"

Arandras stared back, his face flushed. He needed something: a word, a lead, anything to keep him on the trail, free from the meddlesome Quill. *No more deals with devils. Not this time.* He sighed, forced a chuckle, and pulled up a stool.

"Let's start over," Arandras said. "You're a shopkeeper. You have costs and expenses, same as everyone." He spread his hands. "I wish to purchase some information."

Yevin shook his head. "It doesn't work that way. Not even for customers who have names."

"I can pay well."

"No. You can't." Yevin's tone was final. "Just leave."

I could simply take what I need. The thought came unbidden, but Arandras allowed it to linger as he looked Yevin over. The man looked about as strong as any fifty-year-old scribe. If it came to it...

Yevin saw his regard and seemed to guess its meaning. For a moment he said nothing, merely returned Arandras's gaze. Then his brows rose. "Are you a sorcerer as well?"

The question took Arandras by surprise. *As well as — oh.* "Your correspondent is a sorcerer," he said. "Of course he is." A thought struck him. "Is he Quill?"

An annoyed expression flitted across Yevin's face, there and gone again so quickly that Arandras wasn't sure he'd actually seen it. Then a smile touched the corners of his mouth. "You don't have the slightest idea, do you?" He laughed, a mocking, grating sound. "Who put you up to this? A friend? A girl? Please tell me you're not here embarrassing yourself because of a girl."

Images flashed through Arandras's mind: Tereisa's wondering, delighted laugh the day he'd pledged to marry her; Tereisa naked in the moonlight, brow arched, her finger beckoning him closer; Tereisa's body huddled on the steps of their house, the breeze tugging at her blood-streaked hair in ghastly counterpoint to her stillness. *Embarrassing myself? How dare you?* Rage filled him, and he found himself leaning over the desk, fists planted either side of the half-written page, breathing hard. "Never say that again," he growled. "Do not *ever* say that again."

Yevin stood, leaning closer so that their noses almost touched. When he spoke, the words were barely more than a whisper. "Get the hells out of my shop."

The words burrowed into Arandras's ears, penetrating his madness. A memory arose in sympathetic echo: Onsoth leering down, his eyes filled with spite; Arandras standing in response, opening his mouth to reply; then those same words, spoken with the same soft fury.

He stared at Yevin, and he stared at Onsoth; he stood on both sides of the desk at once, staring across it at himself. Perhaps this was what Onsoth felt, why he was always so angry. Perhaps he'd lost someone once, same as Arandras, and now had nothing left save his memories and his rage, no course of action that might ease the ache or answer even one of the questions on which his life now stood.

But I do.

The sensation of solid timber pressing against his knuckles brought him back to the present. He straightened slowly, measuring Yevin with his gaze. The creases about the man's eyes and mouth ran deep. His shoulders had a slight stoop to them. His arms were thin. He would be no match for Arandras. More than likely, Arandras would not even have to lay a hand on him. The mere threat would probably be enough.

Yevin stared back, his face expressionless. But as Arandras watched, he slowly sat back down; and just before he dropped his gaze, Arandras thought he saw a flicker of fear.

The sight cut him open, laid bare the snarl around his heart. Before him sat Yevin, cowed if not yet cowering; behind him in the city, Narvi and the Quill pursued their own advancement; and somewhere out in the world, Tereisa's killer went about his business, unaware and unconcerned. And here he was, breaking a man's will as though by doing so he could somehow right a wrong.

Yevin's hands began to twitch, the confidence slowly draining from his face. But the snarl within, once exposed, could not be covered over again.

This is wrong. No matter what hangs on it. It's wrong.

It was better to make a deal with devils than become one himself.

With a grimace, and a shiver that had nothing to do with his damp clothes, Arandras turned on his heel and walked out of the shop.

PART 2:
THE COMFORT
OF YOUR TEARS

CHAPTER 9

I found him alone in the upper room, perched on his threadbare
mat; yet his bearing was that of one seated upon a throne. "The
soldiers approach," he said.

"They are even now at the door," I returned. "Master, why will
you not act? Even rats defend themselves at need."

His smile was like the morning sun gentled by wisps of cloud.
"If I have done wrong, no defence will serve me. If I have acted well,
none is required. All else is the province of knaves and fools."

Alas, his words fell on my ears like seed upon stone. Even now,
I can scarce approach their edge. Then, I was only a boy.

— Jeresani the Lesser, *The Passing of Herev Gis*
(account disputed by the Gislean Provin)

THE WOODTRADERS' BUILDING HAD ORIGINALLY been constructed with five floors. The sixth had been added only a
few decades ago, during the time of Guildmaster Vorace's
uncle. The architect had done his job well. To the rival companies
on either side, and to the rest of the city across the river, the new
floor atop the building appeared indistinguishable from those beneath it. Inside, however, the compromises that had been made to
present an unblemished facade were plain. Narrow corridors and
low ceilings made everything feel cramped. Where on other floors
the main hallway formed a square of four perfectly straight lengths,
here it twisted and turned like a vine grown wild. Most uncomfortable for Eilwen was the stairway. The architect had apparently been
unable to find the space needed for a true staircase, and had chosen

instead to reduce the number of steps but increase their height to almost twice that of those on the lower levels. Eilwen took the steps gingerly, her leg already beginning to twinge despite the early hour.

"Remember, say as little as possible," Havilah murmured as they reached the top of the stairs. "Answer whatever questions are put to you simply and without speculation. And watch them. This is as delicate for whoever killed Kieffe as it is for us."

The masters' meeting room looked south, past the Tienette to a vista of towers and rooftops and, away to the left, the fields and pastures beyond the city's edge. The quarter-height windows ran the length of the wall, enough to light the room without need for lamps, but too little to overcome the sense of confinement brought on by the low ceiling. Most of the masters were already seated around a polished jarrah table ornamented with gold filigree. A second, more sparsely populated ring of chairs surrounded the first: the adjunct's row, one place for each master's assistant.

"Havilah. About time." Vorace leaned forward, resting thick forearms on the red timber table. He turned his shaggy head to Eilwen. "This is the one who found him?"

"This is Eilwen, yes."

"Guildmaster," Eilwen said, steeling herself to meet his regard. Vorace's scrutiny was known throughout the Guild: aggressive, almost physical, buffeting in its intensity as though the spark animating his soul was too fierce to be contained by even his bearlike frame. Yet as Eilwen stood braced beneath his gaze, she found her attention caught by the droop of his eyelid, the deep lines of his cheeks, and the snowy tufts of his brows. *He's getting old. How have I not noticed that before?*

As if aware of her thought, Vorace gave a throaty chuckle and turned to Havilah. "Sit, sit," he said, jerking his thumb at the vacant space between Caralange and Laris. Eilwen followed Havilah's lead, seating herself in the adjunct's row behind him. The place behind Caralange stood empty, but on the other side Pel leaned across, offering a ponderous nod in greeting. Further around from Laris sat Soll, the treasurer, and old Phemia, the seneschal. Other than Caralange, only Phemia was alone.

"A man is dead," Vorace said. "Tell me what we know."

"The victim's name was Kieffe." Havilah leaned forward, and Eilwen could picture his expression as he glanced around the table, hands laced in front of him. "It seems he had already been dead for several hours by the time Eilwen found him."

Eilwen kept her expression carefully neutral as the others glanced at her. Havilah had told her he was going to do this. *Indulge their curiosity early, then move the discussion along.* With luck, any inconvenient interest in her reasons for investigating Kieffe would be swallowed up in the general eagerness to find the killer.

"And what can you tell us about him?" Vorace said, his gaze flicking back from Havilah to Eilwen.

"Me? Nothing, really," Eilwen said. "I didn't know him at all."

"But you must have. You let yourself into his room."

"I didn't know it was his room." The denial came without thought, the words tumbling over each other in their haste to get out. She took a breath and forced herself to slow down. "The steward's rolls had that room assigned to Master Havilah. I was trying to find out why."

"By letting yourself in."

Eilwen forced herself to hold the Guildmaster's fierce regard. "I knocked, but there was no answer."

"Strange that Ged would make such an error," Soll said, his words soft and precise. "How do you suppose that came to pass?"

"I have no idea. Perhaps you should ask him." Though if they did, the man might recall her comment about wanting the key to investigate an anomaly. "Perhaps it was just a mistake."

"If I may," Havilah said. "The issue at hand is Kieffe. Eilwen is here to tell you what she saw, not to be interrogated."

"Yes, yes, fine." Vorace waved a hand. "Go on."

"The room was empty," Eilwen said. "I mean completely empty. Swept clean. Someone had boarded up the windows. I didn't even realise he was there at first." She trailed off. That first moment of recognition had shocked her into stupor. The shame of being found like that by Havilah still burned. *It's not like I've never seen a corpse before. Gods, it's not like I haven't made a few of my own.* But she never lingered after a kill, never sat with the body as it began its slow decay. She couldn't. Not after the *Orenda.* "I'm sorry. It's just…"

still a little raw."

"The body was unmarked, save for a few spots of blood just about the nose." Havilah said.

Vorace grunted. "What would cause that?"

"I can think of several poisons," Havilah said. "Witch trumpets, for instance, or bluespine. Tana's curse."

Anxious lines creased Soll's high forehead. "Tahisi poisons."

"Mostly, yes."

Vorace turned to Caralange. "Can we find out?"

The sorcerer cleared his throat. "Perhaps the Quill —"

"No," Vorace said. "No outsiders. Not yet."

"I'm no fleshbinder," Caralange said, his raspy voice making the words sound more like a threat than an admission.

"One of your cadre, then."

Caralange scowled. "Vorace, even the Quill struggle to pluck poison from a corpse, and that's when it's fresh. You might as well have the Gatherer's priests ask his ghost what killed him, for all the good it will do."

Matching the sorcerer's scowl, Vorace leaned forward to argue the point. Eilwen turned away, sweeping the room with her gaze, examining each master in turn. Laris sat with her head bowed and hands folded in her lap, apparently uninterested in the debate. Behind her sat Pel in unconscious mimicry, eyes closed, chin resting on his chest. Soll conferred with his adjunct in low tones, his face hidden from Eilwen's view. Old Phemia looked uncertainly from Caralange to Vorace and back again, plainly out of her depth. Vorace's adjunct had a stylus in his hand and a wax tablet on his lap, and was watching the discussion with the avid attention of a magpie hunting for insects. All she could see of Havilah was his back.

Which is it? Which of you killed Kieffe? Surely the person responsible was in the room right now. It was inconceivable that anyone below the rank of master could pull together something like this: to suborn at least one Guild contact, maybe several, and then have a man killed to destroy the trail. *Maybe it's not just one of you. Maybe it's two, or even more —*

"Fine," Caralange said abruptly, jerking Eilwen's attention back to the conversation. "I'll have Orom look at the body, for all the good it'll do."

"Good." Vorace turned, settling his battering-ram gaze on Laris. "Tell us about Kieffe."

Laris exhaled softly. "He was a trader. He'd been away from Anstice for several years, most recently in Neysa." She gave a tight smile. "He deserved better."

"Any enemies? Here, or in Neysa?"

"I don't think so." The Trademaster spread her hands. "Kieffe looked after dozens of accounts. No doubt he made people unhappy on occasion, but no more than Eilwen here in her time. It's part of doing business."

"So is this, perhaps." Soll gestured across the table. "We have Master Havilah, after all."

"We do not kill people, Treasurer," Havilah said levelly.

"Of course," Soll said, with a smile that might have been either mocking or apologetic. "But others might not be so scrupulous."

"This is foolishness!" Phemia broke in. Eilwen looked up in surprise as the old seneschal turned her anguished gaze around the table. "How can this have anything to do with Neysa? This man was killed right here. In our own home!"

Vorace laid a hand on her arm. "Phemia —"

Phemia shook it off. "Don't 'Phemia' me!" She wrung her wrinkled hands. "This was done by one of our own people. A Woodtrader. Three have mercy, we've a killer in our midst!"

The pain in the old woman's words was impossible to miss. Phemia had been seneschal for as long as Eilwen had been a Woodtrader, managing the innumerable mundane details involved in keeping the Guild running. Even now, as the years slowly wore her away, she continued to serve, continued to worry on behalf of the Guild.

And now, someone at that same table was betraying her, and everyone else like her.

For the first time, the wrongness of it struck Eilwen full force, like a blow to the gut; and a spark of anger flared inside. Vorace was speaking now, trying to calm Phemia's fears, but Eilwen scarcely heard a word. The rage grew, hot and primal, filling her up like wine in a skin. Her body felt light, insubstantial, supported not by the chair but by the air all around her. *Whichever of you has done this, I swear I'm going to find you, and when I do, I'll —*

No!

With an effort of will Eilwen pulled back, gasping for air. Not that. Those days were over. She was not a killer, not any more. She closed her eyes, slowing her breathing and unclenching her fingers from the edge of the seat. *Not again. Not ever again.*

"Eilwen? Are you unwell?"

Blinking, she raised her head. The entire room was staring at her. Pel sat to her right, his brow furrowed in ponderous confusion; before her, Havilah's face was smooth save for a single questioning eyebrow. Eilwen gazed at the sea of faces, unsure what to do; and as she did, the anger stirred anew, inviting her back into its arms.

"I'm sorry," she said, pushing herself unsteadily to her feet. "I need to step outside."

It was seven paces to the door. She covered them in silence, propelled by the pressure of a dozen eyes at her back. Only when she closed the door behind her did the conversation resume, in tones too low to overhear. She sagged against the wall and closed her eyes.

Even now, one of the masters in that room was betraying the Guild. Yes, and betraying her, too. Because she was no longer the killer, no longer the traitor. She was not, *would not be* that person any more.

She was the Guild's, and the Guild was hers.

~

With nowhere in particular to go, Eilwen found herself making her way down the stairs and out into the building's inner garden. Several moderate-sized trees spread twisted branches over the bright flowerbeds and patchy grass: myrtles for the most part, likely selected for their tolerance of shade, which allowed them to flourish despite the high, enclosing walls. The eucalypt outside her own rooms stood at the far end of the garden, its leaves barely shifting in the sheltered air, but Eilwen ignored it, seating herself on a low, weather-worn bench and straightening her leg with a sigh.

Usually, apart from some initial discomfort on rising, her leg only pained her later in the day; but today her climb to the sixth floor had set it off early. *My token of the* Orenda, she thought, wincing as she rubbed the gnarled flesh around her knee. *My traitor's mark. No matter how far I run, this will remain.*

Whatever else it was, she could not call it unjust.

"Went well, huh?" Brielle stood before her, a lazy grin on her face.

"Oh, absolutely," Eilwen said. "Still going well right now, I imagine."

"Ha." Brielle sat. "Do they know who did it?"

"No." Eilwen glanced down the row of doors and windows facing onto the garden. Havilah's suite was dark. *Still going well. Oh, yes.* "But we're going to figure it out."

"Are we? How?"

The words hung in the still air. "I don't know," Eilwen said carefully. Brielle gave a sharp sigh, and Eilwen narrowed her eyes. "Are you all right?"

The last of the grin slipped away, leaving a furious glare in its wake. "No, damn it, I'm not all right," Brielle hissed. "It's not supposed to go like this. Enemies out there, yes. Of course. But not in here."

"I know." They were Woodtraders. United in common interest. Without that, what was left?

"They should have locked down the compound the moment you found that body. Nobody in or out. Drop everything until they find the murdering bastard."

There were a dozen reasons why such a course could never have worked. Eilwen settled for the most obvious. "They who? The Guild doesn't have the people for that sort of thing. All they have is us." *And no idea which of us can be trusted.*

"I've seen this before, you know," Brielle said. "In other houses. Other companies. Hells, I learnt it from my ma before I could talk. This is how it starts." She bared her teeth. "Distrust is death, Eilwen. There's a reason that's a saying."

"We'll find the killer," Eilwen said. "We will."

Brielle stood. "We'd better."

She strode away, leaving Eilwen alone with her thoughts. *Distrust is death.* It was true enough, as far as it went. But trust was no less dangerous, in its way. And in any case, death was cunning. It came in innumerable guises, each unique, and sometimes even removing the mask wasn't enough.

Unwelcome memories of the *Orenda* stirred within her. She had trusted, then: trusted deeply and wilfully enough to silence the doubting whisper in her heart, until at last Tammas had confessed his divided loyalties to her face, admitting that he worked not only for the Guild but also for a clandestine band of sorcerers whose name he wasn't even supposed to know, but who called themselves *Oculus*. And then he had died, and the *Orenda* had died; but she, gods be cursed, had survived, a traitor to the Guild and to Tammas alike. A traitor to all, yet reviled by none.

Afterwards, of course, she'd tried to find out why. To her surprise, the egg she'd taken from Tammas had come to her aid. Though he'd claimed it was just a trinket, on rare occasions it would stir, dark sorcery pulsing deep within as it sensed the approach of those it considered friends — other servants of the Oculus. But none of the Oculus she confronted could tell her why the *Orenda* had been sunk, or who had given the order, and as her disappointments mounted, her questions had gradually ceased to matter.

Killing was so much easier when you didn't have to talk first.

A lamp flared to life in Havilah's suite, and a moment later Eilwen saw the Spymaster's form pass before the window. She left the bench, crossing the uneven lawn to his door. It opened as she drew near, revealing Havilah's dark hand beckoning her inside.

"You were waiting?" Havilah said, reaching behind her to close the door.

Eilwen shrugged. "What happened?"

Havilah gave her an appraising look, then turned and pulled out his chair. It squeaked as he sat. "Little," he said. "You were there for the interesting part."

Relief filled Eilwen, the release of a tension she hadn't noticed was there. *Thank you for not asking.* She gave a slight nod, and he returned the gesture with a knowing eye. "That was the interesting part? Seemed like a lot of noise for not much result."

"True. Nobody gained, but nobody lost, either."

"So what was decided?" Eilwen said, sliding into a second chair.

Havilah gave a dismissive wave. "Nothing important. That whole meeting was just for show."

"What?" Eilwen stared. "Well. Great. Of course it was. Thanks for telling me beforehand."

"Don't misunderstand me. I didn't say it was unimportant." Havilah leaned forward. "This is a dangerous game, Eilwen. Kieffe's body is in Phemia's chill-chest right now. Appearances are the main thing keeping you and me from joining it."

Eilwen shivered. "I know."

"You did well up there," Havilah said, his tone softening. "Of course we'll investigate now. Everyone expects that. So long as nobody thinks we're going to find anything, they'll leave us alone."

"Who's us?"

"You. Me. Guildmaster Vorace."

"Vorace is on our side? And you still let him go after me like that?" Eilwen bit off the question, angry at the whine in her voice. Of course Vorace had challenged her. Anything less would have invited suspicion. She grimaced, brushing the question away. "Please, just tell me what's going on."

Havilah folded his hands. "Do you trust me?"

"Of course I do." But she'd doubted him, there in the corridor outside Kieffe's room with the steward's key in her hand. Did she doubt him still? She wasn't sure. *Distrust is death, yes. But only sometimes. Only when it's not warranted.* She tapped her fingernail against the hard wood of Havilah's desk. "Tell me the rest of it. Like where you were while I was turning up a corpse."

"In a chocol house," Havilah said. "Varek's, on the Isle. I was watching a woman."

Eilwen waited.

"Fair skin," Havilah continued. "Pale eyes. Iron-grey hair. Looks about fifty on first glance, but probably closer to sixty. Likes cloves and nutmeg in her chocol, which she prefers cooler than most."

"Three Rivers' new dance partner?"

"If so, she's not exactly single-minded in her affections. She must have met with half of Anstice in the last few days. Guilds, trading houses, moneylenders. A few I didn't even recognise. It looked like she was already well into the city's smaller merchantry. None of the other majors came to visit, but she received couriers from both the East Mellespen Syndicate and the Crimson Sails."

"She's talking to everyone," Eilwen said. "Everyone except us."

"Yes," Havilah said. "Unless..."

Eilwen grimaced. *Unless.* "If someone from the Guild has already spoken to her, but is keeping it from the rest of us..." She trailed off. What would that even mean?

"She wasn't the naive rustic, either," Havilah continued. "She had a confidence about her. The sort that comes when you know you're in a position of strength, and you're so used to it that you don't even think about it any more."

"She's buying," Eilwen said. "She has to be. If she was selling, she'd wait a while before seeing someone new, and she wouldn't bother with the minors at all. Playing them off against each other only works if she's a buyer."

Havilah shook his head. "I don't think she's playing them off. As far as I could tell, most of them walked away with some sort of agreement. If she's buying, she's getting a whole lot of merchandise from a whole lot of people."

Spreading the risk. It made sense, if your venture was too delicate or too large to entrust to a single supplier. But what could be so large as to require the services of every trading company known to Anstice?

"One other thing," Havilah said. "The night you found Kieffe, I managed to leave the chocol house just before she left. I followed her along the river and down the western thoroughfare, but I lost her outside the old wall."

"You lost a sixty-year-old woman?"

"That's what I said."

"Ah, hells. A sorcerer, then."

"Maybe," Havilah said. "Maybe not. But it's a possibility to be aware of."

Eilwen shivered. *A sorcerer. Just like Tammas's other master. Gods, please let it not be them again.* The old hunger stirred within her, loathed but precious. Grimacing, she thrust it aside.

"That's the real question," Havilah said, and Eilwen realised she'd missed the beginning of his thought. "If we're being singled out for exclusion, we need to know why. And if not..."

"If we've taken on a new order, there'll be evidence of it," Eilwen said. "Especially if it's big. Cargo unloading at the dock. Wagon movements. Something." She looked up. "Get me the records and I can cross-check them. I know what to look for. If someone's hiding something, I can find it."

Havilah gave her an odd look. It took several moments for Eilwen to identify it as pride. Something shifted in her throat, and she coughed and looked away.

"What records would you need?" Havilah said. It was not so much a question as a prompt.

Contracts. Ledgers. Bills of lading and receipt. Things a member of Havilah's department had no business requesting, not even with a murder to investigate. Ask for them now, and they might as well announce from the rooftops what they were up to. Eilwen shook her head. "Forget it."

"It's a good thought," Havilah said. "I had a similar idea. That's what I was talking to Ged about, when…" He gestured, and Eilwen nodded. *When you heard I'd taken the key, and came looking for me.*

"And?" she said.

"Nothing. Your clock was the most noteworthy request he'd had for weeks."

Eilwen blew out her cheeks. "Unless he's in on it, too." And that was the barb at the end of every dangling line. When it came right down to it, everyone was suspect. *Distrust is death.*

"So," Havilah said. "You're a master. You're running some sort of operation behind everyone else's back. Something big enough to kill for. What else are you doing? What's your endgame?"

A twist of fear slithered through Eilwen's belly. *Gods, what do I know about masters? I was just an assistant buyer, when… when it was me.* But then, perhaps there wasn't so much difference between them. Betrayal was betrayal, after all.

"No matter how many people are involved, they won't be able to do everything themselves," she said. "They'll need help from others. That means buying people off, or calling in favours, or making threats. Probably all three. Find someone being leaned on, and we can follow it back to whoever's doing the leaning. That's easier said than done, though."

"What else?"

Eilwen frowned. "Assume that woman of yours really has tried to contact the Guild, but this rogue element has somehow intercepted her. That's a significant risk. Yet they've been careful enough to keep this whole thing undetected until now. That means they're ramping things up. The final play can't be too far away."

"And that final play is?"

An image of Vorace's lined face returned to her mind. "Control of the Guild," she said, suddenly sure. "Vorace has a controlling stake, but no children. The succession is unclear. Someone's trying to position themselves as the obvious successor." She paused, and the final piece slid into place. "They're going to kill Vorace."

"Well." Havilah's nod held approval. "Don't ever let anyone tell you you're not much of a spy."

"Gods. That's it, isn't it?" Even though she'd figured it out, her mind seemed reluctant to take it in. "What are we going to do?"

Havilah's expression betrayed nothing. "Whatever needs doing."

The old hunger plucked at her thoughts, whispering of death, but there was no power in it. She nodded her assent.

"Find out who killed Kieffe," Havilah said. "That's your job now. Leave the day to day stuff to Ufeus. Don't involve him in this." He held her gaze. "Everyone expects an investigation. That gives you a certain amount of leeway. All the same, tread carefully. Whoever's behind this will be hoping to avoid a second dead body, but that won't stop them if they feel they have good enough reason. Don't give them one."

"Is that official?" Eilwen said hopefully. "That bit about Ufeus? I mean, if you're looking into what this chocol woman is up to, maybe you want Ufeus back reporting to you."

"No. Ufeus is yours. If I cut you out now, it'll be twice as hard to get you back in. And if your investigation takes you to any of my people, you'll need the authority to compel their cooperation."

The question spilled from her lips before she could stop it. "Why do you trust me, then?"

Havilah smiled faintly. "You're not the conspiring type."

Oh? What type am I? This time she caught the words before they could make it out; but something of her thoughts must have reached her expression. Havilah leaned forward.

"We'll find them," he said. "I know you're used to working alone, but you're not alone in this. If you need anything, just say the word. I'll be here."

She felt as though she should say something in response, but the words wouldn't come, so she just nodded again.

"All right." Havilah stood. "Let's take back our Guild."

~

Murder always left Clade with a feeling of failure.

He paced the length of the study, his back straight, his steps regular and unhurried. His feet fell softly on the rich carpet, except for the three steps near the window where they slapped against stone. Interruptions had been few: a meal shortly after sunrise and another no more than an hour ago, each announced with a soft knock at the door, each too small to satisfy.

Half of the low table still lay where it had fallen. The other half had been shoved aside in the rush to attend to Garrett and now rested upside-down against the shelf on the far wall, its short legs sticking up in the air like death-stiffened limbs. The chair on which Garrett had died remained in place, almost unmarked. The wound had let surprisingly little blood, and the stain merged with the pattern in such a way as to be almost indiscernible during the day. Only when evening came and the lamps were lit did the discolouration become apparent.

He had slept poorly. In his dreams, small details assumed a peculiar significance: the jolt as the bookend struck Garrett's head; the man's hand flopping onto his lap as the life seeped out of him. He killed Garrett, and he killed him again; and as his mind repeated the events over and over, distorted memories of past kills began to bleed into the sequence. He pursued a group of sorcerers on the run from the Oculus, and found them sitting in his study. Garrett was a hostage, awaiting a ransom that never came. He was attacked, assaulted from behind with no weapon at hand but a piece of carved marble. And throughout it all, the god waited, always watching, always just out of sight.

He should have found another way. He had seen Garrett's mask of respect begin to slip, had recognised the danger for what it was.

But he'd failed to act in time, and this was the price.

And if murder was unavoidable, well, Clade had a box tucked away in the cellar for exactly this eventuality. A clean death, untraceable, even by the god. Yet he had failed even to make use of that.

I was twice startled, first by the success of my binding, then by Garrett. My discipline failed, and haste filled the breach.

But such thoughts were useless now, and the reproach in his gut was an unwelcome guest. He put it away with an inward sigh.

At least this time I won't find myself saddled with a new name.

It had been dissenters, the first time: malcontents seeking freedom from Azador. Their leader, Niele, had been foolish enough to put her grievances to paper. When her treatise was inevitably discovered, the group ran, and Clade had been dispatched in pursuit. On his return, the Council had called him Requiter, lauded his ingenuity, his ruthlessness. In truth, he'd done little more than follow directions. Every turn taken by the fugitives, every change in course, every stratagem to throw him off the trail: all had been laid bare by the god, its presence magnified and given voice by the twisted lump of black rock entrusted to him by the Council. He'd come ashore at Neysa with little more than the rock, the clothes on his back, and a blade strapped to his leg. Three days later, the deserters were dead.

Clade had never killed anyone before, but that day he darkened the eyes of two men and two women. Niele never even saw him. He took her from behind, snapping her neck before she had a chance to react. The second and third were messier. One landed a blow across his ribs, cutting open his side; but then the man fumbled the knife and Clade stuck a dagger in his throat. The fourth was young, not yet bound. He begged for mercy before he died. Clade would have spared him, given the choice, but his orders were clear and the god was right there.

Afterwards, he felt none of the nausea that his training had warned him of. Looking down at the lifeless bodies, he was filled instead with profound melancholy. The feeling stayed with him for weeks, haunting his thoughts throughout the return journey. Standing at the rail, staring out over the sea, he'd resolved never again to take a life with his own hands.

Garrett was the eighth.

Someday there would probably be a ninth.

Resolutions were futile. He was a murderer. He had been ever since that day near Neysa. Atonement was a mirage, a false hope peddled by fools and charlatans. If there were gods somewhere who judged men for their crimes, then he, Clade, was guilty. One victim more or less made no difference.

No matter that my cause has changed. No matter that a copy of Niele's treatise now hides under the carpet beneath my bed. Blood is blood, no matter what.

There was nothing to gain from regrets. He'd more than likely have to kill again before this was through. His life — any life — had space for only one absolute. Eventually, a choice was always required, and he had made this choice a long time ago. Far better to accept it and move on than to agonise over things that could never change.

A magpie alighted on the windowsill, pecking at it briefly before swooping down to the street below to scavenge for food. Clade stood by the window, and watched, and waited.

～

The summons came the following morning.

For some reason, Estelle had chosen a small, bare suite on the second floor. The room was dusty and airless; thick with the presence of the god. A wrapped object lay on the table before her. She watched him enter, her lined face expressionless save for a slight droop about the eyes. *She's tired. Is that good or bad?* He seated himself in silence.

When she spoke, her tone was formal. "Clade Alsere. You are summoned to give answer for the death of Garrett Drasso two days past. Answer will be given in the presence of the Council and in the sight of Azador."

She lifted the wrappings to reveal a misshapen black mass about the size of a cannonball. Lamplight bounced off the irregular planes at odd angles, defying his attempt to make out its precise shape. Tiny flecks of green and orange seemed to float just beneath the surface. Clade nodded, unsurprised. Though its deformities were different, the object was unmistakably a twin to the rock once given him by the Council. A greater locus of Azador.

The god's presence ballooned outward, filling the room like a cloud, invisible yet palpable. Clade felt it pressing down on him, wrapping itself around him as though trying to find a way inside. His gorge rose; he coughed once, then gagged, clamping his jaw shut as the acid taste of hours-old breakfast washed past his throat and into his mouth.

Estelle placed a hand on the stone and the pressure eased. Clade swallowed hard, forcing the contents of his stomach back down. She frowned at a thin stack of papers on the table before her, then looked up.

"Tell me what happened."

"Garrett attacked me," Clade rasped. He glanced around, looking for a jug of water, but the only other furniture in the room was a low bookcase, its shelves empty save for dust. "I was forced to defend myself."

"You know I need more than that," Estelle said. "Attacked you how?"

Clade shrugged. "Some sort of binding. One I didn't recognise."

"Tell me about it."

He paused, as though going over the event in his mind. "I don't know," he said at last. "I dodged as he cast it and it split the table. There was no physical manifestation of any kind. Nothing to indicate the spell's foundation."

"Theories?"

"To be honest, I've been a little too preoccupied with almost getting killed to give it much thought."

"Hmm." Estelle examined her papers, touched the stone again. The earlier oppressiveness had lifted somewhat; the god's presence, though still discomforting, was now more brooding than stifling. A frown crossed Estelle's brow, and she stared intently at the stone.

Clade coughed, swallowed, and waited.

Estelle looked up. "Garrett cast the binding. Then what?"

"He began to cast it again."

"The same binding? Are you sure?"

He allowed himself a short glare. "No, I'm not sure. I didn't have the luxury of making myself sure."

She waved her hand, conceding the point. "He began another binding, then. Is that when you struck him?"

"Yes."

"With a marble bookend."

"Yes," Clade said again.

"From behind."

"No."

She frowned. "I have the physician's report here. It describes a single wound to the back of Garrett's head. How did you come to strike him there?"

"Very simply. He turned away at the last moment."

Estelle looked at him expectantly, waiting for him to go on. Clade met her regard in silence. Further embellishment would do nothing for his credibility; on the contrary, it would simply invite contradiction. Truth was bland, dreary, boring. Meaningless elaboration was a sure sign of a nervous storyteller.

"This is the third Oculus death in Anstice in the past year," Estelle said. "The rest of us would be forgiven for starting to feel a little nervous."

Clade snorted. "The others had nothing to do with me." Bes had been knifed in an alley by some passing gutter dweller, while Farna had managed to fall under a stonecutter's wagon on East Bridge. "It's all in the reports."

She turned back to the stone, her brow furrowed in concentration, and suddenly Clade understood. *You can scarcely hear it. Even with that thing, you can barely tell it's there.* The god shifted about the room, restless, the swirling motion-without-motion forcing Clade to press his hands against the table to steady himself. Yet Estelle stared at the twisted rock like one straining to hear a whisper in a crowd, oblivious to its agitation, unable to discern whatever it was that Azador sought to convey.

At last she removed her hand and sat back. "Clade Alsere," she said. "In the sight of Azador, it is my judgement that this hearing be suspended and transferred to Zeanes, there to take place before the entire Council. You will depart this city tomorrow —"

"No."

Estelle gaped. "I beg your pardon?"

The words seemed to come of their own volition. "Forgive me, Councillor, but I cannot leave Anstice. It is imperative that I stay in the city."

"Explain."

Clade moistened his lips. The shock of his interruption was already gone from Estelle's face, replaced by a strange mixture of offence and curiosity. Azador, too, was still, waiting for his response. He hesitated. Once he opened this door, there was no closing it again. He could speak now and remain in Anstice, bring the resources of the Oculus to bear on the elusive urn, and in doing so multiply the risk of exposure a hundredfold. Or he could play it safe and remain silent, returning to Zeanes and biding his time until another opportunity arose.

Assuming it ever did.

So much for avoiding attention.

"Councillor, I believe I am close to determining the location of a Valdori golem army."

A surge of greed broke over him, voracious and potent: the lust of the god. He jerked his hand back from the table, away from the stone, retreating inward and barricading himself against the storm. He heard a distant gasp, saw Estelle flinch back from the rock as if burned. She spoke, but the words were muffled, as though his ears were wrapped with wool. He hunched down in his chair, eyes closed, and waited for the assault to pass.

"Clade." A hand touched his shoulder, shook it. "Clade. Are you ill? Answer me."

He blinked up. Estelle's face hovered just above his own. He straightened, suppressing a groan, and loosened his defences a fraction. Greed still filled the room, pungent and foul, but the first intense burst seemed past. He brushed Estelle's hand away and took a deep breath.

"Clade. Say something." Concern touched her voice. "Are you ill? What happened?"

"Nothing." He shook his head. "It's nothing. An old complaint. I'll be fine."

"I'll call a physician. We can conclude this later."

"Thank you, no. There's nothing the physician can do." Clade met her gaze, held it. "Let me stay in Anstice. Give me more time."

She looked at him as though trying to measure the weight of his words. "Who else knows?"

"Nobody. Garrett was assisting me, but he didn't know what we were working on. Estelle, I'm sorry for keeping this from you. I'd hoped to wait until I had everything in place." He shrugged. "Surprise you."

Again the measuring look; then, like the slow but irrepressible sunrise, a smile crept over her face. "A golem army," she whispered, her eyes lit with excitement. "This time, Requiter, you have truly outdone yourself."

His answering smile felt flat, inadequate to her exhilaration; but if she noticed anything amiss, she gave no sign.

CHAPTER 10

Once upon my travels, I met a man who claimed to have found the secret to happiness. "'Tis simple," said he, kneeling beside the tavern wall. "One merely beats one's head against the stones, like so." I observed that such a practice, though no doubt providing some fleeting satisfaction, seemed an unlikely path to lasting happiness. "Ah, 'tis true," said the fellow, pounding industriously at the wall. "But think of the joy I shall possess when I stop!"

— Eneas the Fabulist,
One Hundred Truths and Ninety-Nine Lies

THE QUILL SCHOOLHOUSE IN ANSTICE was impossible to miss. Situated on the crown of a small hill, the old estate house brooded over its former fields, now crammed with the wood and brick and stone of tenements, townhouses, and cramped, winding streets. Its fluted marble columns and high arches recalled the graceful lines of ancient Valdori architecture, but the blunt corners and floral motifs revealed its true provenance to be the early Coridon period, no more than a few centuries past. Viewed from the east, the dirty white pillars seemed to hover just above eye level, like a storybook temple caught in the moment of being lowered to earth.

It was, Arandras supposed, the sort of visual metaphor the Quill would approve of.

The journey from Spyridon had been less wearisome than Arandras had expected. Mara had not been planning to travel for another day or two, but the prospect of saving several scudi by joining the party on one of the Quill's horses proved sufficient incentive for her to rearrange her plans. She struck up an immediate rapport with Narvi, quizzing him as they rode about the Quill, sorcery, and his travels throughout the Free Cities and elsewhere.

"In Kharjus, the Quill operate most of these," Mara said as they queued at a turnpike on the first evening. "My father used to tell me the reason the roads were so smooth was because the Quill used sorcery to keep them that way. Then I came here and discovered sorcery had nothing to do with it."

Narvi chuckled. "Anyone can build a road if they have the will. Most places, only the Quill have enough vision to do something that goes beyond a city's borders."

"But not here."

"Yes. Thanks to the republic." Narvi launched into a history of the Coridon Republic, its rise in the wake of the Confederation Wars that also saw the establishment of the Gislean Provin, and its eventual collapse in the War of Freedom that gave birth to the Free Cities. "This area owes it more than most people like to think. Standard coinage, for one thing. Roads like these, for another. Dozens of small things that make trade between the Free Cities vastly easier than anywhere else in Kal Arna."

Not to mention the fact that most of the so-called Free Cities are anything but, Arandras thought as they filed past the guards in Spyridon red. The border between Spyridon's territory and that belonging to Anstice still lay another day ahead, just this side of Poet's Corner, Anstice's southernmost tributary.

On the second night, conversation turned to Arandras's time with the Quill, and he sat in silence as Narvi told Mara about Tereisa and her death. Mara seemed to read far more in his expression than the bare events outlined by Narvi, and he found himself staring at his hands, watching the play of firelight over palms and fingers. When he bedded down, sleep seemed as remote as the moon; but the next morning he woke feeling unexpectedly refreshed, as though a weight he hadn't known he was carrying had somehow been lifted.

The remainder of the journey was at once tiring and invigorating. He rode alone as much as he could, falling behind the others to enjoy what passed for solitude on the road. On the third day, as the sounds and smells of horse became familiar enough to ignore, he found himself increasingly attentive to the high, piping birdsong, the scent of eucalyptus, even the breeze on his face. The evening found him sore but content, pleasantly exhausted and soon asleep.

Entering Anstice the following afternoon was like donning an old set of soiled clothes. The noise of the city and its wild mix of aromas hung about Arandras in uncomfortable folds. He sat gingerly in the saddle as they rode past the outlying redoubt, reluctant to move, as if by keeping still he might pass through the clamorous miasma untouched; but the further they entered, the thicker it became, brushing against his face and leaving a gritty taste on his palate. He grimaced, torn between an urge to spit and a reluctance to open his mouth.

Not until they passed the heavy timber gate and dismounted in the grounds of the schoolhouse did Arandras feel capable of breathing normally again. The patch of lawn between the front of the building and the outer wall was barely a dozen paces wide, but in the middle of the crowded city it seemed an oasis. Short rows of saplings stood on either side of the path, their slender arms swaying in the breeze like boys playing soldier before the low, heavy schoolhouse.

"Recent plantings," Narvi said, as if there were some confusion as to how trees might come to be growing in rows. "There's more out the back. You'll like it there."

Arandras gathered his bags and said nothing.

The house sprawled atop the hill like a giant that no longer possessed the energy to stand. With the exception of the northernmost wing, the entire structure was only two stories high; but what it lacked in height it more than made up for with its spread. Inside, wide, low-ceilinged hallways stretched away at odd angles and curved out of sight. Even the doors seemed unusually square, with heavy, overlong lintels that emphasised their breadth.

Narvi led them down a long, gently curving corridor that smelled faintly of damp fur. A series of engraved images ran the length of the wall in a narrow, waist-high band, the scenes too small for Arandras to make sense of without stopping. Lamps hung in pairs on either side of the hallway, low enough to put Mara at risk of striking her head if she strayed too far from the centre. Passing Quill eyed the group with mild curiosity or else ignored them altogether, hurrying by on errands of their own.

"Friendly bunch," Mara muttered, and Arandras smiled.

They came to a broad staircase, the shallow steps worn smooth by centuries of use. Stone leopard's heads stared at them from the bottom of each banister: symbols of Anstice, now hung with tassels in the ochre and black of the Quill, the lips of one curling as though preparing to snarl, the other impassive. Narvi gave the expressionless one a perfunctory pat as he passed.

The stairs emerged onto a wide, rooftop courtyard. Climbing plants roamed free over the rough stone walls, their dark leaves dotted with pale, red-throated flowers that filled the courtyard with a delicate fragrance. The west side of the yard lay open to the setting sun, affording a view of the grounds behind the schoolhouse and the rooftops beyond. One of the city's nine surviving redoubts stood a short distance away, its ruined top caught by the sun in such a way that it seemed for a moment to be lit with an inner flame.

"Make yourselves comfortable," Narvi said, dropping his bags by one of the deep, rectangular pots that lined the walls. "Fas is expecting us. I'll only be a moment." He turned and disappeared back down the stairs.

Mara dumped her bags and ambled to the railing at the courtyard's edge. The open display of any weapon larger than a dagger was forbidden within the city, so she'd been forced to pack her cutlasses into one of her bags, though the protruding hilts left little doubt as to what lay within. She looked different without the blades hanging from her hips; simpler, somehow, yet no less dangerous, as though the potency of the weapons had, in fact, derived from her all along, and now she had simply drawn it back. *Like a panther sheathing its claws, but losing none of its swagger.*

He joined her at the rail, one hand raised against the sun. The schoolhouse grounds sloped away beneath them to the outer wall, the lawn dotted with saplings, some still small enough to be guarded by stakes and rags. By the wall, a gaggle of children in ochre hoods played a game Arandras didn't recognise; something involving a wicker ball and an arrangement of squares marked out on the grass with sticks. As he watched, one of the children snatched the ball from another, who responded with a piercing squeal and was immediately shushed by a large woman hovering nearby.

"I suppose one of those is Narvi's," Mara said, nodding at the children.

"Mm-hmm." Arandras peered down, but they were too far away to distinguish faces beneath the brown hoods. Some would be the children of sorcerers and scholars who worked here; others would be students at the schoolhouse, their places paid for by those among the city's wealthy and influential who thought a Quill education desirable for their son or daughter. *A brood of future Quill and their friends. And so the Quill ensures its continued prosperity.*

"It's not too late to change your mind," Mara said.

"And do what? Give up?" Arandras shook his head. He'd tried everything else there was to try. The Quill were the only option left.

Voices sounded from the stairway, followed a moment later by Narvi and another man, taller than any of them, with thick brows and short grey hair that fringed the dome of his head. The newcomer strode toward them with a broad smile, his hand raised in greeting, Narvi hopping in his wake to keep up.

"Arandras, Mara, this is Fas. He —"

"Damasus Fasurathal," the man said, clasping Arandras's arm. "Call me Fas, won't you? Of course you will."

"Fas oversees all our research projects here in Anstice," Narvi said, slightly out of breath.

"I hear you worked for us in Chogon for a time," Fas said. He leaned in, closer than Arandras found comfortable, and peered into Arandras's face. "Thinking of coming back, perhaps? We can always use a good linguist."

"No," Arandras said, shuffling back half a pace to restore an appropriate amount of space between himself and the other man. "Thank you."

"Ah? Well, of course, you are your own man now." He turned to Mara, eyes flicking up and down. "Delighted, I'm sure," he said. "Narvi was vague on your area of expertise. Are you a linguist too?"

"Not exactly," Mara said, an edge of amusement in her voice.

"Then what —"

"She's with me," Arandras interjected.

"Not exactly that, either," Mara said smoothly.

Arandras glared at her from behind Fas's back. Her response was a cocked eyebrow and a grin. Fas frowned and looked confusedly between her and Arandras.

An awkward silence followed.

Narvi gestured toward the tables. "Shall we sit?"

"Well," Fas said when they were seated, his fingers drumming a tattoo on the table. "This is quite the puzzle. Three dead Quill, a copied journal, and an untranslatable urn. Needless to say, we're keen to find out what's going on." He bent toward Arandras. "As are you, I understand."

"I want to find whoever's looking for the urn, certainly," Arandras said. Even with the table between them, the man seemed able to make him feel crowded. *Would it kill you to just sit still?*

"Just so." Fas nodded as though some point was now settled. "Narvi will head up the project. You'll both be on the team, of course, along with whoever else I can spare. We have rooms being made ready for you, including a work area. There's a secure coffer where you can leave the urn overnight — Narvi can show you there on the way. We expect —"

"No," Arandras said. Fas blinked at him in confusion, and Arandras felt a small measure of satisfaction.

"I'm sorry," Fas said. "No to what?"

"No to your *presumptions.*" The words came out harder than he intended, but there was no opportunity to pause and try again. "This is not a Quill operation, Damasus, and I am not part of a Quill team. The urn is mine, and I will retain custody of it throughout. I've agreed to provide access to Narvi and his colleagues, and to work with them to decipher its meaning. That's all. I will not subordinate myself to your people, I will not even accept payment, because *I am not working for you.* Is that clear?"

Silence settled over the table. Fas pressed his lips together, surprise shifting rapidly to cool politeness. Beside him, Narvi gazed skyward, his face a mixture of frustration and embarrassment.

"For the record, I will accept payment," Mara said.

Fas ignored her, turning instead to Narvi. "Is this acceptable to you?"

"Yes, yes, it's fine," Narvi said, in the tone of one seeking to dismiss an unpleasant matter as quickly as possible.

"Very well." Fas summoned a thin smile. "You've had a long journey. I suggest you rest tonight and begin work tomorrow. Narvi can show you to your rooms."

I'll stay elsewhere, Arandras almost said; but a pleading glance from Narvi stopped the words on his lips. He hesitated, aware of Fas's already chilly regard. So far, the man's displeasure had been unavoidable, but aggravating him further would make a poor start to their time here.

It's just a room and a bed, I suppose. It needn't mean anything more than that.

"Fine," Arandras said. "I'll pay you one scudi for each night I stay."

"As you wish." Fas stood. "If there's nothing else?"

There wasn't.

They rose from the table and began collecting their bags, Narvi with an air of relief, Arandras still thinking about the conversation just finished. Mara glanced from one to the other, a satisfied smile on her face.

"That went well," she said as Fas disappeared down the stairs. "Free lodging, just for joining you two on the road. I should do this more often."

Narvi made a face. "I'm sure we'll find something for you to do."

Mara gave an easy shrug, then bent and hoisted her main bag to her shoulders. "Lead the way."

They headed for the stairs in single file; Narvi followed by Mara, then Arandras. Arandras paused at the top, glancing back at the vista of city roofs. The sun was precisely on the horizon now, a great orange ball perched between distant hills.

It's just a room and bed. That's all.

There was a murmur of conversation from the stairway, followed by a burst of cheeky laughter from Mara. Then her voice floated up from somewhere below. "That reminds me. When's dinner?"

With a faint smile and shake of his head, Arandras lifted his bags and followed the others down.

~

The accommodation provided by the Quill consisted of a cell-like room near the kitchens, a straw pallet, and a small chest with the key still in the lock. Not trusting the urn to the chest, Arandras slept as best he could with it stashed beneath the thin pillow, its round body pressing uncomfortably against him. A high grille in the door admitted the thin light and smoke-tinged perfume of the scented candles burning in the passageway; and, as dawn approached, the sounds and smells of the kitchen returning to life. The clatter of pans drove away any vestige of slumber, leaving him weary, bleary-eyed, but inescapably awake.

He found Narvi at the back of the schoolhouse on a bench over-looking the grounds. A small girl in an ochre hood sat on the grass beside him, giggling at something in her hands.

"Look, Papa!" the girl said, proffering a clay doll for inspection. "It worked! She's wet all over!"

Narvi turned the doll over in his hands. "So she is."

"It's the dew," the girl announced, in the serious tone of one relaying privileged information. "It comes in the night and makes everything wet."

Narvi caught sight of Arandras and waved him over. "Now, who's this, sweet? Do you know?"

The girl looked up, uncertain. A hand shot out and grabbed Narvi's ankle.

"It's all right," Narvi said. "This is Uncle Randas. Do you remember him?"

Arandras crouched before the girl. "Hello, Katriel," he said gravely. "What do you have there?"

"Doll," she said, clutching it to her chest.

"Ah, I see. Does she have a name?"

Katriel shook her head, then nodded, then shook her head again. "Doll," she repeated.

Arandras chuckled. "You've grown big," he said. "Last time I saw you, you were only —"

"Where's Aunty Treesa?"

Arandras blinked, his train of thought gone. Katriel gazed up at him, eyes wide with transparent curiosity, but in his still-sleepy state

Arandras could think of nothing to say.

"She's not here, sweet," Narvi said, reaching for her hand. "Up you get. Time to go to lessons. You can talk more with Uncle Randas later."

With a last puzzled frown at Arandras, Katriel trotted off toward a cluster of other children, leaving Arandras and Narvi alone. Arandras lowered himself onto the bench with a sigh.

"No word from her mother?" he said, looking out at the walled lawn and its collection of slender saplings.

Narvi might have shaken his head. "No."

"I'm sorry."

"No need," Narvi said. "We're fine. Really, we are."

They considered the lawn in silence.

"Katriel reminds me of her," Arandras said. "Something about the nose, I think."

"Yes," Narvi said. "Her laugh, too."

Yes, that too. Arandras had met Narvi's lover only a handful of times before she left Chogon, abandoning her newborn for the seclusion of a monastery in the foothills of the Kemenese. *What would it be like, to be reminded every day of the one you had lost? To hear her voice, see her expressions and mannerisms each day in the face of a child?* He glanced sidelong at Narvi, remembering his smile as he listened to Katriel explain the dew. If the girl brought him pain, he hid it well.

But then, nobody had taken Katriel's mother from them. She had left of her own choice. *The girl might be a reminder of rejection, perhaps, but not loss. Not like mine.*

"Well. That urn's not going to unriddle itself." Narvi stood, grunting as he stretched his back. "Let's make a start, shall we?"

The workroom set aside for their use was situated on the upper floor, near the end of one of the house's shorter wings. A waist-high bench ran around three walls, with stools drawn up against it; on the fourth wall, two large, glass-fronted frames hung from hooks, the kind in which charts or maps might be displayed. A circular table filled the centre of the room, its timber a dull brown, surrounded by a mismatched collection of chairs. Daylight streamed into the room through half a dozen narrow windows along one wall, allowing the chandeliers hanging from the ceiling to go unlit.

Two figures glanced up at their entry. Both wore the bronze Quill feather, though neither brooch had the gold-tipped point marking an Elector.

"Arandras, allow me to introduce Bannard and Senisha," Narvi said. "Bannard, Senisha, this is Arandras, the man with the urn."

"Pleased to meet you, sir," said the man, Bannard, squinting at him from beneath an unruly mop of dark hair. Angry red scabs marked his arm and one side of his face, the flesh around them still pink.

"Just Arandras will do fine," Arandras said, trying not to stare. The man's wounds looked at least a week old, but if he'd seen a fleshbinder they might only have happened a few days ago. "What happened to you?"

"Unbinding gone bad. Halli took the worst of it." Bannard shrugged, apparently unfazed by either his own injuries or those suffered by his colleague. "Narvi says you used to work in the Greathouse archives, in Chogon," he said, with palpable enthusiasm. "Is that true?"

"That was a long time ago," Arandras said. "I'm not with the Quill any more."

"Oh, no, I know. But you must have seen some amazing things."

Arandras had little interest in discussing his time at Chogon. "What's your area of expertise?"

Bannard shrugged again. "Research. Figuring stuff out. Whatever comes along."

"And you?" Arandras said to Senisha, though he thought he already knew the answer. *Sorcerer: check. Researcher: check. Which leaves only...*

"Librarian," Senisha said, in a voice barely more than a whisper. *Check.*

"What about your friend?" Senisha said, her brows curving upward.

Arandras blinked. "I'm sorry?"

"Narvi said there were two of you. What does your friend do?"

Oh. Right. "Mara has business of her own," Arandras said. "I doubt she'll be joining us."

Senisha looked confused, but Bannard seemed even less concerned by Mara's absence than he was by his own injuries. "Splendid," he said. "Where's the urn? That's what we're all here for, isn't it?"

All eyes turned to Arandras. He reached into the pouch hanging from his belt, his hand closing over the urn's rounded form. *This is worth it. It is.* Slowly, he drew it out, placing it on the table and pulling away the wrapping.

There. That's wasn't so hard.

"Oh, my. Oh, that's a beauty," Bannard said, leaning close and squinting. "Do you know what it reminds me of?"

"Some sort of spirit ossuary?" Arandras said.

"A Yanisinian spirit ossuary — huh." Bannard eyed him appraisingly. "You've done some digging already."

"But this can't be Yanisinian," Narvi said, frowning at the urn. "There's no way a Yanisinian piece would be this well preserved."

"True enough," Bannard said. "That metalwork could only be Valdori. How far did you get with the inscription?"

Arandras shrugged. "Not very. It seems to fit the general form of a benediction, but that's about all I can tell."

"What's a spirit ossuary?" Senisha said.

"A receptacle for a dead man's spirit," Bannard said. "That's what the Yanisinians believed, anyway."

"But this is Valdori, right?"

"Right."

"So, the Valdori had spiritbinders, didn't they?" Senisha's brow furrowed. "What if they actually... made it work?"

"I had the same thought," Arandras said. "But it's not big enough, is it? I mean, the sorcery required to draw out a spirit would have to be incredibly complex, if it's even possible."

"Not exactly," Narvi said slowly. "The urn wouldn't necessarily have to extract anything. Something else could do that. The urn would only have to keep it contained." He frowned. "But even then, you're probably right. Imprisonment would likely be complex enough all on its own."

"What if it didn't need to be imprisoned?" Senisha said. "What if it wanted to be there?"

"Huh?" Bannard's squint turned incredulous. "You don't get to stay in your body when you die, no matter how much you want it. Why would an urn be any different?"

"I've never heard of the Valdori using spiritbinding for simple imprisonment," Narvi said, shaking his head. "That's not what it was. It was always about... I don't know, making use of the spirits somehow."

"If it existed at all," Bannard said.

They fell silent, all standing around the table and contemplating the urn. Eventually, Arandras pulled out a chair and settled into it.

"So," he said. "I guess this could take a while?"

～

Eilwen stood on the Guild's private quay, her eyes half-closed against the sunrise, and waited for Pel.

She'd slept fitfully, her dreams filled with images of Tammas. She'd spent years trying to banish the memories, but somehow they always returned: his stride, his crooked grin, the way his beard tickled her ear whenever he pledged his love. Yet when she thought back on it now, it seemed to her that her affection had been won not with smiles, nor even with endless silver-tongued promises, but with the sword-callus on Tammas's thumb.

For a long time, she'd thought of Tammas as just another bravo: a hired sword employed by the Guild to guard the more valuable shipments, too stupid for anything but strutting around a caravan in the hopes of discouraging equally stupid bandits from trying to seize their goods by force. Eilwen had seen too many fools with knives and clubs as a child to be impressed by one more. As a rule, the only intelligence to be found in most armed bands was possessed by either the captain or his second; or, if the company was particularly fortunate, both. Tammas was neither, and therefore not worth her attention.

Then one afternoon, in thick forest a half-day's travel from Fanon, the strutting failed. Eilwen was riding in the lead wagon when they encountered the fallen tree blocking the road; a moment later, an arrow thudded into the post beside her head and she dived to the ground, scrambling beneath the now-stationary wagon for cover.

By the time she crawled out again, shivering with cold, the battle was done. Bodies littered the verges of the road, the blood in their wounds already beginning to congeal. But there were more dead bandits than guards; and when her gaze fell on Tammas, stripped to the waist, pouring wine over a cut in his shoulder, the look he gave her was at once worshipful and ravenous.

They reached Fanon as night fell. Eilwen lingered by the wagons as the vehicles were secured, waiting for Tammas to emerge; but it was he who found her, sneaking up behind her and snaking his arm about her waist. Later, in the moonlight, he cupped her face with his hand, brushing his callused thumb against her cheek, and her breath hitched at the gentleness of his touch, as though he were taming himself just for her.

She'd been little more than a girl, really. What chance had she had? Looking back on it now was like hearing a story about someone else. The person she'd been back then was gone, washed away by seawater and blood. What happened could scarcely be considered her fault.

Except, of course, that it was.

Tammas had known just what to say to win her belief. And she'd wanted to believe him, wanted it more than anything in her life. Then the *Orenda* sank, and her belief sank with it; not just in him, but her capacity to believe at all. Ever since, she realised, she'd found ways to make do without belief.

Until Havilah.

It was strange to have an ally. There was no attraction between them, so far as she could tell; certainly, there was none on Eilwen's side. But there was something else: a common goal, and with it, a shared confidence the like of which Eilwen hadn't felt for a long time. It was true, what Havilah had said. She wasn't the conspiring type. Even the most minor of conspiracies required trust, and trust was something she no longer gave.

Yet here she was, entrusting her life to Havilah as they hunted the Guild's betrayers.

It felt good.

She strolled the length of the quay, enjoying the cool morning breeze off the river despite the faint smell of rot. The Guild docks

were deserted: the first boat wasn't scheduled to arrive until a couple
of hours before midday, leaving the space empty save for Eilwen and
a pair of cormorants at the quay's edge. Eilwen turned before she
got close enough to spook them, ambling back the other way as the
birds chattered to each other behind her back. Her leg was at its best
at this time of day, barely troubling her at all so long as she kept her
movements slow and small.

Eilwen had spent the days since the masters' meeting hunting
down as much information about Kieffe as she could. But the records she'd been able to get her hands on were disappointingly scant.
Ufeus had been unable to turn up anything beyond the standard
contract signed by every member of the Guild on joining. If Kieffe
had ever submitted a trader's report to Pel, none of it had ever been
sent on to Ufeus or Havilah. And her requests to the other masters
to turn over whatever information they had on the murdered man
— relayed on her behalf by a scowling Ufeus — had earned her a
smattering of trivia and nothing more.

After several days spent scouring intelligence reports for even
a passing mention of the man, she'd conceded defeat. Whoever
Kieffe had been working for had covered his tracks too well. She
had no option but to start asking questions and hope her ignorance
wouldn't be enough to undermine the investigation right from the
start.

I did all right with Dallin. She'd confronted him with no prepa-
ration at all, goaded by the bickering between Ufeus and Brielle,
and she'd come away with the lead that had given them Kieffe. And
this would be easier; this time she already knew the people she'd be
talking to.

A horn sounded from the public docks across the river and a
passenger ferry eased away from shore, its prow turning east toward
Borronor's Crossing and the sea. As though in response, a flurry
of wings rose behind her, followed by slow, deliberate beats as the
cormorants flapped past her head and up into the haze-smudged
sky.

The heavy slam of the main building's rear door pulled her back
to her surroundings. Pel slouched toward the quay, a simple fishing
rod slung over his shoulder and a rough wooden bucket in his other

hand. *Ah. At last.*

Pel's dogged interest in angling was legendary among Guild traders. As far as Eilwen knew, the man had never actually caught anything; yet every morning after breaking his fast, Pel would haul his bucket to the river's edge and stand there, line in hand, for the better part of a bell. Some speculated that the pastime was merely a ploy to secure an hour of solitude, a notion derived largely from a junior trader's claim to have witnessed Pel casting empty hooks into the water. Others countered that such an action might just as readily be explained by the man's general absent-mindedness, leaving the traders roughly split between those who believed their adjunct preferred the company of fish to that of other people, and those who considered him simply incompetent at his chosen sport.

Eilwen had been part of the former camp, though her own reserve after the *Orenda* had seen her gradually drift from the social circles of her fellow traders. But the awkwardness of disturbing the man's solitude seemed worth the chance to speak with him alone and informally. If he turned her away and she was forced to find another time, it would hardly make their subsequent conversation any more trying than would naturally be the case.

She turned, resuming her stroll along the quayside. Pel had already cast his hook and now swirled the rod slowly in mid-air, dragging the line through the water below. He frowned, leaning over to peer into the murky depths.

"A fine morning," Eilwen said. Pel found such observations inane, she knew, but she needed something to open the conversation. She halted alongside him and turned to survey the river. "Any bites?"

She sensed Pel shake his head, and found herself picturing the expression of pained disappointment that was likely crossing his face even now. Gathering up her resolve, she pushed the image from her thoughts and ploughed on.

"I wanted to ask you about Kieffe," she said. "What was he working on before he died?"

Her question was met with silence. Eilwen folded her arms and resisted the urge to turn her head. The swirling motion beside her slowed, then stopped.

"I don't know," Pel said at length. His voice sounded rougher than usual.

Eilwen frowned. "But you're the adjunct," she said. "You know what all the traders are doing."

"Not Kieffe."

"What, then?" *Someone must have told the man what he could buy or sell.* "Are you saying he worked directly for Trademaster Laris?"

Pel shifted in what might have been a slow shrug. "Maybe," he said.

Eilwen waited. "Or?"

"Maybe he wasn't a trader at all."

Eilwen risked a sidelong glance. "What does that mean?"

Pel heaved a lugubrious sigh. "Not all of our traders are really traders," he said ponderously. "Sometimes another master needs to put someone in another city. Secretly."

Secret even from the rest of the Guild? The revelation was unexpected, but somehow Eilwen was only mildly surprised. *A few weeks ago, I'd probably have been shocked.* "Which masters?"

"Master Caralange," Pel said. "And Master Havilah."

Havilah. Of course. Disquiet whispered through her breast, but she pushed it away. *It's not him. It can't be.*

Which left Caralange, and Laris.

"I suppose if I asked Laris who Kieffe was really working for, she'd be happy to tell me?" Eilwen said, not sure if she was being sarcastic or not. The masters' meeting would have been the perfect opportunity for Laris to dump Kieffe on someone else. But she'd told everyone the man was just a trader, which suggested it was probably true.

So why wasn't Pel saying the same thing?

Her suspicions rising, Eilwen turned. "Why are you telling me this, Pel?"

Pel looked up, and their gazes locked. His fleshy face was drawn. *He's worried. Kieffe's death has him rattled, and he's decided... to trust me? Oh, gods.* She nodded once, swallowing hard, and he looked away.

"What else can you tell me?" she said softly.

He took a long, slow breath. "There's a shop. An importer from Tan Tahis." He paused. "Qulah."

"I know it," Eilwen said. Qulah's was on the Fanon road, not far from the new estates in the south part of the city. She'd visited it regularly in her early days with the Guild, but she'd barely been back in the years since her promotion to trade factor.

"I was there last week. Kieffe came in. When he saw me, he left."

Eilwen waited, but nothing more was forthcoming. *All right.* "One other thing," she said. "I need access to the trade reports and transaction logs. I know Kieffe's dealings probably aren't in there, but there'll be other things, details I can use to track down what he was doing..."

But Pel was already turning away. "Only Laris can give you that," he said with exaggerated patience.

"I know, I just thought..." She trailed off. *Thought what? That Pel could go behind Laris's back to get me the entire trading record for the past year, just so I can trawl through it and figure out what I'm even looking for?* She shook her head, feeling foolish. "Never mind."

Pel frowned at the water before him. With a slow, deliberate hand, he lifted his fishing rod and began to swirl it back and forth above the river.

Qulah's. It was more than she'd had an hour ago. And it was something she could pursue without feeling like the whole Guild was looking over her shoulder. *Maybe I can get some solid information before I start parading my ignorance before Laris and Caralange.*

"Pel," she murmured. "Thank you."

She left before he could reply. Not that he would have. It was Pel, after all.

~

The way to Qulah's took Eilwen down the eastern thoroughfare, past the building she always avoided. *The Oculus building.* Without the egg, she had no way of distinguishing Oculus from innocent, or untrained token-bearer from sorcerer, and as she approached her usual detour she slowed, contemplating just walking on by. But the thought was foolishness, of course. She'd often come this way before, with and without the egg. The risk was not so much that she might kill someone there and then in the street, though there had been dark moments when that had seemed possible. No, the true danger was subtler, more incremental: a reminder of debts unpaid, and a reawakening of her hunger for justice. A first step down the treacherous, well-worn path that led only to more death.

She grit her teeth and took the detour.

Qulah's Emporium was a low, single-storey affair with a flat roof, sandwiched between a weathered brick warehouse and a run-down, multi-level tenement. With its lead glass windows, elegantly carved cornices, and wide, deep-blue enamelled door, Qulah's stood out like a beacon of refinement among its ramshackle neighbours. Even the marker stone bearing the site's city-ordained lot number was polished to a finish smooth enough for Eilwen to see the silhouette of her own reflection. Behind it, a neatly-trimmed shrub grew from a shallow box, its leaves the same dark green as the plants on either side of the door.

Very nice, Eilwen thought as she pushed open the door and stepped inside. *Qulah, you've done well.*

Inside, the shop was no less impressive. Rich, red carpets lined the floor, thin but beautifully patterned. Eilwen ducked around a large floor lamp, glancing idly at the ivory jewellery, carved black-wood flutes, and other Tahisi exotica arranged tastefully on the low shelves. A faint, vaguely spicy scent tickled her nostrils and she smiled. *Oh, I remember this.* She closed her eyes and breathed deep.

"Can I help you?"

Lungs full, Eilwen opened her eyes and looked around. A young Tahisi man no taller than herself stood at her side, a solicitous smile on his face. She let out her breath with a rush and gave the youth a slight frown. "I'd like to speak to Qulah, thank you."

"Of course," said the youth, his smile unwavering. He gestured in the direction of a side counter. "My uncle will be right with you."

Uncle, is it? Eilwen glanced about the shop. A second Tahisi youth spoke in low tones with a moneyed, thin-haired man in the next aisle, while a third surveyed the store from a vantage point by the far wall. The last time Eilwen was here, Qulah's only assistant had been his curt, unsmiling brother. *So the kids are finally earning their keep. I wonder if Qulah's brought them all the way in?*

The soft click of a side door pulled her from her thoughts, and she looked up to see Qulah crossing the floor toward her. The man's hair was a little greyer than she recalled, and his jowls a little heavier, but his unhurried movements and air of calm attentiveness were just as she remembered them. His shirt was the colour of ink and hung to his knees; but Eilwen could tell from its drape that the fabric was pure cotton, not the half-linen weave she would have expected of an ordinary shopkeeper. *Just a humble merchant. Oh, yes.*

Qulah halted before her, his head inclined in greeting. "I know you, do I not?" Though his skin was half a shade lighter than Havilah's, his accent was almost identical. He studied her face, then broke into a smile. "Eilwen Nasareen. Of the Woodtraders, yes?"

"Qulah. It's been too long."

"So it has. Yet here you are." Qulah spread his hands in a gesture encompassing both forgiveness and welcome. "I trust your visit is not simply a result of taking a wrong turn on the way to your favourite chocol house."

The corners of Eilwen's lips tugged upward. "You still haven't added chocol to your selection of wares? I'm disappointed, Qulah."

Qulah waved a dismissive hand. "There are a hundred and one stores in this city where chocol may be obtained. I have no interest in becoming the hundred and second." He indicated an array of jars on a nearby shelf. "I can, however, offer a fine selection of okra seed. A far superior drink, and only eight scudi per pound."

"Perhaps another time." Eilwen hesitated, unsure how best to broach the purpose for her visit. "In truth, I'm not here to peruse your merchandise."

"Of course not," Qulah said smoothly. "A special order, yes?"

"After a fashion," Eilwen said. "A colleague of mine came to see you last week, or maybe the week before. Ash hair and a narrow face. Name of Kieffe."

"Ah." Qulah stepped closer, his voice soft. "The first shipment arrived yesterday. Would you like to see?"

Shipment? Eilwen inclined her head. "Certainly."

He nodded. "Follow me."

Qulah withdrew a small key from his sleeve and unlocked the side door, ushering her through. The passage beyond was narrow but clean. Daylight filtered dimly through thumbnail-sized holes in the high ceiling. Eilwen matched the Tahisi trader's brisk pace as he led her through the twisting corridor to the adjoining warehouse.

The most valuable of Qulah's wares never appeared in his shop. When the Woodtraders — or, Eilwen suspected, most of the other trading houses in Anstice — needed goods brought in from the south, they could either attempt to arrange it themselves, or they could save themselves the time and trouble and see Qulah. If said items were not technically permitted within the city bounds, the discretion of the Anstice garrison could be purchased for an additional fee, though Eilwen had no idea how Qulah had come to that arrangement. The last time the Woodtraders had attempted to reach a similar understanding with the city garrison, the man making the offer had been lucky to avoid prison.

"My apologies for not recognising you sooner," Qulah murmured as they halted before another door. "Kieffe said he might be returning to Neysa, but he didn't mention that you would be overseeing the order in his absence."

"Oh, I'm not," Eilwen said automatically. "Not really. I just…" She trailed off, thinking frantically. *Overseeing the order? What on the gods' earth are they buying — a herd of Tahisi elephants?* "Several of us are working this assignment," she said, striking out blindly. "Today, I have the pleasure of your company. Tomorrow, alas, it may be another."

Qulah nodded as though unsurprised, but his voice matched her playful tone. "Then I thank Father Earth for today." He opened the door. "There are lamps and sparkers on the wall," he said, taking one for himself. "Watch your step."

The warehouse was even bigger than it appeared from the street. Wooden crates of all shapes and sizes rose in stacked formations like monument stones. Muted traffic noise leaked in from the front of the building; but the two massive railed doors were positioned at the rear, presumably giving access via a more private laneway. The smell of sawdust hung in the air.

"Over here," Qulah called, halting before a smaller stack and setting his lamp down on a pile of hessian sacks. Fetching a crowbar, he began to lever open the lid of the topmost crate. Eilwen gazed at the box with barely restrained curiosity. The crate was long, narrow, and no deeper than it was wide. *Bolts of cloth, maybe? Surely there's more to it than that.*

The lid gave way with a sullen creak, revealing a packed layer of wood shavings. Qulah reached in and brushed the topmost shavings aside. Polished bronze glinted in the lamplight.

"Beautiful craftsmanship, is it not?" Qulah scooped another handful of shavings out of the crate, and the shape of the object was suddenly plain. "Tahisi cannon barrels. Not even the Jervians can produce finer."

Eilwen managed a tight nod. *Cannons. Gods have mercy, what are we in the middle of?*

"Have you decided on a form of payment?"

"Excuse me?"

"Payment. Yes?" Qulah frowned. "Perhaps Kieffe did not tell you."

Eilwen shook her head, still staring at the cannon. "I'm sorry. Tell me what?"

"Kieffe enquired about a discount if he paid with Tahisi coin. I offered two and a half per cent."

"Oh. Right. We're, uh, still working out how much currency we can put together." The gleaming metal drew her gaze like a lodestone. With an effort, Eilwen raised her head. "You said this was the first shipment. When should we expect the next?"

"These were nearby," Qulah said. "I have small amounts of shot and powder on the way as well. They should be here within days. After that..." He spread his hands. "The second consignment will depart Tan Tahis as soon as my message is received. Even if Mother Sea smiles, it will be several weeks at least before those goods arrive. And the third consignment, of course, must first be produced."

"Of course," Eilwen said weakly. *Three consignments. Gods preserve us.*

Qulah lifted his lamp. "Would you like a closer look?"

"Thank you, no," Eilwen said. The warehouse air suddenly seemed stifling. "That will be fine. Thank you."

"The pleasure is mine," Qulah returned, bowing slightly. "I am honoured to be entrusted with your needs. The Woodtraders Guild has no better friend than Qulah."

Maybe not, Eilwen thought, shivering as Qulah replaced the shavings and began hammering the lid back down. *But we've sure as the Hundred Hells got some enemies.*

If only I knew who the bastards were.

CHAPTER 11

Which of these three do you suppose amuses the gods most: your
plans, your fears, or your convictions?

— Kassa of Menefir, *Solitude*

B Y THE END OF THE day, Arandras felt as though his head had
been stuffed full of damp wool and left in the sun to dry. He
bent over one of the books Senisha had fetched from the library, trying and failing to make sense of the page before him. Near
the windows, Narvi and Bannard debated some point of sorcery,
Narvi's calm insistence apparently not enough to persuade Bannard
to the same opinion. Their conversation rose and fell, eating away at
his concentration like water on sand.

It had been much the same all day: long periods of study interspersed with abstruse and sometimes vigorous discussions between
Bannard and Narvi. Now and then Senisha would offer a comment, but mostly she seemed content to listen and read, and to ferry
books back and forth between their room and the library. Only occasionally was Arandras asked to contribute to the discussion, and
even then the questions were largely confined to the circumstances
around the discovery of the urn. His talent as a linguist and his
experience dealing with rare artefacts was neither called upon nor
acknowledged by anyone.

The sky outside the narrow windows was orange gold when Narvi at last called a halt to the day's efforts. Arandras collected the urn

and left without a word, making his way down the curving hallways and out to the narrow strip of lawn and the blessed open air. A whisper of breeze caressed his face, its breath laced with the aromas of the city — beast and man, rotting food and delicate spices — but for once, Arandras didn't care. He breathed deep, drinking in its refreshing coolness and releasing it with a sigh.

"That much fun, huh?"

Arandras's eyes snapped open. Mara stood before him, one eyebrow raised in mock-query. He gave a half-chuckle. "I don't know," he said. "It wasn't so bad, I suppose. I'm just..." He gestured vaguely, not sure how to finish the sentence.

"Tired?"

"That'll do."

"Having second thoughts?"

"Maybe." He frowned. "No, not that. I just feel... I don't know. Out of practice, perhaps."

Mara hooked her thumb over her shoulder at the wide expanse of city. "Want to get away from here for a bit?"

"Weeper, yes."

They strolled down the path between the swaying rows of saplings, Mara with her hands close to her thighs as though holding non-existent cutlasses in place.

"Say what you like about Anstice, you've got to agree they sell better blade oil here than anywhere else," Mara said as they passed through the gate.

"Really?" Arandras said. "I wouldn't know."

"Of course you know." Mara sounded affronted. "I just told you."

"Well, yeah, but that wouldn't be me agreeing with you, would it? That would be you agreeing with you."

"Best approach all round, in my experience."

"Hah."

The breeze faded as they ventured further from the schoolhouse. Lamp-lighters manoeuvred their handcarts around street vendors and their customers, exchanging curses with those who stood in their way. The smell of hot pastry spilled into the street from a pie stand at one corner; further along, a lute player strolled back and forth with two small boys trailing behind. The song was unfamiliar to Arandras, but the tune was lively and the player's voice clear. Someone tossed the musician some coppers and one of the boys darted forward, snatching them off the cobbles as the player grinned his thanks.

"Jasser and Peni are both out of town," Mara said. "Thought I'd try Isaias before calling it a day."

Still trying to sell that damn puzzle box. "Suit yourself," Arandras said. "I think I'll head down to the river." There would be bars and chocol houses there where he might find a game, if he wished. Or perhaps not. After the day's exertion, he had little energy left for the *dilarj* board. What he really wanted was somewhere quiet and out of the way. Wherever that might be.

"I thought you'd want to come along." Mara flicked a coin in the player's direction and watched the boys scramble to pick it up. "Someone here is looking for that urn, right? So wouldn't they start with the local dealers?"

"Would they? Think about the lengths they've gone to. Forged journals, for the Weeper's sake! Seems to me they knew exactly where this thing was."

"All right, maybe they did. But now they've lost it. They don't know who's got it or where it might turn up. How else are they going to find it again?"

It was a good point. He should have thought of it himself. Whatever the plan had been didn't matter any more, now that the urn had slipped through their fingers. Whoever sought it would be improvising, and improvisation was invariably sloppy.

Assuming, of course, that they hadn't simply given up.

"Isaias, huh?"

"For all we know, he might have the name of a buyer in his sleeve right now."

"All right." Arandras took a long breath. "Let's find out."

Isaias's shop was on the southern edge of the old city, just inside the remains of the first city wall. Arandras had only visited the shop once before; most of his dealings with Isaias, and indeed with the other dealers here, took place during their visits to Spyridon, which in Isaias's case occurred two or three times a year. The door was easy to miss, set back from the street between two glass-paned shopfronts.

Arandras tried the handle and the door opened inward, revealing a narrow staircase. Lamplight from an unseen source bathed the wall at the top of the stairs.

"I guess he's in," Mara said.

The stairs creaked under their feet as they climbed, and as they neared the top Arandras heard the sounds of someone in the room above: a tuneless humming, the scrape of a chair, a loud sigh. Then a voice called out to them, genial and familiar. "Come in, friends, come in and be welcome! Isaias is delighted to make your acquaintance."

Weeper save me. Arandras reached the top and turned into the room, Mara at his heels. "Hello, Isaias."

"Arandras! Maransheala!" Isaias beamed at them, his round face a picture of delight. "My dear friends! What a pleasure it is to see you, what an unexpected pleasure, and all the more pleasurable for the surprise! Look who it is, Pinecone!" He scooped up a striped cat with pale ears and pointed its head in their direction. It cast them a disinterested glance. "It's our friends Arandras and Mara. Come all the way from Spyridon just to visit us."

"How are you, Isaias?" Mara said as the cat squirmed free and slunk away.

"How am I? Ah, my dear, fortune is a fickle mistress, a fickle, fickle girl. One moment she lavishes me with bounty, such that I want for not the smallest whit. The next" — Isaias made a flinging gesture with his hands — "she deserts me, and her bounty vanishes as though it had never been." He shook his head sorrowfully; then, like the sun breaking through clouds, the beaming smile returned. "But then, just when she seems to have utterly and finally turned against me, she brings you to my door, my dear friends! How can I hate her? I cannot."

"Mm-hmm." Arandras looked around the shop. Windowed cabinets filled the room, displaying an astonishing variety of objects: books, utensils, weapons, spices, jewellery — even, in a narrow case near the counter, pieces worked with what appeared to be anamnil, the strange, semi-metallic cloth that bore a unique resistance to the effects of sorcery. Below the shuttered windows on the far wall stretched a series of drawers, each sealed with a heavy lock. A green armchair sat in the centre of the room before a hearth, with a bottle of wine and an empty goblet on a small table alongside.

"Pinecone!" Isaias peered behind him, waggling his fingers at a shadowed corner, then straightening when it became apparent that the corner was empty and glancing about the shop. "Pinecone? Don't you want the rest of your dinner?" No response was forthcoming, and Isaias heaved a sigh. "Ah, friends, a queen among cats is Pinecone. Such is her firm opinion on the matter, and I find that I am forced to agree. Yet I confess — and I say this only to you, my dear, trusted friends — that I find myself wondering on occasion whether her fastidious disposition, though entirely appropriate to one of her station, may at times get the better of her otherwise outstanding judgement. A trifling fault, to be sure; and yet, there it is."

"Isaias," Arandras said, and waited for Isaias to look up before continuing. "Could we talk a moment?"

"Certainly, my friend! Isaias would be happy to spend this whole evening in conversation with Arandras and Mara. We could —"

"A few moments should suffice." He heard the impatience in his voice and scowled. *Damn it. Why couldn't it have been Peni in town instead?* "I mean to say —"

"What he means," Mara said smoothly, "is that our business, alas, is pressing. It was difficult for us to find even this time to visit, though of course there was no question that we should; but regrettably, we cannot stay long."

"Of course, my dear. Isaias understands. Always at the beck and call of fickle fortune, are we not?" Isaias spread his hands. "So tell me, my friends, what can I do for you? Is it maps you seek? I have acquired some particularly fine specimens since last we spoke. Or perhaps you have items to sell? Something rare or unusual?"

"In fact, I do," Mara said. She reached into a pocket and withdrew a flat copper box, small enough to fit in the palm of Arandras's hand, its surface streaked with verdigris. "It's a child's puzzle box. I had word from Jasser of an interested buyer here in Anstice, but now Jasser is out of town. Perhaps fortune is smiling on you once again."

Isaias took the box with a frown. "So heavy for a mere child's toy," he said. "I suppose the puzzle is how to open this tiny casket, yes? A clever way to hide something small. A scrap of paper, perhaps, or a small key. Tell me, dear Mara, do you know this riddle's secret?"

Mara grinned. "Do you have a pair of thimbles? Or maybe some small spoons?"

"Well, I… let me see." Isaias shuffled to the counter, depositing the small box on its polished surface and rummaging behind it. He emerged with a small wooden spoon and a matching two-pronged fork. "Will these do?"

Mara took the utensils, one in each hand, holding them by the bowl and prongs so that the stems extended outward. "You have to press in just the right places. On this side, just here, and on the other side…"

There was a click and a snap, and Isaias flinched back. At the side of the box where the spoon pressed, a short needle now protruded, a thin scratch in the spoon's handle tracing its path. Arandras scowled and turned away.

A poisoner's box. Weeper's tears.

With the item's function revealed, the haggling began, but Arandras was no longer listening. He halted before a display case, glaring sightlessly at its contents. *Who in the hells would want to buy something like that? And how can she sell it with no thought for where it might go?* But then, they'd found and sold dozens of knives and daggers over the years. Was selling a needled box really any different?

Yes, he thought. *This is worse.* Yet try as he might, he couldn't say why.

"Not enough," Mara said from the other end of the shop. "Maybe I'll wait until Jasser gets back."

"Ah, my dear, I regret I can offer you no more." There was a pause. "A thought occurs to me, dear Mara. Perhaps Isaias can speak to some people he knows, who can speak to some people they know, who could speak to yet other people in the hope of finding one who may, perchance, be interested in purchasing such a singular item. If such an individual exists, why, perhaps a price may be found that will satisfy Isaias's friends as much as Isaias himself."

Mara nodded. "I'll give you three days before I start shopping it elsewhere. As a token of our friendship, of course." She returned the box to her pocket. "Leave a message at the bar on the corner if you have anything for me."

"Depend upon it, my dear." Isaias beamed, his fingers laced over his belly. "How wonderful it is to be of service to such considerate friends."

"Speaking of which," Arandras said, leaving the display case and returning to the counter, "perhaps we might ask a small favour."

"Of course, my friend, of course! Name it, and it is yours!"

"Just a question," Arandras said. "Has anyone come to you recently looking for a Valdori piece shaped like a small urn? About this big?"

"An urn, friend Arandras?" Isaias gave a sad sigh. "So many people approach me with so many enquiries that I find myself quite incapable of remembering them all. Truly, their sheer volume is all but overwhelming. How it is that so many people come to hear of me, I really do not know."

"Come on, Isaias," Mara said. "We just want to know if you've seen any interest. You can tell us that much, right? Perhaps you've had a sorcerer or two come by, maybe in the last week or so, who asked after an urn?"

"Dear Mara, I would be elated if I could help you in even this very small matter," Isaias said regretfully. "But every one of my customers is a man or woman of discernment and fine character. They come to me in confidence, trusting to my discretion. You would not have me betray their faith, would you? No, no, I know you would never entertain such a motive. Forgive my uncharitable thought, I beg you."

Arandras exhaled through clenched teeth.

"However," Isaias said, and the expression on his face shifted from sorrow to earnest goodwill. "If you should come across a piece such as you describe, do remember your good friend Isaias. Nowhere else in Anstice — nor, indeed, in the whole of Kal Arna — will you find so generous a buyer as he who now stands before you."

Thank you, Isaias, that's very helpful. Arandras glimpsed Pinecone slinking between cabinets and felt a sudden urge to leave before Isaias spotted her too and began another round of babble. He shot Mara a glance and turned to go, but was halted by a sudden exclamation from Isaias.

"But of course! My friends, there is a simple solution to your quandary. An obvious solution, truly, if only one will think of it. You say you seek a sorcerer, one with an interest in Valdori artefacts." Isaias clapped his hands together. "Friends, have you considered the Quill?"

~

The next morning, Arandras returned to the workroom to find Bannard circling the table like a fox. "Took you long enough," he said the moment he saw Arandras's face. "Where have you been?"

Arandras blinked. "What?"

"It's an hour past sunrise!"

"Which is when we're supposed to start, isn't it?" Shaking his head, Arandras produced the urn and began to unwrap it. *Weeper save me from morning people.*

Bannard folded his arms. "You know, we could get a lot more done if you'd leave that thing here, or in the coffer."

"Not going to happen." Arandras tucked the wrappings back into the pouch. "Where are the others?"

"Narvi's tied up with other things." Bannard shrugged, as if to say he couldn't imagine what else might be more deserving of Narvi's time than this. "Said he'd join us later, if he could."

"And Senisha?"

"Here," came a quiet voice from behind him. Senisha shuffled in, a high stack of books balanced in her arms, and slowly set them down on the central table.

Arandras blinked. "What's all that?"

"A bit of everything," Senisha said. "Valdori sorcery. Yanisinian sorcery. Death rites. Metalworking. And these." She picked a trio of slender volumes from the top of the stack and offered them to Arandras. "Minor ancient dialects."

Arandras opened the first one, expecting to find the pages filled with dense writing; but the book held printed text, interspersed with woodcuts to illustrate variations in Valdori letter shapes and writing styles. *Huh. How about that?*

Senisha responded to his surprise with a shy smile. "Do you like it?"

He returned to the beginning, looking for the printer's page. "Is this a new work? Or a printing of an older one?"

"A new one. There's a team in Chogon doing language research now. These three arrived just a few months ago."

"And the printing?"

Senisha looked confused. "What do you mean?"

"How many copies are there? Do you sell them to the public?" Arandras knew the Quill operated a shop in Anstice, but he'd never been inside. *Are there books on the shelves now, alongside the sparkers and chillers?*

"Oh, no, we don't do that," Senisha said. "Each printing is very small. Just enough to send a copy or two to each schoolhouse."

"Right," Arandras said, amused at his own foolishness. Of course the Quill would keep their knowledge to themselves. Start giving it away and there was no telling where it might end.

The morning passed in relative silence. Without Narvi to debate, Bannard kept his thoughts to himself, either unwilling to interrupt Arandras and Senisha, or doubtful of their capacity to appreciate his thinking. Arandras did likewise. He scanned the books Senisha had brought him, searching for similarities to the phrasing and lettering of the urn, but the meaning of the inscription continued to elude him. Here was a variant on the Valdori root word for rest, with an apparent connotation of deep, undisturbed slumber. Here was an unusual term that sometimes meant *substance* and sometimes *spirit*, and sometimes both at the same time. But the context of the inscription and the meaning behind it remained frustratingly out of reach.

The images, at least, were recognisable, even if they failed to illuminate the mystery. Each showed one or more figures against a stylised backdrop. In one, a single figure strode through a forest, arm outstretched to brush aside a branch. In another, a trio stood atop a city wall alongside a smaller figure. Two figures crossed a bridge; one stood surrounded by children in a marketplace; a multitude assembled in a cavern. None carried any distinguishing mark or gave any hint to their identity.

Around midday a servitor arrived, bearing a tray of bread and fruit and a tall jug of lemon water. Arandras put a marker in his book, set it down on the bench and joined the others around the table.

"Any progress?" Bannard asked around a mouthful of pear.

"Not yet," Arandras said. "You?"

Bannard shook his head.

"Those books are remarkable, though," Arandras said. "How long has this research been going on, do you know? There was nothing like that happening when I was there."

"Not long, I suppose," Senisha said. "Those two were both printed last year. But there are lots of teams now, printing books on all sorts of subjects."

"How many is lots?"

"At least a dozen," Bannard said. "Most of them focus on sorcery, naturally. The rest are about different aspects of Valdori history. What happened under which emperor, how they organised their armies, that sort of thing. And languages."

"It's the new magister," Senisha said. "He says we have no idea how much we already know. So he's having it all written down and sent out to all the schoolhouses."

Bannard reached for another pear. "About damn time, if you ask me."

Arandras chewed thoughtfully on a piece of bread. He'd seen the previous magister a few times back in Chogon, but all he could remember of him was the way his eyes only ever opened halfway, as though he were constantly fighting to stay awake. For someone ostensibly in charge of the entire Quill organisation, he'd never seemed to actually do very much. *Sounds like the new guy has no lack of energy, though.*

"So what other sorcerers are there in Anstice these days?" Arandras said. "Besides the Quill, I mean."

Bannard frowned. "I don't know. Why do you ask?"

"Just curious."

"There's a dozen Bel Hennese on the Illith road," Senisha said. "Right next to the building with the bright blue roof. Then there's that crazy woman up near East Bridge who says she can bind clay. Sometimes one of the street kids will ask her for lessons, but they never last long. Oh, and there's another group on the eastern thoroughfare, with fake cannons above the gate —"

"Who more or less mind their own business, same as all the rest," Bannard broke in. "Crazy women aside, of course."

"Is that true?" Arandras asked Senisha.

She nodded. "There's always a few little bands of supposed sorcerers making noise about how dangerous they are, but that's usually a good sign there's not much to them. The ones who keep quiet are the serious ones."

Bannard chuckled. "Who'd have thought?" he said, his tone just short of mockery. "It seems our own librarian is an expert on the sorcerers of Anstice."

Her face reddening, Senisha lowered her eyes and turned away. Bannard shot a glance at her back as she returned to her stool, but made no further comment.

The afternoon sun slanted through the narrow windows, the dusty sunbeams stretching and narrowing as the hours slipped by. Arandras was halfway through the second of a new batch of books — a handwritten volume, at least fifty years old — when the text abruptly ceased its study of Valdori tongues and shifted to a discussion of old Yanisinian. He turned the page, then stopped as a heading caught his eye. *Yanisinian grammar: Fourteen rules of declension.*

Something sparked in his mind, and he looked back at the inscription on the urn. *Surely not.* He scanned the page, looking for confirmation — and there it was. A three-letter suffix, the same as on the inscription's first word. A suffix that had no parallel in any known Valdori dialect.

"Um," he said. "I might have something here..."

The second word was harder, and for a moment he thought he had been mistaken; but there it was, an almost identical word form given as an example of the sixth declension.

The third word was effortless.

Arandras laughed. "Weeper's tears, that's it! No wonder I couldn't make sense of it."

"What?" Bannard's squint was comical for its urgency. "What are you saying?"

"The inscription!" Arandras grinned delightedly at the others. "Each word combines a Valdori root with a Yanisinian declension to

make an entirely new term. You can recognise some of them, sort of.
But you'd never be able to decipher the whole thing knowing just
one language."

"But you can?"

"Oh, yes," Arandras said. "Just give me a minute."

Bannard and Senisha crowded behind him, watching over his
shoulders as he set down the translation, word by word. When he
was done, he picked it up and read it aloud.

"'Here lies the Emperor's first legion. May its spirits rest undisturbed until the end of time.'"

"Spirits?" Senisha said. "What spirits? What does that mean?"

"I don't know." The flush of success slowly drained from Arandras. "Has anyone ever heard of a first legion?"

"I have." Bannard looked as though he had just swallowed something both sour and sweet. "You have too. Everyone has."

"What are you talking about?"

Bannard picked up the urn. "See these figures? They're not people. Not the large ones. The small ones, they're people. The large
ones — they're the Emperor's first legion. Better known to most of
us by another name."

Hells. "Golems," Arandras said.

Bannard nodded. "A Valdori golem army. Tucked away somewhere out of sight for the last two and half thousand years." He held
up the urn. "And this is the key to finding them."

∽

"Nothing," Clade said. *Again.* He leaned across and dropped the
stack of papers by the others. "What next, do you think?"

"The lower shelves, maybe?" Sera looked up from her own pile
of paperwork. "We've barely touched them yet. Maybe that's where
your man is hiding."

They sat together in Garrett's room, alone but for the brooding
presence of the god. The room had been a mess even before they'd
started. Now it looked like the site of a windbinders' duel. Shelves
overflowed with an eclectic assortment of items — bottles, feathers,
coppers, books, even eating utensils and items of clothing — and
in and through and among it all, endless reams of paper. A few of

the upper shelves stood empty, their former contents now rising in haphazard piles along the far wall where they had been dumped by Clade or Sera after painstaking review. Somewhere in the room, Clade was sure, was an address, or a contact, or something to indicate the means by which Garrett had communicated with the men he'd sent after the urn. All Clade had was the leader's name. Terrel.

And he wouldn't even have had that if Garrett hadn't slipped up.

It had seemed like a good idea at the time. Ignorance bought deniability, and deniability had seemed essential. But with deniability had come dependence; and now, with Garrett out of the picture and Estelle demanding progress, ignorance was a hindrance he could not afford.

And never mind Estelle. This Terrel might have the urn right now and be waiting for Garrett to come and collect it. One way or another, Clade had to find him.

He pushed himself to his feet. The tall bookcase ran almost the entire length of the wall. A long-legged spider hung from the corner of one of the shelves, its web extending over half the shelf's width and encompassing a tin cup, a pair of dice, and a sealed inkwell. Thick sheafs of paper jammed the neighbouring shelf, shoved in among mismatched, yellowing tomes. He pulled the documents free with thumb and forefinger, shaking them off at arm's length. A pair of dead moths fluttered to the ground.

A mercenary named Terrel shouldn't be that hard to find. How many can there be? Not that Clade had much idea how to go about finding out. That was what Garrett had been for. *Damn you, Garrett. Even in death you find ways to hinder me.*

The man's body remained in the cool Oculus cellar, sealed in a eucalypt casket not three paces from where it should have been: Clade's stillbox, a man-sized, sorcery-charged box, its true function a carefully guarded secret, kept for precisely this contingency. It was his hidden die, to be rolled only when no option remained but to remove someone from his path. If Clade had only kept his wits, Garrett might be lying there right now with nobody the wiser. Instead, the stink of his corpse had begun to seep through the wooden casket, its stench filling the thick cellar air; though to Clade, the whole building already seemed full of the scent.

Perhaps the funeral would lay it to rest, or at least provide a fresh distraction. Estelle had described Garrett's death to the others as a self-inflicted wound caused by a binding gone wrong, and announced that the Oculus would hold a formal Tri-God service for him — a surprising decision, and not just because of the cost. The sight of several dozen Oculus sorcerers and retainers following a body through the streets could not help but draw the city's attention. It seemed, however, that their time for maintaining a low profile had come to an end.

"Clade," Sera said. "Can I ask you a question?"

"Certainly." The Oculus aside, only one real resource remained to Clade: his Quill insider, unknown to anyone but him. Not that this was exactly the Quill's speciality either. *The Quill can afford to keep their own muscle. They probably have even less idea about dealing with mercenaries than me.*

"Is it true you and Councillor Estelle have found some golems?"

He looked up, startled. A swell of hunger billowed out from the god.

"It is true! I knew it!" Sera gave a delighted laugh. "When do I get to see one?"

"How do you know about the golems?"

"I overheard Kalie talking to the Councillor. Oh, don't look at me like that, I didn't mean to. I just came around a corner and there they were."

"I see," Clade said. Kalie had been with the Anstice outpost for years, far longer than Clade himself. Her talents as a waterbinder were modest, but she had a calm disposition and methodical approach that stood out among her sometimes fractious peers. Clade had chosen her to pick up some of the organisational load left by Garrett, and Estelle, it seemed, had decided to bring her in all the way. The thought left Clade feeling vaguely nettled, as if a confidence had been violated.

"So?" Sera blinked across the table like an expectant puppy. "What are they like?"

Something in her expression caught his eye, something innocent and trusting and vulnerable. A sudden desire caught him to cast secrecy aside and reveal all, tell her everything about the Oculus and the god, the urge as fresh and unexpected as a spring storm. He raised hurried walls, caught hold of the unwelcome feeling and tucked it aside. Yet some part of it remained, something he couldn't quite name: not love, thank the gods, but something not entirely unlike it.

I invited you in, and you trusted me. You trusted us all. And we turned you into another like us: a vessel for the god, its eyes and ears and hands. A thing for it to use.

And you don't even know it.

He couldn't tell her. Not with his plans at such a delicate juncture. A life had room for only one absolute. Nothing could be allowed to threaten that.

She looked at him, hopeful. Waiting.

Ah, hells. Maybe he couldn't tell her anything that mattered; but he could, perhaps, find a way to answer her question.

"I can't tell you about those ones," he said. "Not yet. And you should forget whatever you heard. You'll be told what you need to know when you need it."

Sera nodded, chastened. "As you say, Clade."

"Good."

"I didn't mean to intrude..." She broke off and looked up. "Wait. What do you mean, those ones?" Her eyes widened. "Are you saying we have *others?*"

Clade hesitated. Technically, the story he was about to tell was no secret. His report had been submitted to the archives in Zeanes, just like any other. Any member of the Oculus could find it if they knew where to look. There was no reason the god would object to him telling Sera, so long as he was careful.

"I saw one," he said. "Once. A long time ago."

"A golem?"

He nodded. "A golem."

He'd been on assignment near Scarpton, tracking down an informant who'd gone quiet. The man, a junior officer in the Scarpton militia, had provided a steady stream of intelligence since being purchased by the Oculus some three years before. He'd sent a message describing plans to look into a strange find in the mountains to the city's south — and then he had disappeared. Someone had to investigate.

Clade had followed the man's trail through the wooded foothills of the Kemenese to a clearing, bordered on two sides by a high
sandstone cliff, its wall streaked horizontally with long, colourful
striations. When first he saw the ruined face and torso staring down
from a ledge, he ignored it, taking it to be a relic of some primitive
and likely extinct tribe. Far more interesting was the patch of earth
at the edge of the clearing, poorly disguised by a few branches: a
makeshift grave, made by someone who plainly had no idea how to
go about hiding it.

It was pure chance that the two Jervians arrived just as Clade
was emptying his bladder into a small copse away from the clearing. They came burdened with timber and hammers, and as Clade
crouched behind a dense bush they proceeded to construct a crude
ladder. With the combination of distance and noise, it was hard to
make out more than a few words of their conversation, but one of
those words was enough to capture his undivided attention. *Golem.*

"It took them the whole afternoon to figure out a way to move
it," Clade said. "In the end they sank rings into the cliff. I can only
imagine it was some kind of stonebinding. They fed some ropes
through and managed to get the thing down."

"What was it made of?"

"I don't know. It had a strange mottled look, one I've never seen
anywhere else. It made a strange noise when it bumped the cliff —
thin, I suppose you'd say, sort of like when you scrape something ce-
ramic, or something halfway between clay and stone. And it looked
like it had been through a war. Its arms and legs were mangled
clumps. The side of its head was a shattered mess."

"Gods," Sera said, her voice little more than a whisper.

"And it was big, too. I didn't realise how big until they got it
down. The torso and head stood as high as a man's breast. Its ear
was the size of a fist."

"Did it... you know, do anything? Move?"

"Not that I saw." Beneath Clade's rapt attention, the head and
torso had remained entirely still. Yet Clade had thought he sensed...
something. A presence. Not at all like the god, yet more like that
than anything else. As though something within the ruined shell

still remained.

Sera shifted slightly, her rapt gaze fixed on Clade. "What happened?"

He shrugged. "The men converted the ladder into a sling and carried the golem away. I followed for a while, but when the forest turned to scrub I had to give up the pursuit. I spent the next few days going from village to village, but I never found their trail."

"Gods. It's frightening when you think about it."

"How so?"

Sera's face twisted into a grimace, one that Clade had seen her use often back in Zeanes. *Come on, you're not stupid,* the expression seemed to say. "Who were those people? Quill, or Bel Hennese? Someone else? What else have they found that we don't even know about?" She shivered. "These golems you and Estelle have found. What if someone else gets to them first? What would they do with them?"

What do you think we *would do with them?* The words hovered on Clade's lips for a moment; then he clamped his mouth shut. Madness, to ask that question with the god right here. Besides, he knew what Sera would say. *She'd say what I would have said, back when I was freshly bound.*

Clade's first loyalty had always been to the cause. The Oculus had shown it to him and he had believed, convinced of their passion and commitment. The Valdori had fallen, but the wonders they had wrought and the blessings they had bestowed were merely obscured, not lost. The Empire could be restored. A new golden age could be established, and this time there would be no fall. This time, it would last.

By the time he learnt the truth about the canker at the Oculus's heart, the parasite god that haunted them all, it was too late. He had thought to commit himself to the cause, but instead he had given himself over to Azador itself; and whether or not it was a god in truth, it plainly lacked nothing in at least one divine attribute. Azador was jealous.

Did it really seek the Empire's return? Perhaps it did, to some extent. Maybe that part was true. But that wasn't its first commitment. Its true loyalty was to itself.

A life had room for only one absolute. Azador's was Azador. *But I still believe. The restoration of the Empire, and all that will come with it.*

Life.

"Oh," Sera said. "What did you say his name was?"

What? Who? He looked up.

"That mercenary." Sera had a paper in her hand and a crease in her brow. "Terrel, was it?"

"Yes, that's right. What is it?"

She smiled. "I think I've found him."

The covered Tri-God wagon pulled up in the Oculus courtyard late in the afternoon, carrying four priests in sable and pearl-grey robes. Clade greeted them with a formal bow, then stood back and allowed Kalie to direct them to the cellar. They emerged a few minutes later bearing the sealed casket on their shoulders. With the ease of long practice they slid it onto the wagon, tying it in place with a series of buckled leather straps. Two remained in the back; the others helped Estelle onto the driver's bench, then swung up after her to commence the slow procession to the temple.

The afternoon air was cool, unusually so for the season. The priests kept the pair of horses to a slow walk, allowing Clade and the other followers to keep pace without exertion. All of the bound sorcerers and numerous servants were in attendance, trailing the wagon in a single, formless mass. Sinon strode nearby, his brawler's frame blocking Clade's view to the left, trading quips with Rathzange, the stoop-shouldered Gislean claybinder, and Ulthor, a servant whose fair skin and hair marked his ancestry as either Jervian or Pekratan. Beyond them walked Kalie and her sister Meline, their gait and posture an uncanny reflection one of the other. Sera walked near the front of the group, just behind the wagon. Clade caught a glimpse of her through the crowd: head bowed, one hand touching edge of the wagon, the other covering her face as though in prayer.

It was a strange thing, when you stopped to think about it. Azador was a god, or so the Oculus were told. Yet whenever something *real* happened — a birth, a death, a vow of marriage or vengeance or reconciliation — nobody ever thought to invoke Azador as witness. Nor did anyone pray to it, or not that Clade had ever heard of. The very notion seemed odd. *One might as well pray to the Council, or to the archon in his palace.* It was understood, somehow, that the god had no interest in the mundane details of individual lives. One could look to the Tri-God in such matters, or the All-God, or even the northern fire cults, and Azador wouldn't care. Such trivia was beneath its notice.

Every other god must endure endless petitions from its followers. Hear my vow. Grant my desire. Witness my pain. Even the Sareans, who held the All-God to be indifferent to its human creations, still clung to the hope of snaring his notice once in life and so gaining passage to his favour after death. *But not us. We expect nothing from our god. We give without hope of receiving back.*

The priests in the wagon ahead might call that sainthood.

Was that what they were? Saints? Clade thought not. Azador was a taskmaster, nothing more. The Oculus expected nothing from it not because of their own virtue but from knowledge of its character. Yet the strange thought remained, buzzing around the inside of his skull like an insect that refused to die.

They reached the pantheon as the first streaks of pink touched the clouds. The god had escorted them through the city and over the Tienette, but the brooding presence lifted as they passed through the filigree gate into the yard with its great three-fold statue. The priests steered the wagon around the giant figures and drew up before the temple. Boys in matching sable and grey hurried out to take charge of the horses and to help Estelle down from the wagon. The priests repeated their earlier process in reverse, unloading the casket and carrying it into the temple. Clade and the others followed them in.

The sanctum was huge. Wide and high at the rear, it narrowed and descended in a series of curved steps to a semicircular platform at the front. Coloured tiles covered the walls and ceiling in a breathtaking sequence of mosaics, each showing a scene from Tri-God scripture: the Dreamer, her hand outstretched to create the world and the heavens, her work stark and beautiful, yet still barren; the Weeper watering the earth with his tears, his sorrow quickening the soil to life and so bringing forth the first trees; the Gatherer, arms raised, imbuing the infant world with the gift of purpose and completion; and dozens more. High windows ran the length of each wall, those on the west admitting the soft light of the setting sun.

The priests set the casket down at the front of the platform. Clade and the others filed down to the front of the sanctum, footsteps echoing in the emptiness, and seated themselves on the low ledges. The vast room could have accommodated hundreds. Their group of a scant two dozen seemed barely worth noticing.

If this was how Azador felt in temples, no wonder it avoided them.

"Brothers and sisters, dry your tears."

The speaker was a priest, but not one of the four who had come for the body. This man was bearded and broad-shouldered, similarly dressed in robes of sable and grey but with gold stitching about the neck and wrists. His voice was that of a practised orator: clear, resonant, with a subtle note of invitation. He stood alone on the platform with the casket, his gaze lifted to the rear of the auditorium as though the room were filled to capacity. With his arms raised, he seemed the very image of the Gatherer come to life.

Priests, Clade thought, impressed despite himself and amused to find it so. *Even mummers and noblewomen care less about their appearance.*

"Brothers and sisters, I say again, dry your tears."

Clade glanced sidelong at the assembled sorcerers and servants. Meline was dabbing her eyes, as was one of the servant girls, but that was all. Garrett had had few true friends, and whatever family he had was up north in Eastcliff. Clade's message informing them of Garrett's death probably wouldn't arrive for weeks.

"Brothers and sisters, I say for the third time, dry your tears. Our brother, Garrett Drasso, no longer weeps with us. He rests now in the halls of the Gatherer, as must we all when our lives here are done, there to await the end of all things."

The priest settled into his discourse, expounding on Garrett's life, his gifts, and which of the Twenty Virtues he had particularly upheld. Clade allowed his attention to drift. He'd met with the priest's acolytes the previous day, half worried that one of them might attempt to speak with the dead man's spirit, as some of the

Gatherer's servants were reputed to do. But either the stories were groundless, or Garrett simply wasn't worth the effort. The acolytes had asked him questions about Garrett's life, which he'd answered as best he could, and then they'd left.

The exercise had been tedious enough the first time and Clade saw no need to attend to it again, the priest's numerous embellishments and exaggerations notwithstanding. *Only half of what I told them was true, anyway. What we're getting now is even less than that.* It seemed appropriate. The man had built a life around wearing masks to gain advancement. How better to remember him in death than this?

His thoughts turned to Sera, and the conversation they'd shared earlier in the day. The uncomfortable feeling that had seized him still lingered, unnamed and uncaptured. Perhaps, somehow, he felt responsible for her. It was he who had trained her, at least to begin with; he who encouraged her on the path, convinced her that she was capable of joining them. But for him, she might still be free.

Or perhaps not. If he hadn't been there, someone else may have taken up his role. Perhaps, in the end, his actions had changed nothing.

Nonetheless, I was there. I am responsible.

But what could he do now? Plan to take her with him, free her as well as himself? The thought was madness. Even if she wanted it, the risk would be far too high. And if she didn't want it, or wasn't sure…

No, the whole thing was impossible. Sera was Oculus now. She belonged to Azador, just like the rest of them. Which meant Clade had to keep her out. Just like the rest of them.

"Garrett has left us," the priest said, his tone that of one drawing important matters to a close. "Yet hope remains. He shared this hope, as do all of us here today. It is written that at the end of time, all things will change. The Dreamer will awaken. The Weeper will smile and laugh. And the Gatherer will release all that has been gathered. On that day, at the end of all days, we will see our brother once more. And we will never be parted again."

The priest bowed his head, and several of the Oculus did likewise. The four casket bearers stood, raising the box to their shoulders and beginning the climb back through the sanctum as the priest on the platform prayed.

"Great Gatherer, we commit our brother Garrett to your care, trusting that you will keep him, and us, until your great task is done. We honour you. We thank you. Amen."

Clade sighed. The ceremony was over. The others stirred, and the hall was suddenly filled with the sound of half a dozen conversations all starting at once. He stood, twisting to stretch the muscles in his back. *Never be parted again. Gods, what a horrible thought.*

"We leave for the burial ground at hour's end," the priest said, his voice rising effortlessly above the low hum. "Those who wish to accompany the body should wait in the yard outside."

The Oculus began to file out in groups of two or three. Clade hung back, watching them as they left. There were no tears now. A good sign.

"Sera," he said, catching her sleeve as she filed past. "A moment?"

Sera glanced up, her expression uncharacteristically sober. She gave a faint smile, nodded.

He drew her away, out of earshot of the others. "How are you holding up?"

"Well enough." The smile on her face turned rueful. "It's funny, you know. I didn't think I believed in this any more. Well, that's not true. It's not that I've turned away from them." She gestured vaguely at the gods depicted on the ceiling. "It's more like... I don't know. I didn't think they mattered so much, I guess, now that I have Azador. But being here, and with the service..." She shrugged.

"That's every priest's job in a nutshell, isn't it?" Clade said. "To convince you that what they're talking about matters."

The faint smile returned, acknowledging the joke. "Not all of them, surely?"

"All that I've ever met."

"You don't do that, I mean."

He cocked his head, unsure of her meaning.

"Oh, I know you're not really a priest. Not in the same way. But it's similar, isn't it? Azador speaks to the Council. They relay his words to you. You lead us here in Anstice." She met his gaze, and something in her eyes spoke of secrets on the brink of confession.

"But you're not like the others. You don't spend all your time trying to convince us to think something. You act as if it's perfectly obvious what to think and just get on with the practical, everyday matters." The twinkle returned to her eye. "That's what I found so appealing, you know. A god that doesn't need its followers defending it all the time — that's a god worth following."

He stared, not willing to believe what he heard. *You looked at me, and thought you saw — what? The confidence of the god? Were my true feelings so easy to miss?* But of course she'd mistaken him, she and all the others. He'd done everything possible to make it so.

"We should go," Sera said, glancing up to the rear of the room. The great sanctum was empty now, save for the two of them, and an assistant priest surveying the room from beside the door. "We don't want to miss the burial."

"Of course."

They made their way up the steps and out to the anteroom. Most of the Oculus were already gone, either waiting in the yard as instructed or returning home, but Estelle remained, leaning heavily on her stick just inside the door. She looked up at their approach.

"Ah, Requiter. Good. Shall we lay our man to rest?"

"Will Azador be there, do you think?" The words came out before he could stop them. He cursed inwardly, immediately regretting them. But Estelle simply smiled as though he had asked about nothing more significant than the weather, and tapped his chest with the top of her stick.

"Of course it will, Clade. How could it not? Azador sees all."

CHAPTER 12

Who among us has not spoken more harshly than we intended, or hastened to mock something only half-understood? Such barbs are seeds, cast heedless into the air; and though nine may fall amid rocks and thorns, the tenth takes root, sending forth shoot and leaves until it stands proud beneath the sun, ready for harvest.

Thus does our past reappear, with knives.

— Tiysus Oronayan, *Histories,* Second Volume

ARANDRAS PEERED AT HIS DISTORTED reflection in the bulbous glass mirror held by the barber, then scowled and waved it away. "I'm sure it's fine," he said, smoothing his clipped hair and scraping his palm against his beard.

The barber grunted and reached for a comb, shoving it through Arandras's remaining hair with enough force to scratch his scalp. After half a dozen such strokes, apparently satisfied with his handiwork, the barber emitted another grunt and pulled the smock over Arandras's head, releasing him from its heavy folds.

A breath of cool, late-afternoon air stole in through the open doorway, momentarily lightening the close atmosphere within the shop. Arandras deposited a pair of copper duri into the barber's meaty palm and resisted the temptation to grunt his thanks. Settling for a nod, he stepped out of the shop and into a narrow alley, following its angled path down to a small riverside plaza just inside the city wall.

Mara sat on a bench near the water's edge, a sliver of sunlight highlighting the top of her head but leaving the rest of her in shadow. The bench faced the powder works and redoubt on the other side of the river; the city's centre stretched away to the right, the view framed by Bastion Bridge and the line of the old wall. A procession of some sort seemed to be approaching the bridge, though it was hard to tell through the narrow gaps in the stonework. *Looks like a funeral train,* Arandras thought, peering at the knot of walkers. *What a tawdry thing to do to someone who's just died. Parading them through the streets like a damn trophy.*

He came to a halt before the bench. The seat was comfortably sized for two, but Mara sat in the middle, her arms outstretched against its back. Arandras squinted down, the sun warm on his face. "Care to move over?"

She grinned and shuffled sideways. "Nice cut," she said as he sat down.

Arandras narrowed his eyes. "Why, what's wrong?"

"Hmm? Oh, nothing." A smirk touched the corner of her lips and he watched her try to push it away. "Not unless you count the bare patch on your cheek…" The smirk won out, and she broke into laughter.

"You're a bad liar," he said. "You know that, right?"

"Whatever you say."

Arandras surveyed the river, wrinkling his nose at the faint smell of rot. Not far from their position, a heavily laden barge made laborious progress against the current, half a dozen polemen straining to propel the boat toward one of the arched channels at the bottom of the outer wall. Even with its oars shipped, the barge seemed too wide to fit through the opening; but as Arandras watched, it glided into the tunnel, slowly vanishing like an illusionist's toy, the curved roof of its cabin perfectly matching the shape of the stone above it.

He let out his breath with a heavy sigh. "We found something," he said.

"You know who sent the letter?"

"No. Something else." Arandras glanced around, but the nearest people were a pair of young lovers giggling on the next bench. He lowered his voice anyway. "It's the urn. We think it leads to a Valdori golem army."

"What?"

"Bannard ran off to find Narvi as soon as we figured it out. They were heading in to see Damasus when I left. Weeper knows who Damasus will want to tell. Someone in Chogon, probably."

"A golem army." Mara laughed. "Gods. No wonder those Quill who dug up the urn were killed for it."

"Yeah," Arandras said morosely. "No wonder."

Of all the wonders wrought by the Valdori, golems had been the greatest. Constructs of earth and stone, shaped like giants, their every action directed by their master. In truth, they were little more than glorified puppets — yet what puppets they were. Depending which histories one read, golems had either hastened, postponed, or triggered the Calamities and the fall of the Valdori. *And now I as good as have an army of them right here in my bag, and tomorrow the Quill will be slavering at my feet.*

Weeper spare me.

The great waterwheels on the other side of the river swung slowly around in their never-ending revolution. One had a missing paddle, and Arandras watched as the gap rose into the air, crested the circumference, then slid downward, diving beneath the surface before emerging and beginning its ascent again.

"It doesn't help," he said at last. "I thought learning the urn's purpose would lead me to whoever was looking for it. But who wouldn't want to find… them?"

Mara gave him an amused look. "You mean besides yourself?"

"Gods. It could be anyone."

"Not anyone," Mara said. "They'd have to know about it in the first place."

"Which only leaves scholars, sorcerers, children listening to stories from their nurses…"

"No. I mean this specific urn, buried in a forest in the middle of nowhere."

The gap in the wheel slipped below the water again. "What's your point?"

"That the problem is no harder today than it was yesterday," Mara said. "And if the urn's not leading you to your man, there are other avenues to try. Find out who else calls Anstice home. Sorcerers.

Groups, independents. Anyone who might be in a position to find
out about the urn and use it."

"And then what? Knock on their door and ask whether they've
killed any Quill lately?"

"We can work that out later. First things first."

A trio of round coracles floated out from one of the tunnels beneath the wall, each following the one ahead like beads on a string.
Arandras had seen them on previous visits to the city: circular boats
made of skins stretched over a wooden frame, each filled with straw
then loaded with cargo and rowed down the Tienette by men from
the villages upstream. On arrival in Anstice, the villagers would sell
the cargo, then the straw, then the wood of the frame; then, having
purchased some goods and a beast to bear them, they would bundle the skins onto its back and make their way home. Sometimes,
instead of buying an animal, they would bring one with them; but
Arandras could see no donkey aboard any of the vessels now drifting past, just casks and crates and straw.

He sighed and stretched out his legs. "I hear there's a madwom-
an down the other end of the city," he offered. "Teaches claybinding,
apparently."

"Oh?"

"Uh huh."

Mara eyed him suspiciously. "And how exactly do you know that?"

"And there's a nest of Bel Hennese just across the river," he continued. "Well, probable Bel Hennese. It's hard to be sure. You know."

She fixed him with a level gaze. "Arandras."

He smiled. "Senisha was telling me about them."

"What, the librarian?"

"The same. Seems to know the shape of the city quite well."

"Huh. Well, good." Mara leaned back, propping her elbows up
on the back of the bench. "Get addresses if you can. It'll make it
easier."

"Make what easier?" Arandras said, but Mara made no reply.

The coracles passed under the old wall and out of sight. Across
the river, a bird alighted on one of the wheels, riding the paddle to
the top and then fluttering away.

"A golem army," Mara said, gazing out over the shadowed water.

"Wouldn't that be something to see?"

But the excitement that had filled Bannard and Senisha and that now tinged Mara's voice was absent in Arandras. The Quill could have the damn golems, for all he cared. They'd be willing to bankrupt every schoolhouse in Kal Arna to buy the urn now. Once he found his man, he'd sell it to them, and good riddance.

"Mara," he said. "The urn... it doesn't really matter. You know that, right? And the golems, they don't matter either. The only thing that matters is finding that man, and..."

Killing him. Arandras froze, the words hanging unspoken in the air between them. But Mara's face showed no shock, no surprise; only a strange resignation. Her hand brushed his arm.

"I know," she said.

He flinched away from her touch, wrapping his arms tightly across his chest. "How?"

Somehow, she divined his meaning.

"We were thieves," she said at last, and her mouth twitched as though in memory of a smile. "Just the two of us. He was good. Fast and supple, like a great cat." She looked away, her voice going flat. "One night we hit a whoremonger. Woman as fat as an oxcart. Didn't realise she had a pet sorcerer." Her shoulders moved in a barely perceptible shrug. "He got caught. They kept him for weeks. Toyed with him. When they finally let him go, he was broken. Just... broken. I had to..." She broke off and angrily tossed her head. "The lawmen didn't want to know. Why would they? We were thieves. So... it was just me."

Arandras waited for her to go on, but she seemed to have run out of words. He swallowed. "Did you...?"

She nodded. "Both of them."

"Did it help?"

A shrug. "It needed doing."

She stared away at nothing, fists tight but eyes dry. Arandras rubbed his lip, not sure what to say. The waterwheels turned and turned, the gap from the missing paddle rising and falling and rising again. When at last she spoke, her voice was so soft that he had to strain to hear it over the lapping of the water.

"No," she said. "It didn't help. But it needed doing."

~

"Golems," Fas said, gazing out at the assembled Quill with an expression that put Arandras in mind of a mummer commencing a long-winded soliloquy. "Here's what we know."

The new workroom was half again as wide as the old room, and twice as long. Some dozen Quill were gathered at one end of the room for the briefing, Narvi and Senisha among them. From his position by the wall, Arandras could see Bannard standing behind Fas, hands fidgeting as he tried — with limited success — to give the appearance of paying attention to the other man's words. *You and me both,* Arandras thought, fighting a yawn as Fas ran through the rudiments of known golem history.

"The Valdori created the golems to serve as soldiers. The secret of their construction remains one of the great mysteries of the Empire, but the accounts we have suggest that some form of spiritbinding was the key." Fas paused significantly, his gaze sweeping the room, and Arandras stifled a laugh. *Weeper, but that man enjoys the sound of his own voice.*

"Golems had no will of their own," Fas continued. "They were created to be bound to the will of a master. A golem could have only one master at a time, and that master wasn't always a sorcerer. The Valdori bound golems to military commanders, typically no more than ten or twelve golems per master. Each squad of golems thus had its own human captain who would direct its actions from a position close enough to be effective but far enough from the fray to maintain relative safety."

Or so they thought. Fas's summary was accurate enough as far as it went, but none of it was even remotely certain. Everything anyone knew about the golems was built on fragmentary records, cautious supposition, and outright speculation. Arandras folded his arms. *A little humility in the face of our collective ignorance wouldn't go astray.*

"What are their weaknesses?" The question came from a tall, fair-haired man whom Narvi had earlier introduced to Arandras as Ienn, a firebinder and swordsman who would likely lead the anticipated field team to retrieve the golems. Ienn had the weathered look of one who spent most of his time under the sky — a rarity among the Quill. "How did people fight them?"

"With tremendous difficulty," Fas said. "Sorcery was the only thing that had any real effect. Even then, it was more about incapacitating the golems than destroying them. Burying them in the earth, say. Or you could go for the commanders, of course, though that had dangers of its own."

"Like what?"

Fas turned. "Bannard?"

"Ah. Yes." Bannard stepped forward, squinting at Ienn. "Um. You have to realise we still don't understand how the binding worked. Golem to master, I mean. But in the accounts where a master is killed mid-battle, the golems tend to react unpredictably. Sometimes they just go dormant and refuse to be re-bound by another master, for anywhere from a few hours to several months. But sometimes it's like their master's last orders stay with them even after he's dead. There are stories of the Valdori having to use their own golems to subdue others that have gone rogue after the loss of their master."

"What about anamnil?"

"Maybe, to break the link between golem and master. It'd be unlikely to harm the golem itself."

"Could a master relinquish his golems voluntarily?" asked someone on the other side of the room.

"We believe so," Bannard said. "But again, we're not sure how."

Truth is, we know practically nothing, Arandras thought as Bannard embarked on a discussion of the urn and what they'd learnt so far. *We assume the Emperor had his own personal coterie of golems to guarantee his position, because it's the only power base we can think of that makes sense. But really, who knows?* Perhaps Tereisa's killer knew more. If he really had set this whole thing up, he'd have to know where the urn led.

Maybe I'll ask him before he dies.

A mention of his own name pulled Arandras's attention back to Bannard. "Arandras solved it, in the end. The inscription is — well, in short, each word is a combination of Valdori and Yanisinian elements. Translated, it says, 'Here lies the Emperor's first legion. May its spirits rest undisturbed until the end of time.'"

"First legion?" repeated a plump woman with a stubbled red-brown scalp and a bandage covering one ear. *That must be the sorcerer who botched the unbinding. Halli.* "There's more than one, then."

"Maybe," Bannard said. "Or maybe the golems are the first legion, as opposed to all the other, regular legions. Again, we don't know."

"Where is Arandras?" Fas said, scanning the room. "There you are. Why don't you come up here and show these fine people the urn?"

Every head in the room turned to Arandras. *Oh, wonderful.* Swallowing his reluctance, he made his way to the front.

"Arandras Kanthesi," Fas said, with a wave of his hand as if he had personally conjured Arandras into being. "Former Quill linguist, and the man we have to thank for bringing this puzzle to our attention." He gave Arandras an expectant look.

With an inward grimace, Arandras reached into his pouch and held up the urn. *Seems like all I do here is show this thing off to one Quill or another. A glorified pedestal, that's me.*

"Good, good," Fas said. "With the team expanding, we'll need to make the urn more widely available. Arandras will supervise its use whenever he's present, of course. At other times, we'll find someone else to take charge of it. Narvi, perhaps —"

"No," Arandras said. *Oh, no, you don't, you sneaky bastard.* "The urn stays with me."

Fas's chuckle seemed pitched not at Arandras, but at the watching Quill. "But you see how many of us are now committed to helping you solve this riddle. Some of these people will be working late into the night, and others will start each day before the dawn. You can't possibly be present the entire time."

"No, I can't," Arandras said. "And neither can the urn."

Fas assumed a regretful frown. "Well. We'll discuss this later." He gestured his dismissal to the assembled Quill. "Enough talk," he said. "Go to work."

The Quill dispersed, some leaving the room as others re-formed into smaller groups and began murmured conversations. Narvi caught Arandras's eye on his way out, but the look he cast was beyond Arandras's ability to decipher. Fas hung back, sitting on a vacated stool and busying himself with some papers.

"What in the hells was that?" Arandras said, glowering at the top of Fas's balding head. "I told you how this was going to work. I retain custody of the urn *at all times.* No exceptions."

"Which was fine as long as this was a three-man project," Fas said, not looking up. "It's grown somewhat larger than that now, wouldn't you say?"

"Doesn't matter. Our agreement stands."

Fas set the papers down and stood. On his feet, he was at least a head taller than Arandras. "I've been very patient with you, Arandras," Fas said, his thumb tapping apparently unconsciously against his thigh. "I took up your problem based on nothing but Narvi's good word for you. I gave you food and lodging. I've tolerated your little eccentricities." He gave a slight sigh. "The only way this works is if everyone's prepared to do their part for the whole. You used to work for us, so I know you understood that once. But I'm starting to wonder if, somewhere along the way, you've forgotten it."

More like seen through it. There was no whole, not really; only men like Fas. Arandras took a deep breath. "I remain very happy to cooperate with your scholars and sorcerers, Damasus, just as when I arrived. But I will retain custody of the urn. At all times."

Fas shook his large head regretfully. "You disappoint me, Arandras," he said. "It seems Narvi misjudged you. Blinded by past friendship, I suppose." He sighed. "Well. Despite your intransigence, we're still prepared to honour our agreement. We are not so unprincipled as you seem to imagine. But if you're not prepared to trust us with the urn, I imagine you can't be very comfortable sleeping under our roof, or eating our food. Perhaps you'd like to find other lodgings for the rest of your stay in Anstice."

"Perhaps I would," Arandras snapped. *Honour our agreement, my arse. The Gatherer himself couldn't peel you away from this now.*

"Your friend, too, I imagine."

"Of course."

"Well," Fas said again. "I wish you a productive day." He began gathering his papers. "The Quill is not your enemy, Arandras. Not unless you make it so."

But Arandras was neither the Quill's enemy nor its friend. He was simply himself. *Our relationship is what you make it, Damasus. Everything else is just words.*

∽

Six days after the meeting of the Woodtraders Guild's masters, Kieffe's body remained in Phemia's chill-chest. Eilwen had no idea what was taking Caralange's sorcerer so long, nor which master was paying for the precious hours of chill-chest time. Ten days of continuous use was typically enough to drain the spell dry, rendering the chest inert until a Quill sorcerer could be brought in, at significant cost, to refresh the binding. *We might need two sorcerers this time. One to replenish the binding, and a second to clean the damn box of any leftover corpse bits.*

There'd been a small memorial service for Kieffe the previous day. Laris had brought in a house priest from the Pantheon to perform the rites customarily reserved for cases where the body had been destroyed. Eilwen had gone along, not so much to pay her respects as to see who else might be there. Unfortunately, Laris seemed to have instructed her entire department to attend, many of whom were eager to ask Eilwen how the investigation was proceeding. The tedious rounds of small talk and polite non-answers left her with little opportunity to scan the gathering for unlikely attendees. At one point she caught a glimpse of Vorace across the room talking with Phemia and Soll, but as far as she could tell, neither Havilah nor Caralange had attended.

The image of the cannon barrel nestled in wood shavings haunted her thoughts. In her shock at the discovery of the weapons in Qulah's warehouse, she'd failed to determine how many there were, or how many were yet to come. *Enough to make it impossible for Qulah to fulfil the order out of existing stock, even back in Tan Tahis. How many is that?* The Tahisi merchant had mentioned shot and powder as well, but had said nothing about gun carriages, leaving Eilwen to wonder if the cannons were to be fixed in place, or perhaps used to arm ships. Then again, there was probably nothing special about a gun carriage. If a Woodtrader couldn't arrange the construction of some timber carriages this side of the Sea of Storms, they weren't trying very hard.

The possibility of a separate transaction to procure carriages invited its own line of investigation, albeit one with a familiar problem: the difficulty of getting her hands on any of the records. Havilah's reports, detailed as they were in many respects, simply didn't have the kind of information she needed. But there was no way to demand the relevant records without the masters hearing about it, at which point the information she sought would likely be excised — unless someone decided it would be less trouble to simply have her removed.

She sat on the edge of her desk, her heels raising hollow thuds as they drummed against the varnished eucalyptus panel. *And then there's the coinage.* The notion of paying in Tahisi coin for even one consignment of cannons was improbable, to say the least. It wasn't as though the Woodtraders kept reserves of Jervian talents and Kharjik bezants and Tahisi minza for contingencies like this. Even if the Guild wanted to make the exchange, Eilwen doubted the local money-changers would be able to offer the quantities required. *In a southern port city like Spyridon or Damara, maybe. Not here.*

Unless, of course, the ultimate purchaser was someone with special access to Tahisi currency — perhaps even someone who had been born in Tan Tahis. Someone like Havilah.

No, it doesn't make any sense. Gods, none of this makes sense. What possible use could anyone in the Guild have for a warehouse full of cannons?

A series of loud knocks broke her train of thought. She grimaced, resenting the interruption. "Not now," she called. "Come back later."

There was a pause, then the knocking resumed, softer this time but more insistent. "Open, please," came a muffled voice she recognised as belonging to Ufeus. "You need to hear this."

Oh, for the gods' sake. "Fine," she muttered, marching over and yanking the door open. Ufeus stood in the corridor, Brielle hovering behind him. "What is it?"

Ufeus glanced over her shoulder. "We should talk inside."

Eilwen took a deep breath. *Of course we should.* "Fine."

"It's Dallin," Brielle said as soon as the door closed. "He's dead."

Eilwen shook her head, trying to recall the name. "Who?"

"Dallin Nourt. You remember. Our man at the Exadius company."

Oh. Shit. She looked from Brielle to Ufeus and back again. "Dead."

They nodded.

Eilwen hesitated. "And, uh... not by us?"

"What? No!" Ufeus glared at her as if she had personally accused him of the man's murder.

"Well, not *us* us, anyway," Brielle muttered.

"Who, then?"

Ufeus stared over her shoulder in stony silence, refusing to meet her gaze, so Eilwen looked to Brielle.

"We don't know," Brielle said. "Apparently a Kharjik perfumer noticed him coughing up blood in an alley just north of the river. The perfumer sent his boy for a Quill fleshbinder, but they obviously couldn't help."

"All right. I'm going to have to take this to Havilah." She'd been hoping to put off speaking to Havilah until she'd figured out what to say about her visit to Qulah's, but news of a contact's death couldn't wait. "Do we know anything else?"

Brielle shook her head. Ufeus continued to stare at the wall behind her as if she hadn't spoken.

"Very well. Thank you, Brielle. Ufeus, a moment."

Brielle padded out, closing the door softly behind her. Eilwen sat behind her desk, stretching her bad leg. "All right, Ufeus," she said. "Let's have it. What's your problem?"

Ufeus blinked. "I'm sorry?"

"You heard me. What's your problem?"

Confusion flickered in Ufeus's eyes. He opened his mouth to speak and then closed it again.

"I mean it," Eilwen said. "Tell me what's bugging you. This is your big chance to say what you really think."

"As you say." Ufeus pressed his lips together. "If you must know, I don't appreciate seeing you in that position. My position."

"Yeah. Life's not fair. But Havilah's the boss, and we both do what he says. What else?"

Ufeus narrowed his eyes. His jaw worked, but he said nothing.

"Come on. You're a grown man. I'd expect petty resentment from children, but not you. What else?"

Colour bloomed in Ufeus's face. "Fine," he snapped. "What in the hells are you doing here? You come in with no idea how this place works. You blunder about, ignoring my advice and burning one of our contacts. Then he gets killed, and you have the effrontery to ask if I arranged it! Me! That life is on you, Eilwen! And why is it I'm still doing everything I was doing before? What are you doing with your time, aside from hobnobbing with the masters? Tell me, Eilwen, what exactly are you good for?"

The onslaught of words piled against her like a breaking wave, the impact no less shocking for the fact that she had goaded Ufeus into them. Eilwen gripped the edge of the desk, her knuckles white. Ufeus glared through slitted eyes, his breath short. She closed her eyes and tried to gather her thoughts.

"You're right," she said at last. "I ignored your advice, and I shouldn't have. You're also right that I haven't truly taken on any of the work you've been doing. That was the plan, but it hasn't turned out that way." She fell silent.

Ufeus raised his eyebrows. "That's it?"

Eilwen hesitated. *Don't involve Ufeus,* Havilah had told her. But he was involved. All of them were, whether they liked it or not. "That's all I can say," she said at last. "If you want to know more, you'll have to ask Havilah yourself. And he probably won't tell you either."

He scowled. "That's bullshit."

"No. It's not." She stood. "I'm not going to thank you for doing your job. I'm going to expect you to keep doing it. Seems we both know that you'll do it better than I could anyway." She lowered her voice. "But one day soon I may ask you to do more, for the sake of the Guild. That will earn you thanks. And not just from me."

"Really."

"Really." She gestured toward the door. "That'll be all."

The scowl on Ufeus's face lingered, but without intensity, as though it remained only because he didn't know what to replace it with. At the door he turned back. "What do you mean, for the sake of the Guild?"

Eilwen waved her hand in a shooing gesture. "Goodbye, Ufeus."

He left, and Eilwen sagged back into her chair. *What exactly am*

I good for? Damn good question. She was floundering, that was the truth of it. The investigation was a giant cloud of fog, and she was lost in its centre. Any ground she thought solid invariably turned spongy beneath her feet. She needed an anchor, some fixed reference point with which to take new bearings. She needed time to sort through her confusion, time to work out exactly what she knew and what she merely suspected.

But first she needed to go and see Havilah.

~

Havilah took the news more calmly than Eilwen expected. "Well," he said. "It's probably not surprising, all things considered."

"But if they know Dallin talked to us, then they know we're onto them."

"Perhaps. Perhaps not." He eyed her contemplatively. "If you're worried about yourself or Brielle, there's no need. If they thought you were enough of a threat, they'd have done you at the same time."

"Thank you," Eilwen said. "That's very reassuring."

"There'd be no point, anyway. Not unless they knew who you'd told about it."

"Yeah, unless they just wanted to make a statement," Eilwen said, but her words lacked conviction. Whoever was running the operation seemed to be doing as much as they could to avoid making statements. "Brielle said a Quill fleshbinder was there when he died. I'll see if I can track them down, find out what they saw —"

"Which will tell you what, exactly?" Havilah said, his mild tone pulling the sting from the interruption.

Eilwen blinked in surprise. "Well, I don't know. I thought we were kind of interested in who might have killed him."

"So we are. But this is not about chasing down every possible lead in the hope of striking it lucky. This is about getting the most information with the least possible exposure." Havilah spread his hands. "If this conspiracy goes as high in the Guild as it seems, we're only going to get one shot at taking it down. Give ourselves away too early and we won't even get that. So, yes, there's a remote chance the Kharjik perfumer said something to the Quill fleshbinder which would give us a clue as to who had Dallin killed. But there's a much higher chance that you asking that question will put you in line for the same treatment."

"I thought you just told me I didn't need to worry about that."

"Neither you do," Havilah said. "So long as you don't alter the equation by turning yourself into a threat."

"So, what then?" Eilwen said, trying and failing to keep the nettled tone from her voice. "We just sit here and do nothing?"

"We wait. We watch. We use caution."

Yeah, right up until we cautiously watch Vorace get killed. Or is that what you want? Is it you, after all? She put her hand to her lips, not trusting her face to conceal her thoughts.

Havilah passed a sheet of paper across the desk. "Read this."

Eilwen picked it up. "Kieffe's autopsy. Finally."

"Orom found evidence of bluespine in the man's heart, or so he says. I don't know how much you can really tell from a week-old corpse, even with sorcery, but there it is."

"Bluespine," Eilwen repeated. "A Tahisi poison."

Havilah met her gaze. "That's right."

She nodded. "You mentioned it at the masters meeting, if I remember rightly."

"I did."

"An odd coincidence."

Havilah made no response. He seemed relaxed, but there was something in his posture now — an awareness, perhaps — that hadn't been there before.

She moistened her lips. "It seems our killer may have a link with Tan Tahis."

He folded his hands on the desk. "Is there something you want to ask me, Eilwen?"

"Are you... Is it..." She coughed, angry at her treacherous tongue, and all at once the anger swallowed her nerves. "Did you kill them?" she demanded. "Are you playing me, Havilah?"

"No." He held her eyes, his regard neither aggressive nor defensive, but an offer to look and be satisfied. His expression was calm, assured, and guileless.

At last, she looked away.

"Talk to me, Eilwen," he said gently. "Tell me what's going on."

She bowed her head. "I went to Qulah's," she said.

"The Emporium."

"Yes," Eilwen said. "Kieffe had been there. The first part of his order is waiting for him in the warehouse right now." She drew a long, unsteady breath. "It's cannons, Havilah. Qulah has boxes of Tahisi cannon barrels just waiting for Kieffe to pay for them, with more on the way. A lot more."

For a fleeting moment, Havilah's calm expression slipped. "Cannons. You're sure?"

"I saw them myself. And there's more," Eilwen said, suddenly desperate to lay everything out. "Kieffe was going to pay using Tahisi coin. Or he was thinking about it, anyway. It sounded like he hadn't decided." She buried her hands in her hair. "Where does someone here get enough Tahisi currency to lay siege to a city?"

Havilah's attention was no longer directed at her. He stared into space, his thoughts turned inward. "The weapons may not be meant for Kieffe," he said slowly. "Probably he was nothing more than a middle-man."

"We need to go back to Qulah's," Eilwen said. "We need to find out exactly what Kieffe told him, maybe take delivery of a cannon and see if —"

"No! Were you even listening a moment ago?" Havilah's eyes bored into hers, pinning her to the chair. "Everything I just told you about minimising our exposure now counts tenfold. This is bigger than the Woodtraders, Eilwen. Nobody buys weapons on this scale without a very specific plan for using them." His mouth twisted in distaste. "Someone in the Guild senses an opportunity, I suspect. A chance to advance their own ambitions by hitching a ride on somebody else's. I doubt the purchaser of these goods even cares who leads the Guild."

"But we care," Eilwen said. "Don't we?"

The Spymaster's expression softened. "Yes. We care."

"So what do we do?"

"You do nothing," Havilah said. "Do not go back to the warehouse. Do not speak to Qulah. Continue investigating Kieffe's death, but tread lightly. Have you interviewed any of the other masters yet?"

"No," she said, feeling foolish. "I wanted to find out as much as I could before talking to anyone who might be involved."

But Havilah nodded. "Better," he said. "And who do you suspect?"

"Caralange. Laris." She hesitated. "And you."

He tilted his head. "Still?"

"Well. Not so much, now."

Havilah gave a slight smile, and Eilwen had the sense of a matter being laid to rest, just as she had on her return from Spyridon. She'd struggled to find the word for it before, but this time she knew what it was, and the thought brought an unexpected tightness to her throat.

Forgiveness. This is what it feels like to be forgiven.

"I spoke to Pel," Eilwen said, dragging her attention back to the Spymaster before she could embarrass herself further. "If Kieffe wasn't working for Laris, the only real alternative is Caralange." She shrugged. "Phemia's an old woman. She's given her life in service of the Guild. And Soll…"

Havilah nodded. "Phemia has neither the energy nor the inclination to mount something like this. Soll doesn't have the imagination. And Caralange, I think, lacks the subtlety."

Eilwen frowned, considering. Maybe he did, at that. "You think it's Laris."

"The Trademaster supplies most of Soll's coin, the majority of Phemia's goods, and a decent chunk of my intelligence. She's got far more opportunity than anyone else to mislead us all. And she's been butting heads with Vorace over the direction of the Guild ever since he pulled us back to the Free Cities, in the wake of the *Orenda* incident. I've been waiting for her to pull something like this for years."

"Wait. You're telling me you suspected Laris right from the start?"

Havilah folded his hands. "I did."

Eilwen stared. "Then why didn't you just say so? Gods above! I thought we were supposed to be on the same side. Why make me run around in the dark like that?"

His expression was almost sympathetic. "Why do you think?"

Because you weren't sure I'd hear it. Because you needed me to get enough distance to see it for myself. Havilah watched as her understanding dawned, the compassion in his eyes confirming the truth of her inference. As she stared back, a second insight crashed in on the heels of the first. *That's why you picked me. You wanted someone with an in to Laris and her people, someone who could get you to her.*

You cold-blooded son of a bitch.

Havilah leaned forward. "Do you remember what I told you the first time you sat in that chair? I said I needed people who could be uncompromising in the Guild's service. Sometimes that's hard, for you or for someone else. But it's not about either of us. It's about the Guild."

He paused, eyeing her expectantly. Eilwen tried to speak, but her tongue seemed frozen in place. She managed a rough nod.

"Good," he said. "Now, suspicion is all well and good, but we need proof. And we need to gather it carefully. Are you with me on this?"

Havilah's the boss, and we do what he says. The words rang in her ears. She'd said them to Ufeus not even an hour ago. And it was even more than that. This role — this chance to serve the Guild like she should have served it years ago — it was hers because of Havilah. Because of his authority. The two went together. Either she accepted that authority, or she gave up this chance to do something right and found some other way to spend her life.

Gods, Havilah, all I wanted was to trust you. Why do you have to make it so hard?

"Yes," she said. "I'm with you."

CHAPTER 13

Curse the gods if you must, but do it on your horse.

— Halonan proverb

T HE GLOWING GLASS SPHERE SAT on a low wooden pedestal in Clade's study, its gentle radiance filling the otherwise dark room with a soft, warm light. A second orb lay on a cushion beside it, this one dark, larger than the first but no less smooth. Clade perched before them on the edge of a padded chair, head bowed, his fingers laced over the hair at the back of his neck.

She called me a priest.

The memory of Sera's words haunted him. *You're not like the others,* she'd said, and he'd smiled, not yet seeing her true meaning. Then she'd told him. *A god that doesn't need its followers defending it all the time — that's a god worth following.* She'd looked up at him then, like one enlightened believer to another, inclining her head in silent gratitude for the part he'd played in opening her eyes. As if Azador was a god in truth, and he its loyal minister faithfully guiding her to her own salvation.

It made him want to scream.

Enough! With an effort of will, Clade pressed the feeling down. He summoned walls, jamming them one against another and driving the errant emotion within. It beat against the walls of its cage, desperate for release. *No. I am master here, not you.* Slowly, grudgingly, it subsided. He straightened in his chair and took a long, slow breath.

Control. Without it, he was lost. It made no difference what Sera thought, or Estelle, or anyone else. Truth was no less true for being hidden. *You mistook me, Sera, and I regret that. Perhaps, one day, I may have opportunity to repair that error.*

But not today.

He tucked the penned emotion away, ignoring its diminishing protests, and turning his attention to the orbs before him. The lightglass was a thing of beauty: a Bel Hennese piece about the size of a cannonball, its steady inner glow giving it the appearance of something otherworldly. Clade had discovered it in a corner of the building's cellar shortly after his arrival in Anstice. The find had been unexpected, to say the least: the great walled island of Bel Henna was an entire continent away, and the Bel Hennese were notoriously close-fisted with their sorcery. How exactly it had come into the possession of the Oculus was a mystery. *And twice the mystery that it then failed to make the journey back to Zeanes.* A wry smile touched his lips. Perhaps he wasn't the first overseer in Anstice to carry a secret.

The orb's light glinted off the surface of its twin, a fresh piece untouched by sorcery, commissioned by Clade from one of the city's leading glassworkers and collected the day before last. It was larger than the lightglass, and though it was hard to tell, Clade thought the glass fractionally clearer. Alike, yet different. Equivalent in substance and in craftsmanship, but differing in form. An ideal test for his redesigned binding.

He'd made several adjustments to the binding, refining some of the unfamiliar pieces whose purpose he now thought he understood, and strengthening the structural elements beneath. Comprehension of the spell as a whole continued to elude him. The means by which sorcery was made to act upon sorcery still defied his grasp, even though he himself had done it, shifting the chiller binding from one mug to another. But neither piece had emerged intact; and what truly mattered, other than the success of the spell, was the safety of the source. Only if the bound twin emerged from the process unscathed could Clade be satisfied.

Thus would he free himself of Azador's suffocating grasp. No spiritbinder now lived who might dissolve the link directly. This spell, this transfer of a binding from one object to another, was the only way.

He slowed his breathing, clearing his mind and extending his awareness toward the lit sphere. The glass was entirely free of runes, giving no clue to the structure of the binding within. Clade pressed in, slipping past the first strands and sinking into the tight web of sorcery.

The binding flexed beneath his mind's touch, dense and complex and strangely elegant. He chose a line at random and traced it through the elaborate weave. It mirrored the surface in a gentle arc, then dived into the binding's heart, curling this way and that as it danced around neighbouring strands. Other lines joined it, converging on what seemed to be some sort of nexus, then flaring out in new, unexpected directions.

Clade hopped from one strand to the next, marvelling at the remarkable construction. The design was unlike anything he had encountered before: a single, irreducible whole, entirely unlike the modular, compartmentalised approach to spellcraft with which he was familiar. It was as though some unformed essence of sorcery had been mixed with liquid glass and the two materials simultaneously wrought together to craft a single, perfectly balanced object. *Is all Bel Hennese sorcery like this? Or is this simply what's required when working with glass?*

Reluctantly, Clade withdrew his awareness. The unlit globe on the floor seemed a crude thing now, dull and lifeless. He frowned, struck by the improbability of what he was trying to do. Whatever the means used to create the binding, it was part of the sphere now. One might as well try to extract a man's bones from his body as remove the spell from the glowing ball before him. *But no, a binding is a binding. And I have done this once already.*

He knelt before the spheres, settling himself on the floor, and set to work.

Last time, a piece of the mug had broken off, the apparent result of too much energy seeking to pass through too narrow a binding; so now he built a larger, wider base covering almost an entire hemisphere, adding a quartet of supporting conduits that snaked around to the far side of the orb. With the foundation securely in place, he commenced work on the spell itself, building the spur down toward the floor and the waiting globe, pausing at intervals to review his progress and assess the integrity of his work, examining both the correctness of each detail and the balance of the whole. Piece by piece it grew, curving ever downward as though tracing the path of a falling arrow, until at last it reached its end, the tip hanging invisibly to one side of the target globe.

Clade slid the lightless sphere into position... and cursed. It seemed the refined spell was not as large as he'd expected. The sorcerous spur hung half a hand's breadth above the orb's surface, too far to bridge with the final connection.

He reached behind him, groping blindly for something to use as a makeshift platform, but his fingers met only air and the cold stone floor. The bookshelf stood tantalisingly out of reach against the wall. He dared not go over and fetch a book. The binding was incomplete, held in place only by the proximity of his focused intent. Any movement of more than a step away would put it out of his mind's reach and risk a potentially destructive collapse.

Ah, hells.

There was nothing else for it. Gritting his teeth, he slid his hands beneath the unlit globe, the glass cool and smooth against his skin. He lifted it from its cushion, raising it onto his fingers to give it the necessary height and fitting it into position beneath the dangling spur. Then, lips pressed in concentration, he began the final piece.

The first link was the hardest, involving a manoeuvre akin to threading a needle at arm's length; but with that in place, the remaining links followed quickly. Soon it was done and the completed binding hung before him, a woven cable of sorcery connecting the shining sphere on the pedestal to the lifeless globe in his hands. Clade pressed his awareness against it, working his way down the binding, checking his handiwork for flaws. None were evident. The binding was sound.

This had better work. The thought of either sphere shattering was too dire to contemplate. *One in my hands and another in my face. Perfect.* Fear tickled his stomach and he pushed it away, unable to spare the attention needed to deal with it properly. *Sitting here waiting isn't going to achieve anything. Best just cast it and have it over with.*

Clade drew a deep breath, clenched his eyes shut, and activated the spell. A series of faint clicks sounded somewhere before him and he grimaced, bracing for the worst.

After half a dozen heartbeats, he opened his eyes.

Light flickered in his hands, dim and fitful, but unmistakably there. The fresh globe seemed too large for the thin glow within; or perhaps the transition between spheres had weakened the binding. Clade set it down on the cushion, sliding his hands out from underneath, and turned his attention to the Bel Hennese orb.

The sphere was dark, empty of sorcerous illumination; and it was intact.

Excitement sparked within him. Clade pushed it down, taking the emptied orb from its stand and turning it over in his hands. The tip of his finger brushed against a raised edge and he frowned, holding the surface to the other sphere's dim light. *That wasn't there before.* The ridge was fine, barely noticeable, running in an uneven line a third of the way around the globe's circumference. A second, shorter line ran roughly parallel to the first, mirroring a third along the sphere's far side.

Superficial damage only. Not ideal, of course, but a small enough price to pay to finally be rid of the god. Excitement welled up in earnest and he frowned again, driving it down, forcing it into a cage. This was a step on the path, nothing more. When he was free of Azador, then he would celebrate. Not before.

All the same, it was a milestone of sorts. *I need only two things to rid myself of Azador. Today, I have one.* It was good to acknowledge progress: a goal achieved, and a job well done. Soon he would do more. But today, he had done this.

And so Clade sat on the floor of his study and allowed himself to feel satisfaction.

~

The feeling faded as the afternoon progressed. Clade sat in his study, examining and re-examining his memory of the binding, heedless of the growing stacks of unattended paperwork. All Garrett's correspondence was now being delivered to Clade, accumulating in improbable quantities like drifts of snow across his desk. Clade paid it no mind. The business of the Oculus no longer interested him. All that concerned him now was locating the golems, and that meant finding the urn.

The scribbled note found by Sera in Garrett's room had given Clade the meeting place used by Garrett and Terrel — an unfamiliar bar known as the Red Rodent — but had failed to reveal the means by which such meetings were arranged. Lacking any other ideas, Clade had penned a message to the mercenary captain, addressing it to the Red Rodent in the hope that it would find its way to Terrel. The message was short, instructing Terrel to await Clade at the bar this evening, and concluding with an implied offer of further employment and generous compensation: sufficient inducement, he hoped, to ensure the man's attendance.

If not, I suppose I'll just have to do it the gull's way. Ask around and hope for the best.

The sun was setting as Clade left his suite and made his way down the stairs. House servitors watched his passage in the sidelong manner common to servants everywhere: a compromise between the twin needs to remain unobtrusive and to be ready to respond if called for. The constant subtle attention paid him by servants and sorcerers alike had taken a while to get used to. Back on Zeanes, he had simply been another sorcerer of intermediate rank, meriting no more attention than the next man. Though his fame as Requiter had drawn a certain amount of idle interest, that name had carried no real weight, and everyone had known it.

The title of Overseer was entirely different. With it came power; limited, yes, but real nonetheless. And that was what he had become in the eyes of those beneath him; not a person, or at least not primarily so. Now he walked among them as an ever-present threat, as one who could overturn their plans at whim. And so, like reluctant worshippers, they sought to appease him with hard work and friendly manner, and hoped he would take no interest in their lives.

Just as he did with Estelle.

As though summoned by his thought, the slow tap of a walking stick sounded on wooden steps below; and with it, the dark swirl of the god. One flight below, and coming his way. Clade increased his pace, assuming an air of distracted busyness. Perhaps Estelle would let him pass without interruption if he made his preoccupation clear.

She didn't. "Clade," she said when he rounded the landing. "Excellent. You've saved me the rest of my climb."

Ah, well. It wouldn't have worked on me, either. "Councillor Estelle. Forgive me, I'm just on my way out."

"It'll have to wait," she said, clearing the final step to the landing and leaning heavily on her stick.

"Your pardon, Councillor, but it can't. There's a matter that requires my immediate attention."

"Yes, right here." She drew him close, lowering her voice so that he had to bend his head to hear her. "What progress in our new endeavour?"

"Some," he said, matching her tone. "Without Garrett around —"

"How much is some?"

More than none and less than all. Clade bit back the retort. "I assure you, Councillor, I am devoting my every waking moment to the matter. As it happens, I'm pursuing a lead right now —"

Clade clamped his mouth shut, but it was too late. Like an eel slipping through water, Azador slid from Estelle and settled itself around him.

Damn it.

"Very well." Estelle stepped back, gestured down the stairs with her stick. "Go. And Clade." He paused in mid-step. "Next time we talk, I'll expect specifics. Understood?"

"As you say."

He resumed his descent with the god's foul redolence hanging around him like a cloud. *To the temple first, then. A few moments should be all that's required.*

The eventide service was already in progress when Clade arrived, passing swiftly through the thickly scented antechamber and into the domed Kefiran tabernacle. He slid quietly into a rear pew, seating himself alongside a hatchet-faced Mellespene woman who coughed at his approach, then scowled at him as though her hacking was his fault. *Don't worry, woman,* he thought. *You'll have the pew to yourself again soon enough.* But, as the melodious prayers wound their way toward completion, the god's unwelcome presence persisted. A low, uneasy thrum stirred in Clade's belly. *What is this?* Azador never endured more than a few moments in a temple. Always it left, vanishing like mist on the breeze. Yet here, today, it lingered, its fetor overpowering even the unpleasant odour of burnt flesh wafting in from the altars out the back.

The song drew to a close. The singers filed up the aisles, silent and graceful. The woman beside Clade stood with an impatient harrumph; he shifted his legs and she squeezed past, glowering back at him as she left. Other worshippers filtered out in ones and twos, and soon the tabernacle was empty save for Clade and the god.

How? How can it still be here? But then, he had never really understood why it left. Had it never been anything more than idle preference? He shivered, suddenly cold despite the close air of the tabernacle. *All those times I thought I was driving it away, yet it could have chosen to stay whenever it wished. Gods.*

There was no point in staying any longer. Terrel was probably waiting for him right now, and Clade could not afford to pass up the meeting, not even for Azador. If the god's unwelcome presence could not be disposed of, it would simply have to be borne.

At any other time the evening air would have been refreshingly cool, but tonight such considerations paled to insignificance beneath the oppressive weight of the god. Clade pushed north toward the Tienette, leaving the thoroughfare when he reached the docks and following the river toward East Bridge. The streets here were narrower than elsewhere in the city, enclosed on both sides by tall, timber buildings. Shouts, catcalls and raucous laughter spilled forth from brightly lit interiors. Others stood in relative silence, their shuttered windows blocking all but a faint outline of lamplight and the occasional squeal or moan. Clade found himself hunching his shoulders as he strode from one building to the next, arms folded tightly against his chest, squinting up at the signs hanging above or beside each door.

When he came to the Red Rodent, he almost kept walking. The shape on the sign resembled nothing so much as a vague pink blob. A second look revealed the long, improbably knotted tail at one end, and a third the almost invisible drooped whiskers at the other. With a mixture of relief and disdain, Clade pushed open the door and stepped inside.

A wall of stale, beery air greeted him. Men sat drinking around rough-hewn tables, their conversations boisterous and harsh. Clumped sawdust covered the floor and the stairs leading to an upper gallery that ran the length of the room. Half a dozen women leaned against the railing, each clad in some variation of low-cut blouse and flimsy skirt. One caught Clade's eye and offered him a slow, gap-toothed smile. He shuddered and looked away.

His gaze fell on a compact man who sat alone at a small corner table, watching him in the appraising manner of one used to assessing others by their appearance. The man's eyebrows rose fractionally in response to Clade's look. Clade returned the gesture with a nod and made his way to the table.

"You're Clade," he said as Clade pulled out a chair. His words were clipped, efficient. "Where's Garrett?"

Clade seated himself with a voiceless sigh. "Garrett's dead."

"Really?"

"Really."

The mercenary's face shifted slightly, into what Clade imagined might serve him as a frown. Clade said nothing, content to wait the other man out. He knew this type. If Terrel wanted answers, he would ask. But he probably wouldn't bother.

"Garrett worked for you."

"That's correct."

The almost-frown cleared. "All right," Terrel said, and sat fractionally back in his chair. An invitation for Clade to say whatever he had come here to say.

Clade folded his hands. Somewhere behind his eyes he sensed a sharpening of the god's attention. "I need you to tell me what happened when you tried to retrieve the urn."

"I told Garrett."

"I know. Tell me."

Another subtle change of expression, one that Clade couldn't read. *Annoyance, maybe.* "We saw the Quill team unearth an object," Terrel said shortly. "We killed the Quill and searched them. The object wasn't present."

"I see." Clade kept his tone mild. "And how long did you wait before killing the Quill?" What had Garrett told him? Days?

Terrel's eyelids flickered. "We attacked at the earliest opportunity."

Clade nodded. *Days.* "You delayed. Why?"

"The Quill had a firebinder. Burned off a mess of scrub before they started digging. We needed surprise to ensure victory."

A barmaid set a tall mug before Terrel and looked inquiringly at Clade. Clade shook his head, waving her away.

"You attacked, then," he said when she was out of earshot. "You killed the Quill. I assume you searched the area."

"As much as we could. We had wounded."

"And later?"

"We returned at Garrett's request." A fleeting pause, gone almost before it began. "We didn't find the urn, but we did find certain other... tokens."

A leering man clomped up the wooden steps toward the prostitutes, accompanied by the guffaws of his drinking companions. Clade leaned forward. "What other tokens?"

"We think someone else may have been present."

"*What?*"

Terrel shifted slightly. "There's no —"

"Are you telling me you *missed* someone?"

"No. There were three Quill, no more."

"Then what?"

Another pause, longer this time. *Hesitation.* "There may have been a third party. One person." A twitch of the shoulders indicated a shrug. "We're guessing, Clade. It was more than a week after the fact. The signs were cold. We might have it completely wrong."

The god hung about him like a shroud, heavy and still, listening. Clade ignored it. "But you don't think so."

Terrel took a long pull from his mug. "I told you we had wounded," he said, wiping his mouth. "Two dead, plus Ven. Damned firebinder put Ven's eyes out, burned up half his face. Poor bastard just kept wailing. We took him to an inn, got him patched up, bedded him down for the night. Next morning, he was dead."

"Wouldn't be the first person to lose his sight and decide life's not worth living."

"That's not it." Terrel's lips curled in what might have been the beginning of a smile, but there was no humour in his eyes. "Ven was still tucked up in bed. With a blanket wrapped around his head."

"Smothered."

"Just so."

"And you didn't think this was worth mentioning to Garrett?"

Another flicker of the eyelids. "Not at the time."

"For the gods' sake. Someone killed one of your men *in an inn,* and you said *nothing?*"

Terrel made no response.

"Who did it?"

A fresh wave of laughter arose as the man in the gallery made his selection: a short, boyish woman with close-cropped hair. Smirking, she ran her hand down his arm, grasping his hand and leading him into a dimly-lit corridor behind the staircase.

"I don't know," Terrel said. "We thought he was sleeping. By the time we found him, the inn was half empty." He took another draught, eyes focused on nothing.

"But?"

Terrel licked the foam off his lips. "Stableboy said one guest left earlier than the others. Before dawn. A woman, riding to Anstice."

Clade waited, but nothing more was forthcoming. "That's it? Did you get a name?"

"She didn't leave one."

"Damn it!" Clade slammed his hand against the table, hard enough to make Terrel's mug jump. Some part of him instinctively reached inward, began raising walls against his rage. Impatient, furious, he swatted the impulse away. "So there *might* have been someone else there when you killed the Quill, is that right? And they *might* have got hold of the urn. And they *might* have found their way to the same inn you did. And they *might* be the same person as this unnamed woman, who *might* have delayed her journey just long enough to kill your man for no particular reason before galloping away to Anstice. Is that about right?"

Terrel's shoulders twitched.

"Sounds like you're saying the urn I'm paying you to find *might* be right here in Anstice. Is that what you're saying, Terrel?"

"More or less," Terrel said.

"Because if that's what you're saying, the next thing I expect to hear out of your mouth is what you're doing to find it."

Terrel stared at Clade for a long moment, his expression unreadable. Clade held his gaze, unblinking, allowing Azador to stare back and take in the man's features. *This is the one,* Clade thought, even though he knew the god couldn't hear his words. *This is the man responsible. If I fail to find the golems, this is the one who let me down.*

Eventually, Terrel nodded. "We'll look," he said.

"I want every antiquities dealer in the city questioned. Every shop examined. I want —"

Terrel raised a hand. "Clade. Half my team is dead. Understand? Another man in my position might just cut his losses and move on, your money be damned."

Clade considered him. "Not you, though."

"No. Not me." A new expression crossed Terrel's face, little more than a slight shift about the eyes. *Entreaty? Concern?* "You must understand that my resources are limited right now. I need time to regroup. Find more men." He pulled a small pouch from his belt and set it on the table. The contents clacked and the pouch sagged open, revealing a smooth, black object the shape of an egg. "Garrett said these were to be returned. There are three in there. One for each dead man." He pushed the pouch across the table.

Clade stared at the open pouch, incredulous. *Gods, Garrett. You gave them locuses? What part of "discreet" did you not understand?* But then, Clade himself had told Garrett that the operation was known to the Council — and, by implication, the god. *Azador might have visited them at any time. I might already be undone.* Weakly, he pushed the pouch back. "Keep them," he said. "Give them to your new recruits."

"No. We're done, Clade. I'll do what I can to find your urn, but that's the end of it. I don't care if you offer me enough gold to buy the archon's palace. I'm not taking another of your jobs."

"I see," Clade said. *Oh, yes, I see.* However much or little Azador already knew, it was here, now. There was nothing for it but to carry on. "Then let me make myself clear. You were hired to bring me the urn. Our arrangement ends when that occurs, and not before."

Terrel drained his mug. "I don't think —"

"I do." Clade picked up the pouch. "It's really very simple. I engaged you to do a job, and you're going to do it." He stood, leaning
over the table until he could feel the other man's breath on his face.
"So go get me that fucking urn."

~

By the time Arandras returned to his room to collect his belong-
ings, Mara had already come and gone. Her own door, several down
from his, stood open, the room empty save for the standard pallet
and chest. No note was present, either there or slipped beneath his
own door, nor had he expected one. Mara had friends of her own in
Anstice who put her up when she travelled here, and for whom she
repaid the favour when they visited Spyridon. Even if they'd invited
him to stay along with Mara, Arandras would have refused. *I don't
know why she didn't go there right from the start.*

Or perhaps she had. Her room looked barely used. He thought
back, trying to recall seeing her enter or leave. They'd returned to
the schoolhouse together from the river the previous evening and
eaten their meals out on the lawn, but Arandras had left first and
come back to his room alone. *Did I ever see her at breakfast? Not that
I can remember.* He chuckled. It would be just like Mara to put the
Quill to the trouble of preparing her a room and then never actually
use it.

Arandras left the schoolhouse with his bags slung across his
shoulders and the urn in its pouch by his side. It felt good to be out
from under the Quill's eye, at least for the night. In truth, he'd felt
lighter all day. *The pretence is gone, that's what it is.* Arandras had
done everything he could to work alongside them, waiting all the
while for the ugly, grasping hand to reveal itself. Now it had.

He struck a path north toward the river but away from the old
city, skirting the old wall as it curved westward in the direction
of Bastion Bridge. Craftsmen's shops and artists' studios lined the
streets in this part of the city, most dark now, though a few were
still lit from within. Small, open courtyards fronted many of the
workshops, offering a place where sculptors and painters might

demonstrate their craft during the daylight hours, some still carrying a faint odour of wet paint. Shadowed signs above other doors proclaimed the presence of etchers, limners, cutters of stained glass, and more besides. The doleful tones of a Sarean horn floated down from an upper window, its stop-start progression marking the player as a beginner.

He could still walk away. The Quill needed him, but the reverse was not necessarily true. *Am I really any closer to finding Tereisa's killer than I was before I got here?* Well, he'd managed to puzzle out the inscription. That was something. And if he was honest, the book from the Quill's library was what had made the difference. But for that, he'd probably still have been staring at the pictures and trying to figure out what all the children were supposed to mean.

And then there were the golems. His golems, insofar as the urn belonged to him and the golems were somehow connected to the urn — or at least, his and Mara's and the others'. He shivered. *Weeper grant I never see the damned things.* Let the Quill run madly about the countryside trying to find them. Arandras wanted no part of it —

The touch was light, the merest brush of a feather at his side. Arandras whirled, his hand closing over a child's thin wrist, catching the arm as it attempted to pull away. The boy hissed, twisting and clawing at him like an imp; then he abruptly reversed direction, lowering his head and pulling Arandras's hand to his mouth.

Arandras jerked away, narrowly avoiding the snap of teeth, his hand striking a glancing blow across the boy's nose. The boy staggered back, and Arandras snatched at the boy's scrawny throat, grasping it on his second attempt. The child's struggles subsided, and he glared at Arandras with the sullen air of one whose efforts to pursue his livelihood had been unfairly impeded.

A pair of women passed by on the other side of the street, their eyes fixed on the paving stones in front of them.

Arandras returned the boy's glare. The child was thin as a reed, and maybe eight summers old. "I'm not your mark, kid," he said.

The boy turned his head and spat.

Arandras tightened his grip. "I mean it. The place I live is lousy with your type. They know better than to try me."

"You're not from here," the boy said, making it sound like an accusation.

"That's right," Arandras said. "You don't know me. Let's keep it that way, shall we?"

The boy made a half-hearted effort to wriggle free, but Arandras's grip was firm. At last the boy shrugged.

Good enough.

A thought struck Arandras, and his grip tightened further. "Who sent you, boy? What are you after?"

The boy hacked a cough, shaking his head and pointing at his throat. Arandras cursed and released his grasp a fraction.

"My ma," the boy said, his eyes lifting to meet Arandras's in a calculating gaze. "Five of us, there are, all hungry, and my ma's sister, and —"

"Bah." *A common street thief, that's all.* Arandras shook his head. Of course that was all. If the Quill wanted to take the urn by force, they'd hardly employ a half-starved pickpocket.

Without warning, the boy locked his hands over Arandras's outstretched arm and lifted his feet off the ground, bringing his full weight to bear on Arandras's wrist. Arandras gasped, dragged lower by the sudden load; then the boy's feet were on the ground once more. Twisting like a cat, he tore free of Arandras's weakened grip and darted away, disappearing into a nearby alley.

Damn it. "Hey! Kid!"

A scuffing sound came from the mouth of the alley. "What?"

Arandras felt for his coinpurse and the urn, and checked the buckles on his bags. All was as it should be. "Where's a good place to stay around here?"

There was a pause. "Black Bear Inn. North a couple of blocks. You can't miss it." There was another scuffing noise, then the sound of scampering footsteps running away down the alley.

Which was as good a recommendation of somewhere to avoid as any he was likely to get. *Right. Anywhere but the Black Bear.*

He resumed his course, taking care to walk with one hand on the pouch at his side. What had he been thinking about? *That's right, the Quill.* Yes, they definitely needed him more than he needed them. All the same, he didn't have much in the way of other leads.

He could, perhaps, make a list of sorcerers in the city and go and knock on their doors. But what would that achieve? He didn't even know what the man he was searching for looked like.

Weeper's breath, I don't even have a name.

No, staying with the Quill was his best bet, at least for now. The more he could discover about the urn, the better his chances of guessing at his quarry's plan. And now that the Quill anthill had been well and truly kicked, the likelihood of them drawing the attention of any other interested parties had increased dramatically. If someone came nosing around after the urn, he could still be there to see who they were.

But at least he could house and feed himself.

He came to a halt. A dozen doors further down the street was a large, noisy inn, likely the establishment recommended by the young thief. But here, hard against what looked to be a small warehouse-cum-theatre, stood a well-lit lodging house, its sign showing a pale bird pulling up a worm. Through the open window Arandras could see a narrow, half-empty common room. Several patrons sat alone, some drinking, one sleeping; near the front, a group of four or five huddled around cups of chocol, speaking in low tones; and there, in the back corner, a pair of elderly Kharjik women faced each other over a *dilarj* board.

Perfect.

With a smile, Arandras stepped inside.

～

Arandras's good mood lasted to the next morning. A misty rain had begun falling some time in the night, making the streets slick underfoot, but Arandras paid it no mind. He strode lightly through the fine drizzle, retracing his path of the previous evening, stopping only to purchase breakfast: a rolled flatcake containing almonds, dates, and several other fruits. He ate as he walked, savouring the sweet flavours, sucking his fingers clean when he was done.

The thin-cheeked woman who ran the lodging house had given him a top-floor room similar in size to the one he'd had at the schoolhouse, but with a low, slanting ceiling. Disappointingly, the cured timber shingles proved unable to occlude the sounds and smells of the street outside, or the slow grey light of dawn. But they were watertight — at least against this half-hearted rain — and, critically, the room was his for as long as he wanted it, untainted by the favour or provenance of the Quill.

By the time he reached the schoolhouse, his hair and beard were slick with moisture. Mopping his face with an equally damp sleeve, he hurried inside and made his way to the new workroom.

"Here he is," Narvi said as Arandras entered, the words apparently directed at Bannard, who sat with several other Quill by the far wall. "See? Nothing to worry about."

Worry about? Arandras looked across to Bannard, eyebrow raised, and the other man scowled and looked away.

"Right, then." The voice belonged to Halli, the woman with the stubbled scalp and bandaged ear who'd asked about the inscription at the briefing. She joined Narvi at the central work table, followed by Bannard, Senisha, and another, unnamed Quill whom Arandras had also seen the previous day: a rat-like man with half a dozen brass and copper rings on his hands. "Shall we begin?"

"By all means." Narvi turned to Arandras. "The urn, if you please."

With the meaning of the inscription now clear, the group's focus turned to the urn's contents. Hour followed tedious hour as the gathered Quill took turns hefting, shaking, and frowning thoughtfully at the small pewter vessel. Narvi and Halli each attempted bindings to establish the nature of the sorcery sealing the lid in place, to no avail. Bannard tapped the urn's bowl with a succession of tools and utensils, and tried to judge whether the resulting tone sounded hollow or solid. The rat-faced man — whom the other Quill referred to as Gord — produced a set of scales and an unformed lump of tin and pronounced the urn to weigh just over one-quarter again as much as the tin; but as nobody could state the precise constitution of the urn's metal, nor how thick it was, the result meant little. Arandras observed the proceedings in silence, his cheer ebbing away as the morning dragged by.

"Maybe it really is empty," Senisha said, balancing the urn on her palm with her eyes closed.

"It can't be." Bannard gave her a look that was half squint, half glare. "People are killing each other for it. How can it be empty?"

"I don't know. It feels empty to me," Senisha said. "What do you think, Arandras?"

Arandras shrugged. They'd spent the whole morning learning exactly nothing. "Maybe."

"Let's take a step back," Narvi said. "We've got an urn and it won't open. What assumptions are we making?"

That it matters. Arandras clamped his mouth shut against the sour thought. Maybe knowing the contents of the urn wouldn't help; but on the other hand, maybe it would. That was the thing about riddles. You never knew what was important until you solved the damn thing.

"What if it's not meant to be opened?" Halli said. "Maybe we're trying to do something it's just not meant for."

"No," Bannard said. "Look at the seam around the top. The lid's a separate piece, without question."

"That doesn't mean it's meant to open."

"And *that* doesn't mean we shouldn't try to open it."

"All right," Narvi said. "Assume for the moment that it can still be opened. What could be holding the lid in place?"

"Sorcery, of course," Bannard said.

"Of course. What else?"

Senisha frowned. "It could be something physical. A mechanism of some sort."

"Good. Arandras?"

Arandras roused himself. "Not likely. A mechanism would make it top-heavy, which it plainly isn't."

"It's sorcery," Bannard repeated. "It's got to be."

A group of giggling children ran past the window outside. Gord glanced around the table. "What about anamnil?"

"What? No," Arandras said. *Weeper help us, what a stupid suggestion.* Anamnil might shield someone from the effects of a binding, or prevent a sorcerer from constructing new spells, but introducing it to a bound object rarely made a difference — and when it did, the outcome was anything but predictable. "No anamnil."

"Not what I mean," Gord said. "Maybe there's already anamnil inside."

Halli shook her head. "I'd be able to sense it. Narvi, too."

"You'd sense our anamnil, sure. That stuff the Falisi weave out of the Gatherer knows what. But what if the Valdori had something of their own? Something nobody can tell is there?"

There was a pause as the group absorbed the idea.

"That would explain why neither of you can find any sorcery," Senisha said. "Wouldn't it?"

Narvi and Halli exchanged dubious glances. "Maybe," Narvi said, drawing out the word. "If the Valdori had such a thing. But that's sheer speculation."

"Perhaps it's not anamnil, exactly," Bannard said, thoughtful. "Perhaps it's something more innate." He gestured at Halli's scarred head. "We know sorcerers have a natural resistance to fleshbinding. It'll be weeks before Halli's wounds heal. Mine are already fading. Maybe this stuff the urn's made from is the same, just naturally resistant to sorcery."

Narvi frowned. "Even if that's true, what could we do about it?"

"Stop holding back," Bannard said. "Blast the thing with as much power as you can. The strongest fleshbinders can affect other sorcerers, at least a little. Same thing here."

"You think I'm holding back?" Halli said. "I've tried everything I can think of, and I can't hear even a whisper of sorcery in that thing."

"So stop listening and start pushing," Bannard said.

"Not so fast," Arandras said. "I've authorised scans, but that's all —"

"Oh!" Senisha blinked. "Other sorcerers!"

Arandras and Narvi responded together. "What?"

"Think about it." Senisha looked around the group. "Imagine the Valdori Emperor. Commander of the greatest sorcerers of his time, who've created armies of golems ready to respond to his every command. Who poses the greatest threat?"

Narvi shook his head. "Who?"

"*Other sorcerers.* Rivals, outcasts, whatever. The only people who could conceivably challenge him."

"Exactly," Bannard said. "So you make it impossible for anyone but the strongest sorcerers to break."

"No, that's not it at all." Senisha selected a book from the stack on the bench. "Just think for a minute. You know exactly what's going to happen if someone gets hold of something they shouldn't. They're going to use the best sorcery they can to try and open it. And no matter how tough you make it, there's always the chance they'll manage to blast their way in." She looked up. "So you create something that sorcery can never unlock. Here."

She laid the book open in front of them. Dense writing surrounded a small, abstract diagram consisting of lines, arrows, and annotations too small for Arandras to make out.

"It's like a finger trap toy," Senisha said. "The more you pull, the more you're stuck. Except this kind feeds on sorcery. Poke and prod at it, and it just becomes stronger. Try blasting it to pieces and it becomes practically invulnerable."

Arandras leaned closer, trying to puzzle out the diagram. "So how do you open it?"

"Something physical," Senisha said. "Fire, probably, or a blacksmith's hammer." She frowned. "It must be a lot weaker now, though. I wonder…"

"Wonder what?"

"If this will work." And she grabbed the urn, pivoted, and hurled it against the wall.

The dull crack as the urn hit stone felt like a blow to Arandras's gut.

"Weeper's tears, what are you doing?" Arandras leapt out of his chair and lunged for the urn as it tumbled back toward them. But Senisha was too fast, snatching it up and throwing it against the wall a second time. A high peal rang out, like a struck bell; and as the urn rebounded, something skittered away at an angle, bouncing across the floor with the soft clink of a dropped coin.

The urn rolled to a stop beside Narvi. Slowly, he picked it up and placed it on the table.

The six of them leaned over, peering into the open mouth of the urn.

"It's empty," Bannard said.

In the silence, Senisha's muttered reply might as well have been a shout. "Told you."

CHAPTER 14

Dissatisfaction, you see, is our natural state of being, as natural to us as breathing. Permit me a simple example. Have you ever lain in bed, half awake, cursing your inability to slumber, only to discover when morning came that, far from being half awake, you were in fact half asleep?

— Daro of Talsoor, *Dialogues with my Teachers*

EILWEN HELD THE SPARKER TO the lamp and thumbed the nub on its handle. A weak glow flickered briefly around the white opal tip, then sputtered out.

Damn it.

She tossed the drained sparker onto her desk and glared out the window. Though the slender hand of the table clock indicated the last hour of the morning, the sun was nowhere to be seen. Heavy clouds crammed the sky, casting a fine, misty rain that seemed to float as much as fall through the air. The tree outside Eilwen's window filtered the dim light even further, leaving her suite as dull and dreary as her mood.

Havilah had instructed her to sit tight. He had questions of his own he wanted to resolve, and until he told her otherwise she was to confine her investigation to the records and reports she'd already been over a dozen times. "We can't afford a single false play," he'd said, just before she left his office the previous day. "If you want to keep Vorace alive, this is the way to do it."

Yeah, Eilwen thought, glancing around her gloomy suite. *I'm going to save my Guild by sitting in the dark with my hands tied behind my back.*

Somewhere in this very building, someone was moving their plans closer to completion. *Not "someone". Laris.* Havilah seemed convinced that the Trademaster was behind Kieffe's death, and Eilwen was prepared to accept the conjecture as a working theory. It made sense, as much any theory made sense. Certainly, the position of Trademaster had far greater scope for such undertakings than any of the other masters, and the woman's reported dissatisfaction with Vorace's leadership offered plausible motivation for what now looked to be an imminent coup. But there was no proof connecting Laris with anything, and the presence of Tahisi cannons in Qulah's warehouse remained unexplained. *And Havilah was already after Laris before this even began. Maybe he's seeing what he wants to see.*

She hadn't told Havilah about the brief conversation she'd had with Laris just before discovering Kieffe's body. Something about the memory had made her want to keep it to herself, and as she left Havilah's office she'd realised why. At its heart, Laris's invitation had been a mirror image of Havilah's the day she returned from Spyridon.

Each of them wanted to use her against the other.

Frowning, Eilwen retrieved the sparker from her desk and tried it again. This time the glow lasted barely a heartbeat before vanishing. When she pressed the nub once more, the answering wink of light was so faint as to be almost invisible.

Damn, and damn again. The binding was spent. She had a taper somewhere among her possessions, but with no light to aid her, the search promised to be lengthy and irksome.

Or she could just go the Quill shop and get the sparker fixed. It wasn't like she had anything else to do. And if while she was there she happened to find the fleshbinder who attended Dallin, well, that would be nothing more than a fortuitous coincidence.

The misty drizzle was breaking by the time she left the compound, though streaky dark-on-light clouds still scudded overhead, threatening further rainfall at any moment. Eilwen splashed through the shallower puddles, huddling in her coat against the unseasonal chill. The cool scent of rain hung over the city like perfume, muting the usual smells of food, fish, and animal dung. Wisps of fog drifted over the river, sliding beneath the bridges as though carried along by the current below.

The Quill shop occupied the entire ground floor of a low building several blocks back from the Tienette. Eilwen stomped her shoes on the thick rush mat just inside the door, blinking at the brightly-lit interior. On one side of the spacious room, a series of angled counters and shelves displayed a wide variety of items: chillers and sparkers; pots, bowls, and vases carrying a variety of bindings; garments that had been made softer, or tougher, or less permeable. On the other side, waist-high ropes marked a small queueing area, with tall partitions dividing the remainder of the space into booths. Groups of two or three sat around small tables within each booth, their conversations too soft to hear. A series of large tapestries, each showing the iconic ochre-on-charcoal feather of the Quill, filled the far wall.

Eilwen entered the vacant queueing area. The high counter at the end appeared to consist of three separate stations, but only one was occupied right now. A girl with improbably rouged cheeks looked up at Eilwen's approach.

"Welcome, ma'am," the girl said. Her auburn hair was cropped short in the Sarean style, but her words held no distinguishable accent. "How may we help you?"

"I have a sparker with a spent binding," Eilwen said.

"Of course. Take a seat in the booth at the end, please. Someone will be with you soon."

Eilwen made her way to the indicated booth. Aside from table and chairs, the stall was empty save for a printed page on the table listing the Quill's services: everything from schooling to fleshbinding to earthworks. She glanced at it without interest, putting her sparker on the table and settling in to wait.

After a few minutes, a grey-haired woman bustled in, a bronze feather pinned above her breast. "Good morning, dearie," she said, dropping into the chair across from Eilwen with a grunt. "Dead sparker, is it?"

"That's right."

"You're sure you wouldn't like a new one?"

"No, thank you." The sparker was only a year old, and this was its first depletion. "A fresh binding will be fine."

"Well, if you're sure." The woman lifted the sparker, her gaze turning cross-eyed as she frowned at the slender rod. "Let's see..."

Eilwen always felt uncomfortable watching a sorcerer perform a binding. Mostly she was able to think of sorcerers as no different to anyone else: people who ate, slept, spent coin, and complained about the weather. But in moments like these the illusion faltered. To Eilwen, the world was dirt and sun and flesh; but a sorcerer saw beneath the world's skin to that which lay beneath, a whole other world of spells and energies she could never hope to understand. To watch a sorcerer in communion with that world was to see someone looking past the veil of the mundane to something transcendent, and to know that she herself could never share that view.

Across the table, the woman licked her lips, her eyes fixed on the sparker as though on the face of a lover. Her jaw sagged open and her lips began to work, widening and relaxing in soundless speech. Eilwen stared, unable to help herself, drawn in by the rapture in the woman's face. *What do you see as you reach below the surface of the world? What secrets do you hold that I can never know?*

Why do the gods bless you with such gifts, and leave me with only scraps?

The woman stirred, lowering the sparker to the table and blinking up at Eilwen. "All done." She thumbed the nub and a flare of light sparked from the tip. "That will be three sculundi and five."

Eilwen counted the silver out of her purse and passed it across. The sorcerer glanced over the bars and bits, then smiled and relinquished the sparker.

"Thank you, my dear. Was there anything else?"

"Um," Eilwen said. "Actually, yes. I was hoping to speak to a fleshbinder."

"Of course, dearie." The woman folded her hands with grandmotherly matter-of-factness. "We only treat minor complaints here, mind. For anything else, you'll have to go to the schoolhouse. That includes unwanted pregnancies —"

"It's nothing like that," Eilwen said hastily. "It's about an acquaintance of mine. He died a few days ago, and I was told a Quill fleshbinder was there at the end."

The woman's brow creased. "I'm sure everything possible was done for your friend, my dear. We're often summoned too late to make any difference —"

"Yes," Eilwen said with forced patience. "I know. I'm not looking to place blame. I just want to hear how he died."

"Oh." The woman frowned. "Well. What was your friend's name?"

"Dallin Nourt. And he was only an acquaintance," Eilwen said. "I'm told a perfumer's boy found him near the river."

"Oh, yes. The Kharjik lad. They brought the dying man here, if you can believe it. Not that it made any difference. By the time they arrived, he was already dead." She scratched her ear. "Dallin, did you call him? I never did catch his name."

"I heard he was coughing up blood," Eilwen said. "Could you tell me how he died?"

The sorcerer chuckled. "A knife in the guts, dearie. It'll do you every time. Well, most times, anyway."

"Oh," Eilwen said. *A knife. How very... mundane.* "Right. I see."

"Not the answer you were expecting, then?"

"I suppose not," Eilwen said. What had she been expecting, anyway? "I guess I thought... that is to say, I wondered if there might have been an element of..."

"Of what? Sorcery?" The woman regarded Eilwen with amusement. "Not this one, my dear. Though there's no telling who held the blade."

"I suppose so."

The sorcerer sighed. "I'm sorry, dearie. I shouldn't make light. If you want to know what happened to your friend, best ask the garrison. Half of them couldn't find their arse with both hands, but the boys in charge occasionally show some wit."

"I wish I could," Eilwen said. A visit to the Quill shop was at least marginally within the bounds Havilah had placed on her. Poking around the garrison house was out of the question, at least for now. "It's not that simple," she concluded lamely.

"It never is," the woman said. "Well. I'm sorry for your loss." She considered Eilwen a moment, then leaned in, lowering her voice. "I probably shouldn't tell you this, but next time you're wondering about sorcerers killing people, don't worry yourself over knives and the like. Look to the nose."

Eilwen looked up. "What do you mean?"

"If a fleshbinder wanted to kill someone, gods forbid, they'd do it nice and quiet. No marks, no evidence. Just a spot of blood in the nose. Nothing more."

Eilwen's heart began to pound. "I thought blood on the nose meant poison. Bluespine, that sort of thing."

The woman shrugged. "I wouldn't know about that, dearie. Blood in the nose could mean a hundred different things, I suppose. But sorcery's one of them."

"Can you tell the difference? Between someone who's been poisoned and someone who's been killed by sorcery?"

"Me? Gods, no." The woman laughed. "I'm not even a fleshbinder. I just rebind sparkers and chillers and the like. There are some who can, though. If not here, then at the schoolhouse."

"Thank you." Eilwen leapt to her feet. "Really, thank you. I'll be back."

~

She hurried through the streets as fast as her leg would allow, pushing past other pedestrians, ignoring their shouted complaints. Fine rain had begun falling again, but Eilwen didn't care. All that mattered was getting back to the compound and finding Kieffe's body.

It's Caralange. It has to be. No wonder he was so reluctant to examine the body. She rounded the corner to Traders' Row, skidding on a stone as the thoughts tumbled through her head. *Did he really get one of his people to do the examination, or did he do it himself?* The gate to the Woodtraders compound stood open and Eilwen darted through, dodging an unhitched cart just inside and narrowly missing a youth with an armful of cloth-wrapped bales. At the entrance to the main building she slowed, picking her way up the rain-slick steps and into the entrance hall.

The stairs to the cellar were located in the corners of the building, away from the main staircase. Eilwen strode down the corridor, her breath shortening as her lungs began to catch up with her exertions.

Water dripped from her face and slid down the back of her neck. She paused at the top of the cellar stairs, hastily shedding her coat and blotting her forehead with her sleeve. It would have to do. Her hair probably looked like a drowned dog's, but so did everyone's today.

Bundling her coat under her arm, Eilwen descended the stairs, her wild energy fading. Her bad leg trembled as she set her weight on it, and she grimaced at a shooting twinge in her knee. She'd be paying for that dash through the city for the next couple of days. But that wasn't important now. What mattered was finding Kieffe's body.

And when I do, then what? How am I planning to get it to the Quill? She cursed, pausing at the base of the stairs. Even if she'd been strong enough to haul a corpse out of the building and onto a cart, it would be impossible for her to move it without half the Guild knowing about it. *Brilliant, Eilwen. Just brilliant. Havilah would be proud.*

Perhaps once she'd located the body, she could think of a way to get a Quill sorcerer in. Or perhaps she could tell Havilah, and the two of them could come up with something.

I should take this to him. Turn around, walk up those stairs, and tell Havilah what the Quill told me. She'd let herself get carried away, just like she always seemed to do, but this time she'd caught herself in time. She'd done nothing to attract attention but run through the rain, and surely not even the most paranoid conspirator could interpret that as a threat.

With a sigh, Eilwen lifted her foot to the first step. A fresh bolt of pain lanced through her knee, and she gasped, rocking back onto her good leg. *All right. Maybe I'll just wait a moment before trying the stairs.* She turned, leaning heavily against the wall. The corridor opened to the cellar just past a corner up ahead. Lamplight spilt from the unseen room, painting the near wall a dirty yellow. *Well,* she thought, relinquishing the wall and balancing unsteadily on her sore leg. *Since I'm down here anyway...*

The cellar was a single, wide hall as long as the building above. Bare stone columns marked the central aisle that connected the stairs at either end. Eilwen limped down the colonnade, past sacks of meal, pots of pickled vegetables, barrels packed with salted meat, rows of wineskins, and the hundred and one other supplies and provisions that kept the Guild functioning. Old iron lamps hugged the pillars' unadorned cornices, filling the cool air with the smell of cheap fish oil.

A recess at the midway point of the hall marked the opening to a further alcove. Its rusted iron-grille door stood open, sagging slightly on its heavy hinges. Eilwen paused at the threshold, glancing inside for any sign of life. Four great boxes of fired clay stood in a row across the back wall, each one large enough to hold a horse: the Guild's chill-chests.

"Hello?" she called. "Is anyone here?"

The clatter of a crate lid on stone answered, followed by a peevish curse. A long-limbed man emerged from the side of the alcove, rubbing his elbow with a gloved hand. "Huh. What do you want?"

"Hi," Eilwen said, reaching for the man's name but coming up empty. *Damn it.* "Um. How are you?"

"Dry," the man said, peering at her over an ugly bristle-brush moustache. "What are you here for? If you're after wool stuffing for your bed, I'll tell you now, it'll be next week at the earliest. Make do until then, or go out and buy your own."

"Thanks, but no," Eilwen said. She pointed her chin at the boxes against the wall. "What's our chill-chest capacity like? We're going to need some space soon."

"Oh?" The man's eyes narrowed. "What for?"

Eilwen spread her hands. "They don't tell me that," she said. "They just tell me to come see you."

The man gave a sour snort. "Right," he said. "Well, you can tell them to cross their legs and hold on. Two of those chests have the usual crap in them, and the third is full to bursting with some sort of Pekratan berry. Seems the archon's dear maiden aunt is about to pay us a ridiculous amount of money for them as soon as she can convince her nephew to release the funds." He pursed his lips. "The fourth is completely shot. You can put whatever you like in it, but it won't do you a lick of good until Phemia gets off her arse and ponies up for the Quill to come fill it with cold juice, or whatever the hells they do."

"I see," Eilwen said. *So where's Kieffe, then?* She considered the chests and raised what she hoped was a conspiratorial eyebrow. "I heard there was a body in one of them."

"Yep. Had it stuffed in there for more than a week." The man spat. "You want to know why that chest is out of action, there's your answer."

"So the body's not there any more?"

"Not since yesterday. That sorcerer came down with a couple of lads and took it away."

Shit. "You mean Caralange?"

"Nah. One of his crows."

"Oh." Eilwen racked her memory. "Orom?"

The man shrugged. "Could be."

"Do you know where he took it?"

"No, and I didn't ask. Out of my chest is fine by me. What's it to you, anyway?"

Only the life of the Guildmaster. Eilwen shook her head. "I don't know. It doesn't matter."

The man gave a porcine grunt. "If they'd just burned the damn corpse when they found it, you'd have space for your... whatever-they-ares. Tell them that. And tell them to hold on." He mimed a squat, crossing his eyes and puffing out his cheeks.

"Yeah," Eilwen said. "Thanks. I'll tell them."

She turned and commenced the slow, limping walk back to the stairs, heaviness pooling in her gut. The body was gone, taken by one of Caralange's sorcerers to who knew where, and with it the evidence that would show the involvement of sorcery in Kieffe's death. *Assuming it was even sorcery that killed him. Gods, for all I know I'm down here chasing geese.*

There was nothing more she could do, at least not on her own. *All right. Up the stairs, then find Havilah.*

Gods grant it's not already too late.

She reached the end of the hall. With a long breath, she turned to the stairs — and stopped short. Caralange stood on the staircase above her, his straggly hair turned radiant by the light behind him. His craggy face was closed, his lips turned down at the corners and his eyes half-hooded.

"Oh," Eilwen stepped aside. "I'm sorry. I'll let you pass."

"No, you won't," Caralange rasped.

Swifter than she could draw breath, Caralange drew out a cloth bag and yanked it over her head. She screamed, beating against him with her fists; but as she gasped for air, something astringent filled her lungs, and her arms fell limp. She moaned and tried to shove the sorcerer aside. Then she was falling, her limbs pinned by something heavy, and the stone beneath her feet was gone, sucked down with her into an endless black abyss.

~

Arandras snatched the urn from under the assembled noses and brandished it angrily at Senisha. "Weeper's breath, how dare you? Do you know what this thing is worth?"

"Probably twice as much as a moment ago," Gord said, grinning behind a be-ringed hand.

"And what if it had smashed all over the floor?"

"I'm sorry, I thought you knew." Senisha shrugged. "Valdori metalwork. It's lasted two millennia without so much as a scratch. A bump or two isn't going to hurt it."

Arandras glared at her. "*Tempered* Valdori metalwork. There are plenty of older pieces that aren't. Some of them about as well preserved as this."

Senisha opened her mouth, then closed it again, her expression suddenly sheepish. "Oh."

Arandras turned the urn over in his hands, examining its surface for any sign of damage. But it seemed Senisha had guessed correctly, thank the Weeper. The metal was unscathed.

"All right," Narvi said. "Did anyone see where the lid went? Maybe something came out when Senisha... opened it."

"Over here." Halli held a small piece of pewter aloft. "I don't see anything else."

She returned to the table, offering Arandras the lid. It was a solid wedge of metal, shaped like a cone with the point removed. A thread-like ridge circled the piece about its midpoint, counterpart to a groove set within the urn's flared mouth. Frowning, Arandras fitted the lid to the urn and gave it an experimental twist.

"Careful," Senisha said. "You don't want to seal it again."

"That's all right. I can always ask you to drop an anvil on it next time."

Senisha reddened and turned away. Arandras ignored her, twisting the lid first one way and then the other. It fit perfectly, screwing in and out with a smoothness any clockmaker would have envied.

"What do we do now?" Bannard said.

Narvi shrugged. "Tell Fas, I suppose."

"Tell him what? That the urn was empty after all and we don't have a damn thing left to lead us to the golems?"

The sound of rain tapping on the windows filled the room. Reluctantly, Arandras set the urn back on the table and returned to his seat. "There's more to this than the urn," he said. "Someone killed three of your people, remember?"

Narvi shot him a glance from beneath lowered brows. "I haven't forgotten."

"So, what are we doing about it?" Arandras looked around the table. "Does anyone have the slightest idea who might have murdered those three Quill?"

"You say," Halli muttered.

Arandras turned. "Excuse me?"

"You tell us they were killed," Halli said. "But by your own account, you didn't see it. How do we know what really happened out there?"

"What in the hells is that supposed to mean?" Arandras stared at Halli, his face growing hot. "I'm a liar, is that it? Or a dupe? Or are you actually accusing me of having something to do with their deaths?"

"I'm saying that all we have is a third-hand report that's even lighter on details than it is on credibility. There's nothing to follow up! Do we have bodies? Do we have any idea where this supposed confrontation took place? The only thing you can tell us for sure is that it was night!"

"Enough, Halli." The voice was Narvi's: calm, measured, and annoyingly reasonable. He turned to Arandras. "The place where they were killed. Could Mara find it again?"

Arandras glared. *You asked that on the way up from Spyridon. You already know the answer, damn you.* But Narvi held his eyes, his gaze somehow at once mild and implacable.

"No," Arandras said at last.

Narvi nodded. "Then what do you suggest?"

Arandras moistened his lips. "The journal page," he said. "The one we both got a copy of, almost exactly the same. You said yours came from Anstice. Where?"

Narvi shrugged. "A walk-in at the shop, wasn't it?" He glanced at Gord, who nodded in affirmation.

"Right," Arandras said. "So you must have some record of who sold it to you, yes? Or someone there who might still remember the purchase?"

"Well." Narvi frowned. "Probably not."

"What do you mean, probably not?"

Gord grimaced. "We get hundreds of walk-ins every month. People trying to sell us scraps of half-faded scribble, or their great-uncle's collection of love letters from his Kharjik mistress, or the Gatherer knows what all else." He waved his hand. "We weed out the obvious rubbish and only pay a few duri for the rest, but it's still more than we can stay on top of. Often we don't get around to looking at something until months after the shop sends it on."

Arandras tried not to roll his eyes, but failed. *That would explain why the seller made a second copy, I suppose. Probably figured the first one had got lost somewhere in the bowels of the Quill. Sent the new one down to Spyridon, where the Quill don't have a shop and need to rely more on the local dealers. Except I got it instead.*

But that only made sense if the seller had wanted the Quill to send out a retrieval party. *Perhaps they didn't have any sorcerers who could retrieve the urn directly? But they did have people to kill the sorcerers —*

"What's this?" Bannard said, pulling Arandras from his thoughts. He squinted at the underside of the lid, his finger tracing a shape against its surface. "There are markings here. Like the letters on the urn, but different." He held it out to Arandras. "Here, see if you can read it."

Arandras took the lid with a grudging sigh and turned it over.

The characters were little more than thin scratches, albeit marked out with the same precision as those on the body of the urn.

There were two rows, one above the other, with half a dozen symbols in each. Arandras cast a disinterested eye over the markings, then rolled the lid onto the table. "Not letters," he said. "Numerals."

"What? Let me see." Bannard grabbed the lid. "Hah, so they are! Two, nine, five... let me write this down..."

Arandras tilted his head back and stared at the ceiling. *Here we go again.* Another damn riddle to consume the Quill's attention. Endless conversations about what it could possibly mean...

"What do you suppose it means?" Senisha said.

"I know exactly what it means." Bannard's face split in a grin. "See how the numbers are arranged? Six numerals in each, with a space between the second and third, and another between the fourth and fifth. They're in pairs. A triplet of pairs on each line. See?"

Oh, great.

"Valdori coordinate notation," Halli said.

"Exactly!" Bannard's expression was rapturous. "This is where the golems are! It has to be!"

The Quill looked from one to another, expressions of disbelief turning to delight. Arandras grit his teeth as Narvi clapped him on the shoulder, gazing at the urn so as to avoid catching anyone's eye. *And just like that, any chance we had of looking into what really matters is gone.*

Narvi stood. "Looks like we've got something to report to Fas after all."

Laughter filled the room. Arandras exhaled heavily, resting his chin on his hands as the others began discussing maps and speculating on the location in tones as bright as the weather was gloomy. Even Halli was smiling.

A hollow trepidation opened within him.

Weeper's tears. There'll be no stopping them now.

By late afternoon, every flat surface in the workroom was covered with maps. The largest, a beautifully illuminated chart of the entire region from the Pelasean mountains to the eastern coast, hung in a great glass-fronted frame on one wall. A fresh collection of books surrounded Senisha, including several scrolls with dark wooden

rollers which, judging by the amount of dust on the chipped handles, hadn't been disturbed for years. Bannard and the others flipped
through volumes and pored over maps, hunting for the key that
would unlock the coordinates and lead them to their prize.

Arandras sat in a corner of the room, a book of Valdori geogra-
phy open on his lap, and tried to think of a way to stop them.

He should have pulled the plug before it ever got this far. He'd
seen it happening, step by inevitable step; just stood by and watched
as the Quill slowly but inexorably steered the project away from his
goal and toward their own. Now they had the golems' scent in their
nostrils, and short of a miracle, Arandras couldn't imagine a damn
thing that would convince them to let it go.

The thing of it was, he wouldn't have minded trading the golems
for Tereisa's killer. He'd have taken that deal in a heartbeat, without
a moment's regret. Instead, he'd managed to give them up with not
a copper duri to show for it.

*Weeper's breath, but I should have dragged a name from that
wretched Library scribe when I had the chance.*

Fas was probably already putting together the retrieval party,
never mind that they still had no idea where they were going. Narvi
had gone off to find him hours ago and was still not back. They'd
want the urn with them, no doubt, which meant they'd want Arandras to accompany the party. He still had some leverage, then — a
few last scraps he hadn't yet frittered away. He'd have to find a way
to make them count.

"It's somewhere to the west, for sure," Bannard said, waving at a
section of the large, glass-fronted map. "Near Tienette Lake, like as
not, or maybe somewhere in the Pelaseans."

"That narrows it down," Halli muttered, glowering at the map.
A long, irregular blob at the foot of the Pelaseans marked the lake
that gathered rain and snow melt from a hundred different mountain streams and funnelled it into the Tienette River. "You could set
every Quill in the Free Cities searching for years and barely cover a
fraction of the ground."

"So we need a better map!"

"Fine," Senisha snapped. "Pick one, then. Or go and fetch the
one from the library that I missed."

A tense silence settled over the room. Bannard scowled and stomped away, throwing himself into a seat before a stack of smaller, unrolled maps.

Well, that's something. The Greathouse back in Chogon had a vast array of maps marked with the old Valdori system of coordinates. In Arandras's time there, the Quill had located no fewer than seven previously unknown sites in the surrounding region, based solely on a series of coordinates found carved in the foundation stone of a collapsed obelisk — though as it turned out, all but two of them had long since been discovered and looted by others. *But it seems the schoolhouse here is not so well equipped for such puzzles. Which might give me time to work something out.*

Until then, he would keep his head down and do his best to avoid any further confrontations with Fas or any of the others. Because apart from his in with the Quill, what else did he have? *Still no name for Tereisa's killer, no face, no address, no letter, just a gods-blighted urn —*

The sound of the door being thrown back pulled him from his thoughts. Fas and Narvi entered the room, the former glancing about with a look of intense satisfaction. But it was Narvi's expression that caught Arandras's eye. The wide grin he'd had when he left was gone, replaced with something altogether thinner, almost forced.

"What's this, still working?" Fas said with a broad smile. "Finding a golem army not enough for one day, eh?"

"We haven't quite found them yet," Bannard said.

Fas brushed the protestation aside. "You've done well, all of you," he said. He picked up the lid from the work table and peered at the markings. "This is where they are, is it?"

"We believe so," Narvi said, his attempted cheer belied by the flatness of his tone, though nobody but Arandras seemed to notice.

"And where is that, exactly?"

Bannard pointed to the map. "Somewhere around Tienette Lake."

"We think," Halli added.

Fas studied the indicated section of the map. "You've made a record of these numbers, of course?"

"Of course," Senisha said. "We made copies for each of us, so if anyone spots something —"

"Good, good." Fas looked from Bannard to Senisha, Halli to Gord. "You've done well," he repeated. "More than enough for one day. Go and enjoy yourselves. But," he held a finger to his lips, "not a word outside this house, you understand? Of course you do."

The others began packing up, ordering the piles of maps and finding markers for their books. Arandras stood, stretching the cramped muscles of his neck and back. Senisha glanced in his direction, but turned away as she noticed Fas heading toward him.

"Arandras," Fas said, one thick hand wrapped around the neck of the urn, the other toying with its lid. "A word, if you please."

Arandras studied the man through narrowed eyes. *This doesn't sound good.* "Of course."

"A golem army, eh?" Fas said, the urn's lid snaking through and around the man's meaty fingers. "Who'd have thought when you arrived that we'd be discussing golems a few days later?"

"Who, indeed?" Arandras said, watching the lid as it appeared and disappeared from view.

Fas caught his gaze and smiled. "These are yours, I believe," he said, offering the urn and its lid to Arandras.

"So they are." Arandras took the proffered items. The room was empty now save for the two of them and Narvi, who stood a couple of paces away, refusing to meet Arandras's eyes.

"We owe you a debt of gratitude," Fas said.

"More than just gratitude, I should think," Arandras said, the words slipping out before he could stop them. *Damn. So much for avoiding confrontation.*

But Fas only smiled again. "Quite so." A fat pouch jingled in his hand. "Perhaps this will go some way toward making up for the delay in finding your mysterious letter writer."

Delay? You've scarcely even tried. "I hardly think that's necessary," Arandras said. "What's lacking is time and attention —"

"Which, alas, are now in shorter supply than ever," Fas said, setting the pouch down and leaning uncomfortably close. "The entire resources of this schoolhouse are now committed to the pursuit of these golems. Once we've retrieved them, we'll be happy to pick up your matter again, but you'll understand that I can't guarantee when that will be."

Oh, I understand all right. The Quill would pick it up again when it became convenient, and not a moment before. "I'm not one of your *resources,* Damasus. As far as I'm concerned, I'm still here to find that man."

"Of course, you're welcome to continue your search as long as you wish," Fas said. "But not, I regret to say, from here."

Arandras blinked. "Excuse me?"

Fas gave an exaggerated sigh. "You used to be Quill," he said. "You understand."

An unpleasant suspicion began to form. "Understand what?"

"That in a search for relics of this magnitude, we can't permit the presence of... well, outsiders."

"But the urn —"

"Remains yours." Fas shrugged. "We have all we need from it now."

You treacherous bastard. "I brought this to you," Arandras hissed. "We wouldn't even be having this conversation but for me."

"And we're grateful." Fas nudged the bulging pouch and it gave a heavy clink. "Take it. With the Dreamer's blessing, we'll have the golems in hand within the month. You'll barely notice the wait."

"No. No way in the hundred hells." Once the golems were located, any last leverage Arandras might have had would be gone. He'd find himself cast aside, with nothing left to rely on but the Quill's honour and goodwill.

Which, truth be told, was exactly where he was now.

Narvi looked up, meeting his eyes at last, his expression both pained and pleading. "Arandras..."

Arandras shoved the pouch away. "Gatherer take your coin. I should never have come to you. Trusting the Quill," he spat the word, "like a damn simpleton. Weeper's tears, what was I thinking? The hells with you all." Face flushed, he barged past Fas and made for the door.

"I'm sorry, Arandras," Narvi called from somewhere behind him. "I couldn't... it wasn't my choice. I'm sorry."

But it was too damn late for apologies. Too late by far.

CHAPTER 15

To bind is simply to impose order upon an otherwise disordered object. There is nothing strange or undesirable in this. Generals bind armies, mothers bind children, and administrators bind cities every day.

— *Forms of Sorcery* (author unknown)

"OVERSEER CLADE?"

The knock on his door was soft but insistent. Clade set Yevin's papers down with a sigh. "What?"

"Message for you, Overseer." The heavy door muffled the servant's voice, but not enough to conceal his anxiety. "Sorry to disturb you, but I was told you wanted all messages tonight delivered directly."

Clade opened the door and plucked the note from the servant's hand. "Thank you," he said, closing the door on the man's nervous face.

The note was from Terrel. He opened it and held it to the lamp's light.

Shops checked. No sign of item. Request support to investigate groups. T.

"Request support?" Clade tossed the note aside. The man had the hide of an ox. Did he think Clade had a battle squad ready to go? *I'm hiring him, for the gods' sakes!*

Anger stirred within, threatening to break out. Clade raised hurried walls, smothering the unwelcome emotion and pressing it into a cage. His outburst with Terrel had won the man's grudging cooperation, but it had been a lapse all the same. Control was essential. *Surrender that, and none of the rest matters anyway.*

It was a central tenet of sorcery: above all else, the success of a binding depended on the qualities of the substance in which it was grounded. A grand timber chest, crafted from the trunk of some great oak or eucalypt, could sustain a binding far beyond anything wrought upon an old, half-rotten branch. Clean water from a mountain stream offered far greater potential than a tannery's polluted runoff. Yet purity was not the sole consideration. Order mattered, too. Estelle had explained it to him once as the difference between a calm, green lagoon and the clear but choppy surface of a windy hillside lake. Despite its impurities, the still water of the lagoon would prove more amenable to the waterbinder's craft.

Clade had found it a strange distinction at the time, foreign to his then-limited experience of sorcery. Yet the more he read about the great works of the Valdori, and the more he practised his own small arts of woodbinding, the more he had come to believe that in fact it was order, more than any other consideration, which most determined an object's capacity for spellcraft.

Which, if true, held critical implications for his own endeavour.

Shortly before departing Zeanes, Clade had found reports, deep in the Oculus archives, of renegades who had fled the Oculus in centuries past. Seeking to free themselves of their heart-bond, they had attempted to place it on another: a beggar, usually, or a peasant child. The results were disastrous. Those pursuing the rogue sorcerers had found not free men and women but cripples and lackwits, picking over the bones of their dead comrades. Some survivors had lost limbs; others could no longer command the limbs they had. Few, it was said, could even remember their names.

Vagrants and urchins. It was hard to imagine a worse choice of recipient. Even among the Oculus, candidates were permitted to attempt the binding only after years of training to learn the required discipline; and for every four who survived the attempt, one did not. Unschooled children and vagabonds would never have stood a chance.

Yet success was not solely about the binding's target. It couldn't be. To join the Oculus and receive the binding directly from the hand of Azador was one thing. But to lift the binding from one spirit and place it on another — that was something else entirely. Any constraint that applied to the target must surely apply to the source as well. If he, Clade, were disarrayed when he attempted the transfer, no amount of order in the recipient would matter.

Even if that recipient was a golem.

So keep yourself in check. Clade breathed deeply, willing his mind to calm. The anger brooded in its cage, not yet gone but no longer threatening to break free. *Terrel is not worth my rage. Only Azador merits that. I will show it to him the day I gain my freedom.*

His fear of exposure, at least, had passed as soon as he'd stopped to think. Anything the god might have seen through the locuses carried by Terrel and his men could be explained by the account he'd given Estelle. *I'd hoped to wait until I had everything in place. Surprise you.* Foolish as it had been to give Terrel the locuses at the time, it now served to make Clade appear unexpectedly credible. *For once, Garrett's idiocy works to my advantage. About time.*

A pile of unread correspondence lay on the floor a pace in from the door; some addressed to Garrett and some to Clade himself; all of it Oculus business and therefore unimportant. Terrel's note rested atop the pile where he had thrown it. Clade picked it up, smoothing the paper against a chair arm, and read it again.

Groups. Groups meant the Quill and the Bel Hennese. Maybe the Three Rivers Trading Company, too, or other traders, local or foreign. There were numerous smaller bands scattered throughout the city also, little clubs of two or three half-rate sorcerers, as well as a variety of individuals who held no loyalties to anyone but themselves. Terrel could look those up himself. *But the big groups...* Clade grimaced. Even with the full backing of the Oculus, gaining entry to a Quill schoolhouse or a Bel Hennese circle would be all but impossible. *There's still my Quill researcher, if I can find something specific to ask for. But even then —*

The bells of the Kefiran temple rang out across the road, the unexpected sound disrupting his thoughts. He crossed to the window and peered down at the dark street. A line of candles bordered the front of the temple, their tiny flames winking in and out like upside-down stars, the faint sound of sung prayer drifting up from the street. *Of course. The Night of the Sea.* The line began to snake behind the temple, the song diminishing as the lights passed out of sight one by one. Clade slowed his breath, straining after the half-familiar, half-exotic music. *Like stillness wrought into song, it quiets all it touches.*

The last candle disappeared. Someone had doused the streetlamps closest to the temple, making the street before it a puddle of gloom. From this angle he could just make out a faint glow around the temple's side. He gazed after it a moment; then he turned, striding from the room to the wide timber staircase in the centre of the Oculus building.

He emerged atop the roof in the cool night air. A soft breeze caught his hair, bringing with it the scent of burnt offerings and the sound of Kefiran harmonies. He leaned on the rough stone balustrade, gazing out at the shadowy dome and its small belfry, now silent.

"It's a beautiful night, isn't it?" A shadow at the end of the gallery resolved into Sera's round form. Her voice was hushed. "So peaceful. It's like they're singing the whole city to sleep."

Firelight blazed behind the temple, spilling orange light over the neighbouring buildings for the span of a heartbeat before dying back down. An altar being lit, perhaps. "I didn't know you were familiar with Kefiran rituals."

"Oh." Sera shuffled her feet. "I'm not, really. I just like the song."

Clade nodded, though the gesture was lost in the dark. "You're half right," he said. "It's the Night of the Sea. The song is the prayer of one lost amid the waves. With his words he begs the All-God for calm, and with his music he beseeches the sea to be still."

Sera settled her forearms on the balustrade beside him and looked out at the street, her posture mimicking his own. "Do you follow the Kefiran ways now?"

"Me? No. I don't think they'd have me."

"Why not?"

"You've obviously never heard me sing."

She laughed. "Some other path, then?"

"No." He shifted his weight against the balustrade, stretching his shoulders. "Maybe there are gods and maybe there aren't. But even if there are, why in the hundred hells would anyone want to attract their attention?" A life had space for only one absolute. "There's not a single god out there that doesn't care more about itself than anything else."

"There's Azador."

"Yes, there's Azador," Clade said. "And what do you suppose Azador wants?"

"I thought I was done with tests," Sera said, playful. "I'm a bound sorcerer now, Clade. Remember?"

Of course she was. As if Clade could forget it.

"I can still remember the day you told us," she said. "Do you want me to recite it for you? Because I can. 'Azador grieves for the fallen Empire. Azador longs for its restoration. That is the purpose for which the Oculus exists.'" She sighed. "That's why people seek gods, isn't it? To find purpose. But we don't need any of that. We've got Azador."

"And what if —" He broke off, clenched his jaw shut.

"What if what?"

The question was soft, gentle, as though she were the one offering succour to him. Clade's throat constricted. "Nothing."

A point of light emerged from the side of the temple, followed a heartbeat later by another, then a third. The Kefiran candle-bearers, silent now, completing their circuit of the tabernacle and filing onto the street. The candles seemed to flare for a moment, then guttered all at once; and in the darkness, the song began anew.

The surrender of sight. Abandonment to the will of the All-God; and with it, deliverance.

"Did I offend you the other day?" Sera's voice was soft, hesitant. "When I said you were like a priest?"

"Offend? No."

"Only it seemed like you were... I don't know. Avoiding me."

Yes, I imagine it did. "I'm sorry."

"It's just... I never thanked you before."

He looked up, but her features were hidden in the dark. "Thanked me for what?"

"For inviting me to join the Oculus. For giving me purpose.

What we're doing — what Azador is doing — it's real, Clade. More real than anything going on down there. It matters, and it's good. And the only reason I'm part of it is because of you." She leaned closer, close enough for him to see the soft glint of her eyes. "Thank you."

He nodded again, his face immobile. "Of course."

The song ended on a single note, long and high. Sera turned back to the balustrade. When she spoke, her voice was wistful. "We should have something like that, don't you think? Something that tells the world who we are. Something beautiful."

I cannot say anything, Clade thought. *I must not.*

He stood wrapped in his thoughts, gazing at the dark emptiness of the street below, Sera silent beside him but for the soft, steady rhythm of her breaths.

～

The morning saw a fresh influx of correspondence. Clade gestured at the pile on the floor and the servant stooped, placing the new messages carefully alongside the old, then stood and cleared his throat.

"Something?" Clade said.

"Your pardon, Overseer," the servant said. "Councillor Estelle wishes me to tell you that she will see you within the hour. She instructs you to await her arrival."

"Does she indeed?" Clade glanced around the room. Papers sprawled across the floor, the pile's edge barely a pace in from the door. Pieces of the table that had stood between the cushioned chairs lay against the wall, legs sticking into the air. "There's no need for her to climb all the way up here. I'll go to her."

"Forgive me, but the Councillor was quite specific. She wishes to see you here." The servant bowed. "Overseer." The door closed with a soft click, its heavy timber not quite enough to mask the servant's receding footsteps.

Clade lowered himself into a chair and tried half-heartedly to corral his frustration. Estelle would no doubt want to hear of his progress. *If only I had some to report.* He'd hoped Terrel might give him something, some other avenue to pursue, but the mercenary had turned out to be as useless as Garrett. *I'm surrounded by fools and incompetents.*

Which, no doubt, was exactly what Estelle would think when he gave her the news.

The pile of unread correspondence lay by the door, offering mute testimony to his negligence. Sighing, he scooped up the papers and deposited them on his desk.

A corner of heavy white paper caught his eye. Frowning, Clade pulled it free. The paper had been folded over on itself in a style common to southeast, but rare among the Oculus. The seal on the back bore the tome and inkpot of the Spyridon Library; and on the front, his name and address inscribed in Yevin's unmistakable hand.

The message within was short and to the point.

C—

Received visitor yesterday enquiring after your identity. I revealed nothing. Man seemed to have intercepted our correspondence; suggest we avoid Three Rivers carriers henceforth. He knew about the urn.

Man was of compact build, bearded, educated. Someone of similar description reportedly departed for Anstice this morning, in Quill company. I was unable to discover his name.

—Y

Clade turned it over, examining the message for a date. None was present. *How long ago was this sent?* It was a four day journey from Spyridon to Anstice, though the message itself would have made it in three. Or perhaps not. Yevin might have traded speed for security to ensure the letter made it through.

Frowning, he read the message again. *Quill company.* Unlikely, then, to be involved with the mystery woman Terrel seemed to think had gained possession of the urn. Maybe there was no woman, and the Quill had somehow slipped the urn away themselves.

Maybe the urn was sitting in the Quill schoolhouse right now.

A dark swirl touched his thoughts and he started, bracing himself to keep it out; but it was still distant, perhaps a floor away, moving at a pace that suggested its bearer was either taking their ease or slowed by age and infirmity. He grimaced. *Here she comes.*

Clade stood, tucking Yevin's note back into the stack. His gaze fell on the horse-head bookend and he paused, running a finger over the cool marble, remembering how it had felt as he swung it against

Garrett's head. His hand closed over it, feeling its mass against his skin, its smooth curve nestling into its palm. It had felt *right*...

"Clade?" Something rapped against the door. Estelle's stick. "Open up, Requiter."

He stood frozen, his hand outstretched; then, abruptly, he shoved the bookend away. It toppled onto a low stack of paper with a muffled thud.

"It's not locked," he called.

There was a low mutter beyond the door; then it swung open to admit Estelle's walking stick, followed closely by Estelle herself.

"Councillor," he said. "I'm afraid I still have nothing solid on the whereabouts of the golems. I'm pursuing all avenues —"

"Never mind that now." Estelle sank into a cushioned chair with a sigh. "I need gold, Clade. How much do we have?"

Clade blinked. "Gold?"

"Gold, yes. Oculus gold. From the reserves here in Anstice. How much is there?"

"I, uh... it will take some time to calculate. Our assets are split across several accounts. I could probably get you a total within a few hours."

"An approximation is fine, Clade. How much?"

He frowned, performing some hurried additions in his head. "About twelve hundred lurundi."

"Twelve." She gave an indelicate grunt. "Well. Fifteen would have been better, but twelve should suffice."

Clade shook his head, lost. "Suffice for what?"

"I'll need you to draw up some letters of credit," Estelle said. She handed over a scrap of paper. "These are the first payments."

Clade ran his eye down the list. *Three Rivers Trading Company: two hundred and forty lurundi. Woodtraders Guild: one hundred and ninety lurundi. Doylen Company: sixty-two lurundi.* In among the larger trading houses were numerous smaller merchants: Scamander Jull, dealer in horses and oxen; the shipbuilding collective known as the Storm Sons, whose shipyard at Borronor's Crossing had produced the last three river galleys purchased by Anstice for patrol of the Tienette; and the local representatives of the Falisi, producers and purveyors of sorcery-resistant anamnil. He looked up. "This covers half the merchantry in Anstice."

"Half the significant ones, anyway."

Unease whispered through his breast, ephemeral as the wind. "What's this about?"

Estelle considered him. "Sit down, Clade," she said, and smiled when he complied. "Tell me, how long have we been here?"

"In Anstice? Twenty years, or near enough."

"Twenty-two, in fact. The first Oculus unit to be established on the mainland. Still more than twice the size of our next largest group, in Scarpton. As for the rest, well..." She gestured dismissively.

"What's your point?" Clade said.

Estelle leaned forward, hands pressing hard against the arms of her chair. "Didn't you ever wonder, why here? Why focus on Anstice and not somewhere on the coast, where we could more easily travel back and forth to Zeanes?"

"We do have units on the coast. You just said so yourself. Scarpton, Neysa, others."

"Yes. But Anstice is, shall we say, our base of operations on the mainland. This is the point on which our ambitions hinge."

Our ambitions? He eyed her, trying to divine her meaning. The god shifted about her head, restless, impatient.

"Oh, come on," Estelle said. "You know our purpose. Restoration of the Empire, and all that. You don't think we're going to achieve it if we remain cooped up on our island, do you?"

"Of course not."

"No. We must expand our influence. That's why we've positioned ourselves the way we have."

"Meaning what?" Clade cast about for an explanation. "The Oculus is moving off Pazia? Moving here?"

Estelle shook her head. "Not moving. Not yet, anyway. And not here. Neysa."

"But you just said that the Neysa unit —"

"Not the unit," Estelle said, and she smiled, thin and wide, like a child about to reveal the best secret in the world. "The city."

The city? A hollow opened in his stomach. He stared, speechless. *You can't mean...*

"Anstice would be ideal, of course," she continued. "Wealthy,

central, powerful. Unfortunately, a little too powerful, and with
rather too many friends. So we're going to take Neysa instead."

Take Neysa. Clade moistened his lips. *You're going to* take *Neysa.
Just like that.*

"Do you see now? An assault on one of the Great Cities is bound
to unsettle the other four, but Anstice is the only one close enough
or strong enough to do anything about it. But if the local merchantry have enough business wrapped up with us, the archon won't be
able to act. The Consulate won't allow it."

"So that's what you've been doing here," Clade said, his voice flat.
"Getting into bed with the traders of Anstice."

"Metaphorically speaking, of course," she said, but there was no
offence in her tone, only amusement. "There are more mundane
considerations, too. To take Neysa we'll need men, food, equipment.
Anstice will act as our supply base, which will bind its merchants to
us even more tightly afterwards. How can they object to a new order
they helped bring about?"

An invasion. Gods. Azador pulsed its satisfaction, and Clade
shivered. No wonder it wanted the damn golems so much.

"So you can see why the golem army is so important," Estelle
said, as though tracking his thoughts. "Not that the garrison in
Neysa is anything special. But next time..." She trailed off, eyes
gleaming, and the god surged.

Next time? They're already thinking about the next *city?* The god's
violent hunger pounded against him, and he fought the urge to cover his head with his arms. *If this boulder truly begins to roll, where
will it end?*

"Clade," Estelle said, and he snapped his head up to meet her
gaze. Her face was a mixture of excitement and confusion. *And
impatience.* "What is it? I thought you'd be pleased."

"I am," he said. "Of course I am. I just... I had no idea. The sheer
magnitude of it. Who else knows?"

"Just the Council. No, it's all right. You'll be joining us soon
enough anyway."

"Of course." The small matter of the unfinished hearing into
Garrett's death seemed forgotten, for the moment at least. Azador's
greed pressed against him, and he suppressed a shudder. *No. I cannot*

allow this to happen.

Estelle stood. "Draw up the letters. I want them delivered to my hand by midday."

"As you say, Councillor."

The door closed behind her, the god's lust hanging in the air like smoke. Clade tracked its retreat as Estelle made her slow path back down the stairs. *Demand. That's all the damnable thing knows how to do. And now it wants a city, and more.*

He hissed out a sigh. The god was a perversion. It had to be stopped.

But until he escaped it himself, there was nothing he could do.

He returned to his desk, retrieving Yevin's message from the stack and pressing it flat. The Quill party would have arrived from Spyridon days ago. By now, the entire schoolhouse should know whatever news they had brought.

Thoughts racing, Clade cleared a space in front of him, located pen and ink and paper.

Time to repay your debt, Bannard. You'd better be worth it.

Back in Spyridon, when Arandras had needed to get away from the four walls of his small shop, he'd had no shortage of havens. The great hill beneath the Library afforded a multitude of vantage points at which he might while away an afternoon, gazing out at the red roofs of the city and the surrounding countryside. The Arcade, set as it was near the top of the hill, offered the best view of all; yet Arandras's favourite spot was a stone bench halfway down the hill, hidden away at the end of a twisting alley, unknown to any save a handful of locals. The bench looked out to the nearby town of Port Gallin — these days, an extension of Spyridon in all but name — and the glittering waters of the Sea of Storms away to the south. A few hours spent watching the ships put in and depart, or contemplating the ponderously slow construction of the new wall and breakwater, never failed to soothe his spirit and calm whatever agitation had taken root within him.

Anstice had no such places. The city stood in the middle of a great plain; featureless save for the Tienette winding its way toward the eastern coast. The river was pleasant enough in its own way, to be sure; but after several hours spent roaming the promenades, staring at the water from one bridge or another, and breathing its dank, faintly rotten scent, Arandras found himself no calmer than he'd been on waking.

The nerve of them, to break off association with me!

He grimaced, pushing away from the rail of Island Bridge and turning south. A thick granite tower thrust skyward in the middle distance: one of the nine redoubts scattered about Anstice that housed the city's army and military supplies. Unlike some, this one seemed entirely intact, with a series of dark spots that could only be windows running around the tower's crown. There would be a view, if only he could get to it. No doubt Anstice's army would be thrilled to have him tramping through their stores and barracks for the sake of a pleasant vista.

Somehow, the possibility that the Quill might drop Arandras from the team had never crossed his mind. The ease with which they'd managed to extract what they needed was humiliating, and his own blindness in cooperating with them only made it worse. *The single greatest work of sorcery in the whole of recorded history, and I just handed it to them on a gods-damned platter.*

It made him want to scream.

All that remained now was for the Quill to find a sufficiently detailed map, one bearing the old Valdori notation, and match the coordinates on the urn with an actual location. They already had a region: southwest of the city, upriver, perhaps as far as the lake but certainly no further than the mountains.

If they didn't own the maps they needed, they'd soon start asking around. Peni, if she wasn't still out of town. Isaias, certainly. They'd want to move quickly, take possession of whatever maps they could find before anyone else could get in ahead of them. After all, there was still someone out there looking for the urn, and presumably the golems. That would be the only danger, though. Nobody else knew about the golems except the people in that schoolhouse…

And me.

His hand closed over the pouch at his side. *I know as much as they do. I have the coordinates. I know the region.*

And I just happen to be on good terms with the one man most likely to have what they need.

Spirits rising, Arandras set out down the western thoroughfare in the direction of Isaias's shop. He arrived with a spring in his step, pushing past the door and taking the narrow stairs two at a time. The shopkeeper's expansive voice bounced down the stairs from the room above, followed by the lower, equally familiar voice of Mara. Isaias must have coughed up the extra silver for her puzzle box after all.

"Certainly, my dear, certainly," Isaias said as Arandras crested the stairs. "A moment, if you please, for Isaias to go and fetch this most lavish sum." He peered up at Arandras's approach, his face transforming in a moment from earnest munificence to delighted welcome. "Friend Arandras, you return! How fortuitous for two such dear friends to visit Isaias together once again. Surely this is an omen of good things to come. Even I, unschooled as I am in the noble arts of augury and divination, can see that it must be so."

With a bob of his head, Isaias bustled through a panelled door to the back room, leaving Mara and Arandras alone. Mara quirked an eyebrow in greeting, elbows resting on the counter behind her. Isaias's cat, Pinecone, lay at the other end of the counter, twitching her tail back and forth above Mara's small, verdigrised puzzle box. A tuneless humming rose from the next room.

"They kicked you out, huh?" Mara said, low enough for Isaias not to hear.

Arandras nodded. "How did you know?"

"I went looking for you this morning. Well, you and breakfast. Thought I should make use of the Quill's hospitality at least once. Fas was not happy to find me hoeing into the honeyed bread, let me tell you."

"I can imagine." Arandras chuckled at the thought. "How much did you get down before he saw you?"

"Not enough," Mara said. "Listen, I've had an idea how to find…" She trailed off as the humming grew louder and footsteps sounded on the other side of the door. "Your old acquaintance," she finished, just as Isaias re-emerged carrying a small, but apparently heavy, wooden box in both hands.

What? How? But Isaias was already depositing the box on the counter and reaching into his sleeve, producing a key with a triumphant flourish. "Now, my dear," he said, fitting the key to the lock, "let us see about your payment." The lid swung open, revealing a small stack of gold and silver bars.

Arandras turned away, halting before the narrow case of anamnil-worked items. Mara had a lead on Tereisa's killer? Suddenly, the golems and the Quill seemed half as important as they had a moment ago. But then, there was no guarantee that the lead would pan out. *And if I don't grab the maps now, the Quill will take them and I'll be left with nothing.*

Still, a lead. At last.

Weeper, but I wish you'd come up with it yesterday.

"There, dear Mara, you have your fee." Isaias snapped the box shut and turned the lock. Pinecone startled at the sound, leaping down from the counter and disappearing behind a display cabinet. "A generous price, if I may say so; but of course Isaias does not begrudge such generosity on behalf of his dear friends, no, indeed he does not."

"Thank you, Isaias," Mara said, pocketing her coin. "A pleasure doing business with you, as always."

"And what of you, my friend?" Isaias said, turning to address Arandras. "What happy need brings you to my shop this morning?"

Arandras took a breath. "I'm looking for a map."

"A map!" Isaias cried. "Splendid! Truly, you have come to the right place. What form of map do you seek? Perhaps Anstice as it was in centuries past, when all fourteen redoubts still stood and the city stretched no further south than this very shop. Maybe a chart of distant lands: Pazia to the east, or Jervia to the north, or the far isle of Bel Henna. Or —"

"Nothing so remote as that," Arandras said. "I have a set of Valdori coordinates I'm trying to place. Somewhere in the vicinity of Tienette Lake."

Isaias beamed. "Of course, of course. If you would be so kind as to tell Isaias the numbers you seek, I will be delighted to scour my collection on your behalf."

Arandras recited the coordinates, omitting the final, most

specific numbers, and Isaias scurried away to the back room once more.

"Is that map going to be what I think it is?" Mara murmured.

"Never mind that now," Arandras said. "What's this idea?"

Mara shook her head. "Not here." She headed for the stairs, glancing back at him over her shoulder. "I'll wait outside. Don't take too long."

The shuffle of papers sounded from the next room, followed by a crash and shouted curse from Isaias. *Don't take too long, indeed. Like it depends on me.* Arandras glanced around the shop, eyes lighting on the green armchair. *That'll do nicely.*

Halfway to the chair his boot crunched on something hard. Frowning, he dropped to a crouch. *Looks like fragments of glass. But where...?* His gaze fell on a nearby display cabinet. An entire side of the windowed cabinet was bare, leaving its contents open to the shop.

The door to the back room banged open. "Arandras, I... Arandras?" Isaias glanced about, confusion filling his round face. "Ah, there you are. Captivated by the Kharjik spice jars, I see. Truly, a remarkable —"

"Do you know your cabinet is broken?" Arandras straightened, peered closer at Isaias. "Weeper's breath, is that a bruise on your neck? What happened?"

"Ah, friend Arandras, 'tis nothing." Isaias offered a game smile. "A result of some, shall we say, overenthusiastic enquiries, nothing more."

Right. If by "overenthusiastic" you mean "hand around the throat". "What were they after?"

"An urn, as it happens." Isaias's eyes narrowed in thought. "Now that Isaias thinks of it, did you not mention such a piece in your last visit? What does this urn —"

Arandras crossed the space between them in a single pace. "Who were they?"

"I, uh, well, Isaias had never seen them before. Fighting men, Isaias thought, though neither introduced himself." He fingered his collar and swallowed. "Decidedly unfriendly, in truth, despite my most welcoming —"

"Did they say anything, or wear any identifying mark?"

"No, no." Isaias shook his head. "Come, let us banish such unpleasant thoughts. I have just the map you're looking for. Come and see!"

He knows it's here. Somehow, the man he sought had learnt of the urn's arrival in Anstice. Arandras's hand went to the pouch on his belt. *Weeper's mercy, why is he always one step ahead?*

"See, friend Arandras! A handsome piece, first drawn by the famed Valdori Cartographer's Guild, reproduced from the original by the Weeping Brothers a mere six hundred years ago and copied only twice since then. Is it not perfect?"

A large sheet of parchment lay partially unrolled, showing the edge of a body of water — Tienette Lake, no doubt. Arandras leaned closer, peering at the tiny Valdori numerals adorning the border. *Looks about right. If the Quill knew this was here, they'd likely be tearing the door down right now.*

"How much?" Arandras said, though he could already tell it would be beyond what he had in his purse.

"Thirty-five luri," Isaias said, and Arandras cursed inwardly. The sum was more than double what the shopkeeper had just paid out for Mara's puzzle box. There was no way Arandras could scrape that much together, or at least not in Anstice. His savings back home would have covered it, but that money was locked away in a Spyridon bank and inaccessible until he returned. *Why in the hells didn't I take Damasus's gold? The man was practically shoving it down my throat.*

"Can I see the rest?" Arandras said.

"Ah, friend Arandras, you know I cannot. There are those who would use such a glimpse to gather what information they seek without compensating Isaias for the privilege!" Isaias blinked as though astonished that such perfidy could even be contemplated. "It is not that Isaias does not trust you, dear Arandras; yet I must treat all of my customers alike, or word will get out that Isaias has favourites — and though this may in your case be true, my dear friend, I nevertheless could not permit such a suspicion to darken the hearts of my other valued patrons."

"Fine," Arandras said. "A favour, then. From one friend to

another."

"But of course! If it is within Isaias's power, it shall be done!"

"Hold this map for me," Arandras said. "I need time to pull together the money. Don't sell it to anyone in the meantime, all right?
Don't even let on that you have it. Especially…"

Isaias's head cocked in the manner of an inquisitive dog. "Especially?"

"Especially to the Quill."

"Ah."

Arandras frowned. "Ah, what?"

"Dear Arandras, you know how much I treasure the confidence
of my friends." Isaias smiled magnanimously. "Discretion above all,
that is Isaias's watchword. Not a word of this shall I breathe to anyone save you and you alone. Truly, Isaias lives only to serve his honoured customers…" The shopkeeper trailed off, his face falling. "Yet
it is not so simple as that. Are the Quill not customers too? Indeed,
if the Quill sought to purchase this map, would they not in fact
be the first and only customers? How then could Isaias deny their
request for the sake of friendship, however boundless? If, in this
matter, Arandras remains a friend and not a customer…"

"All right, all right." *For the Weeper's sake, just stop talking.* "I'll put
down a deposit." He dug out his purse and rummaged inside. There
wasn't much left. "This is all I can spare," he said at last, dumping a
handful of coins on the counter. The rest would be enough to keep
his belly full until his lease at the lodging house ran out, with a few
meagre duri left over to buy a slow ride back to Spyridon on the
back of a merchant's wagon. "Will that suffice?"

Isaias beamed. "Completely, friend Arandras. Isaias will set this
map aside for you until, shall we say, eight days hence? No other will
hear a whisper of it within that time."

A week. It was good enough, Arandras supposed. He'd be out
on the street before then, anyway.

Time enough to figure something out.

⌇

Mara was chewing on a strip of dried meat when Arandras came
down, her long pony-tail dancing from side to side in the breeze.

"Any luck?" she asked, as a heavy, barrel-shaped wagon rumbled past, leaving a ripe scent of fermented apples in its wake.

Arandras scowled. "Perhaps." For all the shopkeeper's empty protestations of friendship, Arandras had never known him yet to renege on an actual deal. To Isaias, even a vow before all the priests in the Tri-God Pantheon would likely fare second best against the sacrament of coin. In any case, there was nothing more he could do. Sooner or later, the Quill would come knocking on Isaias's door, and whatever happened next would be up to Isaias.

"Perhaps?" Mara snorted. "Do we have a location or don't we?"

"Not yet," Arandras said. "But neither do the Quill. I hope." She raised an eyebrow, but he waved the look away. "Later. Tell me about this idea of yours."

"Oh, that," Mara said. "It's simple, really. We go to the registrar's office and ask."

Arandras blinked at her. "We go where?"

"The city registrar," Mara said, as if speaking to a child. "Where they keep all the records. Citizenship lists... minutes of Consulate meetings... who owns what buildings..."

He shook his head.

"That Quill librarian told you where they are, right? All the noteworthy sorcerers in Anstice. So we go to the registrar and get some names. Who runs those places. How many people work there. How promptly they pay their taxes." She shrugged. "Maybe we'll find something useful."

It seemed a long shot to Arandras. Senisha had only mentioned two buildings. There were bound to be more sorcerers in Anstice than that.

Then again, what else did he have to do for the rest of the day?

Senisha had given him streets and landmarks, but not addresses. It took them the rest of the morning to locate the buildings, find the marker stones by the gates, and make a note of the lot numbers. Neither seemed likely to conceal a nest of sorcerers. Ornamental cannons aside, the building on the eastern thoroughfare looked like just another tenement, albeit a particularly unattractive one; and the crumbling facade of the Illith road building, supposedly home to a circle of Bel Hennese, stood in rough, depressing contrast to the soaring blue-roofed residence next door.

By the time Arandras and Mara arrived at the city chambers, the single hand on the tower clock had passed its zenith and was beginning its slow afternoon descent. A winged leopard crouched above the chambers' wide entrance, caught by the sculptor in mid-prowl, the doorway below more than twice Arandras's height. He reached out and touched one of the massive iron doors as he passed, running his finger over the abstract design cut into its surface. The sun-warmed metal was hot to the touch, its grooves deep enough to swallow his finger past the first knuckle.

They passed through the doors into a grand entrance hall. Massive stone pillars supported an ornate indigo-and-gold ceiling, each column sporting a ring of carved leopard heads at its crown. A pale marble staircase dominated one side of the room, curving gracefully out of sight to the upper levels, while the other side opened onto half a dozen different passageways, all unmarked.

Arandras studied the featureless passageways with narrowed eyes. "I assume you know where we're going?"

"More or less." Mara set off down a corridor, one hand at her waist to straighten the cutlass that wasn't there. "This way."

The passage led them through several turns before opening to a light and spacious part of the building, with none of the heavy pillars that marked the front. A sunny courtyard stretched to their right, decorated with boxed plants and timber benches, the flowers' scent so delicate as to be barely perceptible. A painter stood at his board before one of the plants, arguing with an older, balding companion. The two fell silent as Arandras and Mara drew near, waiting until they were almost across the yard before resuming their fierce muttering.

The registrar's office stood at the courtyard's end, across from a softly playing fountain. A counter stretched from one wall to the other, bisecting the room. Cabinets, drawers, and shelves filled the space on the clerks' side; on the other, a handful of waiting enquirers stood in a short queue. Indigo hangings adorned the walls, rich and heavy.

They joined the line, Arandras eyeing the jumble of furniture with a frown. "That one," Mara said, her voice low and close to his ear.

"Huh? That one what?"

"Hush." Mara nodded toward the edge of the room, where a stoop-shouldered clerk glared sullenly across the counter at a woman in a large scarlet hat. The man gave an exaggerated sigh and leaned forward in the manner of one forced to deal with an imbecile. "That one."

"What, the clerk?"

She gave a half-grin. "Trust me."

The line shuffled forward. Arandras glanced at the counter. *Three clerks on duty. Two people ahead of us.* If the sullen one were to remain occupied with the behatted woman for long enough —

"You shouldn't have left, you know."

Arandras blinked. "Excuse me?"

"Last night. The Quill," Mara murmured. "What were you thinking?"

"Hey, it wasn't my idea," he said in a rough undertone. "Damasus kicked me out, remember?"

"And you argued the point with him, did you? Told him all the reasons why he should let you stay?"

Arandras fell silent. In fact, he'd done nothing of the sort. He'd lost his temper and marched out. Perhaps he'd expected it all along — that sooner or later, it would come to exactly that point. "They're the Quill, Mara," he said. "They're so obsessed with their own interests that anything else is either a distraction or an obstacle. You can't work with them, not really."

"That's the Quill you're talking about, is it?"

"What's that supposed to mean?"

"Just that you seem to have a talent for burning bridges lately." She gave him a measuring look. "Tell me, were Druce and Jensine obstacles or distractions?"

"Hey!" The word echoed in the quiet room and he caught himself, lowering his voice to a fierce whisper. "Weeper's arse, Mara. They walked out on me!"

"Next, please." The speaker was a clerk halfway along the counter.

Mara turned to the man behind them. "You go ahead," she said with a forbearing smile. "We just need a moment."

Arandras waited until the man was past. "Jensine and Druce chose to leave, Mara. Their choice, not mine."

She tilted her head. "You don't see it, do you? People don't do things in a void, Arandras. They react to the people around them. To you."

"Yeah, right. That must be why the Quill were so happy to follow my suggestions."

"I'm serious," Mara said. "You don't much care what anyone thinks, I know. You just make up your mind, and you imagine everyone else must do the same. But that's not how most people are. Deep down, most people just want to catch a ride with someone who looks like they know what they're doing."

But they shouldn't! It was all he could do not to grab her by the shoulders and shout it in her face. "If so," he grated, "then *that* is their choice."

She stared back, her face unreadable.

"Their choice," he repeated. "Not mine."

"Who's next?" The words came from behind him. Arandras looked around, and the stoop-shouldered clerk cast him a surly glare. "You waiting or not?"

"Yes," Mara said. She strode past and he watched her go, still grasping after the thread of their argument. At the counter she glanced back, eyebrow cocked. Scowling, he marched over to join her.

Mara already had a scrap of paper on the counter, turned around so that the clerk could read it. "We'd like to inspect the ownership documents for these properties, please."

The clerk sniffed. "Who are you, then?"

Mara smiled. "You don't need to worry about who we are."

"That's precisely what I need to worry about, lady. Only citizens can view documents." The clerk gave a tight grin. "And when they do, that gets added to the file too, so the rest of the city knows when someone's been snooping around."

Damn it! Arandras glared at the man's fatuous smirk. Another Weeper-cursed dead end. *The hells take Mara and her bright ideas.*

"Of course," Mara said, as though the clerk had just offered his sincerest regrets at being unable to help. There was a tap of something hard from the hand that rested on the counter, and Arandras caught a flash of silver between her fingers. "But there are always alternatives, yes?"

The memory of Yevin's shop returned in force, of himself, probing and pushing, hunting for a way around the scribe's clearly expressed will. *No, that's not me. That can't be me.* "Mara," he began, but she turned and touched a finger to his lips.

"This is *my* choice," she whispered.

"It's not mine," Arandras said; but this time he was interrupted by the clerk.

"No. Lady, I can't just... that is, we're not..." He trailed off, staring at the partially concealed coin, his face twitching. "Much as I might want..."

"Sounds like there might be some room for discussion there," Mara said.

The clerk gave a dry cough. "No. I'm not about to... no." But his gaze remained fixed on the coin.

Mara smiled. "Forgive me. We want to see documents for two properties. But I've only offered you one... alternative."

She flexed her wrist and produced another coin from somewhere up her sleeve. It joined the first with a soft clink.

The clerk moistened his lips. "Ah." He glanced at Mara, at the queue of waiting enquirers, at the two silver pieces. Then, abruptly, he scooped the coins off the counter and slouched away.

"What are you doing?" Arandras hissed as soon as the clerk was out of earshot.

"Solving a problem." Mara glanced sideways at the clerk, who was now rummaging through an open drawer. "This is how the world is, Arandras. People react."

He stared at her. "You don't."

She opened her mouth to speak, then stopped. Closed it again. Turned away.

Arandras watched as the clerk closed the drawer, papers in hand, and moved off to another cabinet. *I should leave.* But his feet seemed rooted to the spot.

Damn you, Mara. And damn me, too.

The clerk returned, slapping two bundles of paper onto the

counter. "Two properties," he said to Mara, his eyes flicking around the room. "Be quick about it."

A single glance was enough.

"This one," Arandras said, pulling the papers toward him. He reached into a pocket, fished out the ransom note and unfolded it. The graceful loops, the hard downstrokes: all was the same.

Heart pounding, he scanned the page. A name. There had to be a name. His hand trembled as he set the first sheet aside, began on the second.

There it was.

Clade Alsere. Clade, a sorcerer of the Oculus.

Arandras rolled the name around his mouth. *Clade.*

Clade, the murderer of my wife.

His vision blurred. Somewhere nearby, someone drew a shuddering breath, but it couldn't be him because this was not a moment for tears. This was a moment to savour.

Clade. You and are I are going to meet soon.

I think I will have a lot to say.

CHAPTER 16

The sun is fierce upon our brows, and we grow weary.
The earth is hard beneath our hands, and we grow dismayed.
The load is heavy on our backs, and we grow bitter.
Holy Weeper, grant us the comfort of your tears.

— Liturgy of the Seventh Hour, *Tri-God Book of Prayer,*
Pantheon of Anstice

ILWEN AWOKE TO A THROBBING pain in her knee. She groaned, retching as her mouth registered a wad of mushy cloth jammed between her jaws. Edged timber dug into her shoulders, prompting a further unpleasant discovery: she was bound hand and foot, her wrists behind her back and her ankles to the legs of a hard wooden chair.

Shit.

She sat facing a closed door, near enough to touch if her arms had been free. A narrow gap beneath it provided the room's only light. The close walls seemed to terminate in a low ceiling, though the shadows made it difficult to be sure. *Sixth floor, maybe.* She blinked into the gloom, trying to pick where the walls ended and the ceiling began. *At least they haven't taken me off the compound.*

Her knee burned. She twisted in the chair, straining against her bonds, wanting nothing more for the moment than simply to straighten her leg. But the ropes held her ankles like iron, and at last she gave up, sagging into the seat with a muffled whimper.

Caralange. The memory of those empty, hooded eyes filled her with dread. *Caralange is behind it all. He had Kieffe killed to keep us from finding out, and now he's got me.* Even though she'd suspected him, it still seemed incredible. The man had been a Guild sorcerer for decades. He and Vorace had been friends since childhood.

Yet here she was.

He'd want to ask her questions. Find out how much she knew. Eilwen shivered in the gloom. She'd heard stories of people who'd been interrogated by sorcerers. The weak ones, the ones who broke early, they sometimes came out of it more or less intact if the sorcerer was feeling generous. The strong ones broke too, eventually; but afterwards, they were different. No longer themselves. Sometimes, no longer able to walk, or speak, or eat. Occasionally, scarcely men or women at all.

She began to tremble. *Gods, please, not that. Please spare me that.* She twisted again, frantic now, jerking against her bonds with as much force as she could muster. A shriek rose from somewhere within, burning past her throat; but the gag swallowed its fury, and all that emerged was a long, strangled squeak.

The sound was so unexpected that it startled her into silence. A giggle escaped her, then another; and suddenly she was laughing uncontrollably into the gag. *Ah, gods, I'm hysterical.* A fresh outburst took her and her shoulders shook, tears running down her face. *Oh, gods have mercy. Havilah would be proud.*

Havilah.

The image of the Spymaster stopped her mad rush of thoughts like an icy blast. Eilwen remembered burying her face in his shoulder, there in the dark with Kieffe's body bundled against the wall. *He said he wanted someone uncompromising. Instead, he ended up with someone who falls to pieces every time she hits a bump.* She gritted her teeth, clamping down on the coarse, mushy fabric. *Not this time. Not this time, damn it.*

Eilwen closed her eyes, taking a deep breath and holding it in her lungs. *Get a hold of yourself.* Caralange was going to be checking on her. She needed to be ready for him.

She exhaled slowly, relaxing her shoulders, then the muscles in her stomach. *Better.* Her attention shifted to her arms, her legs, her throbbing knee. Slowly, deliberately, she tensed the muscles of her bad leg, grimacing at the pain, then relaxed them as best she could. *Good enough.* At least when Caralange arrived, he wouldn't find her cowering like a terrified puppy.

And then, if she somehow managed to get out of here...

The old hunger stirred in her gut, soft and sibilant, like an old lover, like a winter's dawn. Fondly, tenderly, it reached out to her as though inviting her back, as though it had turned her away rather than the other way around. She froze, a hare in torchlight, torn between competing desires: to pull back from its seductive call, or to step forward and embrace it.

It reached closer and began to twine itself around her. A shuddering sigh escaped her lips, and she leaned into its touch, savouring the delicious, unclean, sickly sweet taste. *Yes.* Emboldened, it pulled her tighter, a beast returning to its lair, and she groaned, head bowed, as she yielded to its claim.

Caralange was a traitor to the Guild. He deserved to die.

And it was up to her to kill him.

~

The click of a key and the squeak of hinges woke Eilwen from her doze. She blinked up, squinting at the light as the door swung open. The room beyond was narrow but well appointed, with an oppressively low ceiling. *I was right. Sixth floor.* Caralange's own suite, probably.

As though summoned by the thought, Caralange appeared in the doorway, silhouetted against the lamplight. *No sun. What hour is it?* He pulled another chair into view and placed it on the threshold, then sat, stretching his legs. She glared mutely at his shadowed face.

When he spoke, his raspy voice was calm. "If I remove the gag, will you scream?"

Glowering, she shook her head.

Caralange reached out, and though Eilwen was sure his hand stretched no closer than her knee, she felt something brush her ear. "You can spit it out now," he said. "I'd appreciate it if you'd aim to one side."

Eilwen hesitated. *I'd appreciate seeing you wipe it from your face, you bastard.* But any such satisfaction was bound to be short-lived. Besides, it wasn't his discomfort she was interested in. It was hard to be uncomfortable once you were dead.

She turned her head slightly and spat. The wadded cloth landed with a soft splat beside his boot.

"Who do you work for, girl?"

She flinched, rankled by his tone. *Don't react. Don't show him anything.* Forcing a shrug, she responded with what she hoped was a convincing note of confusion. "If you know who I am, you must know I work for Spymaster Havilah."

"Don't give me that. Who do you really work for?"

Eilwen shook her head. "I don't know what you mean."

Caralange snorted. "Unbelievable," he muttered, his anger and loathing suddenly plain. "People tell me you're a smart girl. Now would be a good time to show it."

She stared back in silent defiance.

"Herev's blood!" The sorcerer surged to his feet, striding past her and wrenching her arm painfully around even as the other remained bound. "You bolted out of the Quill shop like your arse was on fire and went straight for Kieffe's body. What are you looking for?" Flecks of spittle struck the side of her face, and she flinched. *"Tell me what you're looking for!"*

The pain in her shoulder was like fire. "I'm looking for the killer!" she gasped, and cursed herself for her weakness.

"Horseshit!" He twisted her arm even further, and she shrieked. "Why?"

"Gods attend, it's the truth! I needed a sorcerer..."

"Why not ask me?"

She shot him a vicious glare through her tears. "Why do you think, you traitorous shit?"

"Traitor, is it?" He dropped her wrist, and Eilwen gasped in relief. "This from the woman found with a dead man after bullying the steward for the room's key. The woman whose so-called investigation has snails running rings around it. I don't know what line you're feeding Havilah, but I'm not so blind."

"I told you, I — wait. You think *I'm* a traitor?"

Caralange settled back with a dark grin and folded his arms.

"This should be good."

Caralange is loyal? Eilwen stared. The man's posture of outraged allegiance defied her disbelief. *Ah, hells.* She looked away, groping for words. *I'm trying to find the real traitor. Yeah, that'll work. Or wait, I know: I used to be a traitor, but I'm not any more!* The sorcerer's grin began to fade, and she gave an abrupt laugh. *That's right, Caralange, you've caught your traitor. Only four years late.*

The sorcerer scowled. "Careful, girl. You're not —"

"I'm working for Havilah," Eilwen said as calmly as she could manage. "We know there's a traitor among the masters, and we're trying to find out who." She found his eyes and held them, willing him to listen. "Ask Havilah if you don't believe me."

He fell silent, his face empty of expression. She returned his gaze, determined not to look away first.

"You suspect Laris, then?" Caralange rasped.

"Damn it, Caralange, I suspect everyone! All except Havilah and Master Vorace."

"Does that include me?"

"Of course it does!"

"And now?"

Yes, Caralange, of course I trust you now. The sorcerer was hardly going to accept that, even if it were true. "Let's just say I'm beginning to entertain the possibility that you might be loyal."

"Bold words from a woman tied to a chair."

She inclined her head.

"Unfortunately, I don't think —"

"Did you examine the body? Or did you let Orom do it?"

Caralange frowned. "Excuse me?"

"Kieffe had a spot of blood, just below the nose. Havilah said that's a mark of several Tahisi poisons, but the Quill told me it can also be evidence of sorcery." She lifted her chin. "So did you examine the body, or did Orom?"

There was a long pause. "I can't," Caralange said at last. "I'm not a fleshbinder."

"But Orom is, right? So Orom could have murdered Kieffe, and then claimed he was killed by poison. Yes?"

Caralange gave her an appraising look. "Hmm." He stood,

pushing his chair back out of sight into the room beyond. "You do realise you've got a hand free?"

Eilwen felt her face grow hot. *A fine spy I make.* Fumbling with the knot, she pulled her other hand free, then turned her attention to her ankles. By the time she limped gingerly out of the narrow room, Caralange was pouring watered wine into tin cups. She accepted one gratefully, slumping into an armchair and massaging her knee.

"So," Caralange said. He seated himself carefully, eyes flicking to her face. "What do you suggest?"

She took a long pull of wine. *No point wondering if it's poisoned.* Dosing her wine wouldn't give the sorcerer anything he hadn't already had when she was tied up. "Orom," she said. "What can you tell me about him?"

"He's one of my sorcerers," Caralange said. "He's a good man."

"I'm sure he is. That's why you let me go when I mentioned him, is it?"

He ignored her and took a mouthful of wine.

"You're not sure about him, are you? Something's caught your eye, but you're not sure if it means anything. What is it?"

Caralange set down the cup, studied its contents. "He goes missing," he said. "Disappears for long stretches. Been happening for a couple of months."

"Where does he go?"

The sorcerer shrugged. "You tell me."

"The room I found Kieffe in. Did he ever —"

Caralange gestured impatiently. "I'm not talking about here."

"Then... what? You're saying he leaves the compound?"

"Herev's bones, you don't know anything, do you?"

"Please." Eilwen leaned forward. "These departures. Are they regular? Frequent?"

"Every few days, lately. He leaves in the mid-afternoon. Doesn't come back until after dark."

"When was the last one?"

"Yesterday."

A meeting with someone outside. Havilah had said something about an old woman meeting half of Anstice. A sorcerer. *Gods, what are we in the middle of?*

Caralange drained his cup, set it down hard.

She took a breath. "What direction does he go?"

"West as far as the thoroughfare. That's all I know." He eyed her speculatively. "You're thinking of shadowing him? I can have one of the others fix you up a little, but I doubt they'll be able to do much for that leg."

"I know. And thank you. I —"

A sudden hammering sounded at the door, followed by a muffled voice. "Caralange? Are you in there? Open up, please."

Glaring at the door, Caralange pushed himself to his feet. Eilwen frowned as he passed. *That voice sounded familiar.*

The hammering continued. "Caralange? Open the door, please."

"Enough," Caralange growled, yanking the door open. "What do you —" The words were cut off by a hiss.

Eilwen rose to see Brielle shouldering inside, a dagger at Caralange's throat. *What in the hells...?*

"Where is she, you dog?" Brielle kicked the door closed behind her. "What have you done with Eilwen... oh."

Eilwen gaped at her, her throat suddenly tight. *You came for me.*

A sudden motion from Caralange sent the dagger clattering to the floor. He drove his forearm against Brielle's neck, shoving her against the wall. Eilwen gave a strangled cry.

"The next blade you hold against me will find its home in your guts." Caralange's brows lowered. "Understood?"

Brielle nodded, her eyes wide. "Yes," she said hoarsely.

Caralange grunted and stepped back. Brielle sagged back against the wall, gasping for breath. Eilwen stood rooted to the spot, wiping her cheeks.

Brielle. Gods. You came.

⁓

Clade slipped into the curved timber pew to the sound of chickens squawking outside. A thin whine cut through the noise in a tone of complaint: a man's voice, Kefiran, indistinct. A baritone answered in the same tongue, its tone calm, cool. At the sound of his voice, the chickens fell silent; then, as though suddenly becoming aware of its impending doom, one of the animals loosed a panicked screech.

Too late now, fowl, Clade thought. *Your master has stumbled, and you are the means by which he may recover himself.* It was the way of the world. Lesser things were sacrificed for greater things. Beasts for men. And men for gods.

The tabernacle was empty; the next service still an hour away. Clade slid along the pew until he could see the entrance without the ark obstructing his view. The temple was no longer proof against Azador's presence — if indeed it ever had been — but he'd decided to have this conversation here all the same. The god might be capable of staying, but presumably it still needed a reason to do so. With luck, it wouldn't even bother them.

This is foolishness. His shoulder bag lay on the pew beside him, the folded copy of Niele's treatise concealed within. *I should be preparing to see Bannard, not wasting time with this.* Yet here he was, endangering his entire project — and for what?

She deserved to know. She'd trusted him, and he'd given her over to that thing. The god. Whatever it was.

Foolishness.

He'd arranged to meet Bannard an hour from now on the jetty near the powder works, the same place he used for his irregular rendezvous with Yevin. In his note, Clade had promised the handsome sum of twenty-five luri for useful information about the urn, and twice that for the urn itself — enough to buy a small house. He'd taken his seal to the Coridon Bank earlier that day and withdrawn the gold from the Oculus account. They'd packed it with lambswool to mask the telltale clink, and he'd taken it back to his suite and hidden it in the desk drawer with the false bottom. Then he'd put the empty bag by the desk, to remind him to —

Damn it.

He'd meant to take it with him, but in his preoccupation with Sera, he'd forgotten. The gold was still in his desk.

That's all right. Irritation stirred within, but it was faint and fleeting, already gone by the time the walls snapped into place around it. *I'll fetch the gold before I head off. It's fine.*

A figure appeared at the entrance, halting just inside and glancing uncertainly about the temple. Dark curls peeked out from beneath the hood of her cloak. He waved her over.

"A travelling cloak?" he said, amused, as Sera slid in beside him. "Really?"

She blushed. "I just thought… you said not to tell anyone…"

"It's fine." Donning a heavy cloak in summertime was hardly the way to avoid attention; but Azador was absent, so no harm done. "I'm glad you could make it."

"Of course I made it," she said, her tone half playful impatience and half something else. "You're the Overseer."

No, no, that's not how I want this to go. "So I am," he said, choosing his words carefully. "But not only that, I hope. I speak to you now not as Overseer, nor even as an Oculus sorcerer, but as a friend." *And as the man who recruited you to the Oculus, and set you on the path that led you here.*

"Yes, of course." Sera sat half-facing him, brow furrowed in concern. "What is it?"

"It's about Azador."

She blinked, earnestness turning to confusion. "What about Azador?"

"I'd like you to read something." Clade drew out the folded treatise. He hesitated. "It will be difficult to take in. Please try to…" *Please what? Set aside everything I and everyone else have ever told you?* He shook his head. "Please do what you can to… consider the text on its merits."

She studied him for a long moment; then, wordless, she accepted the pages and bent to read.

The section he had marked out began a few pages into the treatise. The opening passage — in which Niele set forth her grievances with the Oculus leadership of the day, culminating in a bitter, stinging rebuke against the Council's high-handed disregard for any interests but its own — was no less valid today than it had been in Niele's time, but to begin there would alienate Sera and achieve nothing. The true evil, the one that mattered, was Azador itself; and it was there that Niele soon turned her attention. Clade had returned to her words time and again since first discovering them, poring over them, searing them into his mind. He no longer needed to read them to remember.

What is this creature Azador, this thing we call a god? Whence did it come, and how came we upon it? How is it that none in all the world make mention of its name, save we ourselves? To most of these questions we must frankly admit our ignorance; yet some, I now believe, can be guessed at, and perhaps even answered.

The Valdori fell. If there is one matter on which all men now living agree, this is surely it. The Empire bestrode this continent like a colossus, its people working wonders unseen before or since. If the Kharjik historians are to be believed, the arm of the Valdori stretched beyond even Kal Arna to distant lands now forgotten to us. Yet they fell. How could that which stood so high be brought so low? How could a people possessed of such wisdom and beauty come to such disastrous ruin?

My questions burdened me, haunting my waking hours until I could no longer leave them be. I set out to discover the cause of the Empire's fall, reading all I could find, devouring every tale, no matter how incredible. With the Council's blessing I travelled to the mainland, journeying from one city to another, begging entry to archives and libraries and vaults. Slowly, grudgingly, the fragments I found resolved into the mosaic that follows. I offer the following history to all who choose to hear, inviting any who doubt me to follow in my steps and verify for themselves the truth of my words.

Of the origins of the Valdori, I could find only scraps. Even the site of their great city, Asi-Valdor, remains unclear. Some believe its ruins lie deep beneath the waters of Lake Viho, in the wide western plains. Others place it in the forests of Mellespen or among the peaks of the Kemenese, though the latter seems an unlikely site for so great a population. The northern city of Feoras claims its own foundations to be those of Asi-Valdor, as does Sanam in the south, and Cort on the far isle of Jervia. Some say that a city called Asi-Valdor never existed at all. Yet the empire must have begun somewhere; small at first, like a seed or a phoenix ember, or the pebble that starts the avalanche. Had the fire not come, had the pebble not fallen, how different might the world have been?

Somewhere, somehow, the pebble fell. The Valdori grew and became mighty, excelling in all to which they set their hand. Even now, more than two thousand years after their fall, they remain unsurpassed in every art known to man, from war to engineering to craftsmanship to song, and in sorcery above all. They raised spires to rival the mountaintops. They drew gold and silver and jewels from the earth, and wrought such beauty as to draw tears from the vilest soul. They learnt the secrets of binding light, and blood, and spirit itself. Ever deeper they quested, searching for the strands that make up all things, teasing them apart, until at last they broke through to somewhere else — and found something waiting for them.

I cannot say with certainty what happened. The accounts are too fragmented, and each writer too eager to offer his own interpretation. Was this place truly the Shallows, or merely some lesser realm; or even the Deeps? What manner of creatures did they find? Were they deceived, or driven back, or did they stretch out the hand of invitation? I do not know. All I can say is that when the Valdori sorcerers returned, two beings came with them.

Perhaps the Valdori worshipped them at first. When a people already possess dozens of gods, what difference make two more? Or perhaps the Empire found a way to bend these beings to their will. Whether by grace or subjugation, these two creatures from beyond the veil offered up their strength to the Valdori and the Valdori seized upon it, working wonders ever more spectacular, ever more sublime.

Yet over time the beings grew antagonistic and were separated. Differences emerged between their followers, hardening beneath the passage of years until at last they calcified. The Valdori awoke one day to find themselves no longer one people but two. Grieved and dismayed, they resolved to unite the two once more, and raised up leaders who swore to make it so.

The First Calamity struck in the one thousand and ninety-fourth year of the Empire. One side struck the other, and the other struck back, and by the time they were done the entire southern half of Kal Arna had fallen to ruin. The Valdori abandoned the south and retreated north, shaken and repentant. The Empire was diminished, but this state, they resolved, would be temporary. They would reunite and rebuild, and in so doing they would recover their former glory.

For seventy-three years, there was peace.

Then, somehow, it broke.

The Second Calamity struck in the Valdori year one thousand, one hundred and sixty-seven. Those cities that had survived the first *cataclysm fell to the second. The Empire collapsed; its people dead or scattered, its wonders lost forever. The two beings, freed from whatever obligations had bound them to the Valdori yet still cut off from their home, were left to roam the world as they pleased.*

What became of the first being, I do not know. But the second is well known to us.

I found the name in a dozen manuscripts, accompanied each time with a curse.

Ahazedorai. Worldbreaker.

Clade watched Sera take the final page and lay it face-down on the stack beside her. She sat with her head bowed, her hands perfectly still in her lap. Only a slight hitch in her breath betrayed her appearance of calm.

"This is Niele's treatise, isn't it?" she said.

"Yes."

"It's forbidden to read. And twice as forbidden to own."

"Yes."

She looked up, her eyes bright with tears. "*Why have you shown me this?*"

"You have a right to know what Azador is. What we are." He took her hand. "Why do you think it would want to prevent you from knowing this?"

"Because it's a lie!" She snatched her hand away and wiped angrily at her eyes. "How can anyone know what happened that long ago? Niele might have misunderstood a hundred different things. Or she might have relied on other accounts that were wrong. Or maybe she made the whole thing up. Gods know she had a big enough axe to grind."

"You're right," Clade said. "I thought the same things at first."

"And now?"

Now? He hesitated. "This treatise offers a gift, Sera, to any who will take it. Not truth. Who can say what is true any more, so long after the fact? Of itself, a single account proves nothing. But it offers *the possibility of doubt*. And now…" Now he knew Azador. He'd felt its lust, its rage, the darkness at its core. And he knew what it wanted: not to restore, but simply to conquer. "Now my doubts have been vindicated."

Sera shook her head, incredulous. "You believe this, then?"

"The part about the Valdori? Maybe." Spires to rival the mountaintops seemed a stretch; but then, who could say for sure? "The part about Azador being accursed? Yes."

"But... but you're *Oculus!* How can you say that and still do what you do?"

"The Oculus do not tolerate departures. You know that, Sera."

"So, what then?" She waved her arms in a futile, absurd gesture. "What do you expect me to do? Posture and lie and cut out my heart until at last I turn into you?"

Clade's mouth tightened. *It's the shock, that's all. She needs time.* "That depends," he said. "If anything were possible — anything at all — what would you want to do?"

"Make it so this conversation never happened," Sera said, her voice choking on the last word.

"But if it were true," Clade said, as gently as he could. "What then?"

"I don't know." She wiped her eyes again. "I think I should go now."

"Sera," he said, as she stood unsteadily and turned away. "Wait." But she was already gone, scurrying up the aisle and around the ark, then through the portal and out of sight.

A posturing liar with my heart cut out? That was unfair, Sera. But was it? His lies were hardly in question. As for his heart... No. If his heart were empty, he would not have done this.

She wouldn't go to Estelle, he judged. Not yet. He'd need to speak with her again, though, and soon.

Foolishness. What was I thinking?

Movement at the portal caught his eye. Clade looked up, hope leaping in his breast; but it was merely a priest come to clean the pews prior to the next service. *Hells, how long have I been here?* Longer than he'd intended. He stood, grabbing the treatise and stuffing it in his bag, and hurried out.

When he reached the street he paused, looking up at the Oculus building and the window of his suite. Beneath the window, in the false drawer in his desk, Bannard's gold lay hidden. But it was too late to fetch it now.

Bannard would just have to take his word.

He turned north, joining the late afternoon traffic moving into the city; but although he moved as fast as the crowded street allowed, his thoughts lagged stubbornly behind. *Azador is the enemy, Sera, not me. If you believe nothing else, please believe that.*

I don't want to fight you, too.

~

Clade stumbled to a halt in the shadow of the powder works, gasping to regain his breath. He'd run the final stretch, dodging oxcarts and handcarts and pairs of youths lugging oversized baskets. Midway across Bastion Bridge he had come upon a man of the city garrison and had slowed to a jog, not wishing to appear suspicious. The man had grinned, touching a mocking finger to his leather cap as Clade passed by with his hair flapping against his neck. Clade had felt a moment's resentment, but the feeling was easily contained. Far better to seem ridiculous than be delayed. *I'd wear motley and tie bells in my hair if it got me here on time.*

The sun was gone from the west, and the first stars were beginning to emerge. Ahead on the jetty, a figure paced up and down, its form a black silhouette against the dusky river. Breathing hard, Clade peered into the gloom. *Is it him?* As he watched, the figure halted and shook its head; then abruptly it turned and began striding directly toward him.

Damn it. Clade straightened, taking a long pull of river-scented air and letting it out slowly. The figure stomped up the path, head down and shoulders hunched, seemingly oblivious to Clade's presence in the wall's deep shadow. Clade stood motionless, waiting until the figure was almost close enough to touch.

"Going somewhere?" he said, and the figure yelped.

"Dreamer's bloody daughters!" Bannard glared, his arms about his head as though fending off an attack. "You've been waiting here all this time?"

"Just arrived," Clade said. He placed a hand on Bannard's shoulder and gestured toward the jetty. "Shall we?"

Bannard gave a grudging nod and allowed himself to be steered back toward the water. His arm was tense beneath Clade's hand.

Hardly surprising, I suppose. Any man about to betray his colleagues would be tense, especially one not accustomed to the practice.

They sat on the bench. The great wheels of the powder mill slapped the river in slow, monotonous rhythm. Bannard coughed and rolled his shoulder as though trying to shrug off Clade's hand. Clade tightened his grip.

"So," Clade said. "What do you have for me?"

"You first. Show me the gold."

"It's not here. You'll get it if your information is good." He tightened his grip further. "Talk."

Bannard hissed. "All right, fine. Fine. You're looking for an urn, right?" He took a deep, unsteady breath. "I've seen it."

"You've seen the urn?" Hope lit up within him. He boxed it, tucked it away. "Describe it."

"It's about this high," Bannard said, holding his hands a short distance apart. "It has a wide body which curves in to a narrow neck, then flares out again at the mouth. It's made of something like pewter, but it seems undamaged by the passage of time."

Yes. That's it. "Go on."

"There are a series of carved images around the body, and an inscription. The inscription reads, 'Here lies the Emperor's first legion. May its spirits rest undisturbed until the end of time.'"

The golems. Yes.

"The urn has a lid of the same substance. We managed to remove the lid, but the urn was empty —"

"What? What do you mean empty?"

"Just that." Bannard moistened his lips. "But the lid had some symbols carved into it. Valdori numerals, indicating a location." He fell silent, gaze fixed on the dark river.

"Well? What location?"

Bannard offered no response.

"Bannard," Clade said. His grip on the man's shoulder was like iron. "What location? Who has the urn now?"

The other man folded his arms. "That's all for now," he said. "I'll give you the rest when I see my gold."

"You'll get your gold. I'll see to it. Just tell me who has the urn now."

"No. Gold first."

Damn you! Clade released the man's shoulder, reached for his purse. "Look, I don't have your gold with me, but here's what I have. Take as much as you —"

Cold steel kissed his throat. He froze, his gaze swivelling down. *A knife. The bastard brought a knife.*

Clade swallowed, and felt the knife slice into his skin. "I give you my word that I have your gold," he said hoarsely. "Every last luri. We can go and get it now, if you like."

Bannard spat. "You can shove your gold up the Dreamer's bony arse."

"What?"

"A favour, you said." He gave a bitter chuckle. "That's all. Just a favour. And I was stupid enough not to realise what that meant."

There must be something I can do. Clade's hand lay palm-down on the seat between them. If he moved it, Bannard would see. *But maybe the bench...* "A favour, yes," Clade said, narrowing his thoughts to the timber beneath his hand. "In exchange for —"

"*You turned me into a snake!*" Bannard's hand shook, and the knife bit deeper. "Three years a snake, and I didn't even know." His voice softened. "But a snake has fangs, Clade. And this one no longer belongs to you."

There was no time for elegance. Grimacing, Clade pressed his half-formed binding against the long timber planks. The spell flared to life, then buckled, hopelessly compromised by its lack of structure. The wood beneath Bannard burst up as if struck from below, lifting him into the air on long, jagged fingers. He shrieked, losing his hold on the knife as he rose, then falling back to the bench with the crunch of timbers snapping beneath him. The weapon fell, slicing into the meat beneath Clade's thumb and clattering to the jetty. Clade kicked it into the river with a curse, then twisted around and grabbed Bannard by the throat with his uninjured hand.

"I'm sorry," Clade snarled. "I don't think I heard that last part. Care to repeat it?"

Bannard whimpered and shook his head.

Clade leaned close. "Understand this. You are mine. My very own snake, until I say otherwise. Is that clear?"

Eyes clenched shut, Bannard nodded.

"Say it."

"I'm... I'm your snake."

"For how long?"

Despair filled Bannard's voice. "Until you say."

"That's right." Clade released his grip, glanced at his other hand. Blood oozed from the throbbing cut beneath his thumb. He pressed the wound against his leg, wincing at the pain.

Bannard slumped against the bench, head hanging limp against his chest. He drew a long, shuddering breath.

Clade frowned. *No, damn it. I need you functional, not like this.* He grabbed the other man's chin and lifted his head. "Bannard. Look at me. Do what I ask and you can go. Understand? I'll give you your gold and we'll go our separate ways. All debts settled."

Something stirred in the man's eyes. "When I've done..."

"All I want is information. You won't have to hurt anyone. Just information. All right?"

A listless nod. "All right."

Clade sat back. The man had screwed himself up for one shot, and now it was gone. He sat in the wreckage of the bench like a stuffed doll. *I need to focus his mind. Get him thinking about what will happen if he obeys — and what will happen if he doesn't.*

"I helped your family, Bannard," Clade said. "Got them out of trouble with those moneylenders. Remember?" He paused. "I can find them again if I have to."

Bannard's head snapped up. "You wouldn't. Please, no, leave them out of it."

"I will. So long as you do as I ask. And when we're done, you'll have the gold."

Doubt filled his eyes. "No. You'll just kill me."

"*No, I won't.*" Clade exhaled. "You don't believe me? I'll show you."

"You said you didn't have it."

"I'll take you to where it is." He stood and held out his hand. The man was too unstable now for them to talk out here anyway. One shout and who knew what attention he might draw. "Come with me."

Bannard sat motionless for a long moment, then, slowly, he reached up and took Clade's outstretched hand. Clade braced, readying himself in case Bannard tried pulling him into the water, but the other man simply stood.

Nodding in approval, Clade gestured toward the riverbank. "That's it," he said as Bannard began shuffling down the jetty. "Let's find your gold. And once we're there, you can tell me everything you know about the urn."

CHAPTER 17

The noses of the master perfumers of Kharjus surpass those of all other men, capable as they are of discerning more than fifty distinct scents in a single breath. During the reign of Mazkotto II the Ascetic, in the time of the Kharjik Persecution, the master perfumers assigned words and letters to scents, and so devised a means of communicating one with another unbeknown to the Emperor's servants — indeed, if you will forgive my saying so, under their very noses.

The aroma denoting the house of Mazkotto II can be smelled to this day, in every closet and privy in the land — though it is said that only a master perfumer can tell whether a particular bouquet refers to the Ascetic Emperor himself, his virgin wife, or one or another of the Emperor's illustrious ancestors. Whether or not this last is true, I cannot say. But it is an undeniable fact that in all the years since the Persecution, no Kharjik Emperor has ever again taken up the name of Mazkotto.

— Eneas the Fabulist,
One Hundred Truths and Ninety-Nine Lies

THE ENDLESS STREAM OF PEOPLE, carts, beasts and goods was at last beginning to wane. Arandras sat by the side of the thoroughfare, a cloth wrapped around his nose and mouth, and thanked the Weeper for the night. Despite his efforts, the bitter grit of the road had penetrated his screen, working its way into his eyes, nose, and mouth. At some point he had ceased to taste it; yet its texture remained, a rough, abrasive patina on his tongue and throat like crushed emery.

Across the way and to the right rose a featureless stone building, five stories high, protected by a drab stone wall and a timbered
gate. Two ornamental cannon barrels faced each other atop the wall:
an unusual design, and all the stranger on an otherwise unmarked
and unremarkable edifice. Yet for all its plainness, the building was
clearly in use, with a slow but steady trickle of people moving in
and out throughout the day. Arandras had watched avidly at first,
studying each person in turn; but as the day wore on and the flow
of arrivals and departures continued, his enthusiasm and attention
had begun to fade.

Any one of them might have been Clade. None of them might
have been.

The city garrison had moved him on twice. The second time,
late in the afternoon, he'd been warned not to return or risk a fine
for obstructing a public roadway. He'd come back anyway. The
building was a puzzle, an unsolved text, though not the kind that
required translation. *More like decryption.* Solve the puzzle, reveal
the text, and he'd be one step closer to finding Clade.

A mounted courier trotted by, the Three Rivers insignia on her
saddlebag plainly visible in the combined light of the street lamps
and the three-quarter moon. The horse kicked up its hooves as it
passed, throwing another spray of fine dirt over Arandras's face and
arms. He bit back a curse, wiping sweat and grime from his brow
with an equally grimy hand.

Sorcerer of the Oculus. That was what the registrar's papers had
said. Clade, a sorcerer of the Oculus, whatever that meant. Was
the Oculus an artefact? An order? Some old Valdori god? Arandras
couldn't recall ever hearing the name before. *Narvi might know, or
Senisha.* Not that he was likely to see either of them again any time
soon. *Isaias, perhaps. With the Weeper's blessing, he might actually give
me a straight answer for once.*

He coughed, grimacing at the dry rasp in his throat. *Maybe I
should just go in.* The thought had come at least a dozen times over
the course of the day and refused to die, despite its obvious folly.
There was no guarantee that Clade was inside, and in any case Arandras had no way of identifying him. *Whereas Clade almost certainly
saw me in Chogon, and would likely remember my face if he saw it*

again. No, he had come too far to throw caution to the wind now. He just needed more information...

The door beside the main gate opened again and a man stepped hesitantly out, glancing up and down the moonlit street before closing the door behind him. Something about him caught Arandras's attention, and he peered across, craning his neck to keep the man in sight as a heavy cart lumbered past. The man wore a high-collared coat that obscured his features, but his gait and posture seemed familiar.

Weeper's tears. It's Bannard.

Shoulders hunched, Bannard pulled his coat around him and set off south. Arandras scrambled to his feet, twisting his face free of the cloth, and hastened after him.

"Bannard!" The hunched figure seemed to pause at Arandras's call, then pressed on, his stride lengthening. "Wait, damn it. Bannard!"

Cursing, Arandras dodged around a portly merchant and broke into a run. Bannard stepped sideways, slipping into a narrow alley and out of sight. Arandras sprinted to its mouth, then halted, peering into the dark passage for any sign of movement. Broken crates partially blocked the lane, and the smell of rotten vegetables hung in the air. From somewhere behind the stack came a soft scraping noise, the sound of boot leather on stone, and Arandras smiled. *Got you.*

He rounded the crates to find Bannard huddled on the ground. The man looked up, then instantly flinched away. Arandras eyed him uncertainly, unable to read the man's expression in the dim light.

"I thought it was you," Arandras said. "Didn't you hear me calling?"

Bannard drew a shaky breath. "What do you want, Arandras?"

What in the hells? "I just want to talk. I'm not going to hurt you."

"If you say so."

"Of course I say so. Why would I want to hurt you?" Arandras crouched in front of him. "I just want to talk."

The man would not meet his eyes. "What about?"

"About the building you just came out of." Arandras paused, but

Bannard made no response. "Why were you... oh, Weeper's tears." *You weren't there on Quill business, were you? You were there for some other reason.*

Because you're working for someone else.

Bannard buried his face in his hands and gave a long, shuddering sigh.

"Hey," Arandras said. "Look at me. Look." Slowly, Bannard raised his eyes. "I'm not Quill. You hear me? I don't care what's going on here. I really don't."

The scholar's hollow laugh echoed off the alley walls. "You wouldn't say that if you knew."

"Knew what?" Arandras shrugged. "So you're not really a Quill. You're..." Something cold took hold of his spine. *You're one of Clade's.*

But Bannard was shaking his head. "No, I am a Quill! I am! I just..."

"You just what?" Arandras leaned closer. "Why were you in that building?"

Bannard offered a helpless shrug. "To give information..."

"What information?"

"About the Quill. And about the urn." Bannard's expression shifted to something almost pleading. "And, uh, about you..."

"*Me?* Who wants to know about me?"

"A man. A sorcerer. Does it matter?"

"What's his name?" Arandras asked softly.

"Clade." Bannard paused. "Why? Do you know him?"

Do I know him? The absurdity of the question left Arandras gasping. "Intimately. Not at all. I learnt his name yesterday. What did you tell him?"

Bannard blinked uncertainly. "I, uh..."

"What did you tell him, man? Is it the urn? Does he still want the urn?"

"Yes! Yes, he wants the urn." Bannard turned away, breathing heavily. "I told him about it. Told him what we've discovered." His voice fell, making Arandras strain to hear. "He asked me where it was now, and I... well, I told him."

"You gave him my name."

Bannard nodded.

"What did he say?"

"I don't know. Nothing. He just asked another question."

Arandras sat back on his heels. *Clade, asking about me.* The thought made the world seem upside-down. "Tell me, Bannard. You and Clade. How close would you say you are?"

Bannard shuddered, and in that moment Arandras saw all that he needed to see. "Close? Gods." The Quill closed his eyes, and a tear slid down his cheek. "I wish I'd never met the bastard."

"Then you wouldn't be disappointed if he were to, shall we say, meet an unfortunate end?"

"What, you want to kill him?" Bannard spread his hands. "Be my guest. Only I hope you've got a better plan than just sticking a knife in him."

Arandras frowned. "Meaning what?"

"How many people have you killed, Arandras? Lots? Because he has. And he's a sorcerer." Bannard shook his head. "If you can kill him before he knows you're there, great. But if you hesitate, give him a breath before he dies…" He trailed off, cheeks glistening.

"I see." Arandras shifted uneasily, oddly chilled by Bannard's words. "What would you suggest?"

The hollow laugh sounded again. "An army would be good."

An army. The words burrowed deep into Arandras's mind. *An army, you say.*

Well, now, that might just be an option.

He leaned forward and offered the Quill his hand. Bannard squinted at it, then up at Arandras, blinking through his hair. A muffled sob escaped the other man; then, abruptly, he reached out and clasped Arandras's hand in his own.

"There, now," Arandras said, settling himself on the dirty stone of the alley. "There, now."

Bannard's sobs subsided. He withdrew his hand, wiped the tears from his cheeks.

"Now," Arandras said. "Tell me what Clade looks like."

❧

It was morning, and the schoolhouse was bustling with Quill. Arandras strolled down a wide, curving corridor, glancing from face to face, looking for someone he recognised — or, more to the point, someone who recognised him.

A hand fell on his shoulder. "I'm afraid you're going to have to leave."

Ah, at last.

Arandras turned. The speaker, a tall, weathered man with fair hair, studied Arandras with the lazy attention of a seasoned hunter, confident he had the measure of his prey. Arandras remembered him from the briefing but couldn't recall his name.

"I'll see you out," the man said, nodding back the way Arandras had come. "This way."

"I'm here to see Damasus," Arandras said, resisting the man's not-so-subtle nudge at his shoulder. "Could you tell me where he is?"

The man shook his head. "The schoolhouse is closed to visitors, Arandras. Fas's orders." His gaze flicked over Arandras's form, his eyes crinkling in friendly amusement. "Let's do this the easy way, shall we?"

I'd love to, but you're not giving me much to work with. The man's name bubbled up from the depths of Arandras's mind. "Ienn, isn't it?" he said, and the man gave a languid nod. "I appreciate that this is a sensitive time, but I really do need to talk to Damasus. And I wonder if the rules might be relaxed for someone who could supply you with," Arandras lowered his voice, "a certain... map."

Ienn's attention sharpened, and Arandras smiled. *So you haven't found one yet.*

"What sort of map might that be?" Ienn said.

Still smiling, Arandras gave a regretful shrug. "The sort I should talk to Damasus about."

Ienn inclined his head, conceding the point. "Reth," he called, fixing on someone behind Arandras's back. "Could you find Fas and ask him to join us in the upper courtyard, please?" There was a sigh and a muttered assent, followed by the sound of footsteps receding down the corridor. Ienn turned, gesturing at a nearby staircase. "Shall we?"

The courtyard was the one Narvi had led them to the day they arrived in Anstice. Ienn settled into a seat by the mouth of the staircase, his legs stretched before him and his eyes half-lidded, leaving

Arandras free to wander the rooftop space as he pleased. He ambled to the rail and looked out over the sloping lawn, the sun warm at his back, his shadow stretching almost to where a gardener crouched below, tending to one of the staked saplings.

An army would be good. At that moment, there with Bannard in the alley, the solution had seemed irresistible. Get back in with the Quill, lure Clade to follow them to the golems' hiding place, then use the ancient Valdori constructs to at last take his revenge. There was just one problem: convincing the Quill to take him back. *Two problems, in fact. Even if I do get back on the team, they'd never in a thousand years let me take control of the golems.* At least baiting Clade posed no difficulty. Bannard had already agreed to leave signs for Clade showing the path taken by the Quill, and Arandras had convinced Bannard to stick to the arrangement in exchange for Arandras keeping the scholar's secret.

All the same, there ought to have been a simpler way. Except, try as he might, he couldn't think of one.

Oh, no doubt he could have found someone to put an arrow in the man, or drop a rock on his head, or some such. But that was no good. *I need to look him in the eye. I need him to know who's killing him, and why.* That meant finding a way to render Clade powerless without actually depriving him of his senses. From Bannard's account, the man clearly had a capacity for destructive woodbinding, and likely other sorcery too. And that left Arandras with only two options: another sorcerer to counter the man's abilities, or else anamnil to nullify them. But sorcerer mercenaries were rare, and prohibitively expensive. Anamnil was cheaper, but not cheap enough to make a difference — and in any case, the moment Clade sensed its presence he'd immediately be on his guard. *I might as well hire a herald to announce my presence.*

No, the only reliable way to subdue a man like Clade was with overwhelming force, leaving Arandras no alternative but to seize control of the golems. *But only until Tereisa is avenged.* The Quill could have them afterwards, for all he cared. Weeper knew Arandras didn't want them. Once he'd dealt with Clade, his use for them would be at an end.

"Ah, Arandras." Fas strode across the courtyard, the sunlight bouncing off his bare pate. "Back for your gold after all, I see."

"Actually, no." Surely Ienn's friend had mentioned the reason for his visit. "I'm here to discuss maps."

"Maps," Fas repeated, his face inscrutable.

"That's right. You need one. I have one."

"Is that so?" Fas folded his arms, tapped his fingers against his elbow. "I don't see any parchments under your arm. No scrollcase at your feet. What, then? Have you just recalled a secret cache of maps that unaccountably slipped your mind until this morning?"

"No," Arandras said with forced patience. "But I know someone who —"

"Ah, you know someone. And who might that be? No, let me guess. Someone whose name you can't possibly reveal in advance. Am I right?"

"No, again." *For the Weeper's sake, just shut up and listen.* "The man I refer to is Isaias."

Fas gave a dismissive snort. "We already tried him. And Peni, and Qulah, and every other dealer and fence in the city. Forget it."

"You were misled," Arandras said. "Isaias has the map you seek. It's in his shop right now."

"And how do you know this, exactly?"

"I know because I put a deposit on it the day before last."

Something shifted in Fas's expression. "Is that so?" He chuckled. "I was right to begin with, then. You are back for your gold, and more besides."

"We'll need gold to complete the purchase, certainly," Arandras said. "But that's not what I want."

Fas tapped his foot against the paving stones. "What, then? Spit it out."

The words piled up in Arandras's throat, resisting his efforts to force them through. He swallowed. "I want to get back on the team."

"You what?"

"Back on the team," Arandras said, firmer this time. "I go with the retrieval party. I'm there when the golems are found."

"No," Fas said. "I can't allow —"

"And not just me," Arandras continued. "Mara, too." *If she'll come.* But he'd caught the look in her eye when he first mentioned the golems. *She wouldn't miss this.*

Fas scowled. "You, perhaps, I could make a case for. A former Quill assisting us in the field. That might be accepted back in Chogon. But that woman is an entirely different matter."

"Nonetheless," Arandras said. "If you want the map, she comes too."

"And is that all? Any other conditions on your assistance?"

"One more." Arandras considered the other man. *Ah, hells. It's worth a shot.* "I want a golem."

"You *what?*"

"Just the one will do." It would be enough to justify an interest in controlling the damn things, and if he couldn't figure out a way to get to the rest, even a lone golem might be enough for a half-decent shot at Clade.

Fas shook his head, a disbelieving laugh playing at the corner of his lips. "That's absurd. What in the hells would you do with it? Make it your golem manservant?"

"Why not?"

Fas turned away, still shaking his head.

Don't walk away, damn it! Voice tight with frustration, Arandras called out to Fas's retreating back. "Look, do you want to find the damned things or don't you?"

Fas halted at a side railing, running his hand over his domed head. "You're sure Isaias will give us the map?"

"He'll give it to me," Arandras said. "I'll go alone, or maybe with Mara —"

"No." Fas turned, the angle of the light casting his face into odd relief. "You want to spend my money, then I'm going too. Hells, let's all go. You, me, Mara, Narvi, Ienn..."

No, you fool. "Isaias's deal is with me. He's not going to like having all those others there."

"Nonetheless," Fas said. "If you want the money, we come too."

Oh, very clever. "Fine," Arandras snapped. "You come. We get the map. Mara and I join the party, and I get my golem."

Fas studied Arandras for a long moment. At last, he gave a grudging nod. "Get us the map, and you've got yourself a deal."

❦

Eilwen sat in the garden outside Havilah's suite and yawned. She'd slept poorly the previous night, and the night before that. With darkness came memories of the narrow closet in Caralange's quarters, the gag cutting into her mouth, the hard chair beneath her. But it wasn't her brush with hysteria that haunted her dreams. It was the moment after, the moment she'd tried so hard to prevent ever since burying that accursed egg.

I am not a killer. Not any more. But the words rang hollow, and she knew them for a lie.

In that moment, she would have killed Caralange.

It was the *rightness* of it that tore her awake in the middle of the night. As though murder was something that could be justified. No, more than that: as though, in the right circumstances, it could be *demanded,* and she be nothing more than its hand.

She had welcomed the beast back into her heart, and it was as though it had never left.

But I haven't killed anyone. Not yet. And I won't.

She sat in the shade of the building's east wall, heels scuffing the dirt beneath the low bench. The high, piping call of an unseen bird sounded from the tangled branches above her head, its plaintive chirps hanging unanswered in the mid-morning air. Despite the hour, Havilah's curtains were still drawn. Eilwen glanced along the row of doors and windows. Laris's suite shared this side of the garden with Havilah's, though the Trademaster's door was at the far end, almost in the corner. If Caralange was loyal, as it now seemed he was, the traitor had to be Laris.

Almost certainly.

But there was still an almost. The conclusion was logical, even obvious. Yet they still lacked proof.

A sudden urge filled her to go and find out. The garden door in her own apartment had no lock, merely a latch on the inside and a conveniently placed window beside it. Presumably Laris's was no different. *I could go in tonight.* The broken window would tell the Trademaster that someone had been there, but it wouldn't tell her who...

But no. She'd already skirted Havilah's instructions more than she should have. Impulsiveness was not her friend.

Gods, I should know that by now.

The Spymaster's door opened and Havilah stepped outside, standing at the edge of the garden and rolling his neck and shoulders. Mouth dry, Eilwen stood, allowing herself to be seen. *Now? Or later?* Anticipating reproof was bad enough without having to wait for it. *Can we do this now, please?*

Havilah's eyes narrowed when he saw her, but he continued his exercises with no other acknowledgement of her presence or her implied request. She stood before the bench, feeling increasingly foolish as he stretched his arms and chest and back, then bent over to touch his toes. At last he straightened and turned to face her, tilting his head in the direction of his suite before disappearing back inside.

Well. Her shoulders twitched in a jerky echo of the exercises she had just witnessed. *Good.*

Her father had known only one answer to her childhood infractions. He'd made a point of only striking her with an open hand — fists, he said, were the weapons of bullies and drunks — yet his blows were still hard enough to bruise, and she'd taken to rubbing her face with dirt in an attempt to hide her discoloured cheeks from the other children. Later, when her anger at his maltreatment began to emerge, she abandoned the dirt and began wearing the marks as a badge of defiance, imagining herself to be shaming him by refusing to conceal the work of his hands. Only after he died, claimed by an outbreak of sweating sickness in the same year as the *Orenda,* had she finally realised the truth.

The marks, not the pain, had been her true punishment. There was no such thing as a private rebuke. Only by making her sins known to the world could they be expunged.

But Havilah is not like my father. He will not parade my disobedience before the Guild. He cannot.

She stepped inside and closed the door. As she turned, she found herself rubbing her cheek, and she snatched her hand away.

Havilah was already sitting behind his desk. "Sit," he said, the accented word sounding more like an order than an invitation.

Eilwen sat.

"Repeat to me what I told you," Havilah said.

She swallowed. "Don't go back to Qulah's," she said. "Don't

talk to the masters. Don't —"

"I told you to *tread lightly.*" The Spymaster spoke softly, enunciating each word separately, as though she were the one unfamiliar with the language. "Tell me what you think that means."

"Look, I'm sorry, all right?" Eilwen said, grimacing at the quaver in her own voice. "When I came back from the Quill shop I should have come straight to you."

"No, you should never have gone there in the first place! Burning Mother, what were you thinking?"

"I —" The words wouldn't come. She bowed her head. "I'm sorry."

Havilah exhaled through his teeth. "I'm trying to keep you alive, Eilwen," he said softly. "Do you understand that?"

Passion bloomed in her chest, a heady mix of pain and anger and other things she couldn't name. "And why does that matter?" she demanded. "This is about the Guild, remember? That's what you said. So long as the Guild is protected, who cares what happens to you or me or anyone else?"

Havilah had gone still. "I care," he said.

"Why?"

"For the Guild's sake," he said. "And for mine. And for yours."

She shook her head. *You wouldn't say that if you knew what I was.* But those sins still hung about her neck, secret and unpurged, and there was no longer any way to remove them.

"Eilwen," Havilah said. "Look at me." Reluctantly, she met his eyes. "*We are* the Guild. You, and me, and Ufeus, and all the others. All of us. Without our people, what else is left?"

"And the traitors?"

He pursed his lips. "What do you mean?"

"I don't know. Nothing." She buried her hands in her hair. "Look, I know I let you down. I'm sorry. Can we just leave it at that? Please?"

Havilah frowned, but the expression held more disappointment than anger, and more sorrow than either. "As you wish."

Thank you. She took a breath. "So. What news about the cannons?"

"Nothing yet," Havilah said. "And our woman from the chocol house seems to have gone to ground. But I have received word from someone close to the East Mellespen Syndicate." He leaned forward. "Mercenaries, Eilwen. The Syndicate has taken a contract to supply several hundred siege-ready mercenaries to an unknown buyer. Possibly as many as a thousand."

"Gods." Eilwen stared. "An invasion."

"It looks that way," Havilah said. "I'm hoping to receive confirmation later today." He paused. "Another thing. It seems an old woman was seen several days ago entering the house of the Falisi legate."

"She's buying anamnil." Which meant she expected to be fighting sorcery — or, perhaps, that she wanted to protect her swords from the work of her own binders. "A major city, then. Maybe even one of the Five."

"Just so." Havilah folded his hands. "I spoke to Caralange."

Eilwen nodded. She'd explicitly invited the sorcerer to confirm her story with Havilah, and when her anticipated summons from the Spymaster had failed to materialise after her release, she'd guessed that Caralange had taken her offer up — and in so doing had delivered all of her news ahead of her, leaving nothing for her but rebuke. "What are we going to do?"

"Do you believe him?"

"Who? Caralange?" Eilwen thought back to her interrogation. "He was furious at first. Convinced I was in league with whoever killed Kieffe." She shivered. "I don't think he was acting."

"Which leaves us with Orom."

We have to follow him. Find out who he's meeting. What other leads do we have? The words hovered on her lips. But there was nothing in them except what Havilah already knew. And she was tired of urging action only to be shot down by the arrows of Havilah's caution. *He's going to make the call regardless of what I say. Let him decide and be done.*

"I think we should follow him," Havilah said.

Eilwen blinked. "Oh. Good. So do I."

"We'll use a double tail: you and me, one following the other. When Orom spots the first tail, they drop off and the second takes over."

She shook her head. "Double tail, yes, but not you. You're too easily recognised. Make it me and Brielle."

Havilah's frown returned. "We can't risk bringing anyone else in on this. Not even Brielle."

"She's already in. Didn't Caralange tell you what happened?" Eilwen sat forward. "She came after me, Havilah. Somehow she figured out that he'd grabbed me, and she came and put a knife to his throat. If that's not enough to earn our trust, I don't know what is."

The Spymaster considered her. "You're sure we can trust her."

"Yes. I'm sure."

He held her gaze for a long moment. "Very well," he said at last. "Go. And Eilwen."

She paused, half-risen from her seat.

"Maybe we're going to win this," Havilah said. "Maybe not. But win or lose, the Guild will always need people like you." He offered her a faint smile. "So be careful. Yes?"

It wasn't true, of course. The Guild didn't need the real her.

But perhaps she could at least square the ledger.

"Win or lose?" Her answering smile was fierce. "No. We're going to win."

~

"That's him." Eilwen pointed as a lightly-built man descended the steps from the main building, a canvas bag slung across his shoulder. He glanced around the compound as he walked, eyes darting back and forth. "That's Orom."

Brielle nodded beside her in the gloom of the stable. "Got him." She rose to a crouch. "Boy better not make me late for dinner, or my ma'll have his hide, and mine too."

Orom passed out of sight and Brielle moved to the entrance, pausing a moment before easing out behind him. Eilwen waited for the span of a dozen heartbeats, then followed.

Trailing Brielle was easy. The woman's head rose above most others on the road, bobbing gently in time to her long, easy stride. Eilwen followed at a comfortable distance, watching for the signal that showed Orom had spotted his shadow and it was Eilwen's turn to step up. Caralange had told her that Orom seemed increasingly paranoid about being followed, even within the compound itself, so

Eilwen had decided to give him what he expected, instructing Brielle to stay close and make only a cursory effort to disguise her purpose. With luck, Brielle's striking height would so capture Orom's attention that he would overlook his second tail entirely.

And it wouldn't hurt to show that the investigation was bigger than just her and Havilah, either. *Might make them think twice about killing anyone else.*

Orom led them across the eastern thoroughfare and through central Anstice, choosing a course set back from the river but parallel to it, his brisk pace sparking a dull throb in Eilwen's bad leg. Narrower roads meant fewer people, but the late afternoon traffic was still heavy enough to provide adequate cover. The street bent westward, revealing the glaring sun directly ahead, and Eilwen was forced to squint at the silhouetted heads before her as she hurried in Brielle's footsteps.

They crossed the western thoroughfare. Ahead, Brielle turned toward the river, then west again, her course taking them along the riverbank where vendors with covered trays peddled the day's leftover food: loaves, fruit, lukewarm pies. A Mellespene in a wide-brimmed hat stepped into Eilwen's path, holding out a package of spiced meat wrapped in a grape leaf. Eilwen shook her head, side-stepping and brushing away the proffered food, knocking it from the vendor's hand. He snatched after it with a curse, catching it at his shins and snarling after her in his thick northern language.

She glanced up to see Brielle scratching her earlobe, her head turned in the direction of the river as she walked away. *Damn, he's stopped. Where is he?* Eilwen slowed her pace and cast about the promenade in the slow, unfocused manner of one admiring the view. There he was — buying a pastry from a pale, long-haired Jervian. Eilwen leaned against the wall of a spice shop and pretended to examine her fingernails as Orom watched Brielle stride down the riverbank and away toward the coloured spires of the Tri-God pantheon. Her task done, Brielle was now free to head out to whatever eating house she'd chosen to celebrate her mother's birthday. *And it's not yet sunset. You might even be early.*

Orom waited until Brielle was out of sight. Then he turned, flicking the half-eaten pastry into the river, and resumed his course along the bank. Raising a hand to shade her eyes against the sun, Eilwen followed.

She didn't have far to go. Orom halted at the pale stone facade of a riverside gaming house, where he glanced after Brielle one last time before ducking inside. Eilwen approached the establishment with a frown. The building's rear seemed to open directly onto the riverbank, though access to the outdoor section was barred by high timber fences, their boards warped and faded from years of exposure. *Only one way in, unless I want to try swimming.* Gritting her teeth, she pushed the door open and stepped inside.

The interior was dim, and Eilwen paused in the doorway, waiting for her eyes to adjust. Tables filled the room, each hosting games of dice or tiles or *dilarj*. The scent of roasting meat hung in the air, growing stronger as she approached an open kitchen door halfway along the wall. Players glanced up disinterestedly or ignored her entirely as she picked her way toward the rear, scanning the faces at each table. Orom was not among them.

The back door stood ajar, just wide enough for Eilwen to slip through. Diners sat around tables facing the glittering river or tucked against the high fence, some combining their meals with a game, some not. A man carrying a tray of empty mugs looked at her inquiringly, gesturing at an empty table; Eilwen smiled her acknowledgement but did not move.

Where are you, Orom? He had to be here somewhere. *Where have you —*

A woman's laugh caught her ear. Instinctively, Eilwen backed toward the doorway even as she looked in the direction of the sound. *I know that voice.* Her gaze fell on a man wearing the leather and indigo of the city, seated by the fence with two others, both with their backs to Eilwen. Then the woman laughed again, turning her head behind her high collar to say something to the third figure, and Eilwen beheld the features of Laris and Orom.

Triumph filled Eilwen, and with it, an unexpected feeling of relief. *Havilah was right. Caralange, too.* And what was more, they'd both told her the truth.

Laris said something short and pointed, provoking a chuckle from the unknown man. Eilwen retreated further into the doorway and scanned the dining area. The space was a bare rectangle, with nothing to conceal any part of it. Every table lay in sight of every other. But Laris's table was hard against the fence. *Perhaps...*

She turned, pushing past the gaming tables and out of the building, heading around to the side. The fence consisted of eucalypt boards that had clearly never been treated for weathering. Eilwen ran her fingers lightly across the timbers. Though the boards were no longer flush, the gaps between them were still too narrow to see through. Lowering herself to the ground with the sigh of a footsore traveller, Eilwen leaned back against the fence and listened.

"He's expecting a delivery, but he doesn't know what," Laris said. "Your man will need to press it into his hand, like this. Now, go."

A rough scrape indicated a chair being pushed back, followed by the sound of receding footsteps. A few moments later Eilwen saw Orom retracing his steps along the promenade, one hand resting on the canvas bag at his side.

She gave him something. Damn it. Eilwen watched his retreating form, torn between following him further and staying put. It seemed a reasonable assumption that the sorcerer was on his way to yet more members of Laris's conspiracy. But Eilwen had been swimming in assumptions for weeks; now, at last, she had a chance to establish some facts. With a voiceless sigh, she settled back against the fence, returning her attention to the conversation behind her.

"... wouldn't tell me where he found it," Laris said. "You know how he is."

"Dug up somewhere by his cat, maybe?" The man chuckled.

Laris might have shrugged. "It doesn't matter. Good timing, though. Saves us from a bigger mess."

The man murmured something too soft to make out, prompting a silky laugh from Laris. Eilwen blinked in surprise. *Is this man her lover?*

"Very well," Laris said, her tone teasing. "Tell me where we'll be *seen* tonight."

There was a creak as someone leaned on the table. "How about Crescent Hall?" the man said. "Last performance of the Weeping Sisters choir. I hear the archon himself attended a few nights ago."

"Really?"

"Apparently he hated it," the man said. "Which means that to-night the hall should be full of people eager to wag their heads at the great man's lack of taste."

"To the archon's boorishness!" Laris replied, laughing.

The conversation fell away, and Eilwen shifted awkwardly against the fence, trying to remain silent as she found a more comfortable position. There was another creak, then a new sound, soft and moist, directly behind her. *Gods. They're kissing.* Grimacing, she drew up her legs and rubbed her knee.

When the man spoke next, it was almost too low for Eilwen to hear. "I still think this is too hasty."

"He's after the body," Laris hissed, and Eilwen pricked up her ears.

"So what?" the man said. "There'd be nothing left to see by now."

"Letting him find it at all was bad enough! Now he suspects, and he's started digging."

"So he sent someone after it. That hardly means he's on your tail."

"He sent *three* people. First my old trader, then Caralange, then another of his. Brielle, the tall one."

"So he suspects," the man said. "That doesn't mean he knows it's you."

"No. And I don't intend to wait until he does."

Rage filled Eilwen, roaring in her ears. *Got you, Laris, you bitch.* The man said something, but all Eilwen heard was a distant murmur. *You treacherous, murdering shit. We've got you now.*

"Relax." Laris chuckled. "No mess, remember? Nobody will be able to prove anything, except that Havilah's toy turned out to be a little too clever for him. A tragic accident, nothing more."

"You're sure," the man said.

"I'm sure." A smile entered Laris's voice. "Now, take me out and give me an alibi that even the Gatherer couldn't dispute."

Slowly, the words penetrated Eilwen's whirling thoughts. *An alibi. Gods preserve, it's happening now. They're killing Havilah right now!*

She scrambled to her feet, all thoughts of secrecy forgotten. Heart pounding, she broke into an ungainly run, cursing her weak leg as she raced back up the promenade. *Hold on, Havilah,* she thought, shoving past vendors and ambling pedestrians as the sun's last light slowly leached away. *Just hold on.*

    I'm coming.

CHAPTER 18

Two fears drive us to secrecy: the fear of being understood falsely, and the fear of being understood truly. What are the hazards of deceit or betrayal against such perils as these?

— Jeresani the Lesser, *The Passing of Herev Gis*

THE DOORS WERE THE SAME all along the corridor: thick slabs of timber, each with an iron ring for a handle. Clade halted before one, counting once more to be sure he had the right room, then knocked.

Her voice sounded distracted. "Who's there?"

"It's Clade," he said, and waited.

The bolt slid back and the door opened. Sera stood within, smiling; but the smile was tentative, not at all like her usual infectious grin. Her hair hung in a mess of curls about her neck. "Hello."

"Sera," he said, and the word came out warm and not at all sad, just as he intended. "I was hoping we could talk."

She nodded and stood aside. "Come in, then."

The room was a smaller version of his own suite: a narrow cot, a writing desk half the size of his own, a hard chair, a high window. A handful of cut geraniums in a mug graced the corner shelf above a little pile of misshapen wooden blocks. Clade picked one up with a wistful smile. "Are you still playing with these?"

Sera sat cross-legged on the cot, allowing Clade to take the chair. "Keeps me from getting rusty."

"Was this the one?"

"No, that narrow one on the side." Something in her face softened at the memory. "My first ever successful binding. You said I bent it like a stalk of wheat."

"I remember." *You gave it to me with such delight, such pride. Even then, you were sure that one day you would join our ranks. And here you are.*

"Oh," Sera said, her attention caught by the bandage on his left hand. "What happened?"

"It's nothing, I assure you." Bannard's blade had left a clean cut, and the fleshbinders had already begun weaving the muscle tissue back together as best they could for a fellow sorcerer. "I'll be fine."

The urn is carried by a man named Arandras, Bannard had told him, and at first Clade had missed the significance. Only when Bannard mentioned a dead wife did he make the connection. The husband of someone he'd killed. The sixth. Tereisa. She had cursed him as she died, calling on gods and demons alike to witness his crime. There'd been no need for such invocations, of course. Azador had been right there.

Somehow, this Arandras had gained possession of the urn. He'd brought it to the Quill and together they had unravelled the mystery of the golems, discovering coordinates to a location somewhere north of Tienette Lake. The Quill were already preparing an expedition that would leave as soon as a precise destination could be determined. But Arandras, it seemed, had never been interested in the golems. Even now, he was searching for the killers of the Quill who had uncovered the urn — searching for Clade himself. *Thus does our past reappear, with knives. Tiysus had the truth of it, right enough.*

But what mattered were the golems. Clade had already sent a summons to Terrel and begun assembling a party of his own. *The sisters, Kalie and Meline. And Sinon. That should be enough to deal with whatever the Quill might bring.* When Bannard sent word that the Quill were departing, Clade intended to be ready to follow within the hour.

"I'm sorry for what I said before," Sera said. "You know. That thing about posturing, and..."

Clade nodded. "It's fine," he said; then repeated the words, gentler this time. "It's fine."

"You're going somewhere, aren't you?"

A scowl rose behind his face, but he held it back. He'd told the others to keep the planned journey to themselves. "What makes you say that?"

"The servants. They're preparing food, getting horses ready, all the rest of it." She paused, and for a moment he saw a hint of the old grin. "I didn't know for sure it was you, though."

"I didn't say it was," Clade said; but he did so with a smile, conceding the point. "It's just a field trip," he said, as though it were entirely normal for himself as Overseer to take such a journey. "I'll be back in a week or two."

"I see."

He leaned forward. "Sera. When we spoke yesterday, I asked you a question. But you didn't answer."

Sera bent her head as though examining the backs of her hands. "What I would do. If anything were possible."

"That's right."

"If I tell you my answer, will you tell me yours?"

"Well, I…"

She looked up then, her gaze earnest and urgent. "Will you?"

Clade held her eyes for a long moment. *The laughing child I recruited is gone at last. Oh, Sera, I'm sorry.* He tilted his head. "As you wish."

When she spoke, her voice was a whisper. "I would reach out and touch your brow. I would take away all your doubts, all your confusion, all your misgivings. I would take your hand and walk with you to Azador's sanctuary. And there I would say, 'Here we are. Tell us your will, and we will do it.'"

Clade's stomach was a stone. "I see."

"We could change the world, Clade. You, me, all of us. And Azador. We could make it the way it was meant to be."

"Could we? Or would we just make it the way Azador wanted it?"

"It's the same thing."

Clade said nothing. There was nothing to say.

"And you?" Sera said. The words were tight. "What would you do?"

Take you away from here. Leave the Oculus behind. Send Azador back to whatever distant realm it came from. He shook his head. "You already know."

She exhaled heavily. "Yes," she said. "I suppose I do."

"I'm sorry," he said. Her head was bowed again, her hands motionless on her lap. He gazed at her, trying to fix her image in his mind. *Do you understand that you are my enemy now? But no, you don't even realise that this is a war.*

"I won't say anything," Sera said. "I won't tell anyone, especially not the Councillor. I promise."

"I appreciate that," Clade said. "But I won't hold you to it." *A life has room for only one absolute. Don't make that promise yours.*

She lifted her head. "What do you mean?"

"Nothing." He manufactured a reassuring smile. "I should go. I have some things I need to take care of before I leave."

"Of course."

The old woodbinding block still lay in his hand. He stood, concealing it in his sleeve. "Be well, Sera."

He was halfway out the door when she called out. "Clade," she said, and he paused, looked back. She rose, took half a step toward him. "I, uh... that is, you..." Her mouth worked, searching for words but failing to find them; then, as he watched, her face closed over and she took a long, unsteady breath. "Does Councillor Estelle know about your journey?"

Good. That's good. The more she could harden herself against him now, the easier it would be for her later. *Farewell, Sera, daughter I never had. May we never cross paths again.*

"Not yet," he said. "But she will soon."

$\approx$

They would visit Isaias in the morning. Arandras fumed at the delay, but there was nothing to be done. Fas had made the decision, and that was that.

He's probably in Isaias's shop right now, trying to finagle the map without me. A futile endeavour, or so Arandras hoped. If the shopkeeper was half as helpful to strangers as he was to his dear friend Arandras... well, after a few hours of inane chatter the Quill would find himself back on the street with nothing to show for it. *No cause for worry on that front, then.*

In any case, once again, there was nothing he could do.

He leaned back in his chair, feeling it creak beneath him, and gazed up at the ceiling of the schoolhouse library. Narvi, Ienn, and the rest were off somewhere making preparations for their journey. The plan, so far as Arandras had been told, was to leave as soon as they had a known destination. They would take horses down the Lissil road, following the river as far as they reasonably could; then, when the roads would serve them no longer, they'd strike out on foot through the hilly, scrubby forests that surrounded the lake and upper river.

And if it turned out that the golems were at the bottom of the lake, he supposed they'd all be going for a swim.

Arandras was already set. He'd travelled light from Spyridon; most of what he'd brought was gear for the road which had remained untouched since his arrival, first in his schoolhouse room, and now in the lodging house. With nothing better to do, he'd eventually found his way to the Quill library. It was larger than he'd expected — nothing like the Library in Spyridon, of course, but large enough for a schoolhouse so far from Chogon. Heavy carpets and tapestry-covered walls muted the rustling pages and low murmurs of the Quill, giving the wide room an unexpectedly cosy feeling. But for the feather brooches and ochre and black everywhere he looked, he could almost have felt at home.

He spotted Senisha kneeling beside a half-empty shelf, a set of leather-bound volumes stacked haphazardly by her side. She glanced up at his approach.

"You look lost," she said, her soft voice settling lightly over the surrounding quiet.

"They've got you filling shelves already?"

"Part of the job." She shrugged. "I'd rather this than go trekking off with the rest of you to the Gatherer knows where."

Arandras took in the tall, heavy-laden shelves with a glance. "What do you have about golems?"

"Only what Fas and the others have been poring over for days." She pulled a tan volume from the middle of the stack and handed it to him. "Start with that. There's a section a third of the way in that will give you the basics. I'll fetch you more when I'm done."

Arandras returned to his chair and began to read.

Four books later he leaned back, grimacing as he stretched his cramped shoulders and tried to make sense of what he'd learnt.

The only point on which all accounts agreed was that the golems had been created by the Valdori. Everything else, it seemed, was contested. The golems were soldiers, or workers, or mere curiosities for the rich. The Valdori had made thousands of them, or dozens, or only a handful. The secret to their construction lay in obscure sorcery, or advanced engineering, or the direct intervention of the gods. One particularly fanciful tale held that each golem housed the spirit of a Valdori emperor or empress, men and women so glorious, wise, upright, and so on, that death itself shrank before their majesty. But on the matter of exactly how this miraculous transfer was achieved, the tale remained bashfully silent.

Yet the accounts contained some intriguing claims. The golems could travel underwater. They understood speech, or possibly even thoughts. They could continue to function even after losing a limb. This last assertion Arandras found hard to credit — everyone knew that harm to a bound object disrupted the binding, and the more complex the spell, the greater the likelihood that such disruption would lead to failure. Certainly, it was possible for a binding to artificially strengthen its source object; but surely no golem could survive such catastrophic damage as to have an entire arm or leg torn away.

Of most interest, however, were the descriptions of lords and generals issuing orders to their golems. Arandras pored over the sketchy reports, looking for anything that might help him when the time came to use the golems against Clade. How did one ensure that one's own order was followed and not discarded in favour of another? But such conflicts did not seem to arise in any of the accounts, and Arandras was left to speculate as to the reason. *Perhaps they can only be controlled by the person who made them. No, that doesn't make sense. Not unless the Valdori were blessed with a peculiar abundance of golem-maker-generals.*

There had to be a way. No servant or soldier could function

satisfactorily if their instructions could be countermanded by any-one they met. A golem had to have a master.

"Hello, Arandras." Narvi stood by the seat across from Arandras, fingers tapping nervously on its high back. "Back with us, I see."

Arandras closed the book. *Well, well. Look who it is.* "So it would seem."

"Um." Narvi glanced behind him, then back at Arandras. "Do you mind if I join you?"

"It's your library."

"Yes, of course." Narvi sat gingerly, hands resting on his thighs. "I... well. About the other day." He broke off, shaking his head. "I'm so sorry, Arandras. The way Fas treated you, just tossing you out like so much..." A sharp exhalation. "It wasn't right."

"No, it wasn't."

"If it had been up to me... gods, if it was up to me, we'd be find-ing your mystery letter writer right now." Narvi leaned forward in entreaty. "You know I'd never cast you off like that, right?"

It was impossible to witness the man's naked sincerity and re-main unmoved. "I know it," Arandras said. *If it was up to you.*

A smile broke over Narvi's face. "Good. That's good."

"But Damasus doesn't like me, and you need to keep him happy."

Narvi flinched. "I wouldn't put it quite like that."

"Nonetheless."

"This is still my project, Arandras," Narvi said. "Nothing's changed."

Arandras raised an eyebrow. "Damasus won't be joining us, then?"

"He will," Narvi admitted, his face pinched as though he'd just bitten into something sour. "The team will answer to me, and I'll report to him."

Yeah, that's going to work really well. Something of his thought must have shown in his expression, as Narvi pursed his lips and leaned closer.

"You need a friend on this expedition, Arandras," he said. "Some-one who Fas and the rest will listen to. And frankly, I don't see too many other candidates for the role. So yes, I'm going to keep Fas happy, as you put it, because if I'm not around, you're not going to get within shouting distance of the golems, no matter what Fas told you."

Which was probably true. Arandras gave a reluctant nod. "Fair enough." He wondered if Clade was having to deal with this same nonsense from his people. The Oculus, whoever they were. Bannard had had little to say about them, and in any case Arandras had been far more interested in Clade himself.

Narvi sat back in his seat, stretching out his thick legs with a sigh. "I've got the grooms chasing up some extra horses for us right now. They'll be ready to go as soon as we need them tomorrow. The kitchens will have our supplies ready by then too. We're about as ready to leave as we can be."

"Except for the part about not knowing where to go."

"Not at all. We know exactly where to go." Narvi laced his fingers behind his head. "Somewhere west between here and the mountains. What could possibly be clearer?"

Arandras leaned his head against the chair's high back, his thoughts circling back to the Oculus. Of course it would be the same for Clade. Every group succumbed to the same malaise sooner or later. Clade's would be no exception. *Who is he, I wonder, in the eyes of his peers? A leader, like Fas or Narvi? Or just another thoughtless follower?*

Narvi closed his eyes, twisting around in his chair. "Gods, just the thought of sleeping rough again makes my back ache."

The words stirred memories in Arandras of the early days in Chogon: nights spent in the library there, researching the latest find, or in Narvi's home, Arandras and Tereisa helping to put the baby to sleep as Narvi nodded off at the table. The sight of Narvi and Katriel dozing side by side with identical expressions would give Tereisa the giggles, and she would clamp her hand over her mouth, shoulders shaking, trying not to wake them with her laughter.

I'm sorry also, Narvi, Arandras thought, and that too was true. *We were friends, once. But neither of us is who we once were. You are Quill, more now than you ever were back then. And I...*

Tereisa's laughter echoed through his mind, and he grasped after it; but it slipped away, leaving only a hollow silence in its wake.

I have a dead wife to avenge.

~

The box in the cellar was ancient.

Clade had discovered it as a student, hidden away in the dusty archives at Zeanes. Tall as a man, carved from a single massive piece of black-brown wood, it resembled nothing so much as it did a coffin. Sorcery lay heavy in its grain, and Clade had spent days perched awkwardly before it, tracing out its lines and unravelling its secrets.

The first layer was strong and rigid, like a fine steel mesh twisted through the tight wooden weave. Clade had encountered similar sorcery in other Valdori artefacts: bindings to fortify timber until its strength approached that of marble, others to preserve against rot and fire and decay, all on a level far beyond anything he or his teachers could accomplish. The elegance of it took his breath away. That something could simultaneously be so pragmatic and yet so beautiful seemed an impossible grace, like a gift from the gods themselves.

But there was a second layer, too: supple, flowing, smooth as quicksilver yet soft as down. It took days of probing just to find the structure that held it together, and twice as long again before he was able to understand its function. The binding was a screen, designed to occlude light, muffle sound, and absorb motion. Anyone locked within might shout and thrash and beat on the lid as much as they wished, but none of it would escape the binding. Nor would anything pass inside, save only a small supply of air through some narrow breathing channels in the lid. Whether it had been built originally as a form of punishment, a refuge for the seasick, or even to house a brood of particularly noisy hens was impossible to say.

Clade dubbed it a stillbox.

When he came to Anstice, he requisitioned the stillbox from Zeanes under the pretence of a non-existent research project. He installed it in the cellar, attaching a note with instructions to leave the box undisturbed. When asked, he claimed to be conducting a lengthy experiment into the properties of decaying flesh. After a while, the enquiries ceased, and the box was left to gather dust in the corner of the cellar, empty and unremarked.

It was his hidden die, salted away against the future, the kind he hoped never to have to use. Yet the security it offered — the promise of a clean kill, even of one already bound to Azador — was simply too great to pass up. He'd hated himself for it, at least at first; hated the unspoken truth that if the need arose he would put a fellow Oculus in there, qualms be damned. Its presence in the cellar allowed him to sleep easier at night, and he'd hated that, too.

It lay flat in the deepest corner, hidden from the doorway, boxes and crates stacked around it. By now, Clade imagined, everyone else had probably forgotten it was even there.

"Dusty, isn't it," Estelle said with a sniff as she peered around the cellar.

"A little." Clade stepped in behind her, allowing the door at the base of the stairs to swing closed, and raised his lamp. Light flared off jagged stone walls and a low, rough-hewn ceiling. The chamber was rectangular in shape, about twice as long as it was wide, and was filled with crates and chests of all shapes and sizes. Shadows in the far corner tugged at his eye, but he resisted the urge to look.

"Very well, Clade," Estelle said, arms folded. "Let's see these gold reserves."

Clade set his lamp down on a stack of crates. The low light hid the lines of her face and the grey in her hair, peeling years from her appearance. He was reminded of the day he first met her, the day the Oculus recruiter had knocked on his own door and told his parents all the things he could have if they'd just let her take him away with her. She'd been younger then than he was now. Not much older than Sera, really.

Estelle quirked an eyebrow. "What is it? Are you unwell again?"

Clade shook his head. *Don't be a fool. You know it has to be done. Leave her alive and you'll feel her at your back all the way to the golems.* But his hand refused to move.

"Clade?" The concern in her voice was genuine. "Talk to me. What's wrong?"

"Have you never wondered, Estelle?" His voice sounded harsh in his ears and he paused, coughing to clear his throat before continuing. "Have you never wondered about Azador?"

Her eyes narrowed. "Wondered what?"

"Everything. What is it? Where does it come from? What does it want, really? What does it want with us? Why does it require us to —"

"Enough!" She was angry, but there was something else in her voice as well. *Fear?* "You know the answers as well as any other Oculus sorcerer."

"Yes, I know the answers. 'Azador grieves for the fallen Empire. Azador offers the Council guidance and wisdom.' But that's not the whole truth, is it?" He stepped toward her. "It doesn't include the part about it *binding every single damn one of us to its consciousness!*"

"*Not another word —*"

"It's not here, if that's what you're worried about."

Estelle stopped short, her gaze piercing. "What do you mean?"

"I can sense it," Clade said. "I know when it's with me. I know when it's with someone nearby. It's not here."

She looked at him, silent, her expression unreadable.

"And do you know what I sense when it's near?" he said. "Greed. Azador lusts, Estelle. It longs for control. It longs for power. Above all, it longs for the golems." He softened his tone. "It doesn't grieve. Maybe it did once. I don't know. But all it has now is rage and darkness, and a vast, insatiable hunger."

Estelle said nothing for a long moment. Then, slowly, she nodded. "I know."

He blinked. "What do you mean, you know?"

"I know." She smiled at his expression. "Some of the answers are true. 'Azador offers the Council guidance and wisdom.' I know."

Clade stared, waiting for her to go on. "And?"

"And what? It doesn't matter." Estelle laughed. "Don't you see? *Azador is ours.* It can't act in the world on its own. It needs us. So we do enough to keep it happy, and we enjoy the benefits of having it around."

Something hollow opened within him. "Enjoy the benefits," he repeated.

"Its knowledge and experience, of course," Estelle said. "But more than that. How long do you imagine a double agent can stay hidden when Azador can see anyone whenever it wishes? And if they try to run, how far are they going to get?" She reached out, grasped his arms. "Azador is good for us, Clade. Without it, we'd just be another pathetic little band of sorcerers with delusions of someday rivalling the Quill. But here we are, on the brink of something great."

"Invasion," he said, his voice flat. "Conquest."

"Power," she returned. "Our power, not Azador's. Yours and mine. There's a vacant Councillor's seat with your name on it. You can be part of this."

"To what end?"

"To whatever end you like! That's what power means!" She stepped forward, eyes alive with excitement. "Think what we could do!"

The light caught her face, and for a moment she looked like a goblin from a children's tale, all grasping leer and hard, gimlet eyes. He shuddered. *If Azador could take physical form, this is the shape it would assume.* She reached a hand to his face and he turned away in disgust.

"You're one of us, Clade," she said to his retreating back. "You're Oculus. You can't escape that."

He turned. "Perhaps I can."

"No. Azador will find you. No matter how far you run, it'll find you."

"It won't. I've found a way to cut it out."

Her confident expression faltered. "They'll send someone after you. Hunt you down."

"Then I'll cut it out of them, too."

Her eyes darted to the door, then back to his face. *Yes. You understand.*

Clade moved his weight to the balls of his feet. "I can make this easier for you, if you'll let me."

She swallowed. "If you kill me, Azador will be here in a heartbeat."

"I know."

Estelle glanced around the cellar, her breaths growing faster, shallower. *Looking for water to bind, Councillor? There's none here. Just you and me, and that box in the corner.*

"I would really rather not hurt you," he said.

She hissed, baring her teeth in a snarl. "What's the plan, then? Lock me up down here? Someone will find me before you even make it out of the city."

Clade gestured with his chin. "There's a box. Long and narrow."

A quick glance over her shoulder. "I see it. What's inside?"

"Nothing. Yet."

She nodded once. "I see. Then what?"

"Then I leave."

Estelle nodded again, almost panting now. Her eyes flicked from Clade to the door, around the cellar and back to Clade again. She flexed her hands. "No."

"Estelle —"

She whirled and grabbed a small jewellery chest, hurling it across the cellar. Clade cursed and ducked. The chest crashed off the wall behind him and burst open, spraying tiny gems like raindrops across the bare stone floor. Estelle cannoned into him, biting and kicking, scratching at his face. He reeled back, skidding on the gemstones and scrabbling for purchase. She stomped on his instep, clawed his eyes; then somehow she was past him and racing for the door.

He lunged after her, grasping blindly. His questing hand found an ankle and closed desperately about it. Snarling, Estelle tore herself free and spun around; but her foot slipped on some gems and she stumbled, smashing headlong into a heavy, iron-bound chest. For a brief moment she seemed to hang in the air; then, with the faintest of whimpers, she collapsed.

Clade scrambled across, dropping his knee into her back and twisting her arm around. Her hand was limp. *Shit, no, not yet.* He reached for her neck, fingers groping for the artery, bracing himself for the arrival of Azador. *Tell me you're not dead.* For a moment he felt nothing; then a faint pulse fluttered against his fingertips, weak but regular, and he breathed a sigh of relief.

All right. Now to get you into the box. He pushed himself to his feet, wincing as he touched the gouges in his cheek. *Damn you, Estelle. I told you I didn't want to hurt you.*

She was heavy, but not as heavy as he'd expected. He dragged her across the stone floor, manoeuvring her onto the side of the timber box and tipping her inside. She flopped over the edge like a rag doll, coming to rest on her back, her head dangling sideways.

He reached for the lid, then hesitated. Locked in that box without food or water, she'd likely survive for days before thirst finally took her. A quick death would be better than what he was giving her, but that mercy was out of his hands. In any case, the end result would be the same.

Estelle was his ninth.

"I'm sorry," he said.

The lid fit into place like a gear in a Rondossan clock. Clade latched the box shut and smoothed the note affixed to its side. Walls raised and ready, he waited for the first pangs of failure to crawl up out of his gut, as they always did in the wake of a murder. But this time, strangely, they were nowhere to be found.

All he could find was sorrow.

CHAPTER 19

A death in time saves ninety-nine.

— Giarvanno do Salin I

EILWEN BARRELLED AROUND THE CORNER, racing down the corridor and launching herself at Havilah's door, pounding and yelling. Her leg was throbbing, but she barely felt it. "Havilah! It's me. I need to see you right now!"

She paused, breathing heavily, willing him to open the door. *To be alive.* But her only answer was a cold, empty silence.

"Havilah! Open up! Hav—" She broke off mid-word, brushing her sleeve over her eyes. "*Damn* it."

The door was locked. She tried the handle anyway, shoving against the door with her shoulder, then beating futilely with her fists.

"Eilwen?" Ufeus stood in the corridor, a wary expression on his face. "What are you doing?"

"Where's Havilah?" Eilwen marched up to Ufeus, pointing at the unyielding door. "Is he in there?"

Ufeus shrugged. "Presumably. Why?"

"Follow me."

There was a passage to the garden only a few doors down. Eilwen strode outside and around to the suite's garden-side door, Ufeus trailing in her wake.

"Havilah!" She beat against the door with the palm of her hand.

"Are you there?" The door was as solid as its inner counterpart, and the latch...

... was open.

"That's not normal," Ufeus said as the door swung slowly ajar.

Oh, gods have mercy. Stomach churning, Eilwen peered inside, but the room's interior was cloaked in shadow. She reached out and poked gingerly at the door, nudging it all the way open.

Havilah lay sprawled on the floor, his outstretched hand just short of the door.

"Gods! Havilah!" Eilwen rushed into the room, grasping his hand and pressing it between her palms. "Talk to me. Please. Say something."

Ufeus followed her in, hissing through his teeth as he reached the desk. "Ware the box," he said, and pointed.

It was small and flat, the size of three fingers pressed together, the faint carvings on its copper face impossible to make out beneath the verdigris. A wicked-looking needle jutted from its side, its tip coated with a viscous, dark goo.

Poison. Turning Havilah's hand, she found a pinprick wound just behind his thumb. The bead of blood was already dry.

Too late. His hand slipped from her grasp and fell limp to the floor. *I'm too late.*

Hot tears stung her eyes. "Damn you, Havilah. Damn you, damn you, damn you!" Her fists rained down on his unresisting back and shoulders. "Why did you have to die, damn it? *Why did you have to die?*"

Strong hands pulled her back, resisting her efforts to twist away. "Eilwen. Eilwen!" A hard shake, enough to snap her out of her frenzy. "He's gone, Eilwen. Do you hear me? He's gone."

Her legs gave way beneath her and she sank to the ground, the desk at her back. Ufeus crouched before her. When he spoke, his voice was hard.

"Look at me, Eilwen," he said. Slowly, reluctantly, she met his gaze. "You are the adjunct. Do you understand? That means you're in charge."

She stared at him dully. *In charge.* The words worked their way through her thick, muddy thoughts. *Yes. I am in charge.* She nodded.

"We need to tell Master Vorace," Ufeus said. "We need to inform all the masters, tell them —"

"No," Eilwen said, her voice little more than a croak. She coughed. "No," she said again. "We tell nobody, not yet."

"Gods, Eilwen. We can't keep this a secret —"

"I mean it." She glared up at him. "Nobody."

"Eilwen —"

She grabbed his forearm. "Remember what I said before? About needing your service for the sake of the Guild? Well, guess what? Today's the day."

Ufeus pursed his lips. Even in the gloom, the doubt in his eyes was unmistakable.

"I'm not crazed, Ufeus. But I am, as you just pointed out, in charge."

He frowned. "When?"

"I don't know! I need to think."

"You've got tonight," he said at last. "If you haven't told the masters by sunrise, I'll tell them myself."

Eilwen scowled. "Fine. But until then, nobody. Understood?"

He gave a short, grudging nod.

"Good." She waved a hand. "Now go."

She sagged back against the desk. The air was heavy and still, pressing her down like a great, suffocating mantle. A tap sounded somewhere nearby — someone knocking on Havilah's door, then a muttered comment as the visitor moved away. Their footsteps sounded hollow, false, as though conjured by some part of her mind that could no longer convince even her.

Something damp brushed her neck. She reached up to find her collar soaked through. Trails of tears lay thick on her cheeks, and her eyes felt swollen and raw.

"Oh, Havilah," she said, and the quaver in her voice was like that of a child. "Why did you have to die?"

The memory of their first conversation in this room swam before her eyes. The kindness in Havilah's face as he confronted her about her kills. The trust. She smiled through a fresh outbreak of tears. *You believed in me,* she thought. *I didn't even believe in myself. Didn't see any reason why anyone should. But you did anyway. Even though you knew what I was doing, somehow you managed to see past it.*

But then, he hadn't known her true secret. Would it have made a difference if he had? She wanted to believe that it wouldn't, that he would have seen her clearly even through that. But maybe betrayal wasn't the sort of thing you saw through. Maybe it was the sort of thing that was still there at the end, when all the lies and distractions and subterfuge was stripped away.

The kind of thing that defined who you were.

Nobody had known her. Not truly. But she'd known all along.

She was Eilwen Nasareen, and she was a killer.

She groaned, burying her face in her hands. *I tried, Havilah. I tried so hard to become who you thought I could be.* She saw Orom walking away down the promenade, saw herself watching him leave, deciding to let him go. When the time had come, she'd chosen wrong, and now Havilah was dead because of it. *Because of me.*

But she knew who was behind it, now. And even though she'd failed to save Havilah, she could still save the Guild.

Laris. The Trademaster had reached out to her, offering her support as Kieffe's body lay cooling on the other side of the corridor wall. Even then, she'd been playing her. *When did it start? Did she agree to my transfer because she thought she could use me against Havilah?* Eilwen had been a pawn all along, a piece to be deployed wherever she could best serve someone else's ends; and the fact that Havilah's interests aligned with the Guild's made it no less true of him than it was of Laris. It was how the game was played, and she'd been dragged onto the board without even realising it, way back when Havilah first called her into this room.

This was not her game. But there was a part of it which was familiar. She'd been trying to fight it, trying to keep it locked away and pretend it wasn't there. *Because Havilah asked me to.* But she was tired of fighting. And she was tired of pretending that she didn't know that sometimes, some things just needed to be done.

Havilah had seen that, too. Uncompromising, he'd said. *This will be my gift to you, Havilah. My gift to the Guild. This part of the game I know all about.*

Eilwen pushed herself to her feet, grasping the desk to steady herself. Havilah's body lay sprawled before her. In the darkness, she could almost imagine him to be sleeping.

She left by the garden door, pulling it carefully closed behind her. No stars shone in the sky, though a silver-grey patch of cloud showed where the moon struggled to break through. The eucalypt outside her own suite rustled softly in the faint breeze, the whisper of its leaves calling to her like a lover.

The iron trowel was just where she'd left it, in a box of unsorted oddments. She hefted it, frowning at its lightness and the dirt still clinging to its blade. But it had been enough to dig the hole in the first place; and it would be easier the second time, with no roots to cut through.

She tied back her hair with an old ribbon. Then, kneeling beneath the gently shifting branches, she set to work.

Laris's suite was almost a mirror image of Eilwen's. On the wall where Eilwen had shelves, Laris had chosen to hang a trio of small pastoral pictures with ornate gilt frames. The desk itself was free of personal effects — only a few bundles of paper marred its otherwise empty surface. On the other side lay the back room, Laris's bedroom. The intervening door stood open, revealing the edge of the bed and a long coat hanging from a hook in the wall. Unlit lamps hung from the ceiling in both rooms.

Eilwen swung the garden door closed behind her, brushing the fallen glass against the wall with her boot. Then she pulled a chair into the centre of the room and settled in to await the Trademaster's return.

She was calm, calmer than she'd felt for a long time. One dagger hung at her side, a second nestled in her boot, and her loop of sharpened wire lay tucked beside her other ankle; and wrapped in lambskin beneath her shirt, the black amber egg. She'd buried it, thinking to bury her killing self with it, but it had been a fool's hope. The beast had been in her all along. Still, it felt good to have the egg with her, even though she wouldn't need it tonight. It reminded her of other nights like this — nights of delivering death to those who deserved it. *Nights of atonement.*

Eilwen stretched her shoulders, her neck, loosening the muscles of her arms and torso. She had forgotten what the anticipation was like. This was her gift, her calling. Her opportunity to do good. How could she have lost sight of that? It was justice and penance both, and both equally satisfying. *I deserve this no less than she does. Attend me, gods, and see how I make amends.*

She felt as though she had been stumbling through a desert, parched and sun-sick; but now, at last, an oasis had appeared before her. It was time to drink deep.

Somewhere inside, some part of her twisted away in revulsion. *Not this,* it begged. *Not any more.* But the voice was weak, lacking in conviction, and easy enough to ignore.

Footsteps approached from the corridor beyond, halting before the door. There was a scraping noise as someone fumbled with the key; then it slotted home, clicking the lock as it turned, and the door swung open.

"Hello, Laris," Eilwen said, a wide smile on her face. "I'm so glad you're back."

Laris froze in the doorway, her form silhouetted against the softly-lit corridor. "Eilwen? Is that you?"

"I was starting to worry. Thought maybe you'd decided to give up this life of trade and join the Weeping Sisters yourself."

The Trademaster's flinch might have gone unnoticed if Eilwen hadn't been expecting it. "Leave now, please. Leave or I'll call someone —"

"Oh, I don't think so." Eilwen smiled again. "I don't think you want anyone else overhearing the conversation we're about to have."

Laris considered her for a long moment. When she spoke, her tone was lighter, as though she too was smiling. "As you wish." She stepped inside, pulling the door closed behind her. "You won't mind if I light some lamps?"

"Be my guest," Eilwen said, then chuckled. "I'm sorry, how rude of me. Be my host."

Light flared in the gloom. Laris inclined her head in welcome, but the muscles around her eyes and jaw were tense. A second lamp added its illumination to the first, and the Trademaster placed it on the desk and perched herself beside it, just out of arm's reach. "What is it, Eilwen? Have you discovered something?"

"You might say that," Eilwen said. It felt like her manic smile would never leave. "For one thing, I figured out who the lying, murderous whore of a traitor is."

"Really." The word was cool, a perfect facsimile of politely feigned interest.

"Really. Imagine my surprise," Eilwen said cheerfully. "It's you!"

"Now listen, Eilwen —"

"No, you listen to me, you duplicitous bitch!" Her smile vanished as though it had never been. "You murdered Havilah. Oh, I know all about your alibi. Don't even try. You killed him."

Laris's face was smooth. "I suppose that makes you Spymaster now."

"Oh, you'd like that, wouldn't you? A new Spymaster who just happens to be in your debt. No. Sorry. Not going to happen."

"Debt?" Laris raised her eyebrows. "Why would I need anything from you? I've got my own people to find things out. And you'd be surprised at what they've discovered."

Listen, some part of Eilwen whispered feebly, the word barely even a suggestion. *Talk. Anything. Just don't kill.*

She shook her head.

"Change is coming, Eilwen," Laris said. "I don't know the exact shape of it, but there's a new power out there. One to rival even the Quill. And where the Quill seeks influence by making itself indispensable, this group prefers a more, shall we say, direct approach."

There was an edge in Laris's tone that Eilwen hadn't heard before. A thrill ran down her spine. "Does this group have a name?"

"They call themselves the Oculus."

Eilwen shuddered, and the dissenting voice within her whimpered once and went quiet. Images of the *Orenda* flashed before her. The horrendous crack of the ship splitting in two, as though torn apart by two enormous hands. The screams of her shipmates as they plunged into the icy water. Acid stung her throat and she swallowed hard, willing her stomach back down. The black amber egg lay heavy against her side.

"I see you've heard of them," Laris said.

Eilwen coughed hoarsely. "And what have you done about them?"

"What do you think? We've sold them timber, of course." Laris shrugged. "Among other things. They're planning an invasion, that's plain enough to anyone with half a brain. Not here, obviously, or why start trading with every house in the city? But somewhere near-by. Rull, maybe, if they're starting small. Neysa if they're not."

"Gods. You want to be their *allies?*"

"Allies? Don't be ridiculous." Laris laughed. "Just their suppliers."

Eilwen pressed her hands to her head. *The Oculus, invading?* It was too bizarre to be true. *Gods help me, why can't they leave me be?* But they had, hadn't they? This time they'd needed a more powerful tool, and they'd settled on Laris.

A wild laugh bubbled up. *Here we sit, two traitors to the Guild. Two pawns of the Oculus. I was hunting myself all along.*

How Havilah would weep if he were here.

"Explain to me," Eilwen said, her words slow and deliberate, "how any of this makes the slightest shit of difference to Havilah."

Laris frowned. "Eilwen, you need to look at the bigger picture."

"No. This isn't about sorcerers, or invasions, or any of the rest of it. This is about you pulling yourself up the ladder and cutting down anyone you find in your way. Trademaster isn't good enough for you, is it? You want to be in charge of the whole damn show."

The Trademaster surged to her feet, her face filled with contempt. "Havilah was a fool —"

"Havilah was a good man!" She was shouting now, and she didn't care. "He believed in the Guild. He believed in me! All you believe in is yourself!"

"Havilah was holding the Guild back! Vorace still is! But the Guild is bigger than them, and it's a damned sight bigger than you. What in the hells have you ever done for it?"

"This," Eilwen said, and drove her fist into Laris's stomach.

Laris doubled over, gasping for air. A tiny knife tumbled from her sleeve and clattered across the floor. Staggering, Laris turned for the door, but Eilwen was too fast. Springing from her chair, she launched herself at the other woman's retreating form, driving her to the ground. Reaching into her boot, she withdrew the loop of sharpened wire, and as Laris raised her head to gasp for help she slipped it around her neck and pulled it taut against her throat — tight, but not tight enough to kill.

"Hush, now," Eilwen said, and she could feel the smile stretching her face once more. "Hush."

For a frozen moment they held there, Eilwen kneeling on Laris's back, Laris wheezing beneath her. Eilwen thought of Havilah, still slumped on the floor of his office. Dead, without even knowing why.

See what I do for you, Laris. I tell you why.

"Havilah didn't like me doing this sort of thing," Eilwen said conversationally, tightening the wire collar fractionally around Laris's neck. "If he was here now, he'd tell me to let you live. Probably." She shrugged. "Shame he's not here."

"I have gold," Laris rasped. "Whatever you want, it's yours."

"My dear Laris, I think you've misunderstood. This has nothing to do with me. This is about *justice*."

"If you do this, there'll be no place for you here."

She laughed. "Do I look like I care?"

Another rasp. "Can't... see..."

Eilwen laughed again, and pulled.

There was a moment's resistance, then the wire sliced through Laris's throat. She convulsed, shaking as blood began to pool beneath her. Eilwen knelt at her side. "Oh dear," she whispered. "Looks like you've made a mess after all."

She released the wire and resumed her seat, settling back to watch Laris's life bleed away. *Thus are you avenged, Havilah. Thus do I deliver justice.*

And the beast within her opened up its mouth and sang.

Dark, streaky clouds thrust gold-edged fingers across the brightening eastern sky. Arandras yawned, rubbing his heavy eyes and cursing his foolishness at subjecting himself, yet again, to the irrational whims of the Quill.

The others were already there — even Mara, to whom Arandras had dashed off a note the previous afternoon in the hope that she would receive it in time. She leaned languidly against the wall across from Isaias's shop, cleaning her fingernails with a dirk, a faint frown creasing her forehead. Narvi and Ienn had found a fruiterer somewhere along the way and were talking softly over a bag of figs. Fas stood before the locked door, arms folded, his foot tapping out his impatience on the cobbled street.

Morning people, all of them. Arandras blinked hard and tried to convince himself to wake up.

The street was beginning to fill, the early morning traffic of household staff and foodmongers pushing Arandras to the side. He shuffled across to where Mara stood, resting his back and the sole of one foot against the wall with a sigh.

"Doesn't like waiting much, does he?" Mara said, gesturing at Fas with her chin.

Arandras grunted. *Serves him right for getting us all out here so early.*

Mara switched the dirk to her other hand. "You ready for this?" she said, a hint of amusement in her tone.

"Sure," Arandras said. "When Isaias opens up, I'll just yawn at him."

She chuckled. "I like you better when you're half asleep."

Huh? Arandras gave her as sharp a glance as he could manage, but her attention was entirely focused on the dirk as she flicked its point out from beneath a nail. The remark had sounded like it meant something, but he was damned if he had the slightest idea what. Closing his eyes, he leaned his head against the wall. *Weeper's breath, I hate mornings.*

Fas stepped forward, hammering on the door with his fist. "You have customers, Isaias!" When the door failed to swing open he exhaled sharply, fists on his hips, and muttered something inaudible.

"'Doesn't he know who I am?'" Mara murmured, and Arandras coughed a laugh.

A loud rattle from the door jolted Arandras alert. It swung open to reveal Isaias caught in the middle of a prodigious yawn. "About time," Fas said; but with eyes clenched and mouth agape, Isaias showed no sign of hearing.

The yawn ended. Isaias looked blearily at each of them in turn.

"Huh," he said, the utterance as much a sigh as a word, and his expression shifted to a watery smile. "Welcome, friends. Come in, won't you? Come, come."

They climbed the stairs without speaking, Isaias breathing

heavily as he led the way. On reaching the top he made a beeline
for the green armchair in front of the hearth, collapsing into it with
a loud exhalation as Arandras and the others filed into the room.
Narvi and Fas cast uneasy glances at the narrow, anamnil-filled cabinet and found positions on the other side of the room, their Quill
brooches catching the first rays of sunlight through the window
above the counter. Mara sauntered past, unconcerned, as Ienn halted at the top of the stairs, his arms folded.

"My friends," Isaias said, rubbing his drooping eyelids and smiling beatifically. The cat, Pinecone, slunk around the corner of the
armchair and disappeared behind the counter.

"Hello, Isaias," Arandras said. "Sorry to burst in on you like this."

"Ah, Arandras, do not trouble yourself with such trifling considerations. Isaias is always delighted to welcome such dear friends as
yourselves."

Arandras glanced at Fas, who gestured impatiently but at least
had the sense not to speak. *Thank the Weeper for small mercies.* He
scratched his beard, trying to think past his own haze to find the
appropriate opening. "We, uh, are here to purchase a map."

"How wonderful!" Isaias said, the exclamation both enthusiastic
and entirely devoid of recognition. "Isaias is already longing to hear
more. Pray, continue."

"Understand, please, that I'm here under my own auspices,"
Arandras said. "As you can see, I have gathered some other, ah, as-
sociates in this venture, but I remain the sole holder of the project's
key asset." It was not quite a lie. *The urn is the key asset, and it's mine.*
Never mind that the Quill no longer needed the physical object.
"These gentlemen are here to supply funds, nothing more."

Isaias blinked mildly. "I see. And now, perhaps, you would be so
kind as to describe this map you wish to purchase?"

There was a coolness in the shopkeeper's tone that Arandras
knew from long experience. *The last thing I did was give him money
and tell him not to reveal the map to the Quill. And now here I am,
at an hour we both detest, shepherded in by no less than three of them.*
Small wonder if the man thought something was up.

"It's fine, Isaias," Arandras said. "Really. Just fetch us the map I
was looking at the other day."

"Which map was that, friend Arandras?"

"The one that —" Arandras broke off. Isaias wasn't budging. *And he's not going to so long as the Quill are here.* Fas gave a loud harrumph, and Arandras raised a hand to forestall him. "I'm sorry," Arandras said to Isaias. "We're wasting your time. We'll leave now."

"No, we damn well won't!" Fas shouldered Arandras aside and planted himself before Isaias. "You know what we're here for. Bring out your maps, man, and don't try to fob us off with the same rigmarole as last time."

Isaias adopted a regretful expression. "Alas, friend Fas, my answer today is the same as it was on your prior visit. Believe me when I say I would be delighted to sell you the object you seek. Truly, such transactions are the heart's blood of this humble shop. Yet Isaias must sorrowfully confess his inability to —"

"Enough!" Fas stepped closer. "There are five of us here. You are alone. One way or another, we're getting what we came for."

"What?" Arandras blinked at Fas. "No, that's not how this works. If Isaias says he's not selling, then he's not selling."

"The hells with that," Fas said, glancing around the shop. "We'll start here, then move to the private rooms. Narvi, check the shelves and drawers behind the counter. Mara, the cabinets. Ienn, you keep Isaias here company. Arandras, you can help Narvi —

"Are you mad?" Arandras stared in disbelief. "You can't just ransack his shop! Weeper's tears, we're not thugs!"

"Seems like a good way to get on the wrong side of the city garrison," Mara said, in a tone Arandras chose to interpret as agreement.

Fas waved a dismissive hand. "The garrison owes us more favours than I can count. This is worth at least a couple."

"If I may," Isaias said. He seemed calm, yet there was a hint of steel in his tone. "Isaias is exceedingly familiar, alas, with customers who allow their enthusiasm to override their judgement, which I am confident, in other circumstances, is truly exquisite." He turned his head, lowering his collar to show the fading bruise on his neck. "Some others visited my shop just a few days ago with a similarly, uh, forthright approach to their negotiations. Nonetheless, they left empty-handed."

Fas paused, and Arandras took advantage of his hesitation to drive home the point. "What you're doing is contemptible," he said. "And if that doesn't mean anything to you, the fact that it's not going to work should. Give me the money and leave. Let me talk with Isaias alone."

"And let the two of you swindle us while we wait downstairs like mugs? Forget it."

Gatherer take you! Arandras clawed at his hair. "Gods, how can you be such a fool? Take your idiot pride outside and let me buy you the damn map!"

Yet as he said it, he felt a pang of doubt. *What if Isaias isn't simply being stubborn?* Clade had been one step ahead of them the whole time. Could he have somehow prised the map from Isaias's grasp? Arandras glanced across to where Mara lounged by the counter and saw the same thought in her expression. *Weeper, tell me we haven't been gulled. Again.*

"*My* idiot pride?" Fas planted himself a finger's breadth from Arandras's face. "Can you even hear yourself? The Emperor of Kharjus is less arrogant than you! No wonder the Quill booted you out the first time around. I wouldn't be surprised if —"

"Excuse me," Mara said, and something in her tone made them all turn around. Isaias gave a stifled hiss.

The shopkeeper's cat hung from Mara's hand by the scruff of its neck, its legs dangling in the air.

"Now, my dear Mara," Isaias said, his voice no longer as calm as it had been a moment ago. "Pray do not do anything you will later regret. Put her down, if you would be so kind."

Mara lifted the cat to a level with her face. "Pinecone, isn't it?" It gave a plaintive meow. "Are you well, Pinecone? Does the big round man over there look after you?"

Isaias coughed. "Mara, my friend, please. Release my beautiful Pinecone." The Quill looked on like a trio of mummers, Fas intent, Narvi pained, Ienn impassive.

Let her go, Mara, Arandras wanted to say; yet somehow the words wouldn't come. Without the map, there were no golems. Without the Quill, there was no luring Clade from the city. And without both of those, there was no vengeance for Tereisa.

And that was the most important thing of all.

Not like this, though. Not this.

Mara's free hand drifted to the hilt of her dirk.

Isaias gave a sudden yelp. "No! Do not harm Pinecone, I beg you!"

She paused, her hand resting on the hilt, an enquiring expression on her face.

"Ah, my friends." Isaias gulped, pressing his sleeve against his forehead. "I do believe I have just this moment remembered a collection of documents I purchased some time ago, from, ah, an eccentric old... well, no matter. As it happens, many of the papers do, in fact, show maps, including one in particular which I recently had cause to set aside. Perhaps I should fetch it, so that we might peruse it together?"

Mara lowered the cat to the counter, but kept hold of its scruff. "What an excellent suggestion," she said.

Isaias heaved himself to his feet, shuffling behind the counter and reaching underneath. There was a click and the sound of something sliding. Swallowing hard, he drew out a long roll of paper wrapped in a soft leather cover.

"Is this, my friends, the object you seek?"

The Quill unfurled the map on the counter and began poring over it. Arandras turned away, retreating to the far corner of the room. *I had no part in this,* he thought, but even in the silence of his mind, the words rang hollow. He hugged his arms around his chest. *Weeper have mercy, what have I become? How do I find a way back?*

A pouch of coins was upended onto the counter with a harsh jangle. Narvi gave Arandras an excited look, pointing at the map and nodding, his eyes bright. Isaias assembled the coins into stacks, smiling now, chattering on about something or other as though he and Fas had been friends for years; but when Mara offered a chuckling comment, the shopkeeper shot her so venomous a glance that even she could not sustain her smile.

Arandras heaved a shuddering breath and covered his face with his hands.

We did it. The Quill have the map, and I have the Quill. Soon, I will have my vengeance.

Weeper forgive me.

PART 3:
TO WAKE IN DARKNESS

CHAPTER 20

There is a secret song in every man's heart that says, *I am better.* I am better than my family. My family are better than my friends. My friends are better than my neighbours, and even my neighbours are better than others more distant to me.

My city may overflow with fools, yet it remains the greatest in the land. My land may hold scarce a handful as wise as me, yet beyond question it is greater than all others. And no matter how vile the men of other lands may be, even they cannot compare in barbarism to those who live across the sea.

What need has mankind of gods? Each one of us is a god unto himself.

— Kassa of Menefir, *Solitude*

THEY RODE OUT AT NOON. As soon as they passed the gates Ienn established a brisk trot, and Arandras settled into the familiar one-two rhythm, relieved to be out of the city at last. The Lissil road was wide, and they rode in file two or three abreast, the rumble of half a hundred hooves sufficient warning for those ahead to clear a path.

Mara's leathers blended well enough with the ochre and black worn by the Quill, but Arandras's faded crimson tunic stood out among the others like old blood. The contrast was unintentional, but it pleased him nonetheless. *Blood, yes. I wore those colours too, but they are long gone now.*

See what lies beneath the facade.

He rode alongside a rangy man with the pale skin of a Jervian and the sun-shy squint of one who rarely ventured outdoors. The man sat his horse with grim concentration, eyes focused on the back of the rider ahead, his lips moving in a silent mantra, or perhaps a prayer to whoever it was that he worshipped.

The incident in Isaias's shop had left Arandras feeling soiled, as though he'd given up some part of himself by remaining silent while Isaias was coerced. Perhaps he had. He'd been more than just a chance bystander. *By my presence and my silence I endorsed their actions. Their shame is my shame, also.*

Once, during his time in Chogon, the Quill had come across a gold serving platter bearing a faded inscription, apparently a gift from one Valdori noble to another. Inexplicably, the plate had been found in the ruins of a slaughterhouse, and it had fallen to Arandras to clean away its ancient coat of muck. He had set it to soak in the milky fluid the Quill used for such purposes, drying it each day and gently polishing it before returning it to a fresh bath.

Most of the grime fell away in the first few days, but a dark, finger-length stain along one side stubbornly resisted his efforts. After two weeks of continual soaking, he was forced to concede defeat. Somehow, the mark had blended with the gold to become part of the object; an amalgam that could no longer be washed away. Whatever had been inscribed in that place was there no longer. The plate had absorbed the stain into its being.

So it was with the Quill. *They don't notice anything awry because that part of them is already sullied.* People like Fas no longer knew what it was to respect the agency of others. To him, those who belonged to the Quill were merely assets to be deployed at will, and those without were either resources to be exploited or obstacles to be overcome.

Now I share that stain. Weeper grant me a way to make it clean.

They crested a hill and a wide valley opened up before them, the silver thread of the Tienette winding its way through fields, pastures, and orchards. The thatched roof of a turnpike booth could be seen halfway up the next rise, with a short queue of foot travellers and covered wagons each waiting their turn to pay the toll and pass through. Far away to the west and southwest, the distant peaks of the Pelaseans jagged the horizon like the broken foundation of some vast but long destroyed rampart. Arandras absorbed the view, relieved that at least they would not be travelling that far. The sooner this was over, the better for all.

Judging from Isaias's map, their goal lay on the shore of Tienette Lake, near what appeared to be a gorge in the cliffs that edged the water. It was a useful, even fortuitous landmark, the kind that would still be evident even after the passage of centuries. Nonetheless, the location was well and truly in the middle of nowhere, at least so far as Valdori remains were concerned. Such ruins in these parts were few and far between. *How big would a place have to be to hide an entire legion of golems?* Arandras had no idea.

A windmill creaked in the breeze beside the road, and he caught the scent of baking bread. Chickens pecked in the yard outside, heedless to the world beyond their low mudbrick wall. An unexpected longing rose up in Arandras as their convey trotted past the modest house. *I could live there, or somewhere like it. Somewhere self-contained, away from the cities and their people and their stains.*

Only maybe not so close to the road.

A rider moved up from the rank behind, taking position between Arandras and his Jervian neighbour. "Hey," Mara called with a grin. "Nice day for a ride."

"Easy for you to say," Arandras returned. The dark-skinned Kharjik didn't look to have even broken a sweat.

She gave him a bright smile. "Yes. Yes, it is."

Arandras shook his head and returned his attention to the road.

"Hey," she said again. "We're on our way. The sun's shining. What's gnawing your arse?"

Weeper's breath, you need to ask? He gave her a flat stare. "What you did back there was wrong."

"Ha. Really?"

"Really."

They trotted down the hill, hooves clopping and harnesses jingling, Arandras's horse giving a loud snort as it approached the flat. The Tienette drew near on their right, its water noticeably clearer than it had been in Anstice.

Arandras glanced across. The Jervian seemed locked in a ferocious battle of wills, but whether the man's opponent was the road, the horse, or his own body, Arandras couldn't tell. Mara rode easily, one hand on the reins, her long pony-tail bouncing behind her. She caught Arandras's eye and cocked her eyebrow expectantly, and he frowned. "If you're waiting for thanks, don't bother."

"Is that how this works, then?" She sounded amused, but nettled also. "You get to be all high and mighty about how we got here, but still come along for the ride?"

High and mighty? He took a breath, trying to keep the irritation from his voice. "I can't undo how we got here. Doesn't mean I agree with it."

"Didn't say much against it, either. You went real quiet when you saw it was going to work."

There was nothing to say to that. *I am stained, just as she is. Just as the Quill are.* But they had embraced their shame, whereas Arandras's was fresh and could yet be cleansed.

"It needs doing," Mara said, and he knew what she meant. Avenging Tereisa. Delivering justice where no-one else would. "Remember that."

"I know," he said. "But that can't justify everything."

"Fine." She flashed him an annoyed glare. "Whatever you say. Good to know it's all right to kill a man but not to pick up a cat."

She leaned forward, nudging her mount into the next rank where Narvi and Bannard rode. Narvi said something inaudible and Mara laughed, pointing at a sheep paddock on the other side of the river.

Arandras watched the display with a sense of weary inevitability. There would be no uncomfortable questions there. No embarrassing examination of unacknowledged stains. *Just a mutual reassurance that neither of you is really so bad after all.*

And here they were, riding to find a Valdori golem army. One that the Quill would take possession of and use, just as they used everything else.

Consistent with, yet oblivious to, their stains.

Arandras had thought at first that he would claim the golems just long enough to deal with Clade, and then return them to the Quill. He had no interest in them beyond that. There was nothing else he wanted that such things could provide.

But he realised now that that was impossible. There was no way he could hand them over to the Quill, not any more. To do so would be to stand by and do nothing, just as he had in Isaias's shop, and allow the Quill to impose their will on the world, just as they had on Isaias. *And so would my own blemish become fixed, deepening every day with each new outrage perpetrated by the Quill.*

Only one action remained by which he might still retain a chance of washing his own stain clean.

The Quill could not be permitted to gain control of the golems. *When the time comes, I must take them myself.*

～

The reek of Azador hung above the flimsy table in the centre of the room. Clade wasn't sure which of his assembled team bore the watching god, but it didn't matter. It was here, and its presence fouled his nostrils like day-old vomit.

"Dreamer's arse, I hate waiting," Sinon growled, arms folded across his broad chest. He glared at Terrel, who sat with his two remaining men on one side of the table. "What are you whoresons looking at?"

His words drew no response beyond a flicker of the mercenary leader's eyelids. Terrel's men seemed as disciplined as he — a small mercy, but one for which Clade was grateful.

"Stow it, Sinon," Clade said. Bannard had sent a message that morning advising that a map had been obtained and Quill departure was imminent. He'd promised to send another as soon as they left. *An hour or two, he said. No more. And it's been what — six? Seven?* Clade had assembled his group of sorcerers and mercenaries as quickly as he could manage, anticipating a departure at any moment. Instead, they had been sitting here for most of the day.

What will I do if I hear nothing? Wait longer, or set out anyway? The Quill could not be allowed to get too far ahead of them, but neither could he risk revealing their presence. Perhaps he could send one of Terrel's men to the schoolhouse, if need be. Gods knew none of his would go unnoticed.

Sinon had been a brawler in his youth and still looked the part. His affinity for sorcery lay in none of the primary Oculus disciplines

— water, wood, and clay — but in the domain of air. The man had little talent for reflection and even less for research; indeed, he seemed incapable of completing even the simplest binding. Yet whenever his half-constructed spells collapsed, as they always did, the resulting discharge of power only ever blew out in the direction he desired. Eventually his instructors had given up trying to teach him the finer points of spellcraft and had instead begun training him in the use and control of his sole, destructive gift.

Beside Sinon sat the sisters, Kalie and Meline, both waterbinders, both skilled in the art of neutralising flame. The last thing their expedition needed was a repeat of Terrel's encounter with a Quill firebinder. Still, neither sister had experienced combat before, and Clade planned to keep them to a purely defensive role. Between Sinon and Terrel's men — and, if necessary, Clade himself — the group would have plenty of muscle to deal with whatever the Quill decided to bring along.

Assuming they ever depart. Impatience flickered within him and he frowned, smothering the spark before it could flare into something more. Control. Now more than ever, he needed to maintain control. *From this moment on, I feel nothing that I do not choose to feel. No worry, no doubt, no fear. No sorrow over Estelle. I am a well, cool and deep, and my waters never stir.*

"I need food," Kalie said, pushing her chair back with a screech. Sharp-eyed and unsmiling, Kalie was the type who might have made Overseer one day, despite the off-putting effect of her horrible, throaty drawl. "Anyone else?"

"Always," Sinon growled. The mercenaries shrugged their disinterest and Meline sat impassively, showing no sign of having heard her sister speak.

Clade shook his head. "Be quick."

Terrel and his men had said barely a dozen words since arriving earlier in the day. Clade wondered whether Terrel already suspected what Clade might ask him to do. *One man purchased with gold for each sorcerer loyal to the god I intend to abandon.* But of course, the balance could work the other way, too. *Maybe he's not sure which way I'm going to go.*

The mercenary had introduced his men as Yuri and Hosk, but

Clade had already forgotten which was which. The one on the right was lean and hard, his weathered face and greying temples marking him as likely the oldest man in the room. He leaned back in his chair, his eyes closed, a slight smile playing about his lips as though amused by something only he could hear. The other, a flat-nosed plainsman with braided hair, stared intently at the table as though reading some hidden text in its grain. Between them sat Terrel, hands folded, his face as expressionless as ever.

I could have a word with him once we're underway. Tell him something reassuring. Or maybe not; done badly, a conversation like that could have the opposite effect to what he intended. *No, I'll leave it be for now.* Terrel wasn't so foolish as to commit to anything before he knew the score. Besides, Clade would only need Terrel to kill his sorcerers if something went wrong. If everything went as planned, the golems themselves would be more than adequate to the task.

Despite the necessity, the prospect of killing more of his own left a sour taste in his mouth. There was always the possibility that one or another might share his hatred of Azador, deep down where nobody else could see. But the risk was simply too great. *I must win free, no matter the cost.* No eye or ear or hand of the god could be permitted to interfere.

At least his back was clear. With Estelle out of the way, he could present his journey to the rest of the Oculus as if it were just another field trip, unusual only for his own presence on the team. He'd told the others that the Councillor had been called away on an unexpected errand to a village a day's ride north of Anstice, but that she'd certainly be back within the week. It seemed unlikely that Azador would have another greater locus nearby — besides the one Estelle had brought with her, of course — but even if it did, by the time the god thought to stop looking for the missing Councillor and send a locus-bearer after Clade, he'd be long gone.

Somewhere around the table, a stomach growled. "Weeper's guts," Sinon swore, rounding on Meline and subjecting her to a baleful glare. "What's taking your fat-arsed sister so long?"

Meline swatted at the air between them as though waving away a fly. "Shut it," she said with regal dismissiveness, and Sinon subsided, nonplussed.

Clade permitted himself an inward chuckle. *Now, if those two can just confine their needling to each other and leave the rest of us in peace, this journey might not be too bad.*

"Clade?" Kalie stood at the door, a flat loaf in her hand and a boy of nine or ten summers at her heels. She gave the lad a sideways nod. "Says he's got a message for you."

The boy stepped forward, a worried expression on his face. "Are you Clade?"

"I am." Clade gestured him closer. "What is it, boy?"

"A Quill sent me to find you. I tried, sir, I really did, but I don't know this part of the city very well, and I got lost, and then —"

"Slow down," Clade said. "You're here now. What did the Quill say?"

The boy bit his lip. "He said to tell you that they were leaving right now."

"And when was this?"

He hung his head. "Midday, sir."

"Gatherer's arse," Sinon said. "They've been gone for hours."

"Save your bellyaching for the road." Clade gestured to the door. "Move out now, all of you. Horses are waiting for us in the stables. Go."

Sinon shoved his chair back with a muttered curse and strode from the room, followed by the sisters and the mercenaries. The boy looked at Clade, tears welling in his eyes, his piping voice carrying over the noise of movement.

"He said you'd give me a silver bit, sir. Only my ma won't stop coughing and my sister has to look after her, and —"

"All right, boy." Clade fished a scudi out of his purse and placed it in the boy's sweaty hand. "Did the Quill say anything else?"

"Gods bless you!" The boy gazed at the tiny silver coin in gratitude and relief. "And yes sir, he did. He said they were taking the river road. Only he didn't say which direction."

"That's fine." Bannard had already told him the direction they were headed: upstream toward the lake that gave the Tienette River its name. He made a shooing motion. "Run along now."

The boy darted off, leaving Clade alone in the room. Four or five hours behind. It could have been worse. They'd be able to catch up without much trouble, provided the Quill stuck to the road.

He collected his bag and headed out. By the time he reached the stables, the rest of the group was already mounted, and the god was no longer with them. Clade allowed the hostler to tie his bag in place, then swung into the saddle.

He paused in the courtyard, turning for a final look at the building. Somewhere down in the cellar, Estelle lay sealed in the stillbox. *She's probably shouted herself hoarse by now.* It was, he supposed, a fitting end for the one who had drawn him into Azador's snare all those years ago. Yet her fate gave him no satisfaction. It had been necessary, and that was all.

They rode through the gate and into the thoroughfare. Clade gestured to Terrel, shading his eyes against the late afternoon sun. "Lead us out," he called.

Terrel swung his horse around. "Which way?"

"West. The Lissil road."

As they headed out, the bells of the Kefiran temple began to ring, the peals slow and resonant, like the voice of some unfathomable creature; as though Azador itself were calling him back. *But no, there is not enough rage in it to be Azador.* He allowed a smile at his fancy. *Something else, then. One that wishes me fair journey.*

The sound pursued them all the way up the thoroughfare. When they left the main road to turn west, Clade could still hear the two loudest tones, one slightly deeper than the other, each ringing in turn, the odd, staccato rhythm sounding strangely like laughter.

Eilwen didn't know how long she'd been walking. It had been dark when she started, and it was light now. Had it been dark again? She didn't think so. *Only a day, then.* She frowned. That didn't seem right. Was that really all? It felt like years.

A tall Kefiran jostled her as she passed. There had been a lot of that since it had gotten light. *Crowded streets, lots of buildings. Still in Anstice.* That was good, she supposed. At least she knew roughly where she was.

She'd written a long letter before she left. She remembered that. She'd wanted to apologise to the masters, to Brielle, and yes, even to Ufeus. She'd wanted to apologise to Havilah, too, but of course it was too late for that.

Havilah is dead. There was something odd about the thought, something surprising, as though her mind were unable to make space for such a peculiarly shaped notion. Somehow, it just didn't fit.

There was a weight, somewhere. A leather strap, pulling her shoulder down. *I have my bag.* She must have thought to take it before she left. That was good, too. It meant she didn't have to go back.

Her hands moved over her body, feeling for the items she normally carried on her person. *Purse and dagger. Letters of reference from the Guild. Spare dagger in boot.* Nothing was missing, save the wire from her other boot. And beneath her shirt lay the black amber egg, the lambskin wrap pushed aside so that the egg's smooth surface pressed against her skin.

Twice during her wanderings the egg had stirred, once in the pre-dawn as a carriage rattled past, and a second time in the press of a crowded street. But the beast within her seemed sated for the moment, and she'd experienced the egg's voiceless whispers as though detached from her own senses, watching as it called to someone else. She'd felt neither compulsion nor revulsion, nor even curiosity, just an awareness that now it had found someone, and now they were gone again.

Havilah is dead. Gods. He's dead.

At one point while it was still dark, a pair of youths had approached her, one twisting her arms behind her back while the other began pawing at her breasts. She hadn't struggled or cried out. But when the one behind her relaxed his grip she smashed his nose, and by the time the other realised what was happening she'd already drawn her dagger and sliced open his cheek. She'd left them whimpering on the ground, adjusting her shirt as she walked away, never once having opened her mouth.

I didn't kill them. Gods attend, I didn't kill them. For some reason that seemed important.

Her steps carried her to an intersection and she paused, looking at the streets in sudden recognition. *The Fanon road. That's the eastern thoroughfare.* The city wall loomed to the east and south, the heavy, permanently open gates visible in both directions. *East toward Fanon or south toward Spyridon. Or west, back into Anstice. Or...*

Eilwen looked north up the thoroughfare. The side-street that marked her usual detour was just ahead; and half a dozen lots beyond that, the high grey wall that she always, always avoided.

She craned her neck, trying to get a glimpse of the building itself. *I should leave it be. Leave Anstice and not look back. Never have to worry about that building again.* But there was no weight to the words, not any more. The warning seemed meant for someone else, not her; so she nodded, noting its presence, then shrugged it off, making her way up the thoroughfare and halting before the drab, forbidden wall.

The building might have been five storeys high, featureless save for a roofed gallery along the top level. The gate was timber, similar in colour to the grey stones of the wall, which was surmounted by a pair of ornamental cannons. A small door beside the main gate stood open, and Eilwen glimpsed an equally drab courtyard beyond, empty of sunlight save for the small patch admitted by the door itself.

The egg stirred at her side as though muttering in its sleep and she placed a hand over it, caressing it through layers of fabric and lambskin.

There they are. The Oculus. There were dozens inside, no doubt. Maybe more. *I gave you a ship, and you tore it in two.* Tammas had asked her to smuggle the two oversized crates on board, so she had, never asking what was in them; and by the time he told her the truth, the sorcerers had already emerged and killed half the crew, and there'd been nothing left to do but stave the treacherous bastard's head in and then watch as the Oculus ripped the *Orenda* to pieces. *You killed my ship and let me live. You didn't even have the decency to take me with it.*

And now, if Laris was to be believed, they were on the brink of mounting an invasion. Eilwen found the prospect strangely pleasing. *Out in the open at last. No more skulking around, playing at war in the shadows. An honest fight, there for all to see.*

And for her, perhaps, the same. *Not a murderer, not any more. A soldier.* If only she could have explained it to Havilah. He wouldn't have asked her to stop if he'd known. He would have been proud.

Havilah, who was dead.

Hooves clattered within the courtyard. The gate swung open, revealing half a dozen riders within; and as they came into view, the egg swirled to life, tugging at her awareness. *Sorcerers.* At least two, probably more, and others bearing locuses as well. By the look of their bags, they were provisioned for a modest journey, perhaps to a nearby city like Spyridon. They'd be on the road for days, staying in inns, or perhaps even sleeping rough.

The beast within seemed to stretch, sniffing at the scene before her like a wolf sniffing the air. Then it straightened, eyes gleaming, and gave a growl of assent.

A worthy target.

The riders filed through the gate, halting in the thoroughfare. Eilwen saw one of them raise his hand against the slanting sun. "Lead us out," he called.

A shorter man nodded. "Which way?"

"West," said the first man, glancing up and down the thoroughfare. "The Lissil road."

They moved off, the short rider forging a path through the traffic, the rest following in his wake. Eilwen watched their halting progress down the thoroughfare as jangling bells rang out from a nearby building. Seven Oculus on the Lissil road. It was too good an opportunity to pass up.

She stepped into the flow of pedestrians, allowing them to sweep her back into the city, toward the river. There was a stable near Bastion Bridge where she could purchase a horse for a reasonable sum. It was late in the day to be setting out, but the road was good enough that she could ride into the night if need be. A group like that would be hard to miss outside the city.

See me, Havilah. I am a soldier. I go now to fight the enemies of the Guild.

Look upon me and be proud.

CHAPTER 21

To contest, to argue, to fight — to find that which is yours and no other's — this is what it is to live. Only in death are all men one.

— Daro of Talsoor, *Dialogues with my Teachers*

THE VILLAGE CLUNG TO THE road like barnacles to a ship. Many of the buildings were derelict, hollow shells with sagging, weather-worn roofs and gaping windows. The rest filled Arandras with a sense of weariness, as if those within continued to scrape out an existence simply because they couldn't think of anything better to do.

"Lost a field a while back," the innkeeper said in response to Narvi's enquiries, gesturing in the direction of the Tienette. The river was narrower here, flowing through the bottom of a gorge twice as deep as Arandras was tall. "Landslide. Biggest spring melt in years." He shrugged, narrowing hooded eyes. "Four died."

Despite the feeling of malaise hanging over the village, the inn seemed prosperous enough, a fact commented upon by Narvi and explained by the swarthy innkeeper as deriving from its proximity to the nearby bridge. Though too narrow for anything larger than a handcart, the crossing was the last before the lake at the river's source, a feature which apparently attracted sufficient travellers to support not only the inn but also a good part of the remaining village.

"Don't often get as many folk as you, though." The man rubbed his chin. "Could be a tight fit."

Narvi dismissed the man's concern with an easy smile. "We'll take whatever rooms you've got."

In the end, the innkeeper proved able to offer six rooms, each with space enough to bed two. To Arandras's complete lack of surprise, Fas determined that Quill personnel should be given priority, leaving Arandras and Mara to fend for themselves.

"I could find you space in the stables, perhaps," the innkeeper said, with a frown that suggested he wasn't entirely sure they wouldn't disappear in the night with their pick of the inn's horses.

"No need," Arandras said. The evening was warm, with a light breeze blowing in from the southeast. "We'll find somewhere grassy out back."

Supper was served by the innkeeper's nephew: a tagine of chicken, tomato, honey, and early season pine nuts, seasoned with something that put Arandras in mind of a Sarean spice he couldn't name. He ate quickly, relishing the hot food. *Not bad for a rundown village with every second house a rotting husk. Perhaps there's life in the place yet.* He made little effort at conversation and departed as soon as he was done, leaving Mara to drink and joke with as many of the Quill as would join her.

There'd been scant opportunity for Arandras to revisit their disagreement since their brief exchange the other day. Somehow, Mara always seemed to be occupied whenever Arandras was nearby, often in close conversation with one Quill or another, leaving him no opening even to ask whether something was amiss. Not that he could have done much about it if it was. It was he who had pointed out their failing, and she who had refused to hear it. *If she's expecting me to apologise, she'll have to get used to living with disappointment.*

A vast array of stars glittered overhead, cool and remote in the pitch-black sky. A fat moon hung close to the horizon, allowing Arandras to pick his way across the meadow behind the inn with ease. Selecting a spot free of rocks and tree roots, he wrapped himself in his travelling cloak and lay down, bags beneath his head, breathing deep the fresh scents of grass and wildflowers. *Weeper, but it's good to be out of the city.*

He didn't realise he'd fallen asleep until a hand on his shoulder jolted him awake. "Arandras," someone said, and for a sleep-fogged moment he thought it was Mara, come to confess her wrongs. "Arandras," the voice said again, and this time he noted its low, male tone. "Wake up, damn it."

"Who?" he said, blinking at the shadowy form.

The figure put a finger to its lips. "Hush. It's Bannard. Listen to me, Arandras. I can't do this any more."

Arandras sat up with a stifled groan. "What are you talking about?"

"I'm done. You hear me? I'm leaving, now."

"What? What do you mean, you're leaving?"

"What do you think I mean?" Bannard blew out an exasperated breath. "I can't keep leading that bastard on behind us. I'm done with it."

Arandras rubbed his eyes, trying to think. *Weeper's tears, why is nothing ever simple?* "You leave like this, the Quill might not have you back."

"I know. I'm not going back." Bannard's voiced hitched in the darkness. "I'm a snake. Do you know how that feels?" He gave a bitter chuckle. "Well, I guess you do. Maybe you can live with it. I can't."

"I'm not a traitor," Arandras began, then stopped. *Not the time.* "Forget it. Tell me what signs you're leaving for Clade."

"If I do, then whatever happens next is on you. I have no part in this after tonight."

No part. The words echoed in his mind, recalling his own thoughts in Isaias's shop. *I said that too, but it was too late.* "Please. What signs?"

"Stones," Bannard said reluctantly. "Four the same size to show the points of the world, then a smaller one — white, if possible — to show the direction we took."

Arandras nodded. It was a simple enough method. "Thank you."

"If anyone asks about me in the morning, just say you slept through and didn't hear anything, all right?"

"Hey, if you want out from the Quill, there's no way I'm pointing them after you."

"All right." Bannard coughed softly, as if he wanted to say

something else.

"What?"

"Nothing." A pause. "It's just… you still have a choice, you know. Don't let him turn you into someone you're not."

Bannard rose and jogged away in the direction of the stables. Arandras glanced around the colourless meadow. Mara's curled form lay beneath a sparsely-leafed tree, too distant to have heard their conversation. A soft whinny floated down from the stables, then the sound of muffled clops slowly receding back up the road. Sighing, Arandras stretched out on the soft grass.

I'm not a traitor. I've made my refusal to bend the knee abundantly clear. And if Fas and the rest were making assumptions about his intentions, well, the Quill had a long history of benefiting from others' overly generous assumptions about them. *Let's see how they like getting the nasty surprise for a change.*

He slept fitfully the rest of the night, tossing and turning on the cool grass, unable to quite put Bannard's words from his mind. When the first glimmer of dawn appeared on the horizon he gave up, abandoning the meadow and setting out in search of stones.

He returned to the inn early enough for his absence to go unremarked. Sitting alone in the common room, breaking his fast on a selection of berries, nuts, and honeyed flatbread, he watched as news of Bannard's disappearance rippled out among the group, drawing first amusement, then bafflement at the discovery that Bannard's horse was also missing. When Fas paused to ask if he knew where man and horse had gone, Arandras simply shook his head and took another handful of berries.

At length, Narvi and Fas decided that wherever Bannard had gone, he wasn't coming back. Narvi made arrangements with the innkeeper to house their horses until their return, and they set off on foot, making for the bridge just outside the village.

The small arrangement of stones Arandras had assembled stood on the verge of the road, a round river pebble pointing north toward the narrow timber bridge and the far bank of the Tienette. *I'm not a traitor,* he thought as he passed it, turning onto the pressed dirt track that led to the crossing. Ahead, somewhere among the procession of ochre and black making its way across the bridge, Mara and

Fas laughed in unison.

He couldn't be a traitor. After all, one could only betray those who deserved loyalty, and the Quill deserved no such thing, least of all from him. Yet as he crossed the river, listening to the rushing water below, Bannard's words whispered through his heart, and nothing he could say seemed able to satisfy them.

~

Clade stepped into the other man's path, his voice a low growl. "Back off, Sinon."

Sinon lurched to a halt a hand's breadth from Clade, his foul breath washing over Clade's nose and mouth. The big sorcerer stood rigid, his gaze fixed in a glare over Clade's shoulder. Then he snarled and took a half-step forward.

Legs braced, Clade shoved a hand against the man's thick chest. "I said *back off.*"

Sinon grunted, shifting his glare to Clade. Clade stood his ground, answering the other man's regard with a withering stare of his own. They stood there for a long moment, eyes locked together like swords. Then, abruptly, Sinon broke into a fierce, mocking grin. He stepped back, tilting his head in a derisive nod, and stomped away.

Clade released an inaudible sigh.

Footsteps sounded behind him in the still morning air, receding toward the road. Clade turned. "Terrel," he said. The man stopped, not looking around. "What in the hells were you playing at?"

Terrel's shoulders twitched. "Keeping watch," he said.

"I gave Sinon last watch."

"Experienced in the field, is he?" Terrel said. "Knows the difference between a rabbit's rustle and the sound of a child? Or either of those and a creeping man?"

"I hardly think a group like ours is likely to fall prey to bandits. Not this close to the river."

"I trust the men I know."

In other words, not Sinon. Clade frowned. *Or, perhaps, not me.* "Sinon's the kind that takes that sort of thing personally."

Terrel repeated his slight shrug and resumed his course for the road.

It was their third morning on the road. Bannard's signposts had been sporadic, but Clade had pressed on, assuming that the absence of any indication to the contrary meant they should continue along the main road. Sooner or later they always came upon another cluster of stones piled by the side of a turnpike or relay house, confirming that the Quill party still followed the road somewhere up ahead.

The formation just outside the small village signalled a change.

"North," Terrel said, halting at the junction and peering in the designated direction. The dirt road led to a narrow bridge over the Tienette, then twisted away into forest on the other side. He dismounted, examined the road. "Looks like they went on foot. An hour ago, maybe."

Sinon cursed. "I hate walking."

Irritation stirred within, but Clade boxed it in, smothering it before it could spread. *You have no place in me. Begone.*

As they'd followed Bannard's signposts through the first day and then the second, Clade had begun to wonder at the Quill's intended route. Bannard had placed the urn's coordinates somewhere north of Tienette Lake; yet Lissil, the town to which the road eventually led, lay on the lake's south bank, raising the unpleasant possibility that the Quill might intend to cross the lake by boat as the final leg of their journey. Clade had spent hours wondering how to follow a boatful of Quill undetected, fighting the impulse to worry; but now, it seemed, the problem had resolved itself. He stood at the intersection and gazed toward the bridge, untroubled by any temptation to either concern or relief.

So. North.

We'll need to do something about the horses.

The village's only inn offered food, lodging, and temporary stables for as long as one could afford. The innkeeper, a swarthy man with a guarded manner, grudgingly confirmed that a party of Quill had left their horses with him earlier that morning. By the time Clade and Terrel emerged, the group's horses were unloaded and unsaddled, and their riding gear already bundled for storage. The mercenaries, Yuri and Hosk, sat by the roadside, Yuri scratching in the dirt with his dagger while a dozen paces away, Sinon, Kalie and

Meline stood in a small huddle, their backs pointedly turned toward Terrel's men.

Clade suppressed a sigh. *At least they're not actually fighting.*

"How long?" Kalie asked in her rough drawl as the stableboy led the horses away.

"Two weeks," Clade said. "Then he'll sell one to pay for the rest, and so on." He started back toward the crossing. "Come on."

The bridge spanned the shallow gorge like a strung wire, the timber a drab, weathered grey. As Clade neared the middle, a shape swung into view upstream: a coracle, carried along by the smooth-flowing water at a surprising pace. Two men sat within, one on either side, each holding the shaft of pole, or possibly an oar. The space between them was piled high with straw and rough wooden crates, while in the front, a donkey gazed at the river like a comic figurehead, its ears flicking in the breeze.

For some reason, the sight reminded him of Estelle. *Azador is ours,* she had said, as though the god were nothing more than the donkey in the boat below, proudly imagining itself master of its own course. But what if it was the other way around? *What if you, Estelle, are the donkey, and it is Azador that drives you?*

But then, Estelle was surely dead by now. The god had seemed agitated the last time it visited, staying only a moment before flitting away. *Searching for an explanation, no doubt.* Clade turned from the rail, resuming his march next-but-last to the flat-nosed Yuri, whom Terrel had assigned as rearguard. The respite from Azador's presence was welcome, though Clade knew it was only temporary. Once the god caught scent of the golems there'd be no shifting it.

Up ahead, Terrel made an abrupt halt, the group gathering in a circle around him. A cluster of stones sat beside a low bush, and this time the small one pointed west and south, away from the dirt road and into the forest, parallel to the river.

Meline grimaced. "Must we?"

"Weeper-damned trees," Sinon growled, kicking at the dirt beside the bush.

Kalie gave a disgusted sigh. "For the Dreamer's sake, Sinon. If you can't handle the pace, go home. Otherwise, shut the hells up already." She turned to Terrel, ignoring Sinon's glower and swinging her arm in an exaggerated sweeping gesture. "Lead the way."

Terrel began ordering the party, and Clade shot Kalie a nod of appreciation. The woman had the makings of a leader, no matter her limited capacity for sorcery. *Maybe if I'd made her my adjunct instead of Garrett we'd have been here weeks ago, no Quill any nearer than Lissil, and all of them oblivious to the wonders hiding across the lake.*

He'd still have had to bring her along, though. The only difference was that he'd have known her better when he killed her.

Maybe it was better this way.

The Quill trail wound its way through the towering red gums and the sprays of smaller bushes competing for sunlight at their feet. The ground was rocky in places, but mostly flat. Birds chirped and warbled to each other in the high branches, filling the air with their song; and beneath everything, neither strong enough to draw deep nor faint enough to ignore, the fresh, unmistakable scent of eucalyptus.

Sera would have loved this, Clade thought as they stepped around the trunk of a particularly massive gum. Tiny yellow and white flowers peeked out from behind the narrow spearhead leaves. *She'd have wanted to stop, take it all in. Pick a flower and put it in her hair, like as not.* He pictured her with a blossom behind her ear, grinning her infectious grin, and smiled.

When they stopped for a break, he drew out the woodbinding block he'd taken from her room: long as a finger but twice as wide, its surface as smooth as wood could get without being polished. *You made it bend like a stalk of grass. No splits, no damage. But try as you might, you couldn't quite make it straight again.* An unnatural knob protruded from the block a third of the way down; though what exactly gave it its artificial appearance, Clade couldn't say. The angle, perhaps. Or maybe it was just that he knew how it came to be.

"Where's Yuri?" The voice was Meline's. "He was just here. Wasn't he?"

Clade glanced up. Terrel was looking back the way they came, attentive but not visibly worried. The other mercenary, Hosk, knelt at the edge of the clearing, examining the pommel of his sword.

"Gatherer's balls, I hate it when people run off," Sinon said to nobody in particular.

"There he is," Kalie said, and a moment later Yuri's flat features and braided hair came into view around a knot of trees. The man gestured to Terrel, who seemed to relax slightly. *All clear.*

Sinon gave a contemptuous snort and turned away.

"Break's over," Clade said, slipping the block into his pocket. "Let's go."

They moved out, Hosk in front, Clade falling in behind Kalie in the middle of the group. As they marched, he found his hand returning to his pocket, his fingers tracing the marred wooden form. Though the binding was long since gone, the block still bore its scars. *No matter what she did, she couldn't get them out.*

A breath of wind set the leaves rustling high overhead. From somewhere to their right came the screech of a hunting bird, then another. He ignored them, marching with head bowed, turning the block over and over in his long fingers.

～

Eilwen was relieved beyond words when the Oculus party turned off the main road and struck north over the Tienette. Riding was uncomfortable enough at the best of times, but riding in pursuit of a mounted quarry was far, far worse.

She'd stayed as close as she dared, fearful of losing touch with the sorcerers and missing the moment they turned in a new direction. On the second morning, she'd arrived at a turnpike thinking herself just a few minutes behind, only to find a queue of half a dozen travellers before her and the Oculus nowhere in sight; and for a brief, mad moment she'd thought of galloping past without paying, never mind the archer in his terraced platform beside the road. Twice she'd actually passed the group as they halted by the side of the road, and had been forced to loiter half-hidden in way-house stables as she waited for them to resume their journey.

The previous night she'd woken in terror to the sound of drumming hoofs, convinced that the Oculus had noticed her after all and come back to kill her in her sleep. But the sound turned out to be a lone rider, possibly a Quill, travelling east toward Anstice, and eventually she drifted back to sleep, her dreams haunted by galloping horses that turned to mist moments before riding her down.

But no more. They'd turned north, crossing the Tienette at the last bridge before the river became the lake — or the first bridge, so far as the river was concerned. And they'd gone on foot.

Eilwen led her horse into the nearby village, scanning the ramshackle buildings on either side of the road for any place she might dispose of her mount. High whinnies caught her ear from further ahead, and she followed the sound to an inn on the road's south side. In the small yard before the stables she found a skinny boy hauling on the halter of a feisty dun courser, while a pot-bellied man, presumably the innkeeper, stood back and watched. The smell of manure and horse sweat drifted past on the light breeze.

"Excuse me," she called, and the innkeeper strode out with a scowl, shaking his head and waving his hands in front of him.

"If you're looking to house your horse, you're out of luck," he said. "We're full up."

Eilwen glanced over the rows of stalls. All appeared occupied, and many already seemed home to more than one horse. She frowned. "How about if I'm selling it?"

He eyed the creature speculatively. "How much are you asking?"

Perhaps sensing her determination to sell, the innkeeper offered an amount roughly half what she'd paid for the horse and gear in Anstice. Her half-hearted attempts to haggle the price higher were met with blank refusal and she soon gave them up, slipping the fistful of coins and lengths into her bag and chuckling at the stableboy's disbelieving "What?" as the innkeeper broke the news. She retraced her steps up the road, stretching out her sore leg, grateful for earth beneath her feet once more. The sun was warm on her back without being oppressive, and the sound of the river splashing through the gorge filled her with an unexpected vigour, as though the worst was over and she could finally begin setting her life to rights.

It was, she thought, about time.

The trail left the road on the other side of the river, striking westward along the northern bank. Eilwen crouched beside the departure point, frowning at the trampled weeds. A group had plainly passed this way recently, their path so obvious as to give Eilwen pause. *Have they joined some others? Or did a separate group come this way as well?* She squinted along the broken trail, then up at the dirt road. *Or did the Oculus not take this turn at all?*

Eilwen hesitated. The dirt road wound away northward, likely visiting dozens of nameless, insignificant hamlets before eventually disappearing somewhere near the mountains. The fresh trail to the west, however, led... where? Wherever it was, it seemed nobody had had any need to go there until recently. If the Oculus had just happened to come through right after some other group, well, that would be a damned strange coincidence.

She turned, examining the dirt road. A sapling with a freshly broken branch stood a few paces before the fork. Beside it, a flattened shoot lay trampled into the road. Beyond the divergence, however, the road seemed undisturbed. Eilwen straightened, her decision made. Something had drawn the Oculus out here, and it wasn't a sleepy hamlet in the middle of nowhere.

Hoisting her bag over her shoulder, Eilwen set off into the forest. The trail was wide, unmissable. Surely more than seven people had come this way. Now that she thought about it, that stable back in the village had been peculiarly full. She wished she'd asked the innkeeper about his sudden influx of horses. *What on the gods' earth could attract such a crowd all the way out here?*

There was something wrong about the whole situation. She could almost sense it, like a shapeless smudge hovering just past the edge of her vision. *Something is going on.*

She wondered what Havilah would make of it.

The smell of nearby water drifted in and out beneath the fresh scent of eucalypt. From time to time Eilwen caught the sound of the river echoing from the gorge, but the winding trail never quite brought her close enough for another glimpse. A lush variety of shrubs, bushes, and ferns filled the spaces between the larger trees, forming a thick layer of undergrowth. Eilwen picked her way between them, following the path of torn fronds, bent branches, and broken scrub as it wound inexorably westward.

As the morning wore on, she found herself reaching back to her old training to calculate the value of the timber around her. The largest trees here were massive, their boles wide enough at the base for three or four people to wrap their arms around and still not

complete the circle. Deadfall was sparse, suggesting a relative absence of rot and decay. *Any one of these would be worth ten or twelve
times a regular tree by timber volume alone. And if we could get a
woodbinder in to help fell them in fewer pieces...*

But there was no "we". Not any more. *You're alone now, Eilwen.
Best get used to it.*

She was halfway down a gentle slope when the egg stirred to life.

Eilwen froze mid-step, grasping a branch to steady herself, and
scanned the trees around her. All seemed still. Birds chirped softly
above the faint rustle of leaves, but that was all. *Nothing moving at
ground level. Is that normal?* She grimaced, uncertain.

The sense of someone approaching grew stronger. She dropped
to a crouch behind a leafy acacia, ignoring the protests of her knee,
and peered through the branches. A round-shouldered Plainsman
stepped into view on the trail ahead, and she loosed a soft hiss. *An
Oculus.* He moved silently across the forest floor, knees bent, one
hand on the hilt of his sword, swivelling his head like a tribal dancer.
The egg pulsed against her flesh, but faintly, as though impeded by
some invisible barrier. *Not a sorcerer, then. Just a token-bearer.*

A good start.

The thought came from some other place within her: the beast,
its eyes slitted open, contemplating the man in the same way that
she had contemplated the trees. Its casual hunger filled her, and she
abandoned herself to it, allowing it to carry her along as it assessed
his strengths, his vulnerabilities. *Agile. Quiet. No armour. Short
reach. Leads with his left side.* It stretched lazily, considering its ver-
dict. *Surprise. A knife from behind. Throat or heart.*

She nodded as though it had spoken, easing her dagger from
its sheath. Following was all well and good, but she was here for a
reason.

I'm a soldier on a mission. Here comes my enemy.

The man stopped, straightening, and took a final glance around
the forest. Then he shrugged and turned, disappearing back the way
he had come.

What? No! Come back! She almost called out as he passed from
view, gasping as her anticipation shifted in an instant to aching
hollowness. Inside, the beast howled its disappointment. The egg's

stirring quieted, then stilled completely, and she stood, rubbing her leg as she stared at the now vacant trail.

Branches rustled high overhead. Somewhere away to her left, water rushed over stone. She was alone.

But they were close. Closer than she'd realised. *And that man will be back.* He'd looked like he sensed he was being followed. Somehow or other she'd managed to divulge her presence.

She hugged her arms to her chest, looking anew at the trees and scrub around her. She'd spent her first few years with the Guild thinking about nothing but wood and forests, but in some ways she didn't know them at all. *I can identify the most profitable trees, work out how best to fell them. And I can follow a trail, at least when it's as obvious as this. But when it comes to moving through the forest unnoticed, I've got no idea.*

But then, she didn't want to go completely unnoticed. She wanted to be just perceptible enough to have that man come looking for her again.

I'll just keep doing what I'm doing. Sooner or later, my chance will come.

～

"We're here," Narvi said, peering down at the map in his hand and then up again. "I think."

Arandras pulled a skin from his bag and took a long swallow. The forest came to an abrupt end at the edge of a cliff, below which lay a wide, rocky shore. The placid surface of Tienette Lake stretched out before them, its waters glittering in the mid-morning sun. The air smelt like stone after rain.

"I don't see a gorge," he said.

"No," Narvi said. "But do you notice the line of the cliff? That bend looks like this bit on the map. Which means the gorge should be just past that ridge..."

"Could be something here," Mara called from the lip of the ridge. "But it's choked with rocks. We'll have to go around and down."

Great. Arandras peered over the cliff edge at the rough shoreline. *That's a damn long way to fall.* "How are we going to do that?"

"Over here." Ienn beckoned to them from a dozen paces further along. "Looks like there might have been a path once."

It was the kind of remark which was both strictly true and entirely misleading. Whatever path had once existed, only a series of irregular ledges now remained, most clogged with pebbles or coated in moss, some separated from their neighbours by gaps that made Arandras's stomach churn. *There must be another way.*

"Splendid," Fas said, nodding approvingly at the broken path. "Who's first?"

Narvi looked down the first segment of track, his broad face unusually wan. "Um. Perhaps we should send someone down to, uh, make sure it goes all the way to the bottom."

"I'll go," Ienn said, slinging his bag to the ground. "Don't all run off while I'm gone, now."

The group spread out along the clifftop, taking advantage of the chance to rest and enjoy the view. Arandras found himself a patch of grass half a dozen paces from the edge — far enough to relax, at least a little — and sat with his arms about his knees, gazing out at the expanse of water. A few moments later Fas settled beside him with a grunt, his jaw working vigorously on a strip of dried meat.

"Close now, don't you think?" Fas said around his mouthful of food.

Arandras shrugged. "If you say so." The bend on the map was slight enough to match a hundred different spots along the shore; or it might be nothing more than a slip of the pen, made by any of the cartographers responsible for each copy of a copy since the original. *I'll believe we're there when I'm staring the golems in whatever they have for eyes.*

"You still want one for yourself, do you?"

"Of course. That was the deal."

"So it was." Fas chewed slowly, gazing out at the horizon. "Tell you what. When we get there, you pick out the one you want. All right?"

Arandras blinked. "All right."

Fas grunted, nodded, and reached for another strip of meat.

What in the hells was that? Arandras shot the other man a sidelong glance. *A gesture of conciliation?* The disquiet that had been with him since the village intensified.

I'm not a traitor. A traitor would be leading Clade here to thwart the Quill. Arandras was bringing him here to destroy him. And in any case, the Oculus weren't the real issue, whatever Bannard's misgivings. *I can't let Fas take the golems. Not after Isaias's shop.* And there was no reason why he should. Fas had never asked for the golems. He'd just assumed they were his for the taking.

Arandras was simply assuming them back.

The sun was approaching its zenith when Ienn returned from his climb. "It's passable," he said, a faint sheen on his brow. "Narrow in places, though. Some of you will need help."

On Ienn's advice, a rope was tied around a thick tree above the back-and-forth path. Mara volunteered to go first, stepping lightly onto the trail and out of sight. Ienn followed her progress along the cliff edge, pulling the rope across the low scrub as she descended. Arandras watched it slither from side to side, stripping the leaves from the slender shoots in its path, until at last it went still.

"Clear," came the call from the bottom of the cliff.

Ienn tugged the rope back to the beginning of the track. "Who's next?"

Arandras allowed several Quill to take their turn before he stepped up to the path. Wrapping his hands around the thick, scratchy rope, he edged out onto the first shelf. Patterns of sunlight danced over the pale stone of the cliff, reflected from ripples and wavelets on the lake's surface far below. He narrowed his eyes, focusing on the ledge and the placement of each step as the gentle breeze nudged him against the cliff.

At the first gap he halted, frowning appraisingly. A section of path had fallen away, the resulting space just wide enough to be uncomfortable. On the far side lay a slanting ledge less than half the width of the one he now stood on. *Wonderful. Miss it by a finger and I'll be taking the short way down.*

Grasping the rope in both hands, Arandras shuffled forward. He crouched, feeling the stone's edge beneath the toes of his boots. Then, eyes fixed on the ledge before him, he leapt.

He landed awkwardly, feet scrabbling for purchase on the pebble-strewn shelf. Heart thudding, he hauled on the rope, pulling himself tight against the cliff wall. *Still here. I'm still here.* He edged further along, breathing a sigh of relief as the shelf began to widen beneath his feet. *There. That wasn't so bad.* Swallowing, he loosened his grip on the rope ever so slightly, eyes darting ahead to the next break in the path. *Piece of cake.*

But the first gap was the worst. Thereafter he was able to step across the holes, aided by the downward slope, using the rope only to steady himself when the ledge became too narrow to trust his footing. By the time he reached the bottom he was almost relaxed, stepping from one shelf to the next with such settled concentration that he was surprised to find the cliff end and the shore begin.

"Clear," Mara called as he released the rope. He stepped back, taking in the cliff and the path he'd just traversed. *Yeah. Piece of cake.*

The next Quill began to pick his way down. Arandras glanced westward, his gaze drawn by a hole in the craggy stone about half-way up the escarpment. *How deep does that go, I wonder?* He moved closer, squinting at the dark hollow, boots crunching on the pebbled shore. The cavity was wider at the bottom than the top, but too regular to be natural. *A window, maybe?*

Someone drew up alongside. "Looks almost like the lower half of a triangle, doesn't it?" Narvi said. "I keep thinking it looks familiar, but I can't work out why."

Arandras scratched his beard. Now that Narvi mentioned it, it did look familiar. He peered up, trying to place the nagging sense of having seen it before.

Narvi pointed further along the cliff face. "Is that another one over there?"

The second window was higher and smaller, and seemed to point in a slightly different direction. The rock around it was mottled, rough with crags and creases. Viewed from the lake, it was probably indistinguishable from the rest of the cliff.

The third overlooked a cleft in the rocky wall. Fallen rocks choked the fissure after several dozen paces, a few spilling to the base of a great boulder that looked to have been pressed into the cliff. Narvi grasped Arandras's arm in excitement. "That's it. Get out the urn."

Of course. Arandras dug the pewter vessel out of its pouch, pushed aside its wrapping. There it was, in the band of images etched into its curved belly: a cliff split by a gorge, a man and a golem standing at its mouth; and high in the cliff wall, almost too small to see, a window shaped like the lower half of a triangle.

"This is the place," Narvi said, his eyes dancing; and despite himself, Arandras found himself smiling in return.

The golems. They're here.

CHAPTER 22

Your life is a song in the ears of the All-God, and every past day a voice in your choir. They sing without surcease: harsh or soft, treacherous or beautiful, the forgotten days no less than those remembered.

Today, my friends, you will add a new voice to your choir. Choose it well.

— Herev Gis, *Latter Sermons,* Chapter 28, Verses 43–44
(as ordered by the Gislean Provin)

FOR THE FOURTH NIGHT IN a row, Eilwen slept badly.

Though misty horses no longer filled her dreams, she found herself waking with a violent start again and again, heart racing and dagger drawn, staring in mindless panic at the shadowy trees above her. Eventually, after half a dozen such wakenings, she gave up, raising herself to a sitting position and listening to the called greetings of magpies, lorikeets, and other birds as the grey light of dawn crept slowly over the forest.

Despite the difficult night, she found the stillness of the morning strangely calming. *How rarely have I done this? Alone under the sky with the sunrise, welcoming the day.* There was a power in it, something great and constant and unyielding. *Dawn is the Dreamer's time, before the sorrow of the day begins.* She'd heard the words since childhood, even recited them herself on occasion, but she'd never understood them until now.

The sense of calm stayed with her throughout the morning,

bringing an ease to her steps which she found both refreshing and confusing. What had changed? Nothing she could think of. Perhaps it was something about getting out of the city, and it had taken this long for it to finally work its way into her system. *Though I've been out of Anstice plenty of times before, and it never made me feel like this.*

Maybe the difference was that this time she knew she wasn't going back.

She stopped around midday, sitting on a boulder and chewing some flatbread. The leafy canopy danced above her head, sending shadows scurrying across the forest floor. She smiled, tilting her face skyward to catch the breeze, and felt the egg stir at her side.

It whispered to her like an old lover, crooning to her, murmuring the secret song that only they had ever shared. Her feeling of wellbeing slipped away, replaced in an instant by something cool and dark and intimate. Hunger bloomed in her belly, the kind of hunger that bread did nothing to assuage, and she felt the beast stir. It opened a slitted eye, then stretched, baring its teeth in a savage smile.

He's coming. The token-bearer returns.

Hurriedly, she crammed the last of the bread into her mouth and stepped into the shadow of a large tree. The trail crested a hill just a few paces ahead, and for a moment she considered peeking over the rise. *No. He'd have as good a chance of seeing me first as the other way around.* She slowed her breaths, pressing her back against the tree trunk. Thick ferns crowded the other side of her tree, making a stealthy approach from that side impossible. Anyone backtracking would have no choice but to come right past her hiding place.

She eased the knife into her hand and listened to the egg.

It began to pulse, the rhythm thin but unmistakable. A token-bearer again, no question. With luck, the same one; if not, she'd have to chance her hand. Either way, the same tactics would likely suffice: a single knife thrust between the back ribs into the heart. *Gods grant he hasn't found his armour.*

The pulse strengthened to a throb. The rustling overhead dimmed in her ears, giving way to a strained silence. Something scraped just ahead: a boot on the ground, or just a branch against its neighbour? She tightened her grip on the dagger and held her breath.

A figure stepped soundlessly into view. Eilwen glimpsed a stooped shoulder and dark hair in Plainsmen's braids. The head swivelled away from her, searching the scrub on the other side of the trail. Her arm tensed, ready to strike. *Just one more step. One more... and...*

Her knife slipped into his back as though of its own accord, as if skin and sinew offered no more resistance than hot wax.

The man cried out once and crumpled to the ground. She stooped to retrieve her dagger, wiped it clean on his shirt. Then she straightened, looking down at the body through the beast's eyes, drinking in the sight. The peace she'd felt all morning was gone, but there was nothing unpleasant in its place. Just a different kind of calm.

One down, she thought. *Six to go.*

A shouted hello from beyond the hill pulled her attention back to her surroundings. The man's companions were coming. Eilwen tore her gaze from the body at her feet and started down the hill, away from the approaching voice. If she stuck to the trail, they might think her a better woodsman than she was and not bother trying to find her.

On the other hand, if they decided to split up to search for her, that would be even better.

Once upon a time, she'd have had days of nausea to look forward to after something like this. *Murder always left me feeling ill.* But then, it wasn't really murder, was it? That was what she'd never understood before.

The Oculus were the enemy. This was a war. And she was a soldier.

She smiled and stroked the hilt of her dagger.

⁓

The massive boulder seemed impervious to sorcery, but the Quill earthbinders were able to cut a hollow in the ground before it, forming a trough into which it might be rolled. Arandras was assigned a place behind the boulder with a Quill he didn't know. Two more Quill mirrored their positions on the other side, with the rest of the group divided between three ropes fastened to the mammoth rock. When Ienn called the order, Arandras pushed, those on the ropes pulled, and slowly, grudgingly, the boulder shifted a hand's breadth away from the cliff.

"Again!" Arandras set his feet against the wall, straining against the rock with his entire body. It shifted a fraction, then abruptly lurched forward. He fell to the ground, wincing as he landed on his side, a knuckle of stone digging into his thigh. Grimacing, he stumbled to his feet and looked around.

A dark opening yawned where the boulder had been. Half again as high as a man and wide enough for four or five, the passage stretched away into impenetrable blackness. A cool draught wafted past Arandras's face, laced with a dusty, unfamiliar scent, and he sneezed.

Light flared among the Quill, casting flickering shadows into the passage. "If you've got a lamp or a sparker, fire it up," Ienn said. "If not, stay close to someone who does."

"And nobody touch anything," Narvi added. "First time in is observation only."

The Quill began to file in, lamps in hand, some leaving their bags outside the passage. Arandras watched the procession go by. *Anyone feel like sharing a light?* Narvi and Fas walked past, Fas murmuring something about Chogon's likely reaction to their discovery, and Arandras grimaced. *Maybe that rangy Jervian...*

Mara halted beside him, a slender torch in her hand. "Waiting for someone?"

Huh. Look who's come around. He gave a quick smile of thanks. "Not any more," he said, and thought he saw her lips twitch in response.

They entered the passage on the heels of the last Quill, the group spread out before them, each island of light illuminating another small section of stone; and though most of the passage was still shrouded in darkness, Arandras could see enough to get a sense of its shape.

The space was a cavern, at least three times as wide as the entrance and twice as high, and deeper than the light could penetrate. The walls curved into the ceiling in a giant semicircle of pale, grey-brown rock. Footsteps and voices echoed in the hollow space, as though each person was shadowed by a muttering, foot-scuffing twin just beyond the lamplight. Arandras brushed his hand against a rocky spur protruding from the wall. It was hard, its edges smoother than he expected. His fingers came away coated with a fine dust bearing the same dry scent he'd smelled by the entrance, tickling his nose with hints of leather, and spice, and hot desert sand. He sneezed again, and the sound boomed around the cavern like cannon fire.

"Gods," Mara hissed. "Don't do that again."

The cavern sloped down just enough to be noticeable. Doorless portals pierced the walls at irregular intervals, similar in size to what might be found in any building across the Free Cities, though in this place they seemed absurdly small. Some opened to cramped, windowless cells, others on winding stone staircases leading to some lower level. But there seemed an unspoken consensus among the group: onward, to the end of the passage and whatever lay beyond.

They pressed on. In the dark it was impossible to judge distance. A sudden thought made Arandras glance back the way they had come. All was black, save for a faint smudge of what might have been daylight on a pale wall. *The passage must be turning. Steering us back toward the cliff.* He ran his hand along the wall, feeling for the curve in the rough stone, but it was too slight to detect.

Voices called out from the other side of the cavern, drawing Arandras's attention. Two lamps and a torch had come to a halt before what appeared to be a mound of rocky earth. There was a muted exchange, then a word from Narvi that sounded like either permission or a command; and a moment later, a gout of flame bloomed up from the torch, billowing to the ceiling in a fiery mass of orange and yellow, lighting up the cavern for the space of a heart-beat before winking out and plunging them back into gloom.

Firebinder, Arandras thought, even as he took in what he'd seen. The loose earth was more than just a mound — it extended all the way to the ceiling, sprawling across half the cavern's width like an underground hill. *A cave-in. Hells. I thought the Valdori were supposed to be better than that.*

"Old, I think," someone said as Arandras and Mara joined the rest of the group, gathering before the heaped earth.

"How old, Halli?" Fas said.

The woman shrugged. "Years. Centuries. Who knows? It's not about to come crashing down on our heads, if that's what you're asking."

"Good to know," Arandras muttered.

Mara quirked an eyebrow at him. "Of course, that's probably what the Valdori said, too."

Yeah. Probably.

"All right," Narvi said. "Let's move on."

They resumed their course, skirting the edge of the cave-in, Arandras and Mara now at the fore of the group. Arandras peered into the still, inky blackness, straining for any glimmer of reflected light from something solid. The slope seemed to have levelled off now — either that, or he could no longer sense it in the dark.

Mara shifted the torch to her other hand, causing the shadows at their feet to jump and flicker. Her boot scraped against something and she stumbled, cursing. "Weeper's breath! Why doesn't Narvi just put a firebinder in the lead and have him light the whole place up?"

"Yeah," Arandras said. "Because nothing brightens a dark cave like accidentally setting something on fire." *Or triggering some ancient binding with a grudge against sorcery.*

"We survived a moment ago," Mara muttered. "A little more wouldn't kill anyone."

A dark shape loomed before them, tall and wide, blacker even than the surrounding gloom. Arandras blinked, trying to make sense of the murky object. Then Mara moved the torch, and the shadows resolved into pale stone walls about another empty portal, this one of similar dimensions to the entrance now lost to sight behind them. *Aha. The end, at last.* Mara glanced across, brows raised in anticipation; then she raised the torch and they stepped inside.

At first they could see little more than a smooth section of floor. Then, as the Quill entered behind them with sparkers and lamps, the room's layout became clear. The chamber was roughly square, a stark contrast to the rounded walls and ceiling of the passageway. An uneven bench ran along one wall, apparently carved in place when the chamber was cut from the stone. The other sides of the chamber offered no such amenity — instead, shackles hung from the walls in clusters of four, two just above the ground, two more at about the height of Arandras's shoulders.

"The gods wept," Narvi breathed. "What is this?"

Arandras lifted one of the shackles, causing the chain to clink softly. It was lighter than it appeared, the strange, speckled metal cool and smooth, unmarked by rust or verdigris. He held up the fine circlet, running a finger around its circumference. The band was wide enough to fit around both his balled fists with room to spare.

A simple key protruded from the lock, and he gave it an experimental twist. The shackle shut with a smart click. He opened it again, let it fall back against the wall.

"They're too big," Fas said. "Too big to be human. They must be…"

"For the golems," Mara said.

"Weeper's blessed tears," Narvi said. "Why?"

Nobody answered.

Another doorless opening stood directly opposite the one they had come in. Mara stepped toward it, Arandras close behind. She reached the threshold, then stopped dead with an audible gasp.

Arandras stepped alongside. "What's the — oh." *Oh my.*

Where the first, empty cavern had been raw display of might, this was a soaring expression of elegance and grandeur. He stood on a low platform at one side of the tremendous room. Thin streams of light filtered in from windows and other openings high in what Arandras judged to be the rear wall. Vaulted ceilings rose in dizzying arches, their peaks lost in the shadows above. And before him, like giants frozen in time, like strange formations of earth and clay growing from the rock itself, stood rows upon rows of golems.

They were tall and graceful. They were broad and stocky. They were all alike, and each one was different. They held swords and maces and nothing at all. Most stood facing the front of the room, though some seemed caught in the act of glancing to one side or gesturing to their neighbour. A few were kneeling. One, close enough for Arandras to reach out and touch, had its hand raised as though in supplication.

But the eyes in each expressionless face were the same. Two narrow pits of empty, black oblivion which, if they had ever held a semblance of life, possessed it no longer.

Yet far from reducing the figures to mere statues, the terrible absence invested them with a weight of dignity that was almost painful to behold. That these creatures had once marched and fought at the command of their makers could not be doubted. The sight of them here, now, bearing silent testimony to the unimaginable power of the fallen Valdori, filled Arandras with inexpressible awe.

He gaped at the sight like a moonstruck child. Just one would have been a wonder. Here were hundreds.

Thousands.

Weeper forgive me. I had no idea.

~

"Hello?"

The bellowed word struck Clade's ear like an iron spike. He flinched away, glaring back at Sinon; but the big sorcerer merely stared at their trail, insensible to Clade's distress.

There was no response from the other side of the rise.

Sinon exhaled in aggrieved disbelief. "Gatherer's arse, why can't the man just stay put?"

A look passed between Terrel and Hosk. The lean mercenary gave a minute nod and turned, retracing their path with smooth, economical strides.

"Oh, great, another one. Hells, why don't we all just split up and —"

"You want to be rearguard, Sinon?" Clade said. "Because if I hear one more word out of you, that's where you'll be."

Sinon treated Clade to a filthy glare, then stomped away with a muttered oath.

And Terrel would probably put his own man at Sinon's back anyway. Clade dropped to his haunches, grimacing as he rubbed the muscles in his neck. Kalie and Meline sat together a few paces away, Kalie taking a mouthful of water as her sister examined an acacia leaf in apparent fascination. *Just keep your mouth shut, Sinon. Please.*

"Terrel." The word floated down to them from beyond the rise. Terrel's expression shifted fractionally and he turned, tramping away in the direction of the call. After a moment, Clade followed.

The sight from the top of the rise brought him to an abrupt halt. *Gods, no.* Someone behind him called out a question, but he ignored it, descending the slope with hurried, stumbling steps until he reached the site.

Yuri's body lay face-down on the trail, back soaked with blood, braided hair splayed about his head. Hosk and Terrel crouched beside his prone form, impassive, examining what appeared to be a hole in the man's sodden shirt. Terrel muttered something and the two of them heaved the corpse over, revealing Yuri's slack, flat-nosed face.

Gods. We're meant to be following the Quill, not the other way around. Footsteps halted behind him, and he heard Meline's gasp and Sinon's curse. *What in the hells is going on?*

Terrel rose, hands on hips, and looked down the trail. Clade joined him.

"Talk to me," Clade said. "What happened?"

The mercenary captain sucked in his cheeks. "Knife in the back, straight through the heart," he said. "Killer knew what he was doing."

Clade waited, but nothing more was forthcoming. "That's it? How in the hells did he get the jump on your man?"

Terrel's shoulders twitched in the faintest hint of a shrug. He glanced away, clearly considering the comment not worth a response.

Clade drew a deep breath. "Killer, you said. Just one?"

"Very likely." Terrel's gaze flicked to the body, then out to the featureless forest.

"Where did he pick up our trail?"

Terrel's expression became ever so slightly sour. "Probably when we crossed the river. Maybe earlier."

Exasperation rose within him. Clade corralled it, contained it, shut it up in a box and closed the lid. When he spoke, his voice was steady. "You knew we were being followed." *And you didn't mention it.*

"I suspected," Terrel said. Clade wasn't sure whether the words were meant as correction or admission. "Yuri was trying to draw him out."

Looks like it worked. Another time Clade might have spoken the thought, just to see Terrel's response. But the man had already made clear his desire to have nothing more to do with Clade's project. Antagonising him further in the wake of yet another loss was hardly going to improve the situation.

All right. The Quill are ahead. So who's behind us? More Quill? He frowned. It seemed unlikely. If the Quill had known they were being followed, they'd have been laying traps or diversions, not picking his men off from behind. Besides, opportunistic killing wasn't their style.

Not the Quill, then. Who else?

Oculus, maybe. Perhaps Estelle had survived, somehow, and sent someone after them. But it was unlikely anyone nearby had both the training and the locus to hear the god; and even if they did, Azador's presence with the group had been far too sporadic for it to offer such a person meaningful directions. Which left...

An unknown. A wild die. *A savage, perhaps. A madman. The Gatherer's avenging angel. Who knows?*

"He must still be nearby," Clade said. "Can we flush him out?"

Terrel's lips thinned as he considered the question. "Not reliably," he said at last, and Clade understood his meaning: not without risk of further loss.

"Very well." Whoever the killer was, he was beyond Clade's control. He turned away. "Let's go."

Hosk tugged Yuri's swordbelt free and tossed the sheathed blade to Terrel. Then he stood, slinging the dead man's pack over his shoulder.

Meline shuddered, staring at the body as though transfixed. "Aren't we going to bury him?"

"No time," Clade said. "We move on and we stay close. Deny him another chance to strike. Nobody wanders off on their own."

Sinon gave a grunt of approval. "Finally, someone speaks sense."

"Meline," Clade said. "Look at me." There was curiosity in her eyes, and a strange, almost hypnotic fascination, but no fear. "We need to go. Now."

She nodded, shaking as though rousing herself from sleep. "All right."

Terrel took the lead, assigning Hosk as rearguard. Clade allowed the others to fall in behind Terrel, choosing the second from last position for himself to show the rest there was no need for concern; but as they resumed their journey, he felt the prick of watching eyes at his back.

Not worth my energy, he thought. *Nothing I can do about it now. Think about something else.*

Like the fact that Tereisa's widower is seeking revenge and is with the Quill party up ahead.

He paused at the thought. Could this Arandras have left the Quill party, circled around them and killed Yuri? Clade frowned, trying to remember all he could about the man. They'd never spoken, as far as he could recall. It was a dagger that Clade had been after that time, in the Oculus's first foray as far west as Chogon. He'd slipped the ransom note under Arandras's door, and then he'd left.

The job had gone bad. Arandras had defied instructions and gone to the Quill, leaving Clade with no choice but to kill the woman. She'd seen his face. *And then I had to pay off the guard to find a body in the river and call it the perpetrator.* He shook his head, recalling his exasperation at the man's idiocy. Arandras had as good as killed his wife himself.

But from what Bannard had said, he hadn't learnt his lesson. *A more intractable man you'll never meet,* he said. *Utterly uncompromising.* Bannard had shaken his head, but there'd been a note of admiration in his voice. He'd envied the man his principles, maybe. Was he too principled to kill Yuri? It was impossible to know.

Then again, Arandras had been just another scholar, one who'd sought help from the Quill and, through them, the city guard. Hardly the action of a killer. Still, a man could direct a knife without wielding it himself. And there was no telling how he might have spent the intervening years. Clade exhaled, frustrated at the paucity of his knowledge. *Best to avoid dealing with him at all, if possible.*

They walked, and rested, and walked some more. The sun crawled across the sky, moving gradually lower into their path and forcing Clade to squint against its glare. He was still pondering the riddle posed by Tereisa's widower when they emerged from the forest at the edge of a cliff, the lake sparkling before them under a clear, late-afternoon sky. Terrel crouched by the edge a short distance away, Yuri's sword slung across his back, peering at the stony shore below. At Clade's approach, he gestured to a ledge that slanted down from the top of the cliff, and a rope that trailed over the drop from a short, thick-trunked tree.

"Quill went that way," he said.

"Nice of them to leave us a signpost," Kalie said, joining Clade by the edge. "But I'm thinking we might not want to be quite so hospitable."

Clade nodded. "Scout ahead," he said to Terrel. "See if you or Hosk can make it down without the rope." Perhaps they could at least make things harder for their unwanted tail.

Terrel left to confer with his man, leaving Clade and Kalie on their own. Kalie shot a glance after him and leaned closer to Clade. "Do you trust him?"

"Who? Terrel?" Clade frowned. "Yes, of course I trust him. And so should you."

She bit her lip. "You've seen how they hold themselves apart. I don't think he —"

"Stop." Clade allowed a scowl to fill his face. "Terrel works for me, just like you. I trust him. So should you. Understood?"

Kalie nodded, abashed.

"Good. I don't want to have this discussion again."

He folded his arms and she took the hint, moving away to where Sinon and Meline gazed out at the lake. *Gods, I'm already one man down. The last thing I need is for Kalie and the rest to start suspecting.* He rubbed his chin, the stubble of the journey scraping against the palm of his hand. Birds circled above the lake, high and graceful, their forms too distant to make out. *We must be getting close now. Soon we can deal with the Quill and have done with this charade.*

It's a shame, though. She really would have made an excellent adjunct.

～

Arandras wandered the room, gazing at the golems in awestruck wonder. In the thin light they seemed wrought of shadow and stone, as though some unknown sculptor had laid hold of substances from another realm and somehow transmuted them to physical form. Closer examination revealed neither stone nor fired clay, but something in between, smooth to the touch yet fractionally warmer than the surrounding rock. Arandras tapped a fingernail experimentally against a graven thigh and received a dull clink in response. *Like bone on tin, if the tin was a solid lump the size of a mountain.*

This golem appeared to be a fighter, insofar as any motive or purpose could be ascribed to any of them. Its face lay obscured in shadow above Arandras's head, but its nose seemed a little broader than its neighbour's, its cheeks a little lower. A naked sword hung from its waist, weapon and belt both formed of the same strange substance as the rest of it. Much of its body had the appearance of clothing, but there was no clear point at which garment ended and wrist or neck began. Yet the figure gave an impression of vitality that transcended any suggestion of artifice. The fingers resting on the massive pommel looked like they might stir at any moment, perhaps to extend in greeting, perhaps to swat him away like a bothersome insect. Each seemed equally likely.

The light shifted as a nearby Quill moved away, exchanging hushed whispers with her companion. Arandras chose a different direction, walking slowly across the cavern through ranks of motionless figures. For all the years he'd spent studying the relics of the old Valdori Empire, he realised he'd never truly grasped the magnitude of their accomplishments, or their astonishing, brazen audacity to even attempt such feats. *Who were these people, to have built such things as this? What must their cities have been like? Their learning?* It was no surprise their empire had spanned the continent. The only wonder was that it didn't still.

The golem at the end of the row caught Arandras's eye and he halted before it, gazing at its kneeling form. The oversized face was on a level with his own, upturned as though awaiting a blessing. Its features could never be mistaken for human: the brow was too heavy, the jaw too blunt, and the rough, hairless head larger even than a Pazian roundshield. Arandras gazed into its vacant eyes, wondering what they'd seen and how they'd seen it. The creatures had plainly been capable of distinguishing friend from foe. How much more had they been able to perceive? *Could you hear, golem, when your master required it of you? Could you smell?* Its mouth was closed; Arandras had yet to see one whose mouth was open. *Could you speak?*

There was no expression in the golem's face. All seemed to possess the same inscrutable countenance. Yet something about its posture gave a feeling of purpose, as though its attention had been directed toward something or someone. Like the others, it faced what appeared to be the front wall; yet this particular golem was oriented away from the centre, gazing instead at the corner of the room. Arandras looked around, hunting for another kneeling golem amongst the forest of upright figures. There was one, left knee on the ground, hands clasped above its right; and it too seemed drawn to the same corner.

What are you looking at? Arandras peered into the dim corner. Something was there: a vertical shape, grey against the black. He moved closer for a better look.

The shape resolved into a reading stand, oddly small in this room of giants. Formed of the same half-stone, half-ceramic material as the golems, the stand was fixed to a short platform, similar in height to the one at the room's entrance, just wide enough for a single person.

A dais. The place of the master.

He stepped onto the platform and gazed out across the room. There was the kneeling golem he had paused beside; there the one clasping its hands; there another, and another, all facing directly toward him. Many of the standing figures too seemed oriented toward the stand, though it was only now, when Arandras could see the direction of their heads, that their focus became clear. *This is where they were looking when they were stopped, or put to sleep.* Which meant, perhaps, that it was from here that they might be reawakened.

Arandras squinted at the stand. Its angle shielded it from the light streaming in from the rear wall, leaving it shrouded in shadow. He ran a hand along its smooth, slightly powdery surface, halting when his fingers came to an indentation. The hole was round, about the width of an eggcup at the mouth but narrowing abruptly, making it barely as deep as it was wide. Arandras traced its rim, pressing his fingertip around the familiar shape. It felt just like the urn...

The urn. He reached into his pouch and pulled the bundle free, pushing aside its wrappings and tracing the circle of its lip. *The same. They're the same size.* His hand found the lid, twining it between his fingers. *I wonder...*

He held up the small metal cap, studying it as best he could in the dim light. Then he lowered it to the stand, sliding it across the smooth surface until it dropped into the hole.

The golems stood frozen in place. Arandras scanned the assembled figures, willing one of them to move; but the only motion came from the Quill roaming between them, and the play of light from lamps and sparkers.

Oh, well. It was worth a try. He felt around the indentation. *How do I get this thing back out?*

Someone in the room chuckled. Then came a gasp, and a cry of surprise. Arandras looked up.

The eyes of the golems were glowing.

Tiny points of light filled the dim room like stars reflected in a pool of water, their luminescence as low and steady as a monk's candle. Their tones were earthen: reds and yellows, browns and whites. Yet there was something in the still pinpricks that spoke of distance, as though the minute glints were in truth mere byproducts of some other, entirely unseen phenomenon.

"Nobody move!" The voice was Narvi's. "Did anyone touch something or say something? Anything that might have activated a binding?"

They're not here. Not yet. Arandras wasn't sure how he knew, but the thought felt right. *This is something else. A semi-dormant state, maybe. At rest, but awaiting orders.*

Perhaps I should give them some.

"Everyone move back to the entrance," Narvi called. "Do it now."

Arandras turned his attention to the nearest golem. It held a great mace in its outstretched hand, the weapon upright as though being presented to a general. *Lower your arm, golem,* he thought, pushing the words outward. The book in the Quill library had suggested they could hear thoughts. Now, having seen them, it seemed almost irreverent to imagine they couldn't. *Lower your arm.*

The golem stood motionless, unresponsive. The remote amber glint in its eyes stared at him, through him, past him to nothing at all.

I need its attention. He grasped the edges of the reading stand and leaned forward, projecting his words as best he could toward the golem's upturned face. *Hear me, golem. My name is Arandras Kanthesi. Hear me.* A sea of pinprick lights hung before him, and he raised his gaze. *All of you. I am Arandras. Hear me. Know me.*

"Where's Arandras?" Narvi sounded harried, uneasy. "Arandras! Where are you? Are you all right?"

Arandras ignored him. The golems had been there for millennia. They were hardly going to know Yaran, or Kharjik, or any other present-day tongue. *I need to find a language they understand.*

He took a breath, shifting his thoughts to Old Valdori. *Hear me. Know me. I am Arandras Kanthesi. Know me as your master.* He pressed the words outward, offering them to each figure in the cavern, every pair of glittering eyes.

It felt almost as though he were praying.

Know me. Know me.

A grinding, tearing sound filled the cavern like an avalanche. Every golem in the room stood and turned to Arandras.

WE KNOW YOU.

The words struck him like a blow. Arandras reeled back, stumbling off the dais and collapsing against the wall.

The golems all dropped to one knee with a single tremendous thud. Arandras felt the floor shake beneath him.

ARANDRAS KANTHESI.

MASTER.

CHAPTER 23

We fight with such weapons as we have: steel, sorcery, artifice, and a hundred more besides. When wielded deftly, any one of them may triumph over any other. Even a lamb may slay a dragon on its day.

Nonetheless, only a fool bets against a dragon.

— Giarvanno do Salin I, *Meditations on Power*

THEY BUZZED AT THE EDGE of his consciousness like bees. Arandras could hear the low drone in a corner of his mind, as though his awareness had been invaded by thousands of the humming, whirring creatures. *A vast swarm of insects, each one capable of crushing a house. And all of them awaiting my command.*

Rough hands grasped his shoulders. "What in the hundred hells are you doing?" Fas's angry face hove into view. "For the Dreamer's sake, how hard is it to *not touch anything?*"

"Hey, let him go!" Mara shoved Fas backward, interposing herself between them. Fas's face darkened and he shoved back, eyes pinched in fury. She absorbed the blow with a twist of her torso and grinned, raising a cocked fist. "This what you want?"

"Mara, please." Narvi stepped between them, hands raised in a pacifying gesture. "Fas. Let's stay calm, shall we? Yes? Yes."

Fas stepped back, breathing hard, and fixed Arandras with an enraged glare. "*What did you do?*"

Arandras shook his head. There were words in the buzzing whispers. *A cavern. My brothers and sisters all around. A man argues with the master. Stone and stone and stone.* He clasped his hands uselessly over his ears. The chatter was ceaseless, relentless. It was too much.

Be quiet!

The buzz vanished, leaving blessed silence in its wake. He exhaled softly, probing at the place where it had been. The presence in his mind remained, but softer now, like the faintest touch of gossamer on the back of his hand. *Thank you.*

"Arandras. Can you hear me? Arandras." Narvi's voice was muffled, distant. Arandras blinked at him, lowered his hands. "What happened?"

Laughter bubbled up within. "I bound them, Narvi," he whispered, as though saying it aloud might rob it of its truth. "I bound the golems."

Fas snarled and turned away.

"You bound them," Narvi said, staring at Arandras as though he'd just admitted selling his child. "How could you do that?"

"What?" Arandras shook his head, his euphoria fading. "But this is what we —"

"This is a *Quill* operation, Arandras! Weeper's cry!" He threw up his hands. "Do you have any idea what this means to us? Or the assurances I made just this morning to get you in here? Gods!"

Arandras pushed himself to his feet. "Do you really think the Quill are the best people to control these things?"

"I work for the Quill, Arandras! Maybe you haven't noticed that!"

"And if you didn't?" Arandras jabbed a finger in the air. "Look what they did to Isaias. Give the Quill the golems and that'll multiply a thousandfold! Don't you see that?"

"You think you're any better?" Narvi gave a sick laugh. "Gods, Arandras. Look at yourself. What happened to you?"

"The Quill use people, Narvi. It's in their blood."

"Funny. The only person I feel used by is you."

The words struck home. Arandras slumped against the wall, his stomach lurching; but Narvi was already stalking away, back to where Fas stood glaring at the reading stand. Before them knelt the golems, motionless once more, their massive heads still bowed.

The Quill use people. It was true. That was what they did.

And now, so did he.

It was not some faceless collective that had threatened Isaias, it was Fas, and Narvi, and Arandras himself. When everything else was stripped away, that was all the Quill were. People. Altered, yes — moulded into a form better suited to serve the interests of their masters — but people nonetheless. Narvi and Bannard, Halli and Ienn — they were victims as much as Isaias, even if they didn't realise it. They deserved pity, even compassion. Opponents or no, they were entitled to the same respect he would afford anyone else.

Instead, he had turned around and used them all over again. As though what had been done to them already wasn't bad enough. As if he could use the Quill's own weapon against them without becoming the very thing he despised.

Weeper have mercy. He buried his face in his hands. *I am just like them. Gods forgive me.*

"It's the lid of the urn," Narvi said from the dais, his back to Arandras. "See? There must be some kind of depression there."

"Maybe we can remove the binding if we take it out," Fas said. "If I can just get a hold of it…"

Arandras listened without caring. The golems meant nothing. *Let the Quill take them. Let them kill Clade, or not. I'm done.*

"Got it!" The metal cap flashed in Fas's hand. "Anything?"

The golems remained kneeling, heads bowed, the faint light in their eyes still visible among those nearest the front. Arandras reached for the gossamer presence in his mind and found it undisturbed.

"Nothing," Narvi said.

Fas shrieked in frustration, hurling the lid into the corner of the room. "Out," he snapped, striding off the dais, Narvi hopping at his heels to keep up. "Everyone out. No talk until we're away from *them*."

The Quill dispersed, leaving Arandras and Mara alone. Mara picked up the pewter lid, handed it back to Arandras. "Congratulations," she said. "You did it."

He nodded dully. "So it would seem."

She looked close, a questioning smile on her face. "What? You're not going to let Narvi's little tantrum get to you, are you? They're ours, fair and square."

Yeah. Fair and square. Arandras looked up, noting her choice of words. *Ours.* He sighed. "I bound them, Mara. To me."

Mara shrugged. "So?"

"So I don't know how to unbind them, or bind them to someone else. I mean, I'm sure it's possible — hells, one of the Quill could probably tell me." Not that any of them would speak to him just now. "But it might take a while for me to figure it out myself." He watched as the implications sank in. *And until I do...*

"We can't sell them," Mara said. "Yet."

"Yeah."

She exhaled, setting her torch on the ground and leaning against the wall beside him. They stood there side by side, looking out on the congregation of kneeling golems.

"Impressive, aren't they," Mara said eventually.

"Yeah."

"Can you make one do something? Walk around the room, maybe?"

Arandras sighed. "Probably. But it seems a little..." He trailed off, searching for the right word. *Petty? Pointless?* "I don't know. Something."

Mara waved dismissively. "You need to be confident about controlling them before Clade gets here. Go on, make one of them walk."

Right. Clade. Arandras squared his shoulders. He'd come this far. And Clade would be arriving soon, whether Arandras was ready or not. *Might as well be prepared.*

He scanned the front row. An empty-handed golem caught his eye, about half a dozen places from the end. *Is that one a bit shorter than the others? Could make it easier to speak to when it gets up.* He focused his attention on the chosen figure, doing his best to exclude all the others from his command.

Golem, stand up.

With a grinding rumble and the almost-smooth motion of a novice dancer, the golem rose.

Arandras stood back and pointed away from the dais. *Golem, walk to the corner of the room.*

It set off immediately, its stride long and heavy. When it reached the corner it halted and turned to face the cavern, its weight shifting as it settled into place.

Mara laughed. "Did you see that? It's like a sentry assuming his position."

Arandras nodded, warming to the exercise despite himself. The golem was truly a thing of wonder. *Let's try something a little more complex.* He thought for a moment. *Golem, walk through the portal on your right to the room beyond, and stop beside the shackles you see there.*

The golem rumbled away, Arandras and Mara following behind. It covered the distance at surprising speed, and they entered the chamber to find it already at rest beside the slender restraints.

"Ha, I was right." Mara held a circlet against the golem's wrist. "Big enough to fit over its wrist, small enough that the hand can't slide through."

Arandras nodded again, his interest already fading. The sight of the shackles reminded him oddly of Narvi, and the hurt in his eyes when Arandras told him what he'd done.

No, not hurt.

Betrayal.

We were friends, once. He thought we still were.

The hells with it.

"I have to go," Arandras said, turning toward the exit. "I have to find Narvi."

"What?" Mara grasped his elbow, pulling him to a halt. "Forget it. You don't have to explain yourself to any of them."

Explain myself? He gave a hollow laugh. What could he explain that Narvi didn't already see? "I should never have left Spyridon —"

"No." Her grip tightened. "This needs doing. You won't ever be free of what happened until you look Clade in the eye and —".

"Mara. Listen to me." He held her gaze, imploring her to understand. "How many people has this cost me already? Druce and Jensine. Isaias, probably. Weeper only knows why you haven't walked away yet." He shook his head. "I'm not going to lose Narvi too."

She stared at him for a long moment. Then, slowly, she nodded. "All right," she said. "Fine. Let's go."

He hesitated. "You don't have to come."

"Oh, yeah? You've got every one of those Quill out there ready to throttle you. Might be smart to have someone watching your back." She paused. "Or, you know. Your throat."

A surge of gratitude filled him. "Thank you," he said. "Truly. It's more than I deserve." *Weeper's tears, how little I deserve.*

Mara grinned. "You're right. Perhaps we can take that up when —"

Movement from the passage caught his eye. Arandras turned, but Mara was already shoving him aside, drawing her cutlasses with frightening speed and sprinting toward the doorway. He stumbled, blinking at the shadowy figure beyond even as Mara raised her blades and leapt through the portal.

A blast of air met her in mid-leap, flinging her across the room. She struck the far wall with a crack and slumped to the floor, unmoving.

A man stepped into the portal: large, thickset and scowling. Arandras had never seen him before in his life.

One of Clade's. Oh, shit.

The man lifted his hands, brow furrowed in concentration. Arandras turned to run.

The blast hit him from behind. Arandras raised his arms over his head. He felt himself flying through the air, the cool air caressing his cheek like a lover. Then his body struck something hard, and the world went dark.

∽

The boulder was huge, far too large for Clade and his group to have moved by themselves. The Quill, however, had shifted it for them, revealing a great tunnel curving away into the side of the cliff. No spark of light could be seen within, nor was there any hint of sound. Either the Quill were taking care to stay silent, or they'd gone too deep for any noise to reach the surface.

Large ochre bags lay near the passage, each bearing the insignia of a charcoal feather. Clade rubbed his chin, pondering their significance. *They can't have gone far, or they'd have taken their gear with them.* They'd be back soon, then, looking to set up camp somewhere. *In there?* He frowned. If they camped inside and were

sensible enough to maintain a watch, it would be impossible to surprise them. But they'd left their bags, so they couldn't have chosen a
site yet. Perhaps they'd camp somewhere out in the open…

Sinon picked up a bag and began to pick at a buckle.

"Don't touch that!" Clade covered the distance between them
in two strides and snatched the bag away before Sinon could reach
inside.

A spasm of anger crossed Sinon's face. "Dreamer's arse, what
now?"

"Gods and demons, you really need to ask?" Clade stared, but
Sinon's broad face showed nothing but baffled outrage. "As far as
the Quill know, there's no-one around for leagues. Are you trying
to give us away?"

"Keep it down, will you?" The words were Hosk's, low and terse.
"Stone throws sound further than you'd think."

A sharp retort leapt to Clade's lips, but he caught it and pressed
it down, grasping at the threads of his discipline. "Thank you," he
said at last, his voice thick. "You're right. Sinon, go back to the shore
—"

The words died in his throat. Azador arrived with the force of
a whirlwind, sweeping down on him like an eagle upon its prey. A
surge of greed engulfed him and he stumbled, reaching blindly for
the cliff.

"Clade!" Kalie appeared before him, grasping his shoulders and
grunting beneath his weight. "Are you ill?"

His questing fingers found stone. "I'm fine," he muttered. The
god's hunger pressed down on him like a yoke, but he clenched his
teeth, forcing himself to straighten beneath the load. "I'm fine," he
said again, offering what he hoped was a reassuring smile. "There,
you see? Nothing to worry about."

Kalie eyed him dubiously, but stepped back nonetheless. He
took a deep breath and released his grip on the cliff wall. Azador's
presence settled the matter. Fighting would be hard enough with
the god there at all. Staging a battle through its first sight of the
golems would be madness.

"Here's the plan," Clade said. "The Quill left their bags. That
means they'll be coming back soon. We're going to let them come

all the way out of the gorge. Once they're completely out, we'll cut off their retreat and strike."

He glanced at Terrel, who inclined his head fractionally. *He agrees. Or he doesn't disagree enough to object.*

Good enough.

They left the gorge in single file, Clade bringing up the rear. The rocky shore was narrower here than back by the path. Scarcely a dozen paces separated the cliff from the lake. But the strip was bare, bereft of anything that might offer concealment, and the cliff was steep and featureless.

Clade scanned the terrain. *Nowhere to hide. Unless...* "Kalie," he said, and she hurried over. "How deep is the water?"

She shot him a quizzical expression, then grinned her under-standing. "I'll check."

Two waterbinders, he thought, watching as she knelt by the edge of the lake. Its waters were dark now, almost black, reflecting the dusky sky. *Enough to keep us breathing for an hour, at least.* The water would be cold, though; too cold to get away with just a small air pocket around their heads. *And Terrel and Hosk will want dry hands for their swords, and dry boots to fight in. How long could the girls sustain a bubble that large?*

Kalie straightened and shook her head. "Ankle-deep for at least a dozen paces," she said, and he turned away with a frown, eyes flicking over the barren ground. *Not that, then. What else?*

A hiss from Terrel drew their attention. "Movement," he called softly. Clade jogged back to the cliff, cursing under his breath and gesturing for the others to follow. Though the sun was now out of sight behind the western peaks, the sky was not yet dark enough for stars to emerge. They'd be seen as soon as the Quill emerged. He shook his head, trying to ignore the hollow feeling in his gut. *Maybe they won't look. Maybe they'll just head back the way they came.*

"All right," he whispered. The others crowded around him in a tight circle, and Clade was struck by the uncanny impression of Azador standing among them, pressing close to hear his instruc-tions. "Stay close to the cliff. We wait until they're all out or until we're spotted. Then we move. Kalie and Meline, get to the lake as quick as you can. Keep the firebinders off our backs. Sinon, you take out anyone still in the gorge when they see us. Make sure they don't get back to the cavern. Terrel, Hosk, the rest are yours."

Hosk raised an eyebrow in thinly veiled amusement. "That could be half a dozen or more," he said.

"Yes," Clade said. "Or Sinon could have that many still in the gorge." *Believe me, please. I'm not trying to get you killed.* "I'll come help whoever's hardest pressed." *As much as I can in a place so devoid of wood.* "All right?"

Terrel nodded once, his lips thin. Hosk chuckled and looked away.

A breath of wind ruffled Clade's hair, carrying with it the cool scent of fresh water. He pressed his back against the rough stone, gesturing for Sinon and the sisters to do likewise. Terrel unslung Yuri's sword from across his shoulder and stood it against the cliff, then slowly drew his own. Hosk crouched beside him, his blade already in his hand. From somewhere over the lake came a bird's high screech.

Voices approached. Clade reached around to where Yuri's sword lay propped against the cliff, grasping the hilt in a sweaty palm. How long had it been since he'd used one of these? He rolled his shoulder, trying to loosen the muscles, then froze as a man emerged from the gorge. *Here we go.*

Another figure followed, and another, the ochre and charcoal of their clothing little more than grey and black in the dim light. Clade held his breath, counting the figures as they appeared. *Six, seven. Eight. Come on.* Another two joined the others, and the group turned around, milling about the mouth of the cleft. *Come on. Where are the rest?*

"Hey!" A figure pointed straight at them. "Who's that?"

Shit. "Go," Clade said, and the party sprang into action.

Sinon charged at the assembled Quill, Terrel and Hosk a few paces behind. Cries of alarm rose from the group, the sound echoing strangely along the stony shore, and the Quill began to bunch together, those at the front producing blades, those at the rear crouching to dig into their bags. *That's it,* Clade thought. *Nice and close.* "Identify yourselves," called one of the Quill. "Speak, or be destroyed."

Sinon came to an abrupt halt just short of the group. For a moment, nobody moved; then a tremendous blast of wind burst from
Sinon's position, hurling the Quill backward like wheat on a field.
Terrel and Hosk rushed in on the groaning forms, slicing and stab-
bing at anything that moved.

Fire erupted across Clade's vision. Terrel shrieked and reeled
away, a figure wreathed in flame. *That came from the gorge. Damn
it, where are my waterbinders?* His gaze fell on the sisters standing
ankle-deep in the lake, a pillar of water already rising between them.
It reared from the lake, swaying in the air like an unnatural limb;
then it toppled, cascading into the gorge, cutting off the stream of
fire as abruptly as a blade severing a snake's head. Sinon sprinted
down the gorge after the tumbling water, and Clade allowed himself a moment's relief.

Breathing heavily, Clade surveyed the field before him. One of
the mercenaries was down; the other, Hosk, chased a pair of fleeing
Quill back toward the cliff path. From among the bodies littering
the shore, another Quill staggered to his feet, sword in hand. He
looked around, then set off at a stumbling jog toward Kalie and
Meline at the edge of the lake.

They didn't see him coming. Clade watched in horror as they
directed another jet of water into the gorge, oblivious to the Quill
loping unsteadily toward them. *Hells, no.* Clade broke into a run,
shouting and waving at the sisters, gesturing wildly with his borrowed sword at the approaching danger. They turned, spotting the
man at last. A new limb began to form at their feet, twisting upward
like something blind. *Too late,* Clade thought, feet pounding the
rocky ground in a vain attempt to reach them in time. *Too late...*

The Quill stretched his arm back and swung. The sword sank
deep into Kalie's unprotected chest and she sagged against the blade,
hanging there for an absurd moment; then she fell, sliding sideways
into the lake.

Yelling, the Quill drew back his sword for another swing. *No!
Not both of them, you bastard!* The crunch of pebbles betrayed Clade's
arrival, and the Quill swivelled his head, eyes wide. Clade barrelled
into him, thrusting his blade deep into the man's side. *These girls
are mine.*

The man's cry turned to a gurgle. He shuddered, lips twitching as though trying to form words. Repulsed, Clade shoved him away. The man slid off the blade, splashing face-down into the lake beside Kalie, limbs jerking in a cruel parody of swimming strokes before at last falling still. *That's ten.*

Meline stared at the corpses as though transfixed, shivers racking her frame. "Meline," Clade said, snapping his fingers in front of her face. "Meline. Look at me! There's still work to do."

Silence greeted him, before and behind. He blinked and turned around.

The shore was strewn with bodies. Terrel's charred form lay only a few paces away; further away, past the mass of fallen Quill, three more bodies sprawled by the lake. *Hosk and his runaways. Shit.* Sinon limped slowly from the gorge, his lip curled in triumph, still more corpses behind him. Nothing else moved.

That's it, then, Clade thought. *We won.*

He stirred, waving to get Sinon's attention. "Check for survivors," he called. "If there are others still inside, we may need hostages."

Sinon nodded and bent to the task.

We won. Good. That's good.

From somewhere directly behind his eyes and a thousand leagues away, Azador pulsed its satisfaction.

~

Eilwen crouched behind a slight outcrop in the cliff, just below the first of the odd, window-like openings, and watched the battle unfold.

Her knee throbbed where she'd wrenched it in a mistimed leap during her descent. She'd done it on the very first gap in the path, catching her foot on a spur of rock as she landed, fortunate not to overbalance and plunge from the ledge to her death. At that moment she had seriously considered abandoning her pursuit; but the thought of repeating the leap, only uphill this time, had convinced her to carry on, and she'd finally reached the bottom, sore and exhausted, just as the sun began to slide behind the jagged peaks of the Pelaseans.

The halting pace forced upon her by her leg proved to be a

blessing. When the Oculus emerged from what looked to be a narrow gorge, she was still far enough away to find partial cover behind a rare outcrop. Huddling against the rock, she'd peered into the gathering gloom, relieved that the figures did not seem about to retrace their steps but unable to work out what they were doing.

Then the Quill appeared.

Well. That changes things, she thought, watching as the ochre-and-charcoal-clad figures trickled out of the same cleft the Oculus had appeared from moments before. Just as she had been following the Oculus, it seemed the Oculus had been following the Quill. *Beads on a string, and the Quill the largest bead of all. That explains why they didn't come looking for me. They couldn't spare the time.*

The attack came without warning. The Quill were blasted through the air like wooden pins, hitting the stone with a horrific crunch. Men rushed in to finish them, seeming in the dim light to be wielding blades of shadow, invisible save for when they obscured a stray glint off the lake behind them. A gout of flame spat forth from somewhere within the gorge, engulfing one of the swordsmen; then, in fell answer, a serpentine tentacle rose from the lake and launched itself into the fire.

Eilwen stared, no longer seeing the battle before her. She stood on the foredeck of the *Orenda,* salt spray in her face, watching the same uncanny, impossibly long limbs of water rear from the sea. They towered above the ship, impossibly high in the twilit, cloud-strewn sky, as though the ocean itself were attempting to grasp the heavens. Then they fell, smashing into the *Orenda's* timbers with the force of mountains. Blow after blow hammered the ship, buckling her decks, cleaving her hull. One of the columns crashed down almost on top of Eilwen, flinging her into the water. Clinging to a piece of railing, she bobbed helplessly as the ship split in two and was swallowed by the waves.

Gods preserve me, she had prayed, as the mangled corpses of friends and colleagues floated past. *Gods grant me the chance to make this right.*

And unexpectedly, remarkably, they had.

When she returned to herself, the battle by the lake was over. At least three Oculus remained upright, though Eilwen could see no

Quill still standing. Two of the Oculus stood in conversation, while the third picked through the fallen bodies, presumably checking for survivors. The man stooped over someone, and Eilwen tensed, waiting for the deathblow; but instead, he produced a length of rope and began to bind the Quill's hands. *Odd. Why take prisoners?* A second survivor was found and dragged a short distance from the first. Eilwen shook her head, perplexed. Something still didn't add up.

The Oculus disappeared back up the gorge, dragging their prisoners behind them on a rope leash. The first stars began to emerge in the darkening sky. Only when Eilwen was sure the Oculus weren't coming back did she stand and begin to shuffle up the rocky shore, teeth set against the pain in her twisted knee.

In the dark, some of the bodies could almost have been taken for bundles of cloth, cast onto the rocky shore by a freak wave. Others were impossible to mistake for anything else, the multi-toned flesh of limp hands and ruined faces clear even in the fading light. Eilwen picked her way between the corpses, examining each in turn to determine which were Quill and deserved her sympathy, and which were Oculus and did not.

In death, all men are one. The words came to her unbidden and she frowned, unsure where she had heard it before. A Mellespene philosopher, perhaps. She shivered, strangely discomfited by the thought. *At night, even the living look alike. That doesn't mean they are.*

She slipped her hand beneath her shirt, retrieving the black amber egg from the fold of lambskin into which it had settled. At once she felt it throb in an odd, staggered rhythm. A token-bearer lay at her feet, its beats strong enough for two. Another pulse called from nearby: a second token-bearer, probably one of the corpses at the water's edge. Of the third fallen Oculus, she could sense nothing. *That one must have been a sorcerer.*

Eilwen turned, allowing the egg to settle back into place against her skin. The gorge opened up before her, black against the shadowed walls of the cliff. She peered into the cleft, searching for a glimmer or spark, listening for voices or the scrape of boot against rock.

Her senses found nothing but empty, silent darkness.

The Oculus came out first, then the Quill. And the Quill didn't seem to know anyone else was there. The gorge was deep, then. Deep enough to conceal a group of half a dozen from others further in. *I should be able to stay out of sight easily enough.*

Reaching into her bag, she retrieved a lamp, small and crafted for travel. She lit it with her sparker and closed the window to a slender crack, turning it experimentally to assess its brightness. *Good enough.* Lifting it before her, she shouldered her bag and made her way into the cleft.

She saw the boulder first, the huge, pale stone catching the light of her lamp as though made of chalk. A few steps later, the end of the gorge resolved before her, and with it, the hole in the cliff wall. She paused at the threshold, sniffing the air within. It was dry and smelt of something half-familiar: not quite sand, not quite leather, but something somewhere between the two. Unpleasant, but not likely to suffocate her. She turned her head, taking a final breath of cool, lakeside air, then stepped inside.

Blackness confronted her, a vast, impenetrable expanse, too deep for her thin light to pierce. She froze, filled with a sudden fear that she stood on the edge of a pit. Tilting the lamp downward, she swept the space in front of her with its light. Rough stone lay at her feet, solid and reassuring. She reached down, brushing the floor with her hand, and a fine puff of dust billowed to life around her questing fingertips.

All right. Big space. Big empty space. She took a breath. Following the wall would keep her from getting turned around. And if she was spotted, it would give her something to put at her back.

She set off, one hand trailing along the wall, the other directing lamplight before her feet. The egg throbbed gently against her flesh. The sorcerers were here, somewhere, but not close enough to determine a specific direction. If she could find the prisoners first, they might be able to tell her what in the hells was going on.

She imagined Havilah beside her, nodding his approval. *You're a soldier, Eilwen,* he said. *To defeat your enemy, you need to know what he's planning. Find out.*

The wall fell away beneath her fingers and she halted, turning the lamp into the breach. A stone stairway flickered into view, spiralling downward. A second level. How deep did the place go? Eilwen hesitated, glancing over her shoulder at the vast, empty cavern. Even now, any number of eyes might be watching the slow, stumbling progress of her thin light. The thought sent a chill through her, strong enough to override the ache in her leg, and she turned back to the stairs.

Lower level first. Leave the cavern for when I've got a better sense of the place —

A deeper than expected step caused her to land heavily on her injured leg and she gasped, her knee almost buckling beneath her. *Gods preserve!* She clutched at the rough wall, fighting back a wave of nausea. Teetering, she thrust out her good leg, scrabbling for a toehold. Her heel caught the edge of the step, then slipped, and she landed with a jolt on the next step down, her teeth grazing her tongue as they clacked shut.

Breathing hard, she lifted her lamp. Level ground stretched before her into darkness: a corridor, shadowy and rough-hewn. *Enclosed space. Thank the gods.* Setting her lamp on the ground, she lowered herself awkwardly onto the last step and clasped her hands about her knee. Its throbbing seemed to inhabit her entire body. *I really, really need a bath.* She could see it now: a copper tub, long enough for her legs to lie flat, filled with water hot enough to sting; but then the heat would begin its work, drawing the ache from her leg and filling her with blissful lassitude. She sighed. When all this was over, she'd seek one out. *After all, a soldier deserves her reward.*

Bobbing light in the corridor ahead broke her reverie. Her knee's throb was a pounding in her gut, driving and insistent. *Gods, that's not my knee. That's the egg.* The light drew nearer and she scrambled painfully to her feet, scooping up the lamp. The nearest opening in the corridor was half a dozen paces away. *Too far. Back up the stairs, quickly.*

Eilwen set her foot on the step, then collapsed with a cry as her knee gave way. Someone shouted behind her, and she twisted around to face her discoverer.

The man was one of the Oculus, big and thick-limbed, with a nose that had evidently been broken more than once. His face contorted in a scowl. "Weeper's arse, what are you?" Something flickered behind his eyes, and his expression shifted. "You're the one who killed Yuri, aren't you? Yes, I think you are. And now you're here to, what? Finish the rest of us?" He flexed his arms.

"Wait!" Eilwen lifted a shaking hand. "Please." *Just give me this moment.* Slowly, she began to reach into her shirt.

The scowl returned. "You think I'm daft? Not a chance."

"It's not a weapon." She slid her hand further in, closed her fingers around the bundle. "I'm taking it out now. Please, you'll want to see this."

The man glared at her ferociously, but said nothing.

Slowly, agonisingly, she drew out her hand and opened it before him. In her palm lay the black amber egg.

The man hissed, staring in obvious recognition. "Where did you get that?"

Eilwen considered him. "Are you in charge here?"

He looked her up and down. "If I bind your hands, will you resist?"

She shifted on the step, trying to find a more comfortable position; but her trouser caught on the rough wall, pulling her leg sideways, and she gasped through gritted teeth. *I'm sorry, Havilah,* she thought. *I tried.*

"No," she said. "I won't resist."

CHAPTER 24

Those who make their bed in darkness should not expect to wake in light.

— Herev Gis, *First Sermons,* Chapter 107, Verse 12
(as ordered by the Gislean Provin)

THE GOLEMS WERE EVERYTHING CLADE had imagined, and more.

He walked up and down their lines like a general on parade, lamp held high, marvelling at their grandeur and the elegance of the sorcery that enfolded them. Azador ballooned about him, exultant, its presence so thick that Clade had to check the impulse to cover his nose and mouth with a cloth. Yet somehow, it hardly seemed to matter. Before the majesty of the figures filling the room, the god seemed small and insignificant, a triviality scarcely worth acknowledging.

No two were alike. They varied in size and form, in posture and expression, in the shapes of their hands and the casts of their heads. Clade walked the ranks, marvelling at their diversity and wondering at its meaning. Did the differences between golems indicate variation in function? Or were they purely cosmetic, something to help the wielder distinguish one from another? The sheer artistry of it was wonder enough; yet these were no mere statues, but constructs of earth, sorcery, and spirit. The Empire's elite: warriors and commanders and monks, their spirits captured at death, shorn of personality and woven into the heart of a new being. By all accounts, the resulting creatures were practically indestructible, servants of an empire now dead for more than two millennia.

And they were already bound.

He sighed, leaving the golems behind and entering the adjoining chamber. The binder lay slumped against the wall, unconscious, an oversized manacle locked around his neck. *Tereisa's husband. Arandras.* The man's companion was at this moment being taken by Sinon to one of the cells on the lower level, where the surviving Quill had also been deposited. Clade could feel the faint lines of sorcery connecting the man to the golems: slender, delicate, like young shoots that had just emerged from the soil into the open air. They were things of beauty, rare and exquisite, and he longed more than anything else to destroy them.

Damn you, Arandras. A straight unbinding on this scale would be impossible. And any thought of using the transfer spell with which he planned to rid himself of Azador was out of the question. *The man's hatred would be enough to kill us both.*

In a small pouch hanging from the man's belt, Clade had at last found the pewter Valdori urn. It was smaller than he'd expected, with a rounded base that fit snugly into the palm of his hand. A tangle of conflicting emotions had filled him, pleasure and frustration and bitter amusement, and it took long moments for him to confine them. It was the lid, however, that caught his attention. Hope rising, he'd slotted it into the shallow hole atop the dais; yet no matter how he poked or twisted it, the connection between Arandras and the golems remained.

Which left only two options. He could find a way to persuade Arandras to relinquish the golems voluntarily, or he could kill him.

Killing him would be simpler, no question. The man was a loose end, a by-blow of Clade's former life. His presence here spoke of an unhealthy obsession with Clade, one which the man seemed unlikely to abandon any time soon. In other circumstances, Clade would have killed him without hesitation as a simple investment in the future.

But here, now, the situation was not so straightforward. *I could kill him now and release his hold over the golems. But then what?* The golems would be unbindable for days, perhaps weeks. What if the Oculus sent someone after him? Or the Quill? The journey from Anstice had taken four days. When the Quill failed to return, they might send more sorcerers out to investigate, and this time he would have no chance against them. He grimaced, rubbing the stubble on his chin. The risk was too great. Better for Arandras to hold the golems, at least for the time being, than allow them to fall to the Quill, or to Azador.

Persuasion, then.

Clade set down the lamp and considered the unconscious man. He'd forgotten — he had seen Arandras before, just once, a few days after Tereisa's death. He'd been passing her residence on other business when the door opened and one of the city guard stepped out. Clade had paused beneath a lilac tree, catching his breath in the thin Chogon air, and watched as the guard took his leave. Arandras had stood unmoving for a dozen heartbeats or more, staring vacantly at the yard. He'd been clean-shaven then, his face scarred with the stark lines of unexpected grief.

The lines were still there, but they no longer seemed out of place. The man's face had moulded around them, taking them into itself and giving them a home. Heavy creases marked his brow and eyes. The corners of his mouth turned down in a perpetual frown. A close-cropped beard concealed his cheeks and chin, the dark hair salted with grey, giving him the appearance of one far older than Clade suspected him to be. Even in repose, the man looked tired.

How did Bannard describe him? Intractable. There was little sign of it. Yet he had bound the golems. *Against the wishes of the Quill, one assumes. Perhaps even without their knowledge.* At the edge of the room a golem stood in silent contemplation, pinprick yellow eyes burning deep in its sockets. Clade frowned. *What am I to do with you?*

Azador flitted about his head, pulling at his attention like a restless child tugging its mother's skirts. *Oh, go away, already. Let me think.* The man had to be moved, that much was clear. Putting distance between him and his new army was imperative. And then... what?

"Clade." Sinon stood just outside the chamber, half-hidden in shadow, his fingers tapping arrhythmically against the side of his leg.

"What is it?" The words came out louder than he intended, echoing off the chamber's stone walls. Wincing, he crossed to where Sinon stood and lowered his voice. "Are the prisoners secure?"

"Yeah," Sinon said. "Only, we've got an extra one, and she's not a Quill."

"What? What do you mean, an extra one?"

"I found her on the stairs. She killed Yuri."

Clade raised his eyebrows. "She admitted that?"

"She didn't deny it." The big sorcerer hesitated. "Thing is, she's got a locus."

"Really?" Had Estelle managed to send someone against him after all? But no, there was a simpler explanation. "She probably took it from Yuri's body."

"No, Hosk had that one. I saw him take it."

"So she took it from Hosk on her way in." Though even that would suggest an unusual knowledge of Oculus practices. *Just what I need. Another loose end.*

"Oh." Sinon seemed to deflate slightly. "I just thought... she didn't seem..."

Clade waved his hand. "Lock her up. Keep her separate from the others. I'll talk to her later."

"Already done." Sinon glanced at the slumped figure of Tereisa's husband. "You want me to put him with the rest?"

Yes, Clade prepared to say; but before he could speak, the man loosed a long groan. "Who's there?" he said, his voice thick with grogginess.

Motion at the edge of the room caught Clade's eye, accompanied by a low, grinding sound. The golem raised its foot and stepped forward once, twice, coming to a halt beside Arandras.

Shit. Clade stepped hurriedly out of the light, gesturing for Sinon to do the same. Arandras blinked up, raising his hand to shield his eyes from the lamp. "Who...?"

"You have something that belongs to me, Arandras," Clade called, loud enough to make the words bounce around the room.

Arandras scowled, turning his head this way and that. The chain clanked against the stone wall. "Are you Clade? Where are you?"

"The golems are mine," Clade said. "Give them to me, and I'll let you go."

The man laughed. "Can't. They're bound to me now."

"You can. I can tell you how."

Another laugh, and a shake of the head. "No."

"You must know you're not leaving until you give them over."

Arandras made a filthy gesture. "The hells swallow you."

"I have your friends, Arandras," Clade said, hardening his tone. "The woman who was with you. Some Quill. Give me the golems and they won't get hurt."

"The hells swallow you twice."

Clade folded his arms, pushing away the incessant, seething swirl of Azador's presence and trying to think. *Bannard was right. Intractable. Proud, too.* The man seemed almost to be enjoying himself, as though revelling in the chance to defy. *This one would resist any demand simply because it was demanded. But what if the pressure were removed? What if I offered a choice...?*

The scrape of metal on stone pulled Clade's attention back to the room. Arandras had slumped forward, head lolling, the weight of his neck pulling the chain taut. *Passed out again. Probably.*

Sinon touched Clade's arm. "The cells?" he whispered.

Clade frowned. It was the safe thing to do, no question. With his mercenaries dead, and two bound sorcerers still to dispose of, he could ill afford another loose end. Yet he knew in his gut that if he threw Arandras in a cell, he'd eventually be forced to either kill the man or abandon the golems. *Or, most likely of all, both.*

But the other way, there was still a chance...

"No," Clade said at last. "No cell for this one." He looked across at Sinon. "We're going to let him go."

～

He woke to a raucous cawing beside his ear. Something pecked at his shoulder and he started upright, setting off a flurry of wings and receding croaks. He cracked his eyes open, grimacing at the hard rocks beneath his buttocks, and peered around. He was back on the shore of the lake, the sky above him the dim, expectant grey of the hour before dawn. Blinking blearily, he took a deep breath; then heaved it out again, gasping and retching.

Weeper's breath, what is that smell?

Gingerly, Arandras gathered his legs beneath him. His side felt like one gigantic bruise, all the way from his shoulder to his ankle. He groaned, trying to remember what had happened. *I was talking to Mara when someone came in. One of Clade's men. He threw me against the wall. Then there was someone else, talking... demanding the golems... and then...*

The memory trailed off. *Then they dragged me out here, I guess. But why attack us and then let us go?* He shook his head, trying to think past the fog. *Unless someone rescued us. Someone like Mara.*

That must be it.

He looked up. The shore was bare. "Mara? Where are you? Mara!"

A chorus of harsh caws rose behind him. He turned, wrinkling his nose as the foul smell assaulted him once more; then he gagged, clasping his hand over his mouth and staring in horror at the scene before him.

Bodies lay scattered across the shore, their limbs and trunks marred by ghastly wounds. Hook-necked, eagle-like birds fed on the corpses, pecking at sightless eyes and digging out organs from beneath exposed ribs. One of them looked up from what appeared to be Ienn's corpse, cocking its head and blinking its beady eye as though inviting him to join the feast. He reeled back, unable to watch, unable to look away.

Weeper's cry! How? But there was nothing of the Weeper here, and no mystery as to its cause. *The Oculus.* Clade and his men had come upon them unawares, cutting a swathe through the Quill like the Gatherer's own angels. And he, Arandras, had led them here. *I did this. Gods forgive me. I killed them all.*

But no, that wasn't true. He had struck no blows, darkened no eyes. That burden belonged to Clade, and to those he had brought with him. *He killed them. Not me.*

All I did was give him the opportunity.

It was enough.

He started forward, shuffling into the mess of scavengers and remains. It wasn't until he'd peered at a few faces and moved on that he realised he was looking for someone. *I'm sorry, Narvi. I never meant this.* He wondered what Narvi had thought as they cut him down. *Would you forgive me, if you had the chance?* But Narvi had already forgiven him so much. Could he ask for still more? Tears slid down his cheeks and into his beard. *Ah, Narvi. You deserved so much better than what I gave you.* He looked around. *Where are you, anyway?*

Narvi wasn't there.

Arandras scanned the area. Nine of the bodies were clad in Quill colours, including one near the entrance to the cavern. Three more wore no identifying marks and were presumably from Clade's group. *Nine Quill, out of eleven. Leaving two unaccounted for.*

Hope rose in his breast. Narvi could still be alive.

Who else? He moved from corpse to corpse, arm clamped over his mouth, peering at each in turn. Fas lay face-down near the centre of the group, a trio of scavenger birds squabbling over a gaping wound in his back. Ienn sprawled nearby, his arms spread to the heavens in silent appeal, and beside him the gangly Jervian who had ridden beside Arandras for a time. The man lay curled in a ball, face half-covered by Ienn's hand, and might almost have been sleeping but for the dried pools of blood on the rocks beneath him.

A breath of wind curled the stench of waste and viscera into Arandras's nostrils and down his throat. He doubled over, gorge rising, stumbling out from the carnage and dropping to his knees at the lake's edge, the birds behind him cawing their laughter. The breeze coming in over the water was cool and fresh, and he knelt before it, eyes closed, letting it wash over his face as he willed his stomach to settle.

Narvi was still alive. He had to be. Mara, too, was missing, though that probably didn't mean anything. *They'd hardly bother to drag her all the way out here if she were dead.* Then again, they'd dragged him out here. Arandras exhaled, racking his numbed brain for an explanation. *They want me out here because... well, because they don't want me in there.*

So that's where I should go.

He stood, brushing away the tiny pebbles that clung to his

trousers. Holding his breath, he skirted the feasting birds and made his way into the cleft.

A woman stood half-concealed in the shadows of the cavern entrance. For a moment Arandras thought it was Mara and took an excited step forward; then she shifted slightly and he saw that it wasn't so. She was too short, similar in stature to Arandras himself, and her skin was too light. On the ground before her was a pan, apparently taken from one of the dead Quill. A thought crossed his mind and he peered into the shadows, straining for a glimpse of her feet. As he suspected, they were bare.

A waterbinder. Another of Clade's. Arandras settled back on his heels. How many people had he brought? Somehow Arandras had imagined him following alone, or with one or two companions. He'd never pictured the sorcerer bringing a force strong enough to overpower a dozen Quill. *For all I know he's got twenty more in there. How can I contend with that? I'd practically need an army...*

Which I have.

Arandras felt at the edge of his mind for the place where the buzzing had been, and where the soft, alien presence had settled. *Golems! Are you there? Talk to me. Tell me what you see.*

Silence answered him, lifeless and dark.

He tried again, smothering a murmur of panic. *Golems? Speak. Answer me!*

There was no response.

He probed his awareness, searching for the gossamer whisper of the golems, for anything not of himself; but all he found was the circle of his own churning thoughts, curving back on themselves in an endless, unbroken procession. Whatever he had felt before was there no longer.

Arandras dropped to his haunches and clasped his hands over his head. The golems were gone. They were either out of reach, too far away to hear him, or else they were gone, really gone, stolen away by the same man who had stolen his wife. *Is that what you've done? Was robbing me of Tereisa not enough? Gods witness, Clade, I will find a way to end you. I swear it.*

He pushed himself to his feet. The woman in the cavern might have blinked, or he might have imagined it.

"Hey!" Arandras called, striding toward the woman and waving his arms. "Hello, in the cavern! I'm Arandras. Who are you?"

The woman placed a foot in the pan of water before her. A tentacle of water edged upward from the pan, swaying like a python, and the woman spoke in a soft, lilting tone. "That's close enough."

Arandras halted. "That's very impressive," he said, resisting the urge to stare at the undulating column. "Really. But I need to talk to —"

"There's a note," the woman said, gesturing with her chin. "Just there, under the rock."

Arandras frowned. "I see it." A single sheet of paper, folded in thirds, one end sticking out from under a fist-sized stone. He reached for it, then hesitated.

"Take it," the woman said. "It's for you."

He lifted the rock and retrieved the paper, turning it over in his hands. There, in the hated, familiar script, was a single word. His name.

"Read it."

He unfolded the paper with trembling hands, scanned the lines within. The message was brief.

Your friends will be killed at sunset. Please do not interfere.

Beneath were three names, each written in a different hand.

Halli. Narvi. Mara.

Weeper, no. Not again. Please, not again.

The sun crested the edge of the gorge, its light striking the woman full in the face. She squinted, raising her hand to shade her eyes, and for a moment Arandras saw not her but Tereisa, standing on the balcony and looking out at the sunrise, just as she had on that last morning before he'd come home to find her gone. In his memory she closed her eyes, embracing the light, and he turned away, smiling as he closed the door, leaving her behind. Forever.

Gods, no. Not again.

༄

The thick-limbed Oculus took Eilwen to a small, bare cell with fetters set into the floor. He snapped a shackle about each ankle, pocketed the keys, then departed with her bag, her lamp, and her daggers, leaving her alone in the dark.

Eilwen stretched out her legs as the pulses of the black amber egg slowly faded, leaving only the painful throb of her abused knee. Her chains clinked oddly as she pulled them across the cold stone floor, and she lifted one in her hand, frowning at the strange lightness of the unknown metal. Twisting around, she drew up her ankle and took hold of the shackle, striking it repeatedly against the stone floor. But there was no strength in the blows, and at last she gave a long, shuddering sigh, leaning her head back against the wall and allowing the tears to course down her cheeks.

After a time, she slept.

Havilah walked beside her, his face hidden in shadow, his hands behind his back. They climbed a steep, rock-strewn hill, the scent of salt thick in the air, emerging at last atop a windswept promontory.

"Where are you?" he said.

Eilwen raised her arm against the gale, shielding her face from the stinging spray. Havilah rested his elbows on the timber railing, apparently untroubled by the storm. The wind snatched at her clothing and hair, pressing her backward and reducing her vision to a watery haze. "I don't know."

Havilah shifted beside her and she tensed, anticipating his displeasure; but when he spoke, his tone was sorrowful. "Where are you?"

The wind eased. She lowered her arm and looked onto a roiling sea beneath an angry, crimson-streaked sky. A distant speck rode the waves near the horizon, disappearing from view as it plunged into a watery valley then reappearing as it crested the rise.

Eilwen pointed at the speck. "There I am."

"Yes," Havilah said.

The speck was a ship, no longer distant but close enough to hear the terrified shrieks of those on board. The sea bucked and heaved beneath it, tossing it in the air then slamming up to meet it on its way down. Eilwen saw men and women thrown from its sides into the churning sea. A horrible crack tore the air, the sound of something immense splitting apart.

"It won't last long," Havilah said conversationally, his chin propped on his hands.

Lightning stabbed from the boiling sky, transfixing the floundering vessel. With a great, tearing screech, the ship broke in two, folding as though hinged in the middle and sinking beneath the heaving waves. In the space of a dozen heartbeats it was gone, pulled into the murky depths. Nothing remained above the surface but wild, foaming water.

Havilah folded his arms and looked out over the restless, featureless sea. "Where are you now?"

She opened her mouth to respond, and heard a low, wordless growl. Fear pierced her belly like a spear. Hands trembling, she felt for her mouth. Her fingers closed over a snout, furry and bestial, lips curled in a snarl. Fangs jutted from her lower jaw, curving over her cheeks. Panic rose in her breast and she reeled backward, clutching her face and screaming at the sky.

Eilwen jolted awake to find herself lying sideways on the hard cell floor. Heart pounding, she reached for her face, and sighed in relief as her hands touched smooth, familiar skin. *Thank the gods.* She struggled upright, cursing as her elbow struck a glancing blow on the wall behind her, and hugged her legs to her chest.

The dream's meaning was plain enough. *I am becoming the beast.* It had survived all her efforts to put it down, and in the end she'd come crawling back, surrendering herself willingly to its embrace. *I pushed it away, and it pushed back even harder.* She'd given herself over to it, and it had led her out of Anstice, given her a kill in the forest above, and finally brought her here.

And where am I? Locked in a cell by my enemies, barely able to stand even before they snapped the chains shut.

Defying the beast hadn't worked. In the end, it had just made it stronger. But giving it its head hadn't worked either.

What else is there? What can I do, other than resist or yield?

The surge and ebb of the beast's hunger was like a river: sometimes rushing, sometimes crawling, but always there; sometimes calm for a while but never truly exhausted. No dam she could imagine would be enough to contain it forever. She frowned. *I need something else. A weir, maybe. Some way to control the flow, let a small amount out sometimes, but keep it from becoming a flood.*

Perhaps she had already begun without realising it.

I am a soldier. A soldier fights, but does not kill indiscriminately. She has a mission, a purpose that eclipses her own desires. A soldier is not her own master. She shifted position, causing her chains to clink against the rough stone floor, and loosed a bitter chuckle. *Not her own master. No sooner thought than accomplished. See what progress I make.*

The cell's darkness was complete. After a while, Eilwen fell into a fitful doze, neither fully awake nor truly asleep. When her bladder grew too full to ignore, she relieved herself as far away from her place by the wall as her chains would allow. It had been evening when they captured her, but whether it was now midnight or mid-day or evening once more, she could not say. Her knee pounded, her back ached, and she longed for a cup of water.

When at last the corridor outside the cell began to lighten, shifting almost imperceptibly from black to the darkest of greys, she thought it a trick of the eyes, a conjuration of a mind starved of light. Then she felt the egg throbbing against her side and heard the soft scrape of approaching footsteps. She sat up, blinking sleep-encrusted eyes at the lightening wall, and ran a hand through her tangled mass of hair.

A man appeared in the doorway. He was older than the one who'd left her here: mid-forties, perhaps, with dark, shoulder-length hair and slender fingers. Setting his lamp on the ground, he leaned against the open doorway, considering her with narrowed eyes and a faintly distracted air.

"Please," Eilwen said, her voice little more than a croak. "Could I have some water?"

The man folded his arms. "What's your name?" His words carried the expectant tone of one accustomed to authority.

"Eilwen. Eilwen Nasareen." She coughed. "Some water, please."

"Eilwen," the man repeated. "Tell me, Eilwen. Did you kill my man?"

She hesitated. The man was an Oculus, and not just a token-bearer. But he'd asked the question as though he already knew.

"Yes," she said.

The man's expression didn't change. "Why?"

Something gave way within her. *"Because you're Oculus,"* she snarled, and he blinked in surprise. "You drowned my ship and made me watch. You betrayed everything I cared about. If I could, I'd drive a knife through your heart right now."

A hint of a smile played about the man's lips. "You're not in much position to be making threats."

"Fuck you!" She surged from the wall, reaching for his smirking face with clawed hands. The chains at her ankles snapped tight and she pitched forward, her arms hitting the ground still a hand's breadth from his foot. Something dropped from her shirt, cracking against the stone floor and rolling to a halt just beside her hand.

The man dropped to a crouch, his eyes fixed on the black amber egg. "What's this?"

She snatched the egg away, wrapping her fist around it and holding it against her belly. "That's mine," she said, and glared up at him, daring him to take it from her.

"You didn't get that from Yuri, did you?"

Eilwen shook her head, confused. "Who?"

"No matter." He straightened. "You're not going anywhere," he said, and she could almost see him shunting her aside to a holding area in his mind, the one marked *not important*. He picked up the lamp, turned, and left.

"What?" Eilwen blinked at the empty doorway. "Wait. Wait! What's wrong? Too busy invading cities to stop and chat? Hey, come back!"

The footsteps halted. The man returned, stopping in the doorway and staring at her. "What did you say?"

"I said, are you too busy —"

A presence roared into the room, something huge and ancient, an indescribable mass of rage and vast, insatiable hunger. Eilwen reeled back, the egg in her hand vibrating as though fit to burst apart. The man staggered before her, dropping the lamp with a clang and bracing himself against the doorway, shoulders bent beneath a sudden, invisible weight. Eilwen whimpered, huddling against the wall as it pressed against her, raising her arm in a futile effort to ward it away.

It hung in the air, invisible and ravenous; then it settled about the man in front of her, coiling around and through him as though making itself comfortable in a favourite chair. The pressure eased.

The man straightened slowly, staring at her with an expression of astonishment. She stared back, unable to do anything more than gasp for breath. He put a finger to his lips, indicating silence, and she nodded fractionally. His eyes flicked to the lamp, then back at her, and she nodded again in understanding. *You leave the lamp to show you'll be back.*

He gave her a final stunned look, then turned and walked out of the cell. Eilwen listened to the soft, scraping steps as they receded down the corridor, taking the unspeakable presence with them.

~

The woman could sense Azador.

Clade paced the length of the chamber, shoulders bowed beneath the god's weight, his mind whirling. The notion was crazy. Impossible. The woman had clearly never been bound to the Oculus. She didn't even seem to be a sorcerer. Yet her reaction to the god had been unmistakable. *She felt it as strongly as I did. Maybe more.*

He turned, taking a deep, calming breath, slowing his pace as he retraced his steps. The golem stood motionless in its place by the wall, its wrists and ankles now bound with the shackles that hung beside it. It had made no move to resist when Clade snapped them shut, nor shown any awareness that it was being restrained. A pair of Quill lamps retrieved by Meline burned in opposite corners of the chamber, filling it with a soft, yellow light.

How had she done it? He frowned, going over the sequence of events in his mind. Azador had come, pressing down on him like a great stone, and she... Clade paused, remembering the woman's expression. *She was surprised. No, more than that. Shocked.* She'd reacted as if she'd never felt the god's presence before. She certainly hadn't anticipated its arrival. Perhaps she didn't even know what Azador was.

All the same, she was sensitive to its presence. Add to that her apparent knowledge of their plans to invade Neysa, and what seemed an obsessive grudge against the Oculus, and the woman was... what?

Dangerous, certainly. Volatile, too. She'd wished him dead without knowing a thing about him. Which meant it wasn't him she hated, just what he represented.

Or what she thought he represented.

An idea began to form. Perhaps he could give her hatred a real target. *And maybe, just maybe, she can help me solve some of my other problems.*

Picking up a lamp, Clade left the chamber and headed across the vast passageway, taking the first set of stairs down. The lower level was built around a twisting corridor, with stairs to the cavern at either end. Sub-corridors branched off the main trunk, though none seemed to lead very far. Cells sprouted about the branches like leaves, some with chains and shackles sunk into walls and floors, some without. The Quill prisoners had been confined in one such branch; the woman, Eilwen, was chained in another.

He found Sinon sitting on the bottom stair, a lamp midway between his feet and the mouth of the side passage leading to the Quill. The large man grunted as Clade passed.

Clade gestured at the cells. "Any change?"

"Two of them have been out since morning," Sinon said, his tone one of profound indifference. "Haven't touched their water. Either they're really sound sleepers, or..."

Clade nodded his understanding. *Live or die, there's nothing I can do about it now.* "Fetch me some of the water you left them," he said. "Then take a break. Go and have a look at the golems."

"About time," Sinon said, pushing himself to his feet with an enthusiasm that belied his gruff response.

The sorcerer ducked into the passage, returning a moment later with a cup of water. Then he disappeared up the stairs, Azador going with him. Clade took a long breath, straightening as the pressure of the god eased. *It's getting worse.* When Azador had come upon him in the cell, it had felt like a yoke of iron dropping into place around his neck. And before, in the gorge, he would have fallen but for Kalie. It wasn't just the arrivals, either: the god's ongoing presence was becoming increasingly oppressive, requiring ever more effort to ignore. *The longer we stay, the harder it gets.*

And he still had a spell to build.

Clade rubbed his chin, grimacing as the thought played out to its conclusion. *I can't wait for Arandras. I need to rid myself of the god while I still can.* He set his teeth, resisting the urge to slam his palm against the stone wall. *Damn it, Eilwen, you'd better be what I need, or this whole thing is going to come crashing down like a house of twigs.*

Eilwen sat just as she had on his first visit, back to the wall, her legs stretched out before her. Her eyes flicked up at his approach, then widened at the sight of the cup in his hand. Clade crouched in the doorway, placing the cup on the ground close enough for her to reach. "Water," he said. "As requested."

She scrambled forward, snatching the cup and putting it greedily to her lips; then, with a visible effort of will, she paused, taking only a small sip from the cup. A few heartbeats later, she took another.

"I'd like to start again," Clade said, still crouching. "My name is Clade. I'm sorry for chaining you up, but you did kill my man."

She blinked at him over the top of the cup, waiting.

"Can I get you anything else?"

"Yes," she said. "More water, and then some food. But that can wait." She lowered the cup. "What in the Gatherer's cesspit was that thing?"

Clade seated himself on the rough stone floor with a grunt. "You say you hate the Oculus?" he said. "Then that thing is what you hate most of all."

"Really." Eilwen gave him an appraising look. "What is it?"

"It's a god," Clade said, and the woman raised her eyebrows. "Of a sort, at least. It calls itself Azador. Each member of the Oculus is bound to it."

Eilwen's slow nod suggested that the revelation was not entirely unexpected. "And when you say bound, that's not just a metaphor, is it? There's some sort of, I don't know, sorcerous link between you and it. Am I right?"

"Yes," Clade said, struggling to keep the surprise off his face and out of his heart. "How did you know —"

"Answer me this first." She fixed him with a hard stare. "This god. This Azador. Do you worship it?"

He hesitated. The question seemed to carry a layer of meaning beyond that of the words themselves. "No," he said at last. "Azador is my foe. It believes I am here in obedience to its will, but in fact my purpose is entirely my own." He met her eyes. "I'm here to break its hold over me."

She studied him for a long moment; then, slowly, she nodded. "And if you succeed, what will you do then?"

Clade shook his head. "Your turn. Tell me how you knew about the binding."

The woman shrugged. "Maybe I'm a sorcerer too."

"I don't think so. How?"

Eilwen tilted her head in mock-acquiescence. "With this," she said, reaching into her shirt and drawing out the locus she had dropped earlier. "It tells me who's Oculus and who's not."

He raised a brow. "I've got dozens of those back home. They don't do anything of the sort."

Her expression was almost a smirk. "This one does."

Clade held out a hand. "May I?"

"You don't believe me."

"Let's just say I want to see for myself."

She scowled, turning her head as though about to refuse; then, with an abrupt motion, she reached out and dropped the locus in his hand.

He felt the difference immediately. All the familiar features of the binding were still there — the long, narrow spine through the object's axis; the block-like sections at one end that served as primitive receptor nodes; the irregular spikes at the other that bound the object to Azador — but they seemed twisted somehow, a reflection of a thing rather than the thing itself. Usually the pieces combined to form a basic sensory locus, a contrivance by which the god could monitor the activities of the bearer, even if that bearer had never been bound. In this one, however, something about the sorcery had somehow been... *reversed*.

"It's still tied to Azador," Clade murmured. "But instead of the god looking out, you're looking in."

"I don't know about that," Eilwen said. "It just feels different when there's an Oculus near, or another one of these. A normal one. But I'm not really sensing other people, am I? I'm sensing... it. Or the link to it."

"Something like that." Clade handed the subverted locus back.

"How did it happen?"

"Long story," Eilwen said, her tone curt. "Let's just say I got caught in some ugly sorcery."

Clade let the evasion pass. The woman was beginning to talk freely now, her earlier proclamation of hatred apparently forgotten. *No, not forgotten. But she's looking for something too. Something she wants from this discussion.*

She put the locus away. "Your turn," she said. "What next?"

Next? There was no next, not in his mind. This moment, this place, with Azador and the golems and the binding, was the terminus of all his plans. If he'd ever had hopes beyond this point, he no longer remembered them.

"Azador won't just let me go," he said. "If I get away, it will send people after me. Try to kill me."

Eilwen sat back. "So you'll hide," she said. She sounded disappointed.

"Yes," Clade said. "I'll hide. For a while, at least."

"Then what?"

"I don't know. Gather resources, I suppose. Find some friends."

"Why?"

Because Azador won't give up. Not ever. But that wasn't the real reason. *Because I still believe it can be done. The restoration of the Empire. Renewal of what was lost. Impossible dreams. The cause.*

"The Oculus stood for something, once," he said. "Now it just stands for Azador." He paused, waited for Eilwen to meet his gaze. "I mean to take it back."

Something flickered in her eyes. "A war."

He blinked. *A war?* "Yes, I suppose so."

"You want to fight Azador."

"I do."

Eilwen gave a fierce grin. "So do I."

And there it was. He was not her enemy. Azador was. By allying herself with him, she could strike it down at his side.

If he was fortunate, it might even be true.

He hesitated, allowing his indecision to rise to his face. *Prove it.*

She stared at him, uncertain. Then, slowly, she drew forth the damaged locus and held it out, her hand open.

Clade nodded. "Very well." He waved the locus away. "Keep it. You'll need it for your first task."

She nodded, a bright yearning in her eyes. "What task?"

He smiled. "You've already killed one of my men. How would you like to kill two more?"

CHAPTER 25

To the upright, justice.
To the merciful, compassion.
To the humble, grace.
Holy Gatherer, grant us the assurance of your reward.

— Liturgy of the Thirteenth Hour, *Tri-God Book of Prayer,*
Pantheon of Anstice

ARANDRAS SAT BY THE EDGE of the lake and watched the sun
crawl across the sky. Clade's note lay crumpled in a ball on
the rocks beside him, quivering in the faint, breathy breeze.
Wavelets lapped gently just beyond his feet, the sound as changeless
and unrelenting as the screaming inside his head.

It was Chogon all over again. *You have a Valdori dagger in your
possession. I have your wife. Choose one.* And he had chosen the dagger, not because he wanted it more — *Weeper, no, never that* — but
because this was *wrong,* because accepting those terms was the same
as giving in. He had made his stand, resisted the urge to yield, to
corrupt himself by becoming complicit in the other man's abomina-
ble coercion. If the price for his refusal had been his life, Arandras
would have paid it gladly.

Instead, the gods had taken Tereisa.

And now, beyond all reason, they offered him a chance to choose
differently.

Or perhaps not. Perhaps it was a chance to repeat the decision,
to prove the quality of his character beyond all doubt. *Given all that*

you now know, all that it cost you, would you make the same choice again?

How much is your integrity worth?

The wording of the note did not fool him. The implication was clear. Narvi and Mara were prisoners, somewhere within the caverns, and their lives were in his hands. He could choose to do nothing, allow them to die. Or he could offer a trade. The coin was different this time, but such differences were irrelevant. Golem army or ancient dagger, human life or a single copper duri, it was all the same. Coercion was coercion, whatever clothing it chose to wear.

Yet another man's power could not be wished away. Defiance carried consequences, always. He'd been blind to that in Chogon, or else he'd ignored it, unwilling to believe that the gods would allow him to suffer for doing right. Now he knew better. And in response, he had clung to his principles all the more fiercely, because he had paid for them with the blood of his wife, and neither the world nor the gods could ever exact a higher price.

So why in the hells am I finding this so hard?

His friends languished somewhere beneath the cliff, their captor awaiting his decision. *My friends.* Clade had used that word in his note; whether in hope or presumption, it was impossible to say. But it was true. Mara, who had stuck with him from the first sighting of the misplaced letter, doing the things he couldn't, trying to give him a chance at peace. Narvi, who had never turned him away, forgiving his slights time and again until at last Arandras had found a betrayal too great to overlook. Both had given of themselves, over and over, amassing a debt which he now found impossible to ignore.

He'd never sought such friendships, not since Tereisa's death, and this, right here, was why. Such bonds did not bring strength, no matter what the poets said. *They weaken you, undermine your certainty, arm your enemies against you. They dilute you, thinning you out until you're as much them as you are yourself.* He'd done nothing to lead either of them on, offered no reciprocity to encourage them. Somehow it hadn't mattered. They'd staked a claim on him regardless.

He couldn't let them die. Not like this. Not again.

And if saving them meant turning his back on all he held dear, well, he'd done that already. He'd stood by as Isaias was coerced, his own selfish compulsion triumphing over his sadly ineffectual conscience. He'd betrayed the Quill, treating them as though they were no more significant than the golems they'd come to find. Hells, he'd done the same to Druce and Jensine all the way back in Spyridon. He was stained already, irreparably so. Whatever honour he'd thought he had lay trampled in muck. There was nothing left to preserve.

Arandras bowed his head, expecting tears, but none came. *Of course not.* There was no substance to him, not any more. Perhaps there had never been. *I am an empty shell. No dreams for the Dreamer, no tears for the Weeper, and nothing to trouble the Gatherer when I die.*

All that remained to him was to save Narvi and Mara, to pay whatever needed paying to discharge their debts of friendship. The golems would be part of that exchange, no doubt, if they hadn't been taken from him already. The demands of his conscience had lost their hold on him some time ago, it seemed; bonds of sorcery and ties of obligation would soon follow. *Then I will truly be an unbound man, free from all that hinders and restrains. Nothing will ever have hold over me again.*

And then, with neither weight nor anchor to hold him down, he would simply drift away.

The sun crept westward, sinking slowly toward the jagged teeth of the Pelaseans. Arandras smoothed the note, reading the words one last time, then stood, folding the paper over and tucking it away. The air was still, the lake a sheet of glass, silver and blue. Only the soft caws of scavenger birds disturbed the silence.

Time to go.

A different woman stood in the entrance to the cavern. She was shorter than the other, slight of build, and there was no pan of water at her feet. She looked up at his approach, a flat expression on her face.

Arandras halted at the rock that had borne the note. Something flickered in the corner of his mind. He extended a questing thought, felt it brush against a faint alien presence. The golems. *He doesn't have you yet, then.* Perhaps he had simply been too agitated to sense them before. He was calm now.

He tried sending a command, instructing the golem to speak, but there was no change in the whisper-thin presence. *Too far.* They were just too far away.

"All right," he said. "You win. Tell Clade I'm prepared to offer an exchange."

The woman nodded, not meeting his eyes, and said nothing.

Arandras frowned. "Did you hear me? I said I'm ready to make a deal. That's what he wants, right?"

"You'll have to wait," she said, glancing at him for a moment and then away again. Her voice was toneless, dismissive, as though speaking to a disliked pet. "He'll come out when he's ready."

"No, that's not —" He broke off, took a breath. "The note said I had until sunset. I need to see him before then."

"Relax," the woman said. "Nobody's killing anyone. There's been a change of plan, that's all. He'll come when he's ready."

There was a disinterested conviction in her tone, as though what she was saying was too banal to be worth lying about, and he found himself exhaling in relief. "All right. Good." He would wait, at least for a while. "Can you tell me how my friends are?"

She shrugged. "Alive," she said, and there was something strange in her tone, something almost like regret.

Arandras stepped forward, studying her face. She returned his gaze, looking at him as though he meant nothing more to her than the rocks around him. Her eyes were dull, numb. Lifeless.

She is Clade's, some part of him whispered. *This is what he's like. This is what they're all like. Callous and unfeeling.* He shivered. *Inhuman.*

And he was about to give them an army strong enough to overrun the entire Free Cities, and probably Kefira and the Gislean Provin too.

I can't. The woman stared at him as though sensing the shift in his thoughts. *I can't. Mara, Narvi, I'm sorry. I can't do it.*

He stepped forward again. Clade was inside, but so were the golems. Maybe if he got close enough, he'd be able to reach them, tell them to —

The woman whipped out a dagger and held it before her, her face hard and her lips thin. "No closer," she said. "Not even a step."

They had a chance to kill me before, he thought. *But they didn't, because they don't want me dead.* He studied the woman's taut face. *She won't stab me. She won't.*

"I'm going into the cavern now," Arandras said. "Like it or not, I'm going in. If you want to stop me, you'll have to kill me."

He stepped forward.

~

Eilwen stole through the empty doorway, ignoring the twinge in her knee and edging further into the foul miasma exuded by the so-called god. The egg thrummed against her flesh, pulling her on, urging her to make the kill. She drew back her arm, her fist clenched around the dagger's hilt, and struck.

Sinon collapsed on the rough stone with a thud. There was a flare of alarm from the god; then the presence was gone, vanishing in an instant as though swallowed up by the air itself. She bent over, wiping the dagger clean on her victim's arm and replacing it in its sheath.

The beast within her purred its approval.

She ignored it as best she could. She no longer followed its whims. She was a soldier, and she had a mission to complete.

The golems knelt in rows before her, their attention directed to the far corner. Eilwen stared, captivated by the grand, unnerving figures. This, then, was what had drawn the Quill and the Oculus to such a remote place. They were wondrous, yes, and awe-inspiring, and everything else she'd sensed beneath Clade's words as he described them to her. But more than anything else, she found them terrifying.

With an effort of will she turned away, leaving Sinon's body where it had fallen on the low platform. A solitary golem stood motionless by the wall, shackled hand and foot, its tiny yellow eyes staring sightlessly at the chamber's far wall. A thrill ran up her spine as she turned her back on it and strode from the room. *Don't think about the golem. Think about the mission. The mission is what matters.*

Her task was straightforward enough. Kill the remaining two Oculus sorcerers, then hold the entrance to the caverns. There was a man outside who might approach her or try to enter the caverns; she was to prevent the latter, as Clade would soon commence work on a binding which was absolutely not to be interrupted. The man was inexperienced in combat, or so Clade believed, so she should have little trouble keeping him out.

In return, Clade said, she would be given her freedom. But there had been a look in his eyes and an edge to his words that suggested something more. Perhaps, if she was able to demonstrate her value, they might be able to reach an understanding, maybe even a partnership against the being he named Azador.

The prospect of killing twice more had filled her with an unexpected reluctance. The beast had crowed to the sound of Clade's words, gleeful in its lust, leaving her shaken and dismayed. *This is not how it's supposed to be.* She'd hoped that a discipline imposed from without might provide the strength she needed to corral the beast's mad hunger; yet her very first assignment had it tugging on its chains, eager to gorge itself yet again. *This is not who I am. I am Eilwen Nasareen, and I am a soldier, and the beast serves me.*

The cavern turned, bringing the entryway into view, and Eilwen paused. Meline stood to one side, silhouetted against the daylight, a pan of water on the ground beside her. Even from this distance, Eilwen could sense the heavy, brooding presence of Azador hanging over the sorcerer, causing the egg to buzz at her side and the beast to growl within her like two halves of a strange, conjoined being.

There's the spot, she thought, fixing her gaze on a point just left of centre in Meline's slender back. *Put the dagger there, and then it's done.* She took a long slow breath, shutting out the beast's slavering anticipation, and stepped silently into the invisible cloud.

She was three paces away when a pang shot through her knee, causing her to scrape the ground with her boot. Meline whirled about with a yelp, then yelped again at the sight of the naked dagger in Eilwen's hand. Eilwen leapt forward, and the sorcerer stumbled back and across, her foot groping toward the pan. Lunging desperately, Eilwen kicked the pan away, then spun and shoved Meline against the side of the entryway, her dagger at the other woman's throat.

Meline's wide eyes rolled down toward the dagger, then up again at Eilwen. "Please don't," she said, her voice soft and tremulous.

"Please don't kill me."

Something rose inside Eilwen, savage and exultant; the beast, roaring its delight, revelling in its victim's pleas. It stared at Meline through Eilwen's eyes, lapping up her terrified dismay, sucking it down like a ravenous blood-eel. Sickened, Eilwen slashed the woman's throat and turned away, falling to her knees as her stomach began to heave. She doubled over, retching as Meline slumped to the ground behind her. *No more. Gods, please, no more.*

She grit her teeth, swallowing hard, and forced herself to her feet. She was a soldier, and there was still work to do. *But please, gods, no more killing.*

Meline's corpse lay across the threshold, a puddle of blood at her neck. Grasping her ankles, Eilwen dragged her into the cavern and out of sight. She wiped her dagger clean, then emptied the pan of water over the stained stones, washing the blood away into the shadows of the passage. When it was gone, she tossed the empty pan inside, its crash echoing within the cavern, and took up position in the entryway.

Somewhere inside her the beast nestled down, suckling on the remnants of Meline's fear. Eilwen shied away, desperate to avoid it while the appalling taste still lingered in its mouth, and cast about for some other course on which to direct her thoughts. *Clade.* Her employer, her commanding officer, at least for the moment. The man would be commencing his sorcery around now. A binding to rid himself of his god. She still had only a vague idea what that meant — Clade's explanation had been brief, hastened by his apparently sudden decision to complete the final stage without delay. She'd have to ask him about it later, tease out the snarled implications she sensed beneath the surface.

Perhaps Azador was to him what the beast was to her. *What would I do to rid myself of it?* It laughed, baring bloody fangs in mockery. Shame and despair filled her, and she fought the urge to turn and look at Meline's supine form. *Gods help me, it's getting stronger. No matter what I do, it just gets stronger.*

Please, gods, let me not have to kill again today.

The late afternoon sun slanted through the gorge, obscuring the shore and the lake. When the first flicker of motion caught the edge of Eilwen's eye she blinked, squinting into the glare, unsure whether she had imagined it. Then a man came into view, picking his way over the rocks, raising his head at intervals to glance in the direction of the cavern. Groaning inwardly, Eilwen straightened her back and watched his slow, inexorable approach.

He halted a few paces away and stared vacantly into the passage, then shrugged. "All right. You win. Tell Clade I'm prepared to offer an exchange."

I win. The thought made her want to laugh, but she knew that if she started she might not stop. She nodded instead.

The gesture seemed to displease him. "Did you hear me? I said I'm ready to make a deal. That's what he wants, right?"

She glanced at him, taking in his wild hair and dishevelled clothes. "You'll have to wait. He'll come out when he's ready."

"No, that's not —" The man paused, evidently trying to bring his emotions under control. "The note said I had until sunset. I need to see him before then."

He's worried about his friends. The realisation came from a distant part of her, a place that had somehow gone untouched by the beast. She reached for it, filled with a sudden, desperate longing, but it vanished before she could grasp it.

"Relax," she said. "Nobody's killing anyone." *Not at the moment, anyway.* Laughter threatened to break out once more, and she hurried on. "There's been a change of plan, that's all. He'll come when he's ready."

"All right," the man said. "Good. Can you tell me how my friends are?"

She shrugged. "Alive," she said, though she wasn't even sure of that. But she had killed everyone besides Clade, and he seemed too preoccupied with his sorcery to have found time to kill the prisoners. In truth, a cell was probably the safest place to be right now. *Maybe I should have stayed there, too. If this is freedom, maybe I'm better off in chains.*

The man stepped toward her, uncertain, perhaps sensing the doubt in her reply. Then his expression shifted and the beast surged within her. She pushed it away, staring at him with helpless dread. *Gods, please, no. Not another one.*

He took another step and she drew her dagger, holding it before her as though to ward him away. A red smear on her hand caught her eye. She glanced up to see if he'd noticed. *See, I have already killed twice today. Believe it, and save me from making you my third.* "No closer," she said, extending the dagger fractionally. "Not even a step."

The man gave a slight smile. "I'm going into the cavern now," he said. "Like it or not, I'm going in. If you want to stop me, you'll have to kill me."

He stepped forward and she stepped back, maintaining the distance between them. "You really don't want to do that."

The smile widened and he stepped again. "I think I do."

"No." She nodded sideways to where Meline lay just inside the threshold. "Like I said, there's been a change of plan."

He followed her gesture, the smile falling away as he took in the huddled corpse. Then he scowled, rounding on her as though the weapon in her hand were nothing more than a toy. "Look at you," he hissed, the words filled with loathing. "You're dead already, aren't you? You and all the others. Weeper's tears, there's more life in one of those golems down there than there is in the lot of you."

Eilwen gaped, struck speechless by the twinned forces of revulsion and revelation. *Gods have mercy. Is it true?* The beast within her howled its affirmation and she sank to her knees, overcome.

The dream. I already knew it. This was why the beast had defied all her attempts at control. Eilwen, the old Eilwen, was dead. She had died with the *Orenda,* torn in two like the ship itself and left to drown in the icy waters. What lurked within was not a beast at all; it was her, the new Eilwen, ready now to assume her rightful place.

The dagger slipped from her grasp and clattered to the ground. She fell to her knees, her arms wrapped around her body, rocking and weeping as the man's footsteps receded into the depths of the cavern.

~

Clade crouched before the golem, his face a hand's breadth from its shackled leg, and made fast the foundation of his binding. Azador raged about him like his own personal storm, its endless, seething assault battering his defences with the force of a whirlwind, pressing him to the ground. He resisted its attack as best he could, hunkering down before the onslaught and focusing his attention on the unfinished sorcery before him.

The golem's binding was unlike anything he had ever seen. For the first time in his life, Clade found the language of touch utterly inadequate to describe a piece of sorcery. The lines and whorls sang before his questing mind, bursting with indescribable vitality. A deep, rich light seemed to emanate from the heart of the spell, and the scent of it was smooth and sweet like honey, yet as evanescent as smoke.

But for the weight of Azador pressing upon him, Clade could have happily spent days, even weeks, tracing the lines of sorcery through the great ceramic-stone construct, slowly piecing together its design. *Weeks? Say rather years.* To study the golems and draw out their secrets would be the work of a lifetime. *But not mine. Not yet, anyway.*

Not today.

Clade pushed outward, feeling with his mind for the foundation of his own spell. The base of the binding clung to the golem's thigh, its core a wide, open column surrounded by a dozen smaller conduits, each serving to strengthen and support the main structure. His brief survey of the golem's form had identified no single point that seemed most suited to receive the transfer. As far as he could tell, the spirit animating the golem was not concentrated in any one location; rather, it seemed equally present in every part of its body, darting through the complex weave of sorcery like a crimson thread. In the absence of arcane considerations, he had fallen back on pragmatism to select the spell's focal point: a spot just above the knee, which offered both space enough to fix the binding in place and a convenient height for its construction.

The process was slow, intense, and utterly exhausting. Clade had gone over the binding so often in his mind that every step was dully familiar, tempting him to inattention. Conscious of the danger, he forced himself to vigilance, reviewing each piece as he fitted it in place, pausing regularly to look again at the whole and ensure that no flaws or imbalances crept into the structure. Piece by piece the binding grew, narrowing near the middle then widening again as it arched outward. Sweat sprang up on his brow and back, chilling his skin in the cool underground air. Azador's mad fury roared in his ears; yet he pressed on, deliberately forming each link and setting it in place, until at last the binding was done, all but the final piece that would join the unfinished spell to the sorcery lodged in his heart.

Drained, he sat back and considered his work. Somewhere deep within he felt something skitter and leap, like a tiny inner counterpart to the storm of Azador without. He bore down on the flicker of agitation with a frown, penning it between walls of stone and cutting it loose, reforming his being around the empty space where the tremor had been. *You are no part of me,* he thought, and it seemed he was speaking not only to his fear but also to the suffocating rage of the god. *You do not trouble me. I, Clade, reject you.*

A boot scraped on the stone behind him. Clade shook his head, noting and rejecting the invitation to annoyance. "Not now, Eilwen," he said. "Maintain your post and do not interrupt me again. Understood?"

"Yeah," a male voice said. "About that..."

Clade whirled to his feet. Arandras stood in the doorless portal, his bearded face contorted in a triumphant, lupine snarl. A grinding noise sounded just behind Clade's head, and he glanced back to find the golem turned in his direction, its pinprick yellow eyes staring directly at him.

"Your name is Clade Alsere," Arandras said. The words were both a statement and a question.

"Yes," Clade said. A strange calm flooded through him. "It is."

Arandras gazed at him from beneath lowered brows. "You killed my wife."

"Yes," Clade said again. There was nothing else to say.

Arandras bared his teeth. "*Why?*"

Clade flicked his gaze over the other man. Arandras was at least a head shorter than Clade himself, and was already breathing hard. But the man's stance was poised, balanced. Ready.

"I had to," Clade said. Behind him, the unfinished binding tugged at his thoughts like a load on a pulley. He paused, wrapping a piece of his mind around its form, and moistened his lips. Without his support, the incomplete structure risked a potentially destructive collapse. "I had no choice."

"No," Arandras snapped. "Not true. There's always a choice."

"Not for me," Clade said. "I was bound."

Arandras flinched, his expression shifting to something unreadable. "Meaning what?"

"Bound," Clade repeated, watching for any reaction. "By sorcery."

Arandras growled, shaking his head. "No, you weren't."

"I was. That's why I'm here."

The man's laugh was scornful. "Don't give me that. You're here for the golems." He grinned, the confident cast returning to his shoulders. "And you're here because *I led you.*"

Clade raised his eyebrows. "Bannard —"

"No. Bannard left." The grin remained, but there was something beneath it, something Clade still couldn't identify. "I made the sign at the bridge. I showed you where we left the path."

Clade opened his mouth, then closed it again. He hadn't noticed Bannard among the fallen; but then, he hadn't looked very hard. Perhaps it was true. "Why did you do that?"

Arandras's lip curled. "Why do you think?"

Hatred filled the man's face; yet still there lingered something else, something Arandras fought to keep hidden. *What?* Clade cast about for something, anything, that might crack the man's shell. "I think... I think you blame yourself for what happened out there."

Something lashed out beside him, the motion so quick it was already over by the time he turned his head. The golem's hand grasped the air a hair's-breadth from his arm, the manacle's chain pulled taut. Clade drew a deep breath, willing the pounding in his chest to slow; but as he did, a fresh rumbling sounded from the far doorway. An unchained golem stepped through, its feet stained with blood and fluids. *Sinon.*

"Those deaths are on you," Arandras hissed, his face dark with anger. "You are the killer here. You killed my wife. You killed those Quill. Hells, you even killed your own people. And now you want the golems so you can go on killing, with nobody to stand in your way."

"No." Clade grit his teeth, shoving his frustration into as deep a hole as he could manage. His play for the golems had failed. No alternative remained but to give them up and hope that the gesture could still make a difference. He took a breath. "I'm not here for the golems."

"Bullshit." The free golem took a step into the chamber. Its eyes burned a dark orange.

"Hear me," Clade said. "Yes, I sought them. Yes, the Oculus wants them as a weapon. But *I don't.* Not any more. Take them. They're yours." He opened his arms, inviting Arandras to believe. Beseeching him. "I'm not here on behalf of the Oculus. I'm here to escape them."

~

Arandras laughed. The man's claim was absurd. "Of course you are. That's why you followed us all the way here. To *escape them.*"

Clade hissed through gritted teeth, and Arandras laughed again. Without shifting his gaze, he directed a command to the unrestrained golem. *Take another step.* It did so, rumbling to a halt almost within reach of the other man.

"Wait! Wait." Clade raised his arms. "You don't understand. I'm bound. Beholden to a... I don't know what it is, exactly. They tell us it's a god."

"What's that? The gods made you do it?" Arandras shook his head. "No. You killed Tereisa. Nobody else. You bear the price." *Golem, take another —*

"*Ask them!*" Clade pointed a desperate finger at the golems. "Ask them what they see!"

Arandras paused. Clade stared at him, expectant, his outstretched finger almost touching the nearest golem. *Weeper's breath, he actually believes it.* He sighed, feeling strangely deflated. After all this time, all he had done to reach this point, Tereisa's killer turned out to be nothing more than a common madman. *Deluded, that's all. Almost certainly. Almost...*

He gave Clade a long, measuring look. The other man stood silent, waiting, his finger frozen in the air. Slowly, Arandras exhaled. *Golems, tell me what you see.*

The shackled golem remained silent, but the other responded immediately. A low drone filled his head, the strange almost-sound twisting and warping to form words like shapes in the rock. *Stone and metal, sorcery and stone. My brother in chains. A man argues with the master. Sorcery; the man is more. It watches and listens and hungers. Sorcery; my brother is more. Lamps in the dark. An opening. An empty space —*

Hold. Arandras frowned. *Tell me about the sorcery.*

Sorcery, the golem repeated. *My brother is more; the more is incomplete. Sorcery. The man is more; the more is angry. It watches and listens and hungers. A single strand. A fastening made fast. It beats. Spirit and stone, blood and sorcery.*

Arandras eyed the man before him. *The more is angry.* "You're adding something to the golem," he said experimentally, watching for Clade's reaction. "Some sort of spell."

"Yes," Clade said. "To transfer my binding onto it."

Arandras nodded slowly. Perhaps it was true, then. Perhaps Clade did have some... *thing* bound to him. But that didn't absolve him. "This binding," he said. "You chose it?"

Clade hesitated. "Yes."

"And does it physically compel the movement of your body?"

Clade licked his lips, said nothing.

"Your choices," Arandras said. "Your responsibility."

"I see," Clade said. "And I suppose that justifies your choice now."

Arandras said nothing. *Golem, take hold of the man's shoulder.* The heavy hand reached out, enveloping Clade's shoulder in its massive fingers. The man shuddered, took a long, steadying breath.

"Tell me, Arandras," Clade said. "Have you never made a choice and then regretted it?"

A surge of emotion filled Arandras, too thick for words, and he stared back, struggling to speak past the constriction in his throat. "Are you telling me you regret killing Tereisa?"

Clade opened his mouth, then closed it again; but the answer was there in his eyes. *No.*

Rage filled Arandras. "Answer me! Do you regret killing my wife?"

The other man closed his eyes. When he spoke, his voice was

calm. "You've never killed before, have you?"

Arandras blinked. "What?"

"You said it yourself just a moment ago, didn't you?" Clade seemed to be looking past him, off into the darkness. "I'm a killer, you said. You're not."

"There's a first time for —"

"I've killed ten people by my own hand, now. Your wife was the sixth." Clade gave a small smile. "She cursed me, you know. Oh, not in fear, or at least not much. She was angry, I think. Affronted that such a thing was even possible."

Images of Tereisa flashed through Arandras's mind. Memories of the two of them together, arguing, laughing. *Affronted. Yes, that sounds like her.*

"It does something to you," Clade said. "Killing, I mean. You lose something you never knew you had." He paused. "I can't say I regret what I gained. But I do, I think, regret what I lost."

Arandras shrugged. He was an empty shell. Loss meant nothing to him, not any more. "What did you gain?"

The other man blinked. "I'm sorry?"

"You heard me. What did you gain?"

Clade said nothing, a resigned look creeping into his eyes.

"You sought control, I think. Power over others. The ability to further your own ends. Whereas I..."

Arandras trailed off, his words hanging in the air. *Control. Power over others.* Clade stood before him, his arm locked in a grip of stone and clay. *With this golem I remove your volition, just as you did to Tereisa. Because she, to you, was nothing more than a tool to be used. Just as Isaias was to me. And Narvi. And Druce, and Jensine.* He stared into the face of the man who had killed his wife. *And now you have become the same thing. A means. One by which I may console myself, and consider myself avenged.*

Swallowing hard, he pushed the thought to its inexorable conclusion.

With this act, I become you.

It was as though he stood on the edge of a blade, perfectly balanced, with not the slightest breath of wind to push him one way or the other. Clade's eyes showed neither fear nor hope nor petition nor remorse. The golem stood motionless beside him, awaiting Arandras's command.

The golem. A construct of sorcery. Crafted to resemble human form, but not, in fact, alive. A device, in the truest sense of the word. Something created with no greater purpose than to be used. In truth, little more than a glorified puppet.

This is how Clade sees the world. Filled with creatures like these, all awaiting his touch, his direction. His disposal. The vision called to him, tempting in its simplicity. He reached out, inviting it closer. What relief it would bring, to let go of his foolish reserve and embrace the gift that the gods had given him...

No. Another voice stirred to life deep within and he recoiled, turning away from the mirage in revulsion. Conviction filled him, sure and unshakeable. *That is not who I am.*

He bowed his head. *I'm sorry, Tereisa. I cannot do this.*

Not even for you.

Breathing heavily, Arandras sent a command to the golem. Its grip on Clade's arm loosened, and the man pulled himself free, rubbing his shoulder where the great hand had grasped it. A quizzical expression formed on his face and he opened his mouth to speak.

Arandras raised a hand and the other man subsided. He paused, wiping his eyes, taking a moment to collect himself. When he spoke, his voice was steady.

"Where are my friends?"

CHAPTER 26

If the gods did not ceaselessly disappoint us, by what other token
would we recognise them?

— Kassa of Menefir, *Solitude*

EILWEN KNELT IN THE DARK of the cavern, her racking sobs
slowly subsiding. Rough rock pressed against her knees and
she shifted awkwardly, balancing with her hands as the
muscles in her legs groaned to life. Raising herself to a crouch, she
blinked sightlessly down the passageway and heaved a shuddering
sigh.

The man was gone, vanished into the cavern on his way to Clade,
or the golems, or the prisoners. *Or all three.* He had taken her lamp
with him, leaving her stranded at the top of the vast, black sea. But
she knew the layout of the caverns now. *Follow that wall all the way
down to the manacle chamber, and past that, the golems.* And Clade
would be there, preparing the sorcery that would somehow remove
the so-called god's hold over him.

Assuming, of course, that he wasn't already dead.

I failed. Again. Gods, that's all I ever do. Her only task had been
to stop the man from coming in. Instead, she'd just stepped aside. *I
might as well have invited him down for chocol.* But no, it hadn't been
like that. She'd had him at dagger-point, but she'd stayed her hand,
terrified that if she killed again, the beast within would finally and
irrevocably escape her control.

At least she wouldn't have that problem again.

She was the beast, and the beast was her. She saw that now. The old her was gone, drowned with the *Orenda*. The beast was all she had left. *That's why I kept failing.* She'd been clinging to her old self, not realising that part of her was already dead. By forcing her to confront the truth, the man had shown her the way out.

The beast could not be expelled, but neither could it be allowed to roam free. It was still a child, undisciplined and unformed. And like a puppy, or a colt, or the rawest recruit to the standing army of Anstice, it needed the help of others to guide and instruct it on the long, slow path to maturity.

In short, it required *training.*

Havilah had already begun it, she realised now, selecting her as his adjunct and commencing her instruction before she'd even known she needed it. She wondered if he'd seen her truly all along. *You would have taught me well, Havilah. You would have shown me what it meant to fight well.* But Havilah was dead, and the Guild was lost to her. All that remained was her rage.

And Clade. He shared her rage, if nothing else. And he knew what to do about it. She could do worse than follow him for a time. *He's not you, Havilah. He won't train me the way you would have.* And she'd never trust him the way she had Havilah, not after seeing him so casually order the deaths of his own people. But then, they hadn't been his people, not really. *We share a cause, he and I. We fight on the same side. Better we fight together than apart.*

But now she had failed him too, jeopardising his grand project and possibly his life. Even if he survived, even if he completed his sorcery, there'd be no place for her. Not any more.

She groaned, burying her hands in her hair; but as she did so she felt the beast's growl, low and heavy, bringing her back to herself. She was a soldier now. She had failed, yes, but failure didn't release her from her duty. Breathing deeply, Eilwen pushed herself to her feet, wincing at the ache in her leg. She had to get down there, find out what was happening. Maybe she could still make it right.

Without a lamp, the cavern seemed twice as large, a vast, empty space of silence and dust. Eilwen shuffled down the slope as fast as she dared, feeling for spurs and protrusions with each step, groping blindly ahead with both hands whenever an opening punctuated the rough wall. The egg began to buzz softly at her side, gentle as a purring kitten, and she felt the distant presence of the god waft across her face.

An uncanny babble rose from somewhere ahead, and she froze in startled confusion. After half a dozen thudding heartbeats came realisation: the sound was laughter, distorted by the jagged stone into something monstrous. Gritting her teeth, Eilwen pressed on, stumbling as she kicked against the uneven ground.

At last the chamber came into view, its thin lamplight brighter than a beacon to her hungry eyes. Clade stood within, speaking to someone just out of view; but as she watched, a great, inhuman hand reached out and grasped him by the shoulder.

A golem. Gods, no. He's going to kill him. She crept closer, allowing the stink of Azador to wash over her, trying to catch a glimpse of the man who stood frustratingly out of sight. She couldn't intervene without knowing where he was — a moment's warning would be enough for the man to leave Clade with a crushed arm, or worse. Even allowing Clade to see her might tip the man off. Circling around, she approached the doorway and reached for her dagger.

It wasn't there.

Shit. She'd let it fall near the entrance and forgotten it in the dark. *Now what?*

There was still the small one in her boot. She dropped to a crouch; but as she did so her knee gave an ominous twinge and she hurriedly extended her arms, holding herself steady in a painful half-stoop. *Gods have mercy!* Had she made a sound? She held her breath, her leg burning, listening for a change in either man's voice. A moment passed, then another, and she began to breathe more easily. She straightened slowly, easing the weight on her injured knee with a silent gasp.

All right. No dagger, unless I want to give myself away. She reached down to massage her aching joint as Clade's voice rose in the adjoining chamber.

"It does something to you. Killing, I mean. You lose something you never knew you had."

Eilwen bent her head, but the tears that had come with her

moment of revelation did not return. *What's gone is gone.* There was pain, but with acceptance came a kind of peace as well. Not even the gods could bring back the person she'd been before. *This is me, now. Just this.* And she could still find a way to do some good.

The voices in the other room fell silent. Eilwen shook off her reverie, cursing herself for her inattention. *What just happened?* She stilled her breath, straining her ears for the slightest sound within. *Did he kill him? Why is nobody moving?*

Then the other man spoke, his voice startling for its nearness. "Where are my friends?"

"Downstairs," Clade said, and she thought she heard a note of relief. "They haven't been harmed." He paused. "Though some were injured in the battle."

Silence returned. Eilwen waited, fighting an unbearable urge to creep up to the doorway and glance inside.

"All right," the other man said at last. "Finish your sorcery. I won't stop you. But I'll be taking the rest." Boot scraped on stone, and Eilwen shrank back into the shadows. "Oh," the man said, the edge of his sleeve visible in the doorway. "One other thing. I want my urn back."

There was a whisper of cloth and a faint smack, as of something being caught; then the light tilted as someone lifted a lamp. Eilwen retreated to the cavern's shadowy corner just as the man strode out, lamp in hand, and made for the first doorway in the long side wall. He looked inside and shook his head, then moved on to the next opening and disappeared down the stairs.

Silence descended. Thin lamplight still bled from the chamber, its soft glow undisturbed by movement. A needle of fear slithered through her. *Is Clade all right?* A cry echoed up from the now-dark staircase behind her: the man's voice, his words too distorted to tell whether the call was one of welcome or alarm. Casting stealth aside, Eilwen rounded the doorway and entered the chamber.

Clade knelt before the manacled golem, his back straight, his shoulders rising and falling with the slow, smooth breaths of one deep in sleep. The second golem stood a short distance away, its hand once more by its side. The stench of Azador hung thick in the air. She hesitated, unwilling to break the charged silence.

"What went wrong?" The words were soft and calm, almost melodious, and it seemed to her that the voice was as much Havilah's as it was Clade's.

"I'm sorry," she said to his back. "I couldn't..." She trailed off, swallowing hard. "It won't happen again. I promise."

There was no response.

Eilwen bit her lip. It didn't matter what she said. She'd failed, and her revelation had come too late. She hung her head, waiting for him to tell her how badly she'd fallen short. It was no less than she deserved.

At last Clade spoke, his voice remote. "Arandras will be back to take the golems. All but this one. You're to allow it."

She blinked, hope rising in her breast. "All right."

"My binding is almost complete," he continued. "Its effect may be... unpredictable. You're to stay with me until I say otherwise."

The god's presence billowed around her, making it difficult to breathe. "I will."

"I'd prefer to delay this until Arandras is gone," Clade said, a note of strain appearing in his voice. "But I think that is no longer a viable option."

He fell silent, his breaths slowing further. Eilwen nodded, no matter that he couldn't see it, no matter that she had no idea what she was agreeing to. Against all hope, Clade had given her another chance. And this time, she would not let him down.

The sorcerer took a long, deep breath, and bowed his head.

Something *shifted* around her, vast and inexplicable, as though the air itself broke apart and reassembled in less time than it took her to blink. The god's stifling presence wavered, then snapped back in place with a devastating howl of rage and distress.

Clade screamed, a raw, visceral cry. For a moment he seemed suspended by an invisible thread, his shoulders arched back, his chin thrust toward the ceiling. Then he collapsed, slumping sideways like a rag doll and toppling onto the rough stone.

Eilwen stared at Clade's still form, her heart sinking. Then the beast growled in her belly, low and deep, and she straightened. She was a soldier, and not even the gods themselves would prevent her from seeing her assignment through.

There was a place near the middle of the chamber that seemed good. She could see both doorways from there, and keep an eye on Clade and the golems at the same time.

Folding her arms, Eilwen took up her position.

~

Arandras turned on his heel, picked up the lamp and strode from the room.

It was over.

Behind him, his wife's killer still breathed. It would be an easy thing to turn around, march back in, and have the golem squeeze the life from the man's body. But he knew he wouldn't.

He'd been wrong, before. This wasn't a repeat of what had happened at Chogon. Chogon had been the beginning, and this was the end. If the price for his refusal then had been his life, Arandras would have paid it gladly. Instead, the gods had taken Tereisa; but they had left him his resentment and his vengeance, and he had clung to them, nurturing them, not realising that this was the true price, the true test of his resolve. Little by little he'd forgotten himself, gradually surrendering himself to them; and in return they'd stripped him bare, until at last they'd cannibalised even themselves and left him empty of everything but the crushing weight of his loss.

Or not quite. Somewhere inside, a part of him had remembered, lost among the ashes like a phoenix's egg. Finally, he had found it again, warming it before his frail, dying candle until it roared back to life. A small part of that fire seemed to be with him still, warming him as it pulsed through his veins. He felt somehow both lighter and more substantial, as though he had been asleep for years and now, at last, was awake.

The stairs were steep and winding, but Arandras scarcely noticed. The passageway at the bottom branched twice before it twisted out of sight, his lamp casting odd patterns of shadows across the uneven floor. His sleeve snagged on the wall, and as he pulled it free it threw a puff of dust into the air. He sneezed.

"Arandras?" The voice came from somewhere nearby. "Is that you?"

"Mara?" Arandras hurried toward the voice, paused at a fork in the passage. "Where are you?"

"In here."

The branch turned once and abruptly terminated. Cells lined the walls on either side, the odour of stale urine hanging thick in the enclosed space. Holding his breath against the smell, Arandras shone his lamp into the first cell. Mara sat within, her limbs shackled to chains sunk into the cell floor. She blinked away as he entered, shielding her eyes against the light, but her face bore a wide grin.

"Not dead yet, huh?" she said, and nodded her chin at the front of the cell, beyond the reach of her chains. "Key's there."

"Mara. Weeper's cry, it's good to see you." He found the key and crouched beside her, pulling the manacles free from her wrists. The flesh beneath them was bruised and raw. "Are you all right?"

"I'm fine," she said, but her breath caught as he turned to her ankles, betraying her words. "What's happened?"

"We're free to go," Arandras said. "Where are the others?"

"Right next door," Mara said, hissing as Arandras loosed the final restraint. "What do you mean, free to go? Did he come? Is he...?"

Arandras shook his head. "I'll tell you later. Here, take my shoulder and try to stand."

Mara grimaced, levering herself upright against Arandras's proffered shoulder with a groan. "All right. I'm all right," she said, shifting her weight gingerly from Arandras to her own feet. "Gods, I feel like someone dropped a wall on me."

"Yeah," Arandras said. "Come on, let's find the others."

Narvi lay huddled in the corner of his cell, a nasty gash running from his eyebrow to just below his ear. Arandras removed his restraints, massaging his wrists just above the wounds left by the manacles. A cup of water sat inexplicably at the edge of the cell, and Arandras lifted it to Narvi's lips, tilting it just enough to allow a trickle into his mouth.

"Narvi," he said, searching for even a flicker in the man's half-lidded eyes. *Weeper, please let him be alive.* "Narvi. Are you there?"

Narvi's mouth sagged open, water dribbling over his chin; then he coughed, blinking groggily up at Arandras. "Huh," he whispered. "What happened?"

Relief surged through Arandras. "It's all right. You were hurt, but we're going to get you out. Can you move?"

Narvi grunted. "Head hurts," he croaked. "Ribs, too."

"Arms and legs?"

He shifted experimentally, then gave a ghost of a smile. "All still there."

"Good." The light shifted as Mara moved the lamp, and Arandras settled down on the cell floor, pressing the cup into Narvi's hands. "Just sit tight for a moment. We'll head out soon."

Narvi took a sip of water. "Thought you'd be gone by now," he said, his voice firming slightly. "Off with your new toys."

Arandras shook his head in the near darkness. *You really thought that? Weeper forgive me.* "I —" He broke off, groping for words. What was there to say? "I've done badly by you, Narvi," he said at last. "And not just now. For a long time. I'm sorry."

Narvi gave a long sigh. "So you damn well should be."

Mara's shape appeared in the doorway. "Halli's in a bad way," she said. "Good news is that they left my gear in the cell opposite. Don't see anyone else's, though."

"Still outside," Narvi said, coughing again.

Arandras frowned. "Is she all right to move?"

"Maybe with a little help," Mara said.

"Can you...?"

She gave an amused snort. "What, you're not going to save us all single-handedly?"

They left the cells together, Arandras holding the lamp high in one hand and supporting Narvi with the other, Mara following with an arm around Halli's waist. The stairs almost defeated them. Arandras and Mara had to all but drag the others up in turn, pausing for breath every few steps. At last they passed through the mouth of the cavern and sank onto the rocky ground in exhaustion. Arandras leaned back, gazing up at the darkening sky as the breeze caressed his face.

"We can't go back the way we came," Mara said, retying her long ponytail. "We'll have to just pick a direction and walk. There's bound to be a settlement sooner or later, somewhere we can find a boat."

Arandras nodded. "You pick. I need to go back in and fetch

something."

"Oh? What's that?"

He looked at her, saying nothing.

Realisation dawned. "You mean they're still yours?"

Arandras pushed himself to his feet with a grunt, turned, and re-entered the cavern.

He heard the golem before he reached the chamber. *She watches. It watches. He sleeps. It screams. Stone and sorcery. My brother in chains and chains.*

Silence, he told it, and entered the room.

Clade lay in a heap before the shackled golem. A woman stood behind them, the same woman he had passed on his way in, her face and stance showing a resolve that had been entirely absent earlier. Arandras stared at Clade's still form, a sea of conflicting emotions filling his chest. "Is he... did he finish it?"

The woman bit her lip, uncertainty slipping through her facade; then her expression hardened and she folded her arms. Glaring at Arandras through narrowed eyes, she moved across to stand over the motionless figure, the message clear. *Leave him alone.*

He nodded his understanding. *Don't worry. That man is not my concern. Not any more.*

With a final glance at Clade, Arandras stepped into the adjoining chamber. *Golems,* he said, looking down on them from the low platform. *Attend me.*

An immense grinding filled the room as the golems stood and turned in place to face him. Behind him, the free golem did likewise, though he thought the shackled golem remained unmoved. There was something in the restraints, then, that blocked his commands. *Good. That makes this easier.*

He looked out at the thousands of pinprick lights gazing up at him from the dim room. *Golems. In a moment I will walk out of this cavern. When I do, you will form up behind me in ranks of four and follow me out.* He paused. *Do you understand?*

Their response roared in his mind. *WE UNDERSTAND. MASTER.*

Arandras bowed his head. There was something awful about the title, something breathtaking and terrible, even from mere constructs of earth and sorcery. *How much more so when bestowed upon you by a man or woman no different to yourself?* He shivered. He would never accept such a title from another living person. *Never.*

He turned, making his way back through the chamber and beginning the ascent to the surface. With a sound like a slow, rolling avalanche, the golems followed, marching up from the caverns and out into the cool evening air.

⌒

Consciousness returned with the slinking reluctance of a whipped dog. Clade groaned through the pounding in his head and opened a slitted eye. A rough stone floor stretched before his face, its uneven surface casting tiny shadows in the dim lamplight. Stifling another groan, he levered himself up from the floor into a seated position, then paused, bowing his head against a wave of dizziness. A fine sheen of sweat covered his skin.

Panting, Clade raised a hand to his brow — but the fingers that touched his forehead were not the long, slender digits he knew. His breath caught and he snatched the hand away, holding it up before his squinting eyes.

His entire forelimb was withered. Tendons strained in knotted ropes beneath taut skin. Claw-like fingers curled inward like ghastly parodies. Hand, wrist and forearm alike had shrunk as though drained of both life and flesh, leaving nothing behind but an unresponsive lump of muscle and bone. Clade stared in appalled fascination, unable to take it in. *It's crippled me. The damn thing has taken my hand.*

"Gods, Clade, what happened? Are you all right?" Eilwen crouched before him, her concern twisting to revulsion as she caught sight of his deformed limb. "Gods preserve, what happened to your hand?" Her gaze flicked to his other side. "Are they both...?"

A fresh wave of fear filled him and he raised his other hand, his left; but it remained as it had been, narrow and unmarked save for a cut he had sustained while descending the cliff path. *Thank the gods.*

He reached out tentatively with his good hand and took hold of a crabbed finger. It felt stiff, artificial, like a mummer's false arm. When he tried to pull the finger straight it moved only a little, stubbornly refusing to unbend any further than a half-crook. Eventually he let it go, allowing the withered appendage to fall to his lap and gazing at it with hollow resignation.

His limb was lost. The fingers with which he had first learnt to trace the runes of sorcery; the hand with which he had struck down Estelle and Garrett, and each of his kills before that; ruined, all of it. Even the Quill would struggle to heal something like this, even in one not resistant to fleshbinding. Despite his best efforts, something in the sorcery had failed to balance, and the binding had found its own way to rectify the fault.

He supposed he should be glad it hadn't killed him.

"Did it work?" Eilwen's voice was anxious. "Because that thing's still here, whatever it is."

Clade looked up. "It's still here? You're sure?"

She shot him a harrowed look. "I'm sure."

Tentatively, he lowered his defences, opening himself to the presence of the god. Silence answered, still and undisturbed, beautiful in its emptiness. He probed further, questing outward for any sign of Azador; and there, just on the edge of his perception, he felt a hint of the old, familiar weight. *There.* Eyes closed, he cast about for its touch, like an archer licking his thumb to test the wind. *Where are you?* It was faint, ephemeral, barely moving at all. He could almost sense its direction...

"The golem," he whispered, turning to face the shackled figure. "It's in the golem."

A slow grin spread over his face. *It worked.* There was a slight flutter from the golem, faint as butterfly wings, and Clade began to laugh. *I did it. It worked. I'm free.*

"See me!" Clade threw open his arms, gazing up at the golem's distant yellow lamps. "I am no longer your eyes and ears. I am no longer your *plaything.* I am Clade Alsere, and I renounce you!"

His voice echoed around the chamber. Somewhere far away, Azador's flutter settled into something else, something cooler. Clade nodded.

"You will come for me," he said, pointing at the golem with his unmarred hand. "I know. But know this, Azador. You have an enemy. As you marshal your forces, I marshal mine. As you stretch out your hand, I seek to cut it off. *I am coming for you.*"

There was a pulse from Azador, thin and distant; then the faint presence lifted.

"It's gone," Eilwen whispered.

Clade turned away, his ruined hand dangling at his side. The space where Arandras had brought in the second golem was now empty. He walked to the doorway, peered into the chamber where the golems had been. The room was bare.

"He came back a couple of hours ago," Eilwen said. "Led them out like the damn Kharjik Emperor."

Clade nodded.

As you marshal your forces, I marshal mine. He sighed. *What forces do I have? One good hand and an erratic part-time assassin with a limp. Look out, world.*

Eilwen shifted behind him. "Did you mean what you said just then? About fighting back?"

"Yes," Clade said. "I meant it."

"Why?"

Because I was Oculus, once. True Oculus. An agent of restoration and renewal. And now we are corrupted, turned against our true purpose, and bent by Azador toward our own destruction.

Clade sighed again. There was no way to explain it. Not to someone like her.

He turned to face her. "You've felt it," he said. "You know."

She nodded. "It killed the *Orenda*."

"It did." Though if the reason were good, Clade would have killed the ship himself.

"Why?"

"Because it could. Because the ship had something it wanted." Clade shrugged. "Does it matter?"

A pause. "I suppose not."

He forced a smile. "Come," he said. "There's no reason to stay here any longer."

She picked up the lamp, glancing over his shoulder at the shackled golem. "What about that?"

"It's still bound to Arandras, I would think. But now also to Azador." Frowning, he felt for his purse, loosening the clasp with his good hand and reaching awkwardly inside. Coins clinked and jangled as he dug beneath them; then the jagged edge of the shackle key brushed his finger and he nodded, satisfied. *Here you stay.*

Eilwen flinched and raised her arm. "It's back," she said, her voice taut with strain.

Clade slung his bag over the shoulder of his ruined arm. He had nothing more to say. Turning, he extended his good hand to Eilwen and she accepted it with gratitude, leaning heavily against it. Somewhere far away, at the edge of his mind, Clade thought he heard a scream, or the echo of one: a sound of bitterness, and futility, and vast, unappeasable rage. He smiled.

"Let's go," he said.

EPILOGUE

The world is not as it should be. You know this to be true. Yet this is the only world you have ever seen, so whence comes this knowledge?

— Jeresani the Lesser

THE BOY SLID HIS HAND into the frigid water, shivering as he reached blindly for the concealed shelf and the row of sealed clay bottles.

"Come on!" Jon cast an anxious glance back at the collection of huts that made up their village. "Mother asked us to fetch them before mealtime!"

Noash ignored his brother. It was Jon's fault they were late. Jon had insisted they stop at the mouth of the narrow inlet to skip rocks across the lake, an activity that provided the opportunity to show off his superior strength over his younger, smaller brother. Noash knew better than to try to dissuade him; defiance made Jon angry, and it might be days before he let it pass. Besides, Jon was the eldest, and their mother would hold him responsible for any delay.

His questing fingers closed around a fat clay neck and he drew forth the bottle of cow's milk from its cool storage place, heaving it onto the grass at Jon's feet.

"Now the other one," Jon said. "Hurry!"

Noash returned his hand to the clear pool, setting his teeth against the chill; but as he did so he felt something stir out in the

lake, the ripples of its motion reaching up the inlet and into the pool
to brush against his fingers like an underwater shadow. He gasped,
snatching his hand back and scrambling to his feet.

Jon gave him a startled look, then burst into laughter. "What
happened? Fish nibble your finger?"

"No." Noash gazed down the inlet at the vast, placid lake. The
shore curved away behind a low rise that concealed the first of the
cliffs away to the west. "Something's coming," he whispered.

"Mother will be coming if we don't bring back her milk," Jon
said. "Fetch another one and we can — hey, where are you going?
Hey!"

Noash darted away, heading for the rise that marked the edge of
the village's land, his brother's shouts receding behind him. It was in
the air, now: a hush, as though a hundred men all held their breath
together. *Something's coming.* He pushed himself up the hill, slowing
as the ground steepened, until at last he reached the top, stumbling
to a halt and looking out along the rocky shore.

Strangers trudged toward him, two light-brown men and a dark-
skinned woman; and there, marching beside them, a giant made of
stone and clay, walking with a sound like a millstone. Noash stared
at the great, lumbering shape in amazement. It carried a fourth figure in its arms, holding it close like a mother cradling its child.

The woman nudged the man beside her, the one with the beard,
and pointed directly at Noash. Terror closed over his heart. He
turned and ran, pelting down the hill and toward the village as fast
as his feet would take him.

Jon stood by the pool, shaking his arm dry, a pair of clay bottles
on the grass beside him. He glanced up at Noash's approach and
scowled. "Mother's going to be so angry when I tell her what you
did."

"Strangers," Noash gasped, sprinting past his brother and on to
the village. His father spent each morning out on the lake, catching
the fish that fed them all, but he would be in by now, cleaning his
catch, or maybe mending nets. Noash craned his neck as he ran,
searching for a glimpse of his father's shaggy head. *There, by the
boats.* He veered toward the shore, calling out and waving his arms.
"Father!"

His father looked up, dropping the net and coming out to meet him. "Noash? What is it, son?" He crouched, reaching out his great arms, and Noash was swept into their embrace, burying his head in his father's chest. Then the hands took hold of his thin shoulders, pulling him away, and his father put a finger under Noash's chin, lifting his gaze. "What's wrong?"

"Strangers," Noash said, panting so hard he almost couldn't talk. "Three of them, or maybe four, coming along the shore. And they have a giant made of stone!"

"A giant, you say?" His father gave him a grave look. "How big would you say it was?"

"As tall as our hut, at least," Noash said. "And it made a noise like the stone Uncle Goloth uses to sharpen his big knife." His father nodded, the corner of his mouth quirking in a smile, and Noash gave a frustrated cry, beating his hands ineffectually against his father's chest. "It's true, father! I saw it!"

"I'm sure you did, son," his father said in that familiar, hated tone which meant exactly the opposite. He stood, resting his hand on Noash's head and tousling his hair. "Look, there they are now."

The four strangers stood at the top of the hill, one leaning heavily against a companion. Two were dressed in what looked like the same clothes, grey-black and earthy brown. The tall woman and the bearded man conferred, then seemed to come to a decision. At a signal from the man, the group began the descent toward the village.

There was no sign of the giant.

Noash stared with a mixture of relief and dismay, unable to understand what had happened. "It was there! I know it was!"

"All right, son." One of the other men caught his father's eye, and he nodded. "You run along now and find out if your mother has anything she needs done. We'll go talk to the strangers."

His father gave him a last tousle and moved away, heading out with Uncle Goloth and Old Rob to meet the strangers just beyond the first huts. Noash watched long enough to see them clasp hands, Uncle Goloth greeting them with his usual uncertain grin, his father exchanging a slight nod with Old Rob before turning and gesturing to the village.

"There was a giant," Noash muttered as he walked away,

0

remembering the sound it had made as it moved, the way it turned its head back and forth as though examining the ground before it. "There was. I saw it."

When Noash looked up, he found that his feet had taken him back to the mouth of the inlet that led to the pool. *The pool.* He glanced along the narrow channel to the place where the villagers stored things that needed to stay cold. *That's where I felt it first. In the water.*

He looked out at the lake, then down at the clear water before him. A soft breeze stirred its surface, the gentle motion of the water throwing patterns of sunlight over the rocks below. Noash lowered himself onto the grassy bank, lying on his stomach with his head sticking out over the water. A grey fish no bigger than his finger drifted into sight below, then darted away with a swish of its tail. Clenching his teeth, he stretched out his hand and plunged it into the icy channel.

The sensation came stronger this time, thicker, as though he reached not into water but some other, more syrupy liquid. A thrill ran down his spine. *There's more than just one.* They were moving together, purposeful in their advance. Some might even have been speaking. *A lot more.*

Hundreds.

He sat up, shivering, wiping his hand dry on the grass. Hundreds of ghosts, all trapped in the bodies of giants; and all of them were out there, somewhere, beneath the surface of the lake.

A shadow fell across his lap. "Father's taking the strangers across the lake," Jon announced. "They wanted to go to Lissil, but Father said that was too far, so they decided to just go straight across."

Noash glanced up. "Is there to be a banquet tonight, then?"

Jon shook his head. "They're leaving right away. One of them's really sick, and they think she might die if they don't get help soon."

Noash looked back toward the boats. His father was already there, preparing his small craft for launch.

Jon flopped down onto the grass beside him. "Oh, and Mother's mad."

"They have ghosts trapped in giants of stone," Noash said, hugging his knees to his chest. "Out there, where the water's deep enough to cover them."

Jon gave a solemn nod. He always took Noash's pronounce-ments seriously, ever since the night Noash woke him to tell him their grandmother was saying goodbye before anyone knew she had died. "Who do you think they were?"

Noash shrugged. "I don't know. Just strangers."

"Not the strangers. The ghosts. Back when they were still alive."

Noash recalled the sense of purpose he'd felt in their movements. "Soldiers, maybe," he said. But there was something different about these ghosts, something unusual in the way they felt. Ghosts were usually sad, or angry, or upset about something, and they never seemed to stay very long. The giants had a feeling of calm about them; a still, settled patience. *Almost as if...*

He gazed out over the lake and gave voice to his thought, the words little more than a whisper. "I don't think they ever died."

There was a distant splash, followed by the sound of voices raised in farewell. His father's boat nudged away from the shore, the strangers' weight making it sit lower in the water than usual. Noash watched his father slowly work it out of the shallows, oars dipping and rising in strong, practised strokes, sunlight sparkling off the scattered water. When it reached the deeper waters, the lake's surface rippled as though stirred by a sudden breath of wind, and Noash nodded to himself.

The giants were following.

The boat slid away over the water, leaving a smooth, ever-wid-ening wake to mark its passage. Noash followed its progress until he could see it no more, and thought of ghosts, and giants, and wondered what it would be like to live forever.

About the Author

Like every child, Matt Karlov was raised on stories of the impossible, from the good parts of *Sesame Street,* to *The Hobbit,* to *Watership Down* and beyond. As Matt grew older, he had the good fortune to retain his taste for the fantastic, which soon developed into a deep love of speculative fiction in its many guises. He has been struggling to make room on his shelves for new books ever since.

Matt has been a software designer, a web developer, and a business analyst. He lives in Sydney, Australia. *The Unbound Man* is his first novel.

Visit www.mattkarlov.com to discover more about Matt's writing and the world of Kal Arna.

45969078R00305

Made in the USA
Lexington, KY
17 October 2015